JACK DICKSON

FREEFORM

THE GAY MEN'S PRESS

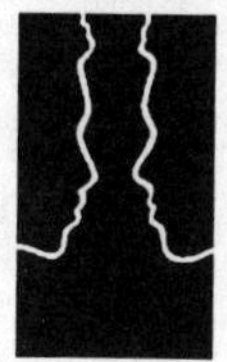

First published 1998 by GMP Publishers Ltd,
P O Box 247, Swaffham PE37 8PA, England

A CIP catalogue record for this book is available
from the British Library

ISBN 0 85449 257 7

Distributed in Europe by Central Books,
99 Wallis Rd, London E9 5LN

Distributed in North America by InBook/LPC Group,
1436 West Randolph, Chicago, IL 60607

Distributed in Australia by Bulldog Books,
P O Box 300, Beaconsfield, NSW 2014

Printed and bound in the EU by The Cromwell Press,
Trowbridge, Wilts, England

One

JAS'S BODY shuddered as tremors shot up his arm. Fist connected with skin and cartilage with a satisfying crunch.

The pinched, acne-scarred face crumpled, contorted by pain, then surprise. "What the fu...?" Blood began to pour from what used to be a nose.

Pressing both hands into the flabby chest, Jas pinned the guy against the wall and hit him again. Cheek this time. Bone sharp as arrow shattered under the blow, the surrounding flesh dissolving into soup. The head ricocheted back, meeting brick. Another punch caught the mouth, rotten teeth glancing off calloused fingers.

The damaged tongue mumbled lisping syllables of protest as the mouth tried to scream. Crimson mucus leaked from dried, crusted lips, split in three places and already beginning to swell.

Anguished whispers, soul-deep, echoed in the alley.

A succession of jack-hammer blows silenced any chance of moans. The face was dog meat...like the brain. Jas grinned, turning his attention to the softer, lower body.

Knee married groin in a union of agony as the writhing torso slumped, breath rushing from lungs in a low, primal groan. Too late he tried to shield the delicate organs, in an instinctive gesture. Shaking near-numb fingers, Jas aimed his left fist at the stomach and fired.

Pitching forward onto the ground fluttering hands still grasped genitals, as the man curled into a futile foetal position.

Other sounds, new sounds. A window opening. "What the hell's goin' on doon there?" The voice was female: the hour was later.

A growl grew low in his chest, resounding in the alley. Ignoring the question, Jas regarded the mess at his feet.

A kid's body...dressed in cheap jeans and a thin, blood-soaked T-shirt...but an adult's crime.

Barely twenty.

Jas looked at the pulped face.

Barely breathing.

Walking around the heap, he directed a kick at the kidney area.

No sound. Another kick, the steel-toed boot sinking into soft, unresisting flesh. Jas thought of other soft, resisting flesh and scowled at Jimmy Mygo.

Barely human.

"Yous doon there?" The voice at the window again. "Eether finish yer fight elsewhere or ah'm callin' the polis!"

Bending, Jas grabbed a handful of bloody black curls and yanked the head upwards. Pus-filled eyelids clamped shut, rivulets of pink snot cascading from a scarlet mass, lips three times normal size. Pulling back his arm Jas delivered a punishing, open-handed slap to the swollen face.

Still no sound. One eye blinked open, cyclops-like.

Jas looked deep into the blood-tinged retina, searching for a soul. He found none. Lowering his head to within inches of Jimmy's, he whispered: "That's for Jo Hunter."

The eye rolled back, its owner retched and sprayed vomit over the shiny surface of Jas's boots.

Voice at the window again, angry now. "Okay, that's it! The polis is gettin' called if yous don't pack it in..."

"No need." Jas straightened and looked up. His face was a mask. He flashed his ID, knowing it was invisible in the darkness. "DS Anderson..." The voice was loud, the words clear, unambiguous. He gave the remains of Jimmy Mygo one last kick. "...but you can call an ambulance, if you like..."

"You stupid bastard!" DI Moira Campbell glared from behind her desk. "Have you got a death-wish or something?" The voice was steel wool. "Why did you tell the damn woman your name?"

"No reason not to, ma'am," Jas replied, staring straight ahead. On the wall, above a filing cabinet, was a small print of Rossetti's 'Ecce Ancilla Domini'.

The DI lifted a sheaf of papers and flicked through them. "I don't suppose you're interested in Mr. My...er, Johnstone's condition." She looked up at Jas.

He shrugged.

"I'll tell you anyway," she went on icily. "Might help it sink in."

Focusing on the Rossetti print, Jas traced the Virgin's long red hair with his eyes.

"You should be grateful he's out of Intensive Care," DI Campbell began. "They've managed to stop the internal bleeding, and save one kidney, but we won't know about brain damage until more test have been run..."

Her words drifted on unheard, as Jas examined Mary of Nazareth's almost unbelieving expression. The look was unworldly, unknowing, un-aware of what lay ahead of her. It was the same look he had seen on Jo Hunter's face, as he'd cradled the thirteen-year-old's head in shaking arms.

DI Campbell's voice droned. "...the doctors' biggest worry is the left eye..."

The night of the attack, he'd been on his way home from a late shift. Dawn was edging furtively into the eastern sky as he crossed the waste ground where Shettleston's iron-works had once stood. Three am and silent...until the scream of a patrol car shattered the calm, scattering nesting birds from the scrub-ground. Instinctively, Jas had run towards it, as the headlights illuminated four figures gathered around something on the ground. They ran too, away from him and straight into the arms of two burly constables...or at least, three of them did. Making his way towards the object of their attention, Jas saw it was a boy...a young boy, almost a child.

Naked from the waist down, the legs were splayed and semen-splattered. What looked like a section of fence-posting protruded from...

Jas studied the Virgin's white, flowing robes. Jo Hunter's jeans, when they'd eventually been found, had been white...or rather, gore-splattered white.

Over the inert body crouched a grinning figure, limp penis in hand. An animal, too intent – or stupid – to run. As Jas approached, he could hear muttered words: 'Mygo...mygo now.'

With one hand, the figure grabbed the boy's lolling head, prising open the mouth. Just as he was about to stuff the hardening organ between pink lips, a second patrol car arrived, followed, in the distance, by an ambulance. On his knees now, Jas shoved the leering figure to one side and reached for the child.

'Hey, man...' The words were twisted, threatening, like the mouth which formed them.

Jas turned to the blank-eyed figure.

'Mygo now. You wanna go, you gotta wait...' He began to masturbate furiously.

Jas ignored him, focusing on the pitiful young body on the ground. The boy's pulse was faint but rapid. He moaned, briefly opened unseeing green eyes before sinking back into unconsciousness. Jimmy Mygo's ecstatic breathing was audible in the background. Instinctively, Jas began to stroke the boy's forehead and mutter soothing, meaningless words. He sat with Jo until the ambulance crew dragged him away...

"DS Anderson!" His superior's sharp voice brought him back. "Have you heard a word I've said?"

"Yes, ma'am."

Moira Campbell's tired grey eyes scanned his face. "You will be suspended from duty, on full pay, for the duration of the investigation. Do you understand?"

"Yes, ma'am." Eyes on the efficient, business-like face: mind in the depths of hell.

"An appointment has been made for you with the police psychiatrist. Tomorrow at 3 pm. Please attend."

"Yes, ma'am."

"Clear your desk, DS Anderson, and remain at home until the investigating officers contact you. Clear?"

"Yes, ma'am."

A sigh. "Anything you'd like to tell me, DS Anderson?" The words were unexpectedly soft.

Tell you? Tell you what? That Jo Hunter's a basket-case at thirteen? That the doctor said he'd never seen internal injuries like it? That Jimmy fuckin' Mygo and his pals got off? Or that I see Jo Hunter's face every time I close my eyes? "No, ma'am."

"Jas!" Exasperation, anger. "For Christ's sake, talk to me! I know how it can be. I want to help...." Di Campbell stood up and walked round to him. "Do you know what you've done?"

Society a favour? Redressed the balance? "Battery, aggravated assault, attempted murder...take your pick. I hope the bastard dies and I'll be sorry if he doesn't." Eyes again on the pre-Raphaelite print.

DI Campbell shook her head. "Get out of my sight!"

A calculator, three pens, a broken Tag Heuer watch and an old cigarette lighter. Jas stuffed the sum total of his three years with London Road Police into an empty carrier-bag.

Emptiness...

He looked at the unbroken watch, the one on his wrist: 6.50 am. Late...too late...too late for a lot of things.

Including regret...which refused to form anyway.

Sound behind, then a voice: "Hey, Big Man! How's the hauns?"

One set of footsteps, then more. Shift changeover. Suddenly the squad-room heaved with life. Curious, admiring voices: "That bent prick got what was coming, Jas...long overdue...fuckin' poofs fuckin' little kids...should've told us, Jas, we could've helped, sorted him out good and proper...you can expect a bottle of malt from the Hunters when they hear what happened..." Approval, back-slapping.

Jas winced, head down. Not sex...not with Jimmy Mygo. Violence...the domination of another human being...male or female, Jimmy didn't care.

Not sex...

Not sex...

Leigh...

A soft voice in his ear, amidst the general racket. "Seriously, Jas...that looks bad. You should drop into the Royal..." DC Ann

McLeod sounded concerned.

Glancing at his right hand, Jas saw it was raw and bleeding again. Blood dripped from his knuckles onto the plastic carrier-bag, shrinking and scattering like mercury. He made a fist, watched as veins pumped more blood out through two small cuts on the back of his hand.

"Looks like teeth-marks," Ann went on. "Get a tetanus while you're at it. Come on..." Hand on his shoulder. "...I'll do my nurse-act, wash it for you first." Joking voice. "Hope Jimmy uses clean needles these days..."

"Lea' it!" He needed to bleed, needed some reminder of what he had done.

Hurt. "Suit yourself, but you should really..."

"S'okay." Mechanically, Jas produced a clean white handkerchief from his pocket. He walked to the First-Aid box on the wall, took out an almost-full bottle of antiseptic. Soaking the handkerchief in the etherous liquid, he wiped all traces of blood from his desk, the floor, the carrier, then wrapped his right hand in the cool fabric.

"Sir?"

A new voice. He looked up. Two uniforms, early twenties, smiling pink faces. Jas stared. Recognition: the same two who had arrived with the ambulance, brought him back to the station, done their duty...

Duty...

Duty...

"We've been thinking, sir..." Educated voice, graduate. "Mrs...McGuire – her at the window? Well..." Awkward, unsure. "Well, sir...she says it was a fight, didn't see who attacked who...what if Jimmy had a blade, sir? You'd only have been defending yourself..." Words spilling forth in a torrent of eager camaraderie. "We went back to the scene – Tom and me..."

Rustling.

The uniform reached into his pocket. A Stanley knife. Old, rusted, through the cellophane evidence-bag. He cleared his throat. "Jimmy's prints, sir..."

Even after only a year's probation, the lies come easy.

Lies...lies...

He was the lie-expert. Jas grabbed his jacket and moved quickly towards the door. He knew what he'd done, wanted – needed – to take the consequences.

The uniform called after him. "We've not given statements yet, sir, but when CIB get here..."

Jas closed his ears and headed for the lift. His hands throbbed like engines, pumping pain into his brain. He jabbed at the call-button, was debating taking the stairs when the doors slid open.

Occupied: greying guy, mid-fifties, braided uniform, big brass...not local. Jas scowled and stepped in. "Sir."

The doors closed.

In the small space, Dettol mixed with the smell of his own sweat and the warm, visceral aroma of fresh blood. Jas thrust hands into pockets. The antiseptic wrapping dropped from fingers to the floor. He let it lie there, then kicked it.

"Rough night, Detective, er...?" The voice was low, powerful. West End vowels.

"DS James Anderson, sir." Jas bent, picked up the bloodied handkerchief, dug his fingernails in.

"Ah..." Comprehension. "DS Anderson. The 'unreasonable force' DS Anderson?"

"Sir." Unreasonable...reasonable: what was the difference? It was all meaningless. Jas scrutinised the illuminated numbers on the control-panel. The lift slowly descended.

"Hmm...you know the procedure, I take it. Keep your nose clean. Get in touch with the federation rep, a good solicitor maybe..." The voice was smooth, the words rehearsed.

Jas glanced at the shoulder pips: Assistant Chief Commissioner, desk-bound, PR-obsessed. Lunches with councillors, smiles for the press. "Sir."

"Maybe..." The ACC continued, "...do a bit of gardening, spend more time with the wife, eh?"

The usual assumption. Jas stared at the shoulder pips. "Live in a flat, sir." The usual avoidance.

Ignored. "The backbone of an officer's life – his home. Kids?"

"No, sir."

"Ah, well...you're young. Plenty of time for all that later." Apologetic. "Sorry I don't know your record better, DS Anderson. You've been with us...?"

"Probation with Gorbals division. Juvenile Crime, two years – Easterhouse. Four months secondment to Lothian and Borders, Vice. Drug squad, four years – attached to Stewart Street. Been here three, DS for two..." Automatic, meaningless.

Laugh. "You've certainly been about a bit, DS Anderson. You're...what – late twenties?"

"Thirty-three, sir..."

"An ambitious young man, I see..."

"Sir." The air in the lift was hot, oppressive. A hand on his shoulder:

"Well, don't worry too much about things..."

The hand patted his shoulder. Jas tensed.

The hand was withdrawn. "Have I met Mrs. Anderson?"

"Not married, sir." The usual half-lie.

A low laugh. "Ah...one of our young bloods, I see. Still playing the field, eh?"

"Sir." Not now...

Chuckles. "Broken a few hearts in your time, I'll bet, James – you don't mind if I call you James?" The voice oozed forced friendliness...and something he couldn't quite put his finger on.

"It's Jas, sir. No one calls me James..."

"As in freeform?"

The lift stopped, doors opened. Jas stepped into the hallway. "Good night, sir." He strode towards the door, nodding to the duty sergeant.

"Can I give you a lift?" Footsteps behind.

Jas shook his head. "Thanks, I'll walk....need some air." Again: "Good night, sir..." For fuck's sake answer and let me out of here!

"Good night, DS Anderson."

Outside, the cool morning air stung his face like a slap. Summer air...it would heat up later. Jas walked quickly out onto London Road and on into the Gallowgate.

Routine...everyday routine. Routine helped fill the emptiness. Sometimes.

Jas surveyed the reassuring normality of early morning Glasgow and smiled...then frowned. His brain was full of nothing. No regret for what he'd done...but no sense of satisfaction either.

He paused by a litter bin, realising he was still clutching the blood-stained handkerchief. Bitten nails had cut through the thick fabric. Giving his hands one last wipe, he looked at the bin, then balled up the soaking cloth and shoved it back into his pocket. His right hand was stiffening, and he began to flex it convulsively as he walked along the road.

Houses were blinking awake as he passed, lights visible in most downstairs rooms. A small milk-float hummed, its cargo rattling and clinking. A lone paperboy ducked and dived up a close ahead, delivering the obligatory copies of the *Sun* and the *Record*, staples in this part of Glasgow, along with white bread and Kensitas Club cigarettes.

Remnants of other unhealthy indulgences strewed concrete front gardens as Jas turned up Appin Road and into Haghill. The scene could've been the aftermath of a Sunday School picnic, if he didn't know better. Crisps were scattered everywhere, their packaging the only reason for their purchase: used to inhale glue and various other noxious substances. Crumpled Kit-Kat wrappers bore testament to sugar-craving and the absent silver paper: used to liquefy heroin or tems – the impoverished user's friend. A couple of bent and blackened spoons lay on dead grass, but no needles. Jas knew syringes were almost as precious as the drugs themselves, were shared by up to five different people for as many weeks, and only discarded when the needles broke off – often in the injector's arm.

Appin Road was busy at 7.15 on a Monday morning: it was busy every morning. For every junkie lying senseless in his bed, there were three awake, jumpy, waiting for a delivery so they too could find oblivion. Temazepam tablets – 'jellies' – were the opium of the drugs underclass. Easily obtainable, they were the spoils of overnight chemist break-ins, or the nocturnal mugging of doctors. Stolen in boxes of up to five hundred, some were used, the rest sold on.

It was a seller's market, the thieves had queues waiting behind closed doors, eager to pay, on average, three pounds a hit. The capsules were opened, the contents heated then injected. Once in the bloodstream, the warm substance quickly resumed its solid form, often causing embolisms.

Haghill roulette.

If you were lucky, the clots headed straight for the brain: permanent oblivion.

Or the solid Temazepam lodged in a limb, where gangrene soon set in. Prosthetics were a booming business in this part of the world.

Jas fumbled in trouser pocket for cigarettes, then remembered he'd given up. Crossing Corsock Street he glanced at the scorched doors and burnt-out buildings. For years, feuding families had waged a war over trivialities, culminating in three shoots in the last year alone. Traffic markings ran down the centre of the street like a thin red line, daring the police – or anyone else – to cross.

Jas crossed. A wheel-less car had taken his attention. Instinctively, he noted the registration but decided not to phone it in. He was suspended: that was someone else's problem now.

Corsock Street gave way to Walter Street, and a row of newly-refurbished, sand-blasted redstone tenements. Brightly coloured, fringed Austrian blinds guarded windows, as though the occupants thought bad taste could keep bad blood at bay. Christ! There were even window-boxes on the top floor. Jas shook his head and smiled. Someone was making an effort, trying to build a life in this lifeless desert.

Property prices were a first-time-buyer's dream in Walter Street: £13,000 for a two-bedroom flat. Insurance premiums, Jas knew, could be as much as a tenth of this. 'Investment potential', the estate agents screamed, 'up-and-coming area'. As he walked past the reinforced primary school, Jas thought they were probably right. He side-stepped a pile of human excrement: the area had no other direction to move in!

Back on Appin Road, he sensed movement in a doorway behind. He turned swiftly, but the shadow had gone. New graffiti smeared the road, still wet:

DEATH TO ALL COPS. DENNISTOUN POSSE.

Jas turned onto Cumbernauld Road and into a small Asian grocer's. Lifting a pint of milk, he walked to the counter.

"That you done fur the day, Mr. Anderson?" The stout, Pakistani woman beamed at him. The same inquiry every morning.

"Aye, Mrs. Rehmandi. That's me aff home." The same response. Jas placed the milk on the counter, searching for change. "That's...?" He looked up at the brown face and saw the expression alter to one of horror.

"Whit ye done tae yer haun?" Concern framed the large eyes. "Ye should get along tae the Casualty."

"Caught it in a door." Jas counted out 33p. "Is the *Herald* in yet...?"

"Looks nasty, son..."

"I'll leave the paper." He put the milk in his pocket. "Tell Ali I'll maybe see him doon the gym later..."

On the corner of Cumbernauld Road and Alexandra Parade, Jas waited patiently for the lights to change. There was no traffic in sight. He stepped onto the road, patting his pocket for keys. He had reached the pedestrian island when the white car appeared, engine roaring, doing sixty at least.

The BMW stood out like an untanned ring-mark. Jas remained still, watching as the powerful vehicle charged towards him.

An inner sense made him suddenly run for the far side of the road. Just as he reached the security of a pub doorway, he heard a swerve, then the sound of metal against metal as the car's front bumper impacted on the iron fence.

A screech, gears grinding into reverse. Jas turned to see the white car facing him, engine revving. It lurched forward, heading in his direction.

He dived to one side.

The car's wheels spun, trying to match his movements but failing. Instinct told him not to run a second time. Staring into the windscreen, Jas tried to see who was driving.

The car screamed into reverse. Another screech as the BMW pulled away and sped off along the Parade.

Jas watched as Mrs. Rehmandi emerged from her shop. "You okay, Mr. Anderson?" The voice was fearful, edged with excitement. "Ah heard the brakes. Wiz it they joy-riders again?"

Staring at a section of mangled fence, Jas raised his head. "Probably just somewan in a hurry," he remarked, irritated he didn't get the reg.

"Well, away you go hame...an' get they hauns seen to!" she admonished, with a smile. A wave.

Jas lifted a bloodied hand in salute. He walked slowly up Kennyhill Road into Eastercraigs. And home.

Two

JAS OPENED the door to his first-floor flat and listened. No sound.

Leigh would be asleep.

Closing the door quietly, he secured two dead-bolts before walking through to the lounge. Jas sank into the deep, padded sofa. A sigh escaped his lips as he leant back on the comfortable cushions. He removed his jacket, tie and rubbed his face vigorously. Pain throbbed in his knuckles. Jas ignored it and closed his eyes.

Jo Hunter's face painted the lids, tattooed on his retinas for ever.

Eyes shot open. Slowly, he rose and unbuttoned his shirt. It was thrown on the floor as he began to undo the belt of his trousers. Soon naked, Jas walked through to the shower.

The familiar icy needles pierced his skin on impact, spreading over his body. Jas stood motionless for a full five minutes as the freezing water cascaded over broad shoulders, down chest and stomach onto legs. Turning head upwards, he faced the faucet. The power jets blasted onto cheekbones, numbing his skin. Jas opened his mouth, feeling sub-zero drops prickle his tongue. He rubbed his angular face vigorously again, then reached for the temperature control. Warm water mixed with cold. Jas seized a bar of soap and began to wash, scrubbing at his hair, then face. Efficiently, he soaped chest, legs, groin. He was about to rinse when there was a soft tap at the door. It opened:

"Finished the Spartan routine yet?"

Deep inside a numb body, his heart began to glow. Sensation flooded in, almost filling the emptiness. Jas grinned.

Leigh made it all worth while...this man was the reason he always took the same route home. Alone. When the shift ended, some of the guys made straight for McGuire's cafe, seeking solace from empty lives in greasy fry-ups. Others wandered further afield, to the Tap Shop down at the docks. A guy could always get a drink there: the pub still kept its early opening hours, from the days when there were thirsty sailors to service.

There were...reasons Jas didn't accompany his colleagues. He blinked soap from his eyes and stared at the major, naked reason.

Five-eleven...four inches shorter than Jas. Long, smooth limbs of honey-coloured flesh. Shoulder-length blond hair secured behind neck in a ponytail. Under the shower's fluorescent light, gold nipple-rings twinkled on a hairless chest. Jas continued to admire, eyes shifting to...

Finely-toned muscle twitched in Leigh's biceps as he clenched fists and stretched in an elegant yawn,

...arm-pits. Jas stared into one deep, blond-tufted hollow. Leigh had the deepest, hairiest pits he'd even known, pits a guy could bury his mouth in, lose himself in. Jas tore his gaze away and smiled. "Aye...ah'm finished." He switched off the shower.

Leigh yawned again, grabbed a towel from the rail and threw it to Jas.

He caught it easily. With quick strokes he dried face and body, then stepped out of the cubicle.

"You missed a bit..."

Jas stood motionless as Leigh began to dab a still-damp chest with towel-edge. He stared at the tiled wall.

The streets, the scum which littered them, the blood, the shattered bone, the anguished relatives and reluctant witnesses...

The towel dropped from his fingers. Leigh was drying lower now, gently patting stomach.

...the clever solicitors who helped 'clients' fight for 'rights' to which they had no real right, the naive jurors persuaded by clever advocates' cleverer words...

The dabbing teasingly avoided his prick, which Jas could feel brushing navel.

...and sceptical of the word of a cop, a judicial system which maintained the archaic 'not proven' verdict which translated into 'we know you did it, we just can't prove it', and allowed trash like Jimmy Mygo to walk free while a thirteen-year-old boy lay comatose in Intensive Care...

Jas closed, then opened his eyes just as Jo's veined image began to form on the lids.

The outside world should stop at the entrance to Seven Eastercraigs. In here, he had power. He had control. He had a life.

Prick twitched against stomach. Jas stared at the top of a blond head. Leigh was part of this life, this world.

A gentle, towel-clad hand stroked the inside of his thigh.

Jas pushed the softness, the gentleness from his mind and roughly pressed the blond head towards his groin.

Strong hands gripped his thighs. A firm mouth opened. Eager lips hardened, moving up and down the length of his prick. Jas groaned. He stood very still, arms braced rigid against the shower cubicle. Better than pleasure, it hurt more than pain. Leigh's mouth moved faster, tongue licking, teeth pausing occasionally to nibble at foreskin, teasing, prolonging the exquisite agony.

Jas closed his eyes: the red tattoo was still visible. He grabbed the sides of Leigh's face and moved the blond head up and down the length of him.

The busy mouth worked diligently, sucking, kissing, exploring.

The red tattoo spidered with cracks, merging with the veins on his eyelids. Jas thrust deeper into Leigh's mouth, jabbing the back of his lover's contracting throat. The soft palate shimmered over his prick as he withdrew, then plunged again. His right hand balled into a fist, pain obliterated by growing ecstasy.

Eventually, sensation exploded deep in his balls.

The red tattoo dissolved into tiny fragments.

His hard body tensed one last time before shuddering into orgasm. Jas screamed like an animal, pumping into Leigh's throat, ignoring the gagging swallows. Tremors convulsed his broad frame. His legs began to buckle. Grasping Leigh's shoulders Jas pulled him into an upright position. He kissed him hard, tasting his own semen in Leigh's warm mouth. He felt the firm body against his own, felt another throbbing erection pressed into his stomach. Jas's teeth slid off Leigh's, tongues entwined, slick with saliva and spunk. Panting, he pulled away and stared into black, dilated pupils.

Jas hoped Leigh knew just what a big part of this life he was.

Leigh blinked, coughed then smiled. "Bad night?" Blue eyes glancing downwards to where Jas was still hard.

Jas sighed. Leigh could always tell.

"Want to talk about it, or...?"

With one hand he pushed Leigh's hair back from the handsome face and smiled. Leigh understood. That was one of the things he valued so much about him...

With the other hand he raised Leigh's right arms and fingered the thick, soft hair in the warm pit.

...this was another thing of value.

He couldn't talk...not now. He had to...act.

Action filled the void. Action took his mind off the emptiness.

Leigh had draped his left arm over Jas's shoulder and was nuzzling his ear. Hot lips kissed an icy lobe. Then words, filling his head. "Will I get things...ready?"

The Game.

The Game...helped, made things easier.

Leigh liked The Game: they both did.

The Game usually worked...Jas hoped it would work again. He couldn't think about what he'd done earlier this morning...and where better not to so than...

He spun Leigh round, slapped the hard, hairless arse and pushed him through to the bedroom.

Hours later, he gazed down at the sleeping form. Leigh's right arm was still handcuffed to the brass bedhead. Reaching over the muscular, tanned back, Jas released the bracelet, running his fingers along the angry weal left by reinforced steel. Leigh mumbled in his sleep. Jas lowered his head and gently kissed the reddening wrist-skin. The bedside clock read 2 pm. Time for the gym.

He dressed quickly, pulling on jockstrap, jeans and a Lonsdale sweatshirt. He debated what to do about his enforced leave which, for all he knew or cared, could turn permanent. DI Campbell's instructions came back to him.

Police psychiatrist: that was something else he could do without. His body tensed. Jas walked back to the bed, leaned over and slowly traced the outline of Leigh's spine.

His body relaxed.

CIB would, no doubt, be in touch either today or tomorrow. He looked at Leigh. Now, that might be a problem. The two-bedroom flat was for show, the spare bed exactly that, surplus to requirements. Fuck them all! Jas ran a hand over his spiky blond hair.

In the kitchen he drank half a carton of orange juice and scribbled a note: 'Back about five. Remember to leave the machine on.'

Grabbing his sports stuff, Jas was passing the phone when it rang. He was about to ignore it but, given the internal investigation, thought the better. He waited patiently as his own gruff voice barked back at him from the answerphone: 'I can't come to the phone now, so leave a message and I'll call you back.'

Bleeps.

Jas noticed the 'Messages' display read '4'.

The voice was low, menacing: Glasgow accents didn't transfer well to telephone. "You're dead, fuckin' cop." Guttural consonants echoed round the hall.

He pressed 'Play'. Other messages hissed at him.

"You're dead, fuckin' cop."

"You're dead, fuckin' cop."

"You're dead, fuckin' cop."

"You're dead, fuckin' cop."

Age: hard to say, the words were whispered. Sex: definitely male. Accent: East End. Ejecting the tape, Jas tucked it under a copy of *Yellow Pages*, putting a new one in. He frowned. Threats were par for the course, but this one was different. He was vaguely irritated. Someone who shouldn't had this number: that meant they had this address, and that meant trouble.

Control...of his life, his territory.

Outside this flat was another world, a world in which he had to function.

Outside this flat he had a job to do.

Outside was contaminating inside.

Jas stared at the now-silent answering machine.

He shrugged, lifted his keys and left the flat.

Walking down Whitehill Street to the gym, Glasgow was an oven. The light blinded him. Jas regretted leaving his shades at home, and squinted in shimmers. Summer, which had been quietly simmering on a back burner, had suddenly boiled into an over-cooked mess of heat, melting tarmac and festering litter bins. No clouds, no wind. June sunshine soldered the sweatshirt to his back.

As he passed Onslow Square, elderly lackadaisical women were exercising elderly, lackadaisical dogs. A gaggle of teenagers had gathered on the grass, rave music shrieking from a ghetto-blaster. Cheap, white baseball caps perched limply on heads, long-limbed boys played a half-hearted game of football; the girls, pale, rapidly-reddening, unhealthy legs below denim shorts lounged languidly against a tree.

The sun was rare in Glasgow, and when graced with its prodigal presence, Glaswegians flocked to pay homage.

Head down, Jas strode towards his destination.

To call it a gym was an aggrandisement. A derelict school housed Dennistoun Sports Centre. Created by a lot of enthusiasm and a meagre grant from the Council, it was stocked with basic, weight-training equipment. No frills, no lockers, no Step Rebok classes, no exercise bicycles, no spandex lycra...no steroids! Just a bunch of guys honing their bodies, pushing flesh and sinew to the limit, refining and perfecting the ideal musculature.

Not for show or vanity. For self-preservation, to work-off anger, frustration, self-pity.

Pushing open the peeling door, Jas went in. The smell of sweat and muscle-rub was overwhelming. He breathed in the odour like oxygen.

"Jas."

It was a statement, not an acknowledgement.

"Rab."

Robert Currie – 'Big Rab' – was general manager, bouncer and part-time trainer. Laid-off from Ravenscraig steelworks five years ago, Rab was built like a smelter and, at 5' 9", six inches shorter than Jas. The nickname had been spawned pre-puberty, when Rab had already topped 5' 8", and had stuck there, give or take the odd inch. Now the 'big' referred to Rab's deltoids, which threatened to burst from the shiny skin which only just held them hostage.

On the slag-heap at thirty-two, Rab had a lot of anger to work off.

"Busy?" Jas paused.

Big Rab shook his bullet-head. "Coupla kids, and that wuman fae Shoprite." He scowled. Females were tolerated here, but not encouraged.

Jas smiled, made to walk past.

"Ah heard about Jimmy Mygo, Jas." The voice was low.

Word travelled fast in Glasgow. Jas continued to walk.

"Ah'll no' say whit ye did wis right..." The words measured, thoughtful. "...but ye wurney the first, and ye'll no' be the last..."

Jas stopped, silent.

"...but why the fuck dae it on duty, man?" The face was quizzical, looking for answers.

"Water under the bridge, Rab..."

The bullet-head shook slowly. "Ah canny make you out, these days..."

You never could. Jas pulled his thoughts away from the obvious. "Ali in?"

"Aye, he's through in the weights-room, but..."

"Catch ye later, Rab." Jas strolled through the swing doors into a long, dark corridor.

Emerging into light, he scanned the small room. Four sets of bar-bells, four sets of weights, a set of scales and a pair of parallel bars. In a corner, an athletic, coffee-coloured figure sat on the floor, head thrown back. Sweat coursed through the ebony hair.

As the door opened, the figure looked up, eyes opalling. "Jas! Christ, man! Thought ah's missed ye.." Anxious, jumpy.

Jas walked over, dumping his bag beside the parallel bars. "Ali."

"Ma maw said you'd be doon here..."

Jas sat down, pulled off his trainers and jeans, replacing the latter with cotton football shorts. A voice at his elbow:

"Man! Ah need tae talk tae ya..." The Asian face was at odds with the accent. He produced a cigarette.

Jas eyed it.

Guiltily, Ali crammed the cigarette back into the packet. "Ah really need tae talk tae ye, man," he reiterated. "Jimmy Mygo..."

"Later, Ali." Jas moved to the centre of the floor. "Count for me, eh?" The press-ups began.

A dark fist held steady below Jas's chest, Ali had reached eighty-five before urgency overwhelmed him. "Listen, ya fanatic: it's yer legs ye should be exercising. The word's oot. Jimmy's brothers are efter ye."

Jas brushed the fist one last time then stopped in the 'raised arm' position, breathing easy.

Crouching by his side, Ali removed his fist and spewed forth. "Y'ken Mick? Works in the Bakery? His brother dis the Johnstones' car. He heard them talkin'." Ali was worried. "Ye really kicked fuck outta Jimmy, didn't ye, Jas. The whole world kens..."

Jas sank to the floor. The white BMW...the phone-calls... He gave a low laugh.

"Ah widney joke aboot the Johnstone brothers." Astonishment, then fear. "They're mad bastards, them. You know that, Jas. The whole faimly's three coupons short o' a blender. Whit did ye want tae gie Jimmy that doin' fur?"

On his feet now, Jas whipped off the soaking sweatshirt and wiped face, then chest. "Ken where the Brothers Grimm are livin', these days?"

Ali shook his head. "Naw...and ah don't want tae. Neether dae you, man. Keep outa thur way, aff the streets fur a while."

"Thanks fur the advice." Back on the floor, Jas clasped hands behind head and began the sit-ups.

Ali moved round, automatically lowering two brown hands to clasp Jas's ankles.

Jas smiled, Ali's concerned face disappearing then reappearing with each fluid movement. "Seen Marie recently?" he asked, casually.

"Yur no' thinkin' a...?"

He felt Ali's grip tighten. "I ken she moved – Southside, somewhere..."

"Jas, it's no' worth it."

If anyone knew the Johnstones' whereabouts, Marie would...

The sit-ups continued.

"Ah wideny think she'd want anythin' tae dae wi' that bunch, no' after..."

"That's exactly why she wull ken, Ali. Marie wants tae put as much distance between hersel' and the Johnstones as she can..." Jas paused, pulled his feet from the tight grasp.

Ali produced the crumpled cigarette, and lit it. "Ye lost touch, didn't yous? She yist tae be yer...er...?" Uncomfortable. He passed the cigarette to Jas.

He waved it away. "Snout, informer, grass, ears on the street." Jas's low voice filled in the awkward silence. "Haven't seen Marie fur aboot a year – not since the court-case."

"A wee cracker," Ali mused, watching as the sit-ups passed one hundred. "Maybe she's still oan the game. No' the sorta face ye'd wanta fuck, these days, though..."

Jas laughed. "There's no' accountin' for taste, Ali. Ah hear she gets by jist fine – acquired a new clientele." He stressed the word mockingly. Ali joined in the laughter. "Like it blindfold, dae they?" He was suddenly self-conscious. "Good kid, Marie. Didn't deserve..." He ended abruptly, and shook his head.

At one hundred and fifty Jas stopped. "Listen, Ali. Ah need a word with her. Don't worry..." Lies, different lies. "Ah'll no' go near the Johnstones, but if ah want to avoid them, ah'll need to know where they are, right?"

Thoughtful, puzzled...then believing. "Ah suppose so." Grudging.

Jas wiped underarms with sweatshirt. "You don't ken, but Marie wull. Think she gave me hur new number, though where it is now ah..."

"Oh, well..." Brightening, relieved. "If yer sure that's aw' yer wantin' it fur..."

"Wid ah lie tae you, ma man?" Jas grinned: face, mind, life a mask.

Consideration, then smile. "Aye, ye've always been straight wi' me, Jas Anderson. Dunno about the phone, but Marie's been rehoused ower at Hutchie E. Sixteenth flair, flat five..." Beneath the coffee skin, reddening.

'Straight'...he'd never been straight with Ali. Watching as dark eyes avoided his, Jas scanned the handsome face. "Marie an' you...?"

Ali looked away, shame-faced.

Jas's voice was soft. "None of ma business, whit you get up tae."

An arranged marriage at twenty-two, Ali and his wife – a pretty girl – lived with old Mrs. Rehmandi over the Cumbernauld Road shop. Apparently, young Mrs. Rehmandi didn't share her husband's interest in more unusual sexual practices.

Ali cleared his throat. "Ye ken how it is, man..."

Jas moved to the parallel bars for chin-ups. "Aye, Ali... ah ken." More than you'll ever know. Jas clenched his teeth and tried to persuade himself Leigh was on a par with Ali's use of prostitutes. He knew he was wrong. He did sixty chin-ups then paused.

"Ma maw said ye'd hurt yer haun," Ali said, eventually.

Easing himself down, Jas examined the bruised fist. The cuts were starting to scab over, but the knuckles glared back angrily at him. "It'll heal."

Ali got up and peered at the two adjacent cuts. "Aye, ah heard the bastard bit ye."

Producing a bottle of liniment from his bag, Jas smeared liquid over chest, shoulders and armpits. His body tingled and shone like steel.

"Gie Marie ma regards," Ali ventured.

Jas pulled on jeans and a fresh T-shirt. "Is she still...?"

Scowl, then a brief nod. "Did detox fur a couple of months, but couldney stick it. The Social took her kids..."

"She still oan methadone?"

Vigorous shake. "Smack – when she can get it. Tems the resta the time. Ah've tried to get'er aff it aw', but..."

Jas fastened belt. "Ah'll seeya, Ali..." He picked up the bag and walked slowly to the door.

"Watch yer back, man," Ali called after him. "Hutchie E's no' Dennistoun. They don't wait fur a full moon ower there..."

"Bye, Ali." He strode from the hot, oppressive gym into a hot, oppressive world.

Glasgow Green was airless as Jas jogged past the People's Palace towards St. Andrew's suspension bridge. Various attempts by the city council to sell off great chunks of the Green to private developers had been thwarted. Some ancient grazing laws were eventually found, by pressure groups, to block plans for up-market housing.

At present indulging themselves in this arcane right were a couple of dossers dozing in the late afternoon sunshine, the obligatory dog-walkers and a group of pre-teen boys, engaged in some furtive activity near a clump of trees. Jas jogged on. Approaching the white iron bridge, he looked up. Who'd want that for a view, anyway?

On the other side of the Clyde, his eyes met Hutchesontown. It wobbled in the heat, draped in a miasma of yeasty steam from a nearby distillery. A sixties dream gone bad, the whole lot was due for demolition. But where do you put ten thousand bread-line tenants when you've sold off most of the council housing-stock?

Slowing to a brisk walk, Jas cut along Adelphi Street, then up towards the old Gorbals Cross. Perfectly good sandstone tenements were demolished for this, Jas thought, glancing up at the dirty cream concrete flats. He'd done his probation here, but his opinion of the area hadn't improved since.

If you treat people like beasts, house them in rat-traps, don't be surprised when they turn rabid and bite your ankles. Jas passed the Gorbals Police Station, carried on into Queen Elizabeth Square and the almost derelict Cumberland Street shopping complex.

Above, the massive Hutchie E block stood on eight concrete legs, a juggernaut defying all architectural logic. Its sister-block had been demolished, after three tries, last summer. Plans were afoot to do the same to Hutchie E, but it was so huge, so immovable, Jas doubted anything less than another Titan would succeed in the attempt. Underneath, most of the shops were boarded-up shells, the few which remained encased in heavy armour-plating. Wan mothers pushed sleeping kids in pushchairs. A few feisty pensioners chatted in little groups, as though there was safety in numbers. An air of quiet resignation, almost peace, was apparent.

Suddenly, the shatter of glass from above. Ahead, a thin youth appeared at the top of stone stairs, which linked flats to shops, and rushed down into the precinct. The face was white, unhealthy, fear-streaked. Almost immediately a gang of five others appeared behind him, shouting, screaming. The sounds of voices and boots echoed in the calm of Cumberland Street.

Adrenalin spurted.

The gang quickly caught up with the escapee near a group of gossiping mothers. Jas quickened his pace towards them, as the white-faced youth cowered in an iron-clad doorway. The five laid into him, aggression ballooning around them.

"Watch the wains!" a tired voice half-heartedly ordered, not expecting compliance. The mothers edged away.

The attack was vicious and short-lived, over before Jas reached the scene. The five scattered, the mothers began to gossip again, pensioners resumed their chat. Jas walked over to the foetal ball on the ground. He crouched down. "You okay?"

The youth, no more than fifteen, was crying softly. He looked up, suspicious, wiping bloody mucus from his nose. "Whit's it tae you, Big Man?" A gash near the hairline was beginning to drip.

Jas shrugged. "Ye could report it. I saw whit happened. The police..."

The boy snarled and spat. "The polis. Get, real man. Whit can they dae?"

Fuck all without your cooperation!

The boy staggered upright. He was under five foot, a skinny runt in a designer leather jacket. "Ah'll sort it oot masel'..."

Jas looked at the slight figure and wanted to laugh. "You an' whose army?"

Fumbling in an inside pocket, the boy produced a small package, wrapped in a dirty rag. He moved in front of Jas, shielding himself, and uncovered his trophy. "Me an' this army..."

The black hand gun was dull and ancient, but undoubtedly real.

"Ken how tae use that?" Jas inquired.

"S'easy," the boy grinned. "Seen it oan the telly..." He gripped the handle and adopted a theatrical, legs-astride stance. He pointed the gun at the ground, and fashioned a sneer. "Go on, cunt...make ma day!"

Jas laughed. "Gotta permit?"

The boy shrugged.

Jas unzipped his sports bag.

The boy froze.

Jas found a notebook and pencil, scribbled down a name. "Gie this guy a ring..." He handed the relieved boy Big Rab's name and number. "That gun's illegal, an' you're too young for a permit onyway. But Rab's gotta practice range. Air rifles, crossbows..."

The boy's eyes brightened. "Crossbows?"

Jas nodded, unloosening the gun from small pink fingers. "Whit wis the kickin' fur?"

"Wull ah get tae fire arrows an' stuff?"

"If Big Rab lets ye..." Jas held the gun, felt its weight in his hand. "Whit were they after ye fur?"

Shrug. "Ma maw owes the tally-man. She canny pay. They're..." Eyes upwards toward the flats. "...his boys."

"Live up there?" Jas gestured above.

"Aye...sixteenth flair...you goat ten pee, Big Man?"

Jas rummaged in his pocket. "Ye ken Marie McGhee?" He gave the boy a pound coin.

He laughed. "Scarface? Aye, ah ken hur – or ma maw diz." The boy eyed Jas scornfully. "Yer no' wanny hur...?"

"Naw..." He pocketed the gun. "...jist an auld friend. Gonny phone Rab, then?"

The boy nodded, eyes shining.

"Tell him Jas said it wis okay..."

"Thanks, man. Want me tae show ye the way?"

Jas shook his head. "Ah'll manage. Now, away you an' phone..." He moved towards the stairs.

"Whit aboot ma gun?" The voice was remembering.

"Ah'll look efter it fur ye, 'til yer permit comes through. Okay?" Jas reached the stairs, turned his head.

"Well...ah suppose so. Ye'll mind an' clean it after ye've used it?"

Jas laughed. The weapon was so dry from disuse he doubted it would even backfire. "Marie's got ma number. Gie me a ring in a couple of years. Ye can have it back then, if ye still want it..."

The boy looked hard at Jas, opened his mouth, then closed it. Pattering footsteps. Then he was gone.

Jas began the climb to Marie's flat.

Three

WINDS SCREECHED through Hutchie E's decrepit skeleton. Jas paused at the thirteenth-floor landing and gazed out the window space. You could see for miles, to the West End and beyond in one direction, up north towards Garthamlock in the other. But no one lived here for the view. You came to Hutchie E when there was nowhere else to go. Like a reluctant parent, it had to take you in. Jas continued up the rusted and cracking stairs. Gaping fault lines breached the walls, contradicting the designer's theory that iron encased in concrete was the building material of the future. Sure, concrete lasted, but damp had seeped in, corroding the iron like bone-cancer. Hutchie E was rotting from the inside out. The foundations were shifting, the whole structure was collapsing.

A crowd of lazy kids meandered down the stairway. On the floor above, voices were arguing: two men and a woman. The latter sounded desperate, pleading.

Jas waited silently in the stairwell.

The talk ceased. Two skinny figures scuttled past. The faces were pointed, rodent-like.

Unlike rats, Jas knew these vermin wouldn't leave the sinking Hutchie E. They had it good here. The police never ventured above the fifth floor.

Two more flights of crumbling breeze-block led to the sixteenth floor. Six doors. Three boarded up: shooting galleries. One with net curtains draping the window-panel, a brave attempt to keep the flag of decency flying. The door of Flat Six was slightly ajar: the sounds of sobbing drifted out. Flat Five was in the far corner. Jas walked towards it. A solid-core door, as yet unpainted. New locks. A spy-hole. No window-panel. No name-plate.

No answer.

Jas knocked again, pressing his face to the spy-hole.

A yellow eye winked back. "Whit dae ye want?" The voice was hoarse, breathy.

"Marie? It's DS Anderson..."

"Ah dinny ken ony DS Anderson. Fuck aff!"

Jas lowered his voice. "DS Anderson – London Road. Remember?" They'd been close, he and Marie... Jas smiled: the nearest thing he'd had to a friend in the days before Leigh.

"Fuck aff, polis!" A harsh laugh. "Ah've had enougha yous tae last me a lifetime."

"Come on, Marie..." He kicked the bottom of the door. It didn't give an inch. "...open up. It's Jas – ah've bin talkin' tae Ali."

Silence. Then: "Ali? Ali who?"

Jas laughed. "Ali-fuckin' Baba! Ali Rehmandi – remember? Ali's worried aboot ye, Marie. Ah wis worried aboot ye tae."

Scrapings, bolts unbolted, chains unchained. Slowly, the door opened a crack. A jaundiced eye peered at him. "Jas? Big Jas?"

"Aye, Marie...can ah come in?"

The door burst open and a thin arm grabbed his. "Get inside, ya stupit fuck...whit ye dain' roon here?" He was pulled into the flat.

In the unlit hall, Marie carefully re-did dead-bolts and the three-foot metal security bar which ran the breadth of the door.

Jas waited. She turned, pressing fingers into his chest.

"Go on through, man."

Jas made his way through to the lounge. Marie followed. The walls were a lurid orange, the carpet new, a static-inducing brown nylon. There was no furniture to speak of. A couple of blankets lay in a corner, along with a blue sleeping-bag. Three large holdalls slouched in a corner, spilling what looked like black PVC. A small TV sat perkily on a cardboard box. The room was tidy and clean. Jas walked to the curtainless window, before turning. "It's bin a while, Marie."

Long, dark hair hung across her face. She wore red sweat-pants and a baggy white top. Large, black trainers housed small feet. She looked impossibly young. Smack...the fountain of youth. At 5' 4" Marie was smaller, thinner than Jas remembered...

She pushed back the hair.

...but the eyes were the same, just a little yellower. Blue pupils stared out of a Dresden face which was pale as the china, hard as the bombing-raids. The mouth was set in a red curl, mocked by the long crescent scar which linked right eye to a birthmark above top lip. Drawn by a crazed dot-to-dot fanatic whose hand had slipped, the wound glared defiantly at Jas.

She laughed. The scar twitched.

"Hid a good look, hiv ye?" Marie walked to the TV and lifted a packet of cigarettes.

Jas had heard about the attack, but not seen the result. Like Dali's 'St. John', Marie had survived wanton vandalism, but apparently rejected any restoration attempts. She wore her damage like a badge, flaunting it.

She jiggled a cigarette in his direction.

He shook his head and moved closer. Gently, he traced the length of the scar-tissue with the back of a finger. It was knobbly, rough beneath his touch.

Remaining stationary, Marie grabbed his wrist. "Didney think you were intae wimmin...but that'll be ten quid, onyway." She grinned. The scar twitched again. "Ah'll dae you a special rate. The punters pay fifteen tae touch it, twenty tae lick it."

Jas laughed, enjoying the rapport. "Easy money, eh Marie?"

She let go his wrist and lit a cigarette. "Maybe the Johnstones did me a favour." She exhaled noisily, blowing a smoke-ring. "Huvney opened ma legs in months. Nae need." She fingered her means of production. "Maest're happy jist lookin', then ah toss them aff. A few are intae the rough stuff..." She pointed to the holdalls. "...but that's nae hassle, eether." She smiled. "Gies me a chance tae dress up!" Marie shook her head, disbelieving. "Corrective Services..." She pronounced the words awkwardly. "Never knew there wur so many weirdos..." She corrected herself. "...gentlemen of exotic tastes, in Glasgow ..." She sat down.

Jas joined her on the floor. "Take aw' sorts, Marie."

An ironic smile. "You'd be the expert, man!" Sigh. "If ah'd kent that earlier, ah couldda retired by noo. As it is..." She looked down at her hands.

"Still oan the junk, ah hear."

She nodded. "Aye..." She puffed on the cigarette. "...but at least ah'm aff the streets." Pause. "'Member Chrissy?"

Jas remembered. "Ah wis sorry tae hear aboot..."

"Jist a kid." The voice was low, tinged with sadness. "Couldney get by on the social, no wi' Tony's habit an' aw..."

At eighteen, Christine McGhee's semi-cremated body had been discovered, naked, three months ago on waste ground. Stabbed twenty-five times. Her common-law husband was currently in custody, awaiting trial.

"Did it tae feed the kids, only the wance. Some psycho...no' Tony." Anger. "Doesney seem fair. At least ah kent whit ah wis dain'..." She looked at Jas.

He nodded.

"The risks..." She pulled off a black trainer and rubbed a foot.

Between toes red puncture marks dotted the white skin. "...we aw' take risks, eh man? The risk ye take tae block-oot another risk can turn oan ye."

Jas frowned. Life was full of risks...of one sort or another. Risks helped fill the emptiness. Marie laughed again. "Aw' this, an' ah'm still alive an' clean as a whistle...'part fae the hepatitis..."

"Lucka the draw, Marie. Ye must have a guardian angel up there, somewhere..." They sat silently together on the floor. Through the wall, from the next flat, an agonised moan.

Marie finished her cigarette, killed it in the ashtray. "So, Big Man – tae whit dae ah owe the pleasure?" She stood up almost jauntily.

"Ah had a word wi' Jimmy Mygo."

Nod. "So ah heard. Wish ah'd seen it. Whit that bastard did tae that wee boay..." Anger, then pity. "The polis chuck ye oot?"

"Suspended, but that's the leasta ma worries. Ali says the brothers Grimm ur efter me. Ah need tae git tae them first, Marie. Ye heard anythin' else?"

Marie walked to the far side of the room, paused. "They'll no' be well pleased," she murmured, "that's fur sure. But ah've a feelin' they'll no' dae much aboot it. Jimmy wiz an...embarrassment tae them."

"They still nickin' cors?"

Head shake, then laugh. "Naw...almost legit, noo, the Johnstones. Big garage – 'valetting' they call it. Flash motors ..."

Jas remembered the spinning wheels and screaming brakes of a white BMW.

"Still runnin' the girls, on the side, though," she continued. "Coupla boys too, nooadays, fae whit ah've bin telt...young boys."

Jas frowned. "Diversification – the mark of the real entrepreneur!"

Marie looked puzzled. "Onyway," she went on, "ah'd stay well oota their way, Jas." Pause. "Hey...ye don't want me tae start snoutin' fur ye again, or anything?" She crouched down.

"Naw...you did yer bit."

"'Cos ah've goat a new guy...."

Jas rubbed the broken skin on his knuckles.

"Toap man." Marie smiled. "Pays better than you ever did!"

"That's between you an' him, Marie...dae ah ken the guy?"

She shook her head. "Stewart Street...canny tell ye onything else."

Jas understood. He got up. "Know where the Johnstones're livin' these days?"

"Movin' aboot, fae whit ah hear. Nowhere near here, though – thank fuck!" Her voice leaked concern. "Don't go lookin' fur trouble, Jas...let it lie."

Watching the damaged face, Jas saw curiosity.

"Nothin' ever bothered ye before, Big Man...why the interest noo?"

"Somewan kens ma home number."

"Ah..." Philosophical. "Get it changed. Ye did that often enough at yer auld place." Sigh. "well...ah'll ask aroon' fur ye – fur auld time's sake, eh Jas?"

"Ye've goat ma number?"

"Still Dennistoun?"

He nodded. "Ah'll let ye know if it changes..."

"Aye...it'll be aroon' here somewhere. Noo..." She glanced at an expensive watch on her wrist. "... ah don't want tae hurry ye, Jas, but ah've a punter at five an'..."

"Sure." He picked up his sports bag and moved towards the door. He paused. "You okay fur money, Marie?"

She laughed and slapped his arm. "Listen, Big Man. Ah'm in clover here. Polis-protection, nae hassles fae the neighbours an ah'm clearin' nine hundred a week withoot tryin'..."

Enough to support the worst habit.

Marie smiled. "...but thanks onyway, man."

"Dae ye get tae see yer kids much?"

The smile faded. "They're better aff withoot me. Foster hames..." Self-pity thrust aside. "Ye keepin' well yersel'?" Marie eyed his broad frame.

"Nae problems."

"Still wi' Pretty-boy?"

Jas laughed. "Aye, Leigh's still around."

Marie grinned. "He must be somethin' special tae keep you happy, Big Man!"

Leigh was special...very special. A warm numbness spread through his veins. The Game...another brand of heroin?

At the door, two sharp knocks, then one long.

Marie pushed past him into the hall. She knocked once.

Two knocks in return.

Marie opened the door. "In ye come, son."

A fat man in a grey suit, clutching a briefcase, crept past Jas into the lounge.

"Ah'll no' be a minute, son," Marie called after him. She turned to Jas. "Look efter yersel', Big Man. Ah'll be in touch..."

He stepped from the flat onto the soundless landing.

As he strode up Abercromby Street towards Craigpark and home, Jas mulled over Marie's words. If the Johnstones were valetting cars, that gave them anonymous access to expensive vehicles. Even if he had got the number of that morning's BMW, no way could it be traced back to them. On the other hand...if Jimmy wasn't part of the new, legit scene, had Jas, in fact, done the Johnstones a favour working him over, saving them the trouble? If Marie was right, and the family were trying to create a facade of respectability, the last thing they'd want was a vendetta with a cop.

Passing the abattoir on the corner of Duke Street, the smell of manure and animals' fear twitched his nostrils.

Jas had seen the Johnstone brothers' handiwork at close quarters many times. Kneecapping was commonplace, castration not unknown. Marie had got off lightly, and she knew it. Snouts who gave evidence in open court didn't usually survive, let alone go on to enjoy an improved lifestyle. Dog eat dog wasn't enough for the Johnstones: they ate their enemies all right, but publicly, showily. Were threatening phone-calls and a botched murder-attempt really their style?

He climbed the steep Craigpark hill easily, sports bag slung casually over one shoulder. His stomach rumbled. Food. he hoped a certain someone had done some shopping. Jas tried to remember if this was one of Leigh's working days.

Work...work.

Both he and Leigh kept work and play strictly divided: Jas, because he knew he had to. Leigh, because...

Jas frowned.

...because it didn't matter.

Nothing mattered outside the doors of Seven Eastercraigs. Leigh wasn't part of this life, this outside world.

Jas closed his mind to the contradiction, the way he'd closed it for the past two years.

Policing was a job...just a job.

Like Leigh's job...

Involved in some vague research for an even vaguer doctoral qualification, Leigh washed test-tubes at Glasgow University's medical school, in exchange for lab privileges. The hours fluctuated, but he was at home most afternoons. Evenings, Leigh worked.

Jas walked on.

Dennistoun was quiet. Windows were flung open, houses gasping for air in the airless afternoon. A few schoolkids straggled home, dragging dusty rucksacks. He was passing a small florist shop when a voice called to him: "Mr. Anderson?" Expected. Respectful.

Jas paused, turned back to the doorway. A young woman – younger than him – appeared, spiral-permed, sunbed-tanned. "Hi, Linda..."

"How's the wee lad doin', Mr. Anderson?"

Jas closed his eyes: the red tattoo was back. He opened his eyes and looked at the orange face. "The same, Linda. Breathing on his own, now, but still in coma..."

"You goin' to see him tonight, Mr. Anderson?"

Jas nodded. Routine...more routine.

She plucked a large bunch of carnations from a bucket near the door. "Take these..." She thrust them at Jas. Water dribbled from the stems onto dry, arid tarmac.

This was a ritual. Linda and her husband knew Jo Hunter's family well. Hounded by the press, the Hunters had moved to another part of town, but were still remembered here.

He took the dripping bouquet, the fourth in so many days. The ward in the Royal was a rainforest of blooms already. "Thanks, Linda..."

"Give Jo our love, Mr. Anderson. I'm sure he'll get better."

Jas nodded a wordless lie and walked away.

Home...

In the Eastercraigs flat, Nitzer Ebb's electronic pulse blasted off the walls. Leigh evidently hadn't left for the lab yet. Jas dropped his keys on the hall table. The answerphone display read '2'. He strolled through to the lounge, dumped the carnations in a vase then made straight for the CD-stack, where he lowered the volume considerably.

"Oy!" An irate voice from the bedroom. "I was listening to that!"

"So was half of Dennistoun!" Jas shouted back. He walked through to the bedroom where Leigh stood, rummaging in a cupboard.

"Got them." He turned, holding two videotapes.

"The trials?"

Leigh nodded, thrusting the cassettes into a briefcase. He knelt down and grabbed some papers. "Editing tonight. Should be enough visual material alone to postulate a link between cortex electro-stimulation and..."

Jas switched off. Leigh's research didn't interest him. Leigh's hard buttocks, encased in faded denim, did. He walked towards the crouched figure, leaned over and stroked the blond head. His prick twitched.

Leigh stood up, pulling a leather jacket from the bed. "Good day at the gym?" He breezed past, heading for the kitchen.

Jas followed.

Opening the fridge, Leigh peered in. "There's some steak left from last night. Salad's a bit low. I'll do you something to eat later, if you like..."

"You'll dae me noo..." Behind, Jas circled the slim waist with one brawny arm. He slid a hand under Leigh's shirt, fingering the pierced, ringed nipples. His erection ground against slim hips.

Leigh laughed. "What's got you so hot?"

Bending his head, Jas kissed the brown neck. "The weather, the gym...you." With the other hand he began to rub hard mounds of muscle.

Leigh turned, manoeuvring his face to catch the kiss.

Jas opened his mouth and plunged tongue deep into a warm cavern. Strong arms were around his neck as he moved forwards and down, lowering the hard body to the floor. He straddled the slender hips, sensing another hardness beneath his thighs.

Leigh's hardness.

He fed greedily on Leigh, sucking in his taste, wanting to blot out the taste of the Gorbals, the taste of the outside. The more he sucked, the harder he became. Leigh's tongue flicked snake-like around his mouth, causing tiny explosions in his brain. Jas moved back slightly, still gorging on hot saliva, and seized two slim wrists, dragging Leigh's arms from around his neck and pinning him to the kitchen's tiled floor.

Leigh groaned into his mouth.

Jas pulled away and stared down.

Leigh's eyes were shut, lips parted and swollen from the fierceness of the kiss.

Jas sighed. This was the usual prelude to...The Game. He paused.

Ever-alert, Leigh's eyelids sprang open.

Jas released the wrists, then watched as a gentle finger stroked his cheek:

"What's wrong?"

He eased himself from Leigh and turned away.

A hand on his shoulder, a concerned, massaging hand.

Work-life: play-life. Separate...always separate.

He wanted to tell Leigh...he had to tell Leigh. Jas stood up and closed the fridge door, breathing hard.

"You working later?"

Jas leant against the table. "No."

Leigh raised an eyebrow. "Thought you were on nights 'til the end of the week?"

Jas sighed.

Leigh stared, then smiled. "I can never keep track of your shifts." He got up from the floor, plucked an apple from the fruit-bowl. "Oh, by the way..." Munches. "...a couple of guys came looking for you. I did my..." Frowning munch. "...lodger-act, told them I thought you were at the gym. They're calling back..." More munches.

Jas clenched his fists. "Police?" Work-life: play-life.

Leigh tossed the apple-core into the bin. "Didn't say, but the suits did..." He made a mock-jealous face. "One of them was quite dishy, though." Wink. "What have you been up to?" He walked into the hall.

By the telephone, Jas told him.

Leigh paled beneath the tan. "Oh fuck, Jas. You stupid..."

"I know, I know. It happened before I could..." He rubbed his face. "I don't know why I..."

Low voice. "I do."

Jas removed hands from face and stared.

"You want to be sacked...you want to take the easy way out and quit the job, rather than..." The sentence hung unfinished.

Jas sighed. The old argument. He didn't want to think about that, not now, now here...

"You've got a death-wish as far as that job's concerned, Jas."

He pushed away the truth. "That's what the DI said. I've been suspended, pending further investigation."

Leigh fumbled in the leather jacket and produced cigarettes. He lit one. "Can't say I'd be sorry if they threw you out..." He inhaled deeply. "...you know how I feel about what you're doing." A frown. "So what happens now?"

Jas's lungs gasped for the exhaled smoke. He shrugged. "Dunno...don't really care..."

"You care all right..." The voice was soft. "...too fuckin' much." Long fingers caressed his arm.

Jas flinched.

Leigh continued to stroke.

Eyes closed, the red tattoo burst into renewed life. Jas was aware of Leigh's hand, gently massaging a bicep.

They stood, saying nothing, for five minutes.

Then Leigh spoke. "Look: I've got to go. You'll be here all evening?" Pause. Hand removed. "I should be back soon."

Jas opened his eyes. Leigh's features swam a little. He shook his head. "Jo...the hospital."

Sigh. "Cut it loose, Jas. That whole things's making it all so much worse. It's over, you did your best for him, but you can do nothing now..."

Do nothing...

Do nothing...

Powerlessness swept through his body. Eyes open, the red tattoo spidered the wall above Leigh's head. Half of him – the old half – wanted the handcuffs, wanted to cuff those slim, hairless wrists, wanted to blindfold those blue eyes and fuck Leigh the way the job fucked him. The other half – the growing half – wanted to feel long fingers in his hair, wanted to gaze down on a passion-filled face, wanted to watch and be watched as he made love to the most important thing in his life, wanted to have Leigh without the bonds, the tethers.

The two halves were threatening to take over the whole.

"Come on, Jas – we can't go on like this."

He blinked, lowered his eyes to the concerned face. "Leave it, Leigh..." A growl.

Hands up, mock-surrender. "Okay, okay..." Reluctant. "... but take it easy, eh?" A hand on his shoulder. "Try to get an early night."

The hand dropped away. "Be good!"

The door opened, then slammed shut. Jas undressed where he stood and made his way to the shower.

A distant buzz, insistent, unrelenting. He walked through to the hall dripping and lifted the intercom. "Yeah?"

Crackles, then a voice. "DS Anderson?" English accent.

"Who wants to know?"

"CIB. We called earlier, DS Anderson. Can we have a word?"

Jas pressed the 'Entry' button. Somewhere below a dog barked, as the main door to the block swung. Picking up the jeans at his feet, Jas pulled them on. The kid's gun, still in the pocket, dug uncomfortably into his thigh. He rubbed wet hair with the sweatshirt while he waited.

The bell pinged.

Jas peered through the security-viewer, then opened the door. "Got ID?" He wedged one bare foot in place and stared.

Two men. Leigh had been right: off-the-peg, badly-fitting suits. One fiftyish, fat. The other smaller, a little younger, in better shape, vaguely familiar. Little and Large.

Large extended a warrant card officiously.

Jas took it, read it, turned it over, gave it back. "Come in." He moved his foot.

The two men walked past him, into the lounge.

Jas followed, still holding the wet sweatshirt. He threw it on a chair and sat down.

Little and Large stood in the middle of the room.

"Take a seat." Jas gestured to the sofa.

Little sat. Large stood. He spoke. "Chief Inspector McNeil..." Nod to the younger man. "...DS Clark."

Clark...Clark. Jas looked straight ahead.

Large went on: "This is just an informal chat, DS Anderson – you understand?"

Jas nodded, catching Little's eyes. He was under scrutiny.

"No need for the federation rep at this stage, I think..." Large produced a blue folder from somewhere. "Concerning the alleged attack on Mr..." He thumbed through papers. "...Mr. Johnstone, I have the statement you gave to DI Campbell, plus those from the two officers who witnessed the alleged assault..."

Jas looked at the floor. Water evaporated from his hot skin.

"Mr. Johnstone himself is still unconscious," Large continued, impassively, "but will be questioned as soon as possible. Meanwhile..." He looked at Jas.

Jas looked back.

"...we have a slight...discrepancy in statements, DS Anderson, which we hope you can clear up for us..." He looked at Jas.

Jas looked back.

"Your account of the fight is rather unclear. PCs Forsyth and Lambie state they found a knife in Mr. Johnstone's hand: you, DS Anderson, do not mention this knife..."

Jas sighed.

Large glanced at Little, who spoke for the first time: "I hear you were quite badly cut up, DS Anderson." The voice was educated, powerful; Edinburgh accent. "Can I see your hand?"

Edinburgh...Clark...Clark. Jas extended his right arms. Water droplets glistened in thick blond hair.

Little took Jas's wrist, stretching out the fingers. He examined the knuckles. "Defensive cuts?"

Jas pulled the arm away.

Little met his eyes again. "A nasty piece of work, this Johnstone, from all accounts. Tooled-up too. Out looking for trouble, no doubt..."

"I've read your record, DS Anderson," Large broke in. "Exemplary, two bravery commendations. High conviction rate. DI Campbell says you're one of her best officers. You've probably made a lot of enemies, over the past nine years."

Jas looked at the floor.

"The civilian witness..." Rustling papers. "...a Mrs. McGuire, is worse than useless. All she saw was a fight."

Jas looked up.

Large looked at Jas. "You're a big chap, but Johnstone had the knife, took you by surprise, Caught you off guard..."

Jas knew what they wanted him to say. He clenched his fists. He'd done the deed: he'd pay the price.

Large cleared his throat. "Well, I dare say it'll all be cleared up when Mr. Johnstone regains consciousness."

Little stood up. "Don't envy you the streets, DS Anderson." He walked to the CD-stack, long easy strides.

Jas followed with his eyes. The voice was familiar...the face both familiar and not-familiar.

"I hear you've got an appointment with the psych-doctor coming up." Little knelt and began leafing through CDs. He looked round at Jas. "You must be under a lot of strain."

Large: "Can I use your toilet?"

Jas nodded, watching Little. "End of the hall..." The obligatory flat-search.

Large trundled from the room.

"You don't remember me, do you?" Voice soft.

Jas tried to place the face. It still evaded him.

Sigh. "No reason you should, I suppose, We only met once, four years ago and even then it was a brief meeting. I'm sorry I wasn't exactly...grateful for what you did for Ricky." Sad smile. "I had no idea you were in the Force."

The face suddenly found a place for itself. Jas frowned. Summer four years ago... Edinburgh. On temporary secondment to Lothian and Borders: undercover, Vice Squad. No choice in the matter.

Ricky...Richard Clark. Almost lifted for the ancient crime of 'importuning' in a cottage on Calton Hill.

Ricky Clark. Fifteen. Sweet kid. He'd given five blow-jobs before he'd offered to suck off the wrong guy. Jas had bundled Ricky out of the toilets, into a taxi and taken him home before the operation really got going.

Home for Ricky was Blackhall. Very respectable. Very middle-class. Very intolerant.

Ricky's father was the image of the area. Jas had smiled, given Ricky a Gay Switchboard card, the phone number of a new gay youth group but not his own name or rank. It was one of the few times he'd got real satisfaction from the job.

Then Jas had stood on the doorstep of Ricky's imposing Blackhall home and watched as Ricky's imposing, Blackhall father had torn the card into so many pieces, hurled Ricky inside then slammed the door in Jas's face.

He frowned as DS Clark extended a hand.

"We'd both like to thank you..." The strong face creased. "...I should have been...man enough to do so at the time."

Jas stared at the hand, stood up then gripped it. "How's Ricky?"

Smile. "Second year medicine in October..." Smile less sure of itself. "...he wants to do research...AIDS research."

Jas squeezed the hand of a man still fighting to come to terms with his son's sexuality...but getting there. "Tell him ah wis askin' fur him." He looked at the bad suit and the tired eyes.

His grasp was returned. "I will. I owe you one...we both do."

The sound of footsteps.

Jas dropped DC Clark's hand and turned.

Large was back. "Your lodger not in?"

Jas dragged his mind from four years ago and Ricky's Clark's tear-stained face. "A student. Works nights up at Glasgow Uni." The usual lie: he'd done it so often it was automatic. "Now, if ye don't mind..." He moved towards the door. "...ah wis on ma way out."

Large fished in his folder. "So, you don't want to alter your statement, DS Anderson?"

Jas shook his head.

"Have a think about it, anyway," Large said. He turned to his colleague. "Come on, Andrew. Let's leave DS Anderson to consider his position."

They walked from the room. Jas followed.

"We'll be in touch..." Large paused by the door, voice low. "You've got a lot of friends in the Force, Anderson. Don't let them down by refusing their help. Good night..." He moved onto the landing and downstairs.

Andrew hung back. "Give me a buzz," he whispered, pressing a card into Jas's hand, "if you ever need anything." He left in a wake of aftershave.

Jas closed the door, looked at the card, then threw it on the hall table.

The walk to the Royal took thirty minutes. In Intensive Care, Jo Hunter's pale, freckled face was the same as usual. Jas talked.

After two hours, a tap on his shoulder.

Jas looked up. A nurse. Black, young.

"Ye'll need to go now, Detective Anderson. It's late..."

Jas stood up and walked silently from the room. He paused at the nurses' station.

"Time for a cuppa?" Beckoning.

"Aye...why not." She took his arm, leading him into a small room. She sat. He sat.

"Milk? Sugar?"

Jas shook his head. "As it comes..."

The nurse laughed. "I like it strong and black too..."

Jas sipped the bitter liquid. "Do the family still visit?"

"Less and less, these days...too painful." The nurse frowned, then nodded over his shoulder. "He does, though..."

Jas glanced behind, through the perspex window which looked onto the ward. A heavy, ginger-haired figure had taken his place at Jo's side. Thick red growth hid most of the face.

"The brother," the nurse explained. "Works the rigs – or, used to. Gave it up to move home..."

Jas studied the face of Jo Hunter's brother and saw a shadowed, parallel morass of confusion and powerlessness. He shut his eyes, then immediately reopened them. "Ah'll get goin'..." He rose.

"Good night, Detective Anderson."

Jas walked swiftly from the ward.

Four

AS HE APPROACHED Eastercraigs, Jas looked up at the first floor of Number Seven. Light and the low hum of a TV wafted out from two open windows into still, sultry evening air.

He opened the main door and ran up two flights of stairs. The hospital always made him tense...and tension made him hard – hard for Leigh, for Leigh's body. Maybe it had something to do with the stench of death and hopelessness which permeated the Intensive Care ward. Something about the powerlessness of all those inert bodies seemed to empower his own.

But tonight was different. He needed something else from Leigh...something which didn't involve handcuffs.

Jas unlocked two double locks, moved swiftly into the hall, then the lounge. He threw himself onto the sofa, burying his face in Leigh's lap.

The sound of the 'Late Show' burned in his ears as gentle fingers stroked his hair.

"Hey...come on..."

He grasped Leigh's waist with blind hands and pressed his face further into warm denim.

"...it's okay." Stroke, stroke.

Then the stroking stopped. Warms palms on each side of his sweating face, tilting it upwards. Jas gazed into Leigh's blue eyes.

"You wanna talk, or..." Blue eyes flicking towards the door. "...get it all out of your system?"

Jas felt a twitch in the denimed groin at the thought of The Game. Not now. "Ah've goat a headache!"

Leigh laughed, leant over and kissed his forehead. "It's always the same...never a cop available when you need one!"

Jas smiled, lowered his head and stared at the outline of Leigh's prick. His own began to respond. He frowned. Not now. Now was for talking. Real talking.

He eased himself off Leigh and stood up. The frown remained in place.

Leigh raised an eyebrow.

Jas sighed, sat on the floor and reached for the TV remote, turning from his lover's curious face. He flicked.

A girl with glasses and lipstick mouthed silently on-screen.

Jas began to talk at her...

...an hour later the girl with the glasses had been replaced by some guy from the Open University. Jas turned and blinked at Leigh through a haze of cigarette smoke. The ashtray on the sofa was almost full.

Leigh smiled. "You've not told me anything I didn't already know. You can't live with a guy for over a year and not pick up on...things. All that working-out, for a start."

Jas coughed, eyeing the cigarette packet enviously.

"You know that...sex-wise, I can't get enough of you. The SM..." Leigh grinned "...came as a bonus, but I knew what you were doing, what you were using it for – even if you didn't." The handsome face sobered. "Christ, it's hot in here!" Leigh stood up and walked to the open window. "The Game's good for all sorts of things, Jas...balancing your life, channelling energies. I use it to...relax – you know that. But it's only a game – we both know that. It doesn't really solve anything..." He opened the window further, leant two bare arms on the sill. "...out there."

Jas stared. "Ye think ah should pack the job in?"

Leigh turned. "Want my honest opinion?"

Jas clenched his fists. He knew what was coming and didn't want to hear it.

Leigh walked back to the sofa and sat down. Sigh. "Okay. I think you should come out or get out."

"It's no' that easy."

Leigh lit another cigarette. "It's never easy. I've never known a gay cop, let alone one like you. Maybe packing-in the job would..."

"Ah...couldney dae onthin' else!"

"Oh, come on! There's all sorts of...options open to you." Smile. "If the worst comes to the worst, I'll support both of us!"

Jas grinned despite himself.

Leigh talked on. "You like the work – anyone can see that ...though Christ knows why..." He fingered the blond ponytail. "...and you're good at it. There's something in you Jas, something hard that shuts down the part I know, lets you do cop-work and do it well..."

Jas stared.

"...at least, there was..." Sigh. "But you should come out. Tell your boss – Moira, isn't it? Tell her."

Jas sighed. "She'd be okay aboot it, but...ah don't ken if ah kin...face the resta the guys." He stared at Leigh, then looked away.

Low voice. "Thanks."

Jas blinked, then glanced at the tanned face. "Whit fur?"

Leigh smiled through a smoky haze. "That's the first time you've admitted any weakness..."

Long fingers brushed his cheek. Jas held the gaze, then broke it.

"...and it's a start, Jas. You'll be very...vulnerable if you come out. Better start getting used to it."

Jas looked away.

Leigh continued. "Ask for a transfer out of Scotland, if you think a new start'll make things easier. You can move anywhere: London, Brighton...I read somewhere that Sussex Police are actively recruiting in the gay press. Okay, maybe your straight colleagues will call you the same names, but at least you'll have the support of the top brass."

Jas closed his eyes. "Ah widney want tae go withoot... you."

Soft laugh. "I'm not tied to the lab. I can do the research at any university."

Jas frowned. "Ah like Glasgow." He opened his eyes.

Leigh wrinkled his nose. "It's okay, I suppose, but..."

"Ye don't understand. Glasgow's parta me..."

"Gay's a bigger part, Jas. You're not being honest with the people you work with – or anyone else, apart from that junkie tart

Marie – and that's bound to cause you...problems."

Jas rubbed at the polished floor with a sweating finger. Leigh was right. Jas scowled: he was a coward. He knew that. He'd thought he could handle everything and had failed miserably. Movement above him. A hand rubbed his head:

"Think about it, eh? As far as I can see, you've only two options." Fingers stroked his ear-lobe. "I can't stand seeing what this is doing to you, Jas, but..." The stroking stopped. "...of course, it's up to you..."

Jas seized the hand and kissed it. There was so much Leigh didn't – couldn't – know. There were more immediate problems: the threats, the Johnstones, the BMW... He inhaled Leigh's warm skin, mind elsewhere.

Sort the Johnstones out. Then sort his life out.

He stared up at the handsome face. Even talking about it had helped.

Leigh winked.

Jas began to harden. He smiled, stood up and pulled Leigh to his feet. "Whit wur ye sayin' aboot there never being a cop around when ye need one?"

In the bedroom, he lounged in a chair while Leigh stripped. Jas watched as the tanned, naked body crouched, pulled back the rug and pressed the loose floorboard. Lifting out a large, metal box Leigh sat it on the bed, opened it.

Jas stared as Leigh produced a leather jockstrap, a gag, two black silk blindfolds, a tube of lube, a heavy chrome harness and two pairs of police-issue, regulation reinforced steel handcuffs.

Jas frowned. The accoutriments of The Game. The props they used to prop up his life outside this flat.

Leigh carefully, lovingly laid each of the eight items on the bed. "Okay?" The voice was low, husky.

"Okay what?"

"Okay, Jas."

"That's better." He undressed efficiently then strolled naked to the bed. "Ye ken white tae dae, Leigh?"

"Yes, Jas." Leigh walked to the window, closed it and the venetians. Crossing to the far wall he illuminated the dark room with one 120-watt spotlight, trained it on the bed. The hot room became hotter.

"Whit are ye, Leigh?"

Leigh knelt at his feet, head bent. "An animal."

Jas watched their shadows, huge on the wall. "What kind o' animal?"

"A dirty animal."

"And...?"

"A bad animal."

"And whit tae bad animals deserve?"
"Discipline."
"And whit dae bad animals need?"
"Discipline."
Jas grabbed loose blond hair and yanked Leigh's head back. "An' whit dae bad animals love?"
The eyes were open, pleading. "Discipline."
Jas hauled Leigh to his feet before he drowned in those eyes. Hot breath on his cheek. "Is that whit ye want, Leigh?"
"Yes, Jas. Please..."
"Begin."
Lifting the jockstrap, Leigh stepped into it, cramming his hard prick into the small pouch. The black straps stretched tight over his buttocks, cutting into white flesh.
"The harness."
Obediently, Leigh picked up the heavy leather and metal restrainer, held it out, then turned.
Jas slipped it over the tanned body, fastening buckles at groin and shoulders. "The handcuffs."
Leigh raised the bracelets, securing one around each wrist. Then he knelt, staring up at Jas. "What about...?" Eyes flicked between Jas, the gag and blindfolds, then back again.
Jas scowled. Two instincts struggled within him. "Ah want to see yer face. Ah want you to see ma face as ah fuck ye." He glanced at the handcuffs. They could stay. Jas tore his eyes from Leigh's. "Get the KY..."
Leigh turned towards the bed.
Bracing one foot against the brass bed-frame, Jas grinned. "On second thoughts..." He pushed Leigh down. In one easy movement he linked each wrist with the bedhead, three feet apart.
Leigh lay there, spreadeagled on the bed, a sacrificial lamb tethered but not longer blind, no longer speechless.
Jas watched as a smile of curiosity flitted over the features before transforming itself into a grin of understanding.
"Get that look aff yer face, Leigh."
Complicity. Using the cuffs for leverage, Leigh raised long, tanned legs over blond head, twining feet between the bars of the bedhead.
Jas stared at Leigh's arse, each cheek bisected by the athletic support's straining leather straps. His balls spasmed unexpectedly. He moved into the bed, kneeling.
Leigh was breathing heavily, and Jas could see seven inches twitching on a honey-coloured, hairless stomach. Gently, he nudged thighs apart, lowered his head and licked one of Leigh's balls.
A sigh filled the room.
Jas continued to lick, enjoying the taste and texture of stretched scrotum under his tongue.

"Let me touch you." Words barely audible.

Jas raised his head from between Leigh's thighs and smiled. "Whit ur ye?" He stared at the handsome face.

Full lips quivered. "Silent."

Jas returned to his task.

When he'd licked and sucked every centimetre of Leigh's balls and prick into a stiff, molten mixture of sweat and spit, he moved back and stared at the arsehole. The small, crinkled orifice was contracting with pleasure. Jas smiled. Spreading a broad palm on each cheek He pressed with shaking fingers, opening the man. Jas glanced up between rigid thighs.

A sticky droplet of precum glued the head of Leigh's prick to the hard stomach.

Jas grinned and moved his eyes further upwards.

Leigh's face was a series of creases, criss-crosses of pleasure and the pain of waiting. The eyes were shut, despite his instructions.

Jas smiled. They could stay like that...for now. His own prick was near to detonation point...but control was something he was good at.

Control was something life had taught him.

Control was something Leigh had helped him focus.

Sliding his naked body to the foot of the bed, Jas lay down and buried his face in Leigh's arse-crack. Tongue played up and down the length of the warm crevice. The pink, crinkled hole opened like a goldfish's mouth. Jas sighed softly into Leigh.

The emptiness was a distant dot.

Nothing else mattered. Only this...

As his tongue began to probe the inside of his lover's warm body, a shriek filled his ears: "No, Jas! No! I'm gonna come if you do that!"

He smiled, moved back a little then spat into the open arsehole, smearing saliva over spasming lips of muscle.

Another shriek.

Jas pulled himself up the bed and knelt beside the shuddering body. "Open yer eyes, Leigh." He kissed a damp forehead.

Eyelids sprang open, blue irises locked with his.

Jas stared into huge, dilated pupils. "Watch ma face while ah fuck ye, Leigh. Ah want to see ye scream when ah make ye come."

Something about the eyes made his heart almost explode. He traced the outline of a pink swollen mouth, rubbed blond sandpaper stubble above the upper lip, then removed trembling fingers.

The expression on Leigh's face was making it impossible to hold off any longer.

He moved to behind Leigh's elevated arse, spat into his hands and began to lubricate his prick. Shivers of anticipation racked his body: saliva dried fast, allowed for friction. He closed his ears to

Leigh's moans and spat again, smearing more saliva around the already slippery, dilating hole. Leigh groaned, inhaled. "Now, Jas..."

Guiding his prick, he plunged into Leigh.

Tight, hard muscle resisted his thrusts. Jas braced a hand against Leigh's arse, withdrew a little then pushed again. Skin dragged, then entry was easy. Elbowing the finely-muscled legs aside, he slipped between Leigh's rigid thighs and grasped a cuffed wrist. He twined fingers of the other hand in the long blond hair which was now slick with sweat.

Leigh grunted softly, pushing up against him.

Two bodies moved in mirrored unison.

Sensation shimmered along the length of his prick as muscles deep inside Leigh's hot body caressed and massaged. His lower abdomen struck Leigh's thighs, slapping, wet sounds. Jas drove into Leigh harder, faster.

The body beneath quivered, the panting sounds quickening.

Jas stared into huge blue eyes, extending body-lock to mind-lock.

Leigh's pupils spoke volumes...pleading, knowing, urging, enjoying.

Slamming against sweat-slicked flesh, Jas could hold back no longer. Pressure which began in his balls was filling his body.

Leigh was saying something inaudible.

Buzzing in his ears, the noise of his heart and the quickening slap of flesh on flesh.

Muscle deep inside Leigh began to spasm.

Jas checked his own pleasure, sensing a climax in the body below. He removed one hand from Leigh's cuffed wrist and laid palm over a throbbing prick.

Deep inside Leigh, muscle contracted in response.

Only seconds now...

At the point of orgasm, Jas squeezed Leigh's erection. "Whit are ye?"

A breathy whisper. "Yours...only yours..."

A bright, red explosion in his balls coincided with Leigh's climax. In his head, Jas screamed as his prick seemed to shatter.

On the bed, Leigh made an ancient, primal sound, pumping semen into Jas's hand.

As warm sticky liquid soldered fingers together, Jas buried his face in blond hair. He felt Leigh's legs move from between the bars of the metal bedhead and wrap themselves around his thighs.

Cooling sweat and lukewarm spunk melted two bodies into one...

Beneath his weight he felt Leigh stir. Jas stretched across the tanned body, fumbling under the mattress for handcuff keys.

On the bed, Leigh was breathing more deeply.

Jas unlocked one manacled hand, then smoothed soaking hair from the handsome face, from the damp, still-closed eyelids. Pink exertion showed beneath bronzed skin. Jas turned Leigh onto his side, took him in his arms and pulled the limp body against his own, a sweating back leaning against damp chest-hair.

Two heartbeats synchronised, gradually slowing. Wrists tight against nipple-rings, softening prick still deep inside Leigh's body, eventually Jas fell asleep...

A distant, soothing purr.

He blinked, immediately awake. The clock showed 11am. At his side, Leigh stirred. A languid moan, movement.

In the hall, the answering-machine beeped into life.

Jas sat up, head fuzzy.

Marie's amplified voice. "Jeez, man! Ye didn't warn me ye'd goat wanna these things..."

Springing from the bed, he made his way into the hall. He picked up the receiver. "Marie?"

"Laugh. "Yer up then, ah...."

Jas broke in. "Anythin' fur me?"

The laugh continued. "No' as much as a guid mornin', ye bad-mannered bastard!"

"Get oan with it, Marie!"

Huffy. "Okay..." Deep breath. "Well, the Johnstones urney sayin' much, fae whit ah hear. " A throaty laugh. "Yer oan the front page o' the *Record*, Jas. Nae names, though..." Rustling. "It sez...er, 'a man is recoverin' in Glasgow's Southern General Hospital after a brutal attack on Sunday night. A police officer has been suspended, pendin' inquiries...' That'll be you, eh?"

"The Johnstones, Marie. Where can ah find them?"

"Sigh. "Wull ye no' leave it, man? Ye've enough oan yer plate withoot..."

"Jist tell me!" Jas saw the 'Messages waiting' display, which had read '2' last night, now read zero.

Resignation. "Huv it yer ain way. They're workin' oota a breaker's yard doon at Barrack Street – by the auld sidings. D'ye ken where ah mean?"

"Aye, Marie. Thanks. Ah owe ye wan..."

"Yer no' goin' looking fur trouble, Jas, ur ye?" Worried.

He laughed. "Ma beef wis wi' Jimmy, no' his brothers..."

"Well...jist watch yersel', Jas. They're big lads..."

"Ah'm only wantin' tae talk tae them, Marie. Thanks fur the word..." Jas paused. "Ali said ye didn't huv a phone – where ye callin' fae?"

Laugh. "Ah'm mobile noo, Jas. The new guy ah'm snoutin' fur

gied it me. Ah canny tell ye the number, though. Naeb'dy kens it but him. Sorry..."

"Nae problem..."

"Guid luck with the polis, Big Man. Ah hope they take ye back. Jimmy'll keep his mooth shut, if he's goat ony sense..."

"Thanks, Marie." He severed the connection and walked through to the bedroom.

Leigh slept on, the deep, peaceful, dreamless sleep of the innocent.

Jas frowned and unlocked the remaining cuff. He knew pins and needles would have set in, and began to massage sensation back into hand and wrist.

A moan.

Jas scowled. Leigh shared enough of his problems: he'd handle the Johnstones alone. He lowered the brown arm, turned, opened the wardrobe, lifting out a navy suit. Lurking in a heap of sweatshirts, the hand-gun, its serial number filed off rendering it untraceable. A single bullet sat in one of its six chambers. Jas slipped the weapon into a trouser pocket.

On the bedside table lay his appointment card for the police psychiatrist: Tuesday – today – at three o'clock. Pitt Street, Divisional headquarters. The alarm clock's hands slouched towards 11.30 am. Jas began his workout.

Fifty press-ups, sit-ups and burpees later, he was showered, shaved and dressed. He opened the curtains. Leigh still slept, his hairless chest gleaming in the noon sun. Walking over to the bed, Jas sat down, running hard fingers over soft, smooth skin.

Leigh snuffled, stretched and kicked the duvet to the bottom of the bed. Lying naked on his stomach, fine blond hair cascaded over shoulders.

Jas smiled. Placing a hand on the brown back, he shook.

Leigh stirred, snuffled again.

Jas shook harder.

Leigh moaned, eased himself up on an elbow and turned. Voice heavy, half-awake. "Thought you'd be sleeping late today..." The slavic cheekbones shone. Leigh patted the space beside him.

Jas toyed with the nipple-rings instead. "Things tae dae. Ah shouldney be that long. You working?"

Leigh moved onto his back. "Tonight. Evening classes..." He scratched his groin, grinned. "Is it worth getting dressed ..." Reaching up, he took Jas's face between palms. "...or shall I wait here for you?"

Gently, Jas removed the hands. "Back about five..." How long would the shrink-visit take?

Leigh sat up and reached for cigarettes. "Where you off to, anyway?" He eyed the suit.

Jas told him, leaving out the Johnstone brothers.

Cigarette lit. Thoughtful, then: "What we were talking about last night..." Smoke exhaled. "...psychiatrists have some sort of...ethic of confidentiality, don't they? You could sound Dr. Freud out on the subject of..."

"The sessions are fur...evaluation. Ah'm no' huvin' some guy ah don't ken pokin' his nose intae ma business."

Leigh puffed lazily and smiled. "It'll be everyone's business if you decide to come out, Jas. Better get ready for that..."

As Leigh talked on, Jas's mind was back with the Johnstones and their car-valetting service. An hour should do it. He'd find out what he needed to know.

"...think we could get away for a couple of weeks, when this disciplinary business has all blown over?" Leigh had moved onto other topics. "Give us a chance to...think."

Jas watched as the slender, naked body slipped out of bed and struggled into jeans. He smiled.

"You know," Leigh continued, "I bet you could get some paid, compassionate leave out of all this..." He zipped up then peered critically at himself in the large mirror on the wall behind the bed.

Jas watched Leigh admire his own body, enjoying the narcissism. Over a shoulder, Leigh met his eyes. "...if you play it right!" He winked and turned. "Two weeks of sun, sand and..." Wink. "...do you the world of good, Jas. Get it all out of your system."

"The sun's here." Jas nodded to the window.

"No sand, though," Leigh countered. "I've always fancied going back to LA – you've never been, I know. Cheap flights, I've got a couple of friends we could stay with. LA's great, Jas...you'd love it!"

Another dirty city, crime rate through the roof and the added hassle of armed police and civilians.

Leigh eyed the growing bulge in Jas's trousers. "Is that a gun in your pocket, officer..." He placed hand on hip. "...or are you just pleased to see me?"

Yesterday's confiscation snuggled against his thigh. "It's a gun..." He withdrew the weapon.

Leigh's eyes widened. He grinned. "Don't shoot me, officer! I'll...come quietly."

Jas laughed, laying the gun on the crumpled duvet.

Leigh stared at it curiously. "Is it real?"

Jas nodded, detailing the weapon's history.

"Don't hand it in," Leigh pleaded. "Let's keep it..." He traced the barrel with a long finger and glanced at Jas, eyes sparkling. "Another...toy never goes wrong."

With a sigh, Jas bent down and tucked the hand-gun under the mattress. "Don't you go near it, right?"

"Yes, boss!" Leigh knelt before him and began to undo the fly of Jas's trousers.

"No time!" Jas growled, as he rose and walked to the door. He needed the tension, if he was to get through the afternoon. Just before the front door, he grabbed shades and glanced at the telephone. "Oh...git in touch wi' BT, will ya? We need the number changed again."

"Sure, boss..."

Leigh's Game voice followed him out of the flat.

Five

AT THE FOOT of Craigpark he paused. The air rippled with heat. Traffic was heavy into town. Jas stood on the edge of the pavement, waiting for a lull in the long procession of vehicles. He loosened his tie.

Behind, in Anfield Place, revving.

Jas turned seconds before the white BMW propelled itself towards him. Acceleration zero to sixty in four seconds. Mounting the pavement, the large car bore down on him, clouds of dust puffing from beneath the tyres.

Jas stepped up onto stone-anchored railings, pressing his body against iron bars.

A sickening thud as the front bumper impacted on concrete, brushing his left foot. Screeching into reverse, the car pulled away, wheels spinning and drove off down Sword Street.

Jas caught sight of the back of the driver's head, eyes moving to the number-plate: obscured. He stepped down from his perch. A hand on his arm:

"Ur ye okay, son?"

A woman, elderly, dragging tartan trolley-bag and a dog.

Jas straightened his tie. "Aye, missus, but thanks for the thought..." He patted the dog.

She shook her head. "Ah couldney get his number, but ah saw the hale thing, son. If ye phone the polis, ah'll tell them whit happened..." Ancient eyes.

"It's okay, missus. Ah think ah ken the driver...or at least the cor..." Jas walked away.

Flash BMW. Car-valetting. The Johnstones...

Duke Street was no cooler. Blood leaked from the ankle-graze. Jas stopped, pulled down a sock and mopped with a handkerchief.

The Johnstones...

He walked on. There were four brothers in total: Liam, Michael,

Jimmy and Neil. Years ago they had all lived with an aging mother at the family home, in Provanmill Road. One police-raid too many had scattered the offspring to the four winds, so much bad seed searching for more fertile ground.

In his forties, Liam Johnstone was the brains of the family – if inbred halfwits could be said to possess brains – and the driving force behind the family's criminal activities. The valetting service was probably his idea, a gloss over the diversification into rent boys. A front – that was Liam: camel-coated and pinky-ringed, he knew all the tricks and never got his hands dirty. If there was an acceptable face to Glasgow crime, Liam was it. A very dangerous man...

"Ony change, pal?"

A scrawny, bare-chested figure lounging in the sunshine. Jas tossed him fifty pence.

He caught it easily. "Cheers! yer a gent, Big Man, a real gent..."

Michael was the trendy Johnstone. About Jas's age, part-owner of a city-centre hairdressers, Michael was gay. He and Jas had come to an uneasy understanding years ago. An orientation in common: nothing more.

Michael liked his meat young and fresh, and didn't particularly care how he got it. But drugs were Michael's first love. Five charges of possession, three with intent to supply, Michael was still dealing, as far as Jas knew. The flashy 'merchant city' salon had been raided twice in the past year: smack, tems, E, and, more recently, crack cocaine, manufactured in a bathtub in Possilpark. Michael was usually off his face and apparently liked it that way. He had done more hours in detox, to avoid jail, than any Gorbals junkie.

At seventeen, Neil Johnstone was just a kid, but legacies passed down early in his family. Hot-wiring and car-radio theft had slipped into reckless driving: Neil had killed a pedestrian two years ago. Marie McGhee had witnessed the 'accident', Jas was the arresting officer. Neil was at present serving a one-to-two stretch in Barlinnie, no doubt learning new skills. Now Neil, like his brothers, was a lost cause.

Jas turned a corner.

Halfway down semi-derelict Barrack Street, sweat pooling on his skin, Jas found what he was looking for. A sign bore the legend 'McKay's Spares' in large, untidy, hand-painted letters. Underneath, in a more professional script, read 'Johnstone's Valetting and Car-Care Service.' Jas glanced at the oil-streaked ground: if you really cared about your car, you wouldn't bring it here. The breaker's yard was a soup of old iron and oxidising metal, landscaped with towering heaps of twisted body-parts. An ancient crane held sway over this domain, this elephant's graveyard where vehicles came to die.

But appearances deceive.

The surrounding wall was topped by double-spiked barbed wire.

A closed-circuit camera looked down from a high post above the gate. High-powered sodium security lights dotted the perimeter fence.

There was something here worth protecting.

Two chained Rottweilers growled half-heartedly from the side of a shabby Portacabin, their services surplus to requirements amidst the high technology.

Under a flawless blue sky, Jas walked through the open gate.

In a corner, behind the Portacabin, lay a fenced-off area, demarked from the general messiness by a triple-link, reinforced-steel mesh barrier. Within, like prized steers, sat four cars: a red Porsche, a Mitsubishi jeep and two BMWs.

Neither were white.

"Can ah help ye, pal?"

A heavy, surly man in overalls oozed from behind a multi-coloured pile of rusting car doors. Sweat and grime etched his features in a dirty pen-and-ink sketch. He carried a sledgehammer. He was not a Johnstone.

"The boss in?" Jas nodded towards the enclosure.

A smiled slashed the dirt-smeared face. "Wantin' yer cor valetted, sir?" The large chest heaved, lungs opening. "We dae a collection service, sir. Door-tae-door. Complete internal and external cleanin', colour-wax and polish, upholstery shampoo, metal-work buffin'. The executive treatment." The man ended his prepared speech, the smile fixed. It sat uneasily with the sledgehammer.

Jas laughed. "Ye dae manicures as well?"

The smile didn't slip.

"A word wi' yer boss?" Jas repeated.

The man shrugged, lumbering to the Portacabin. He opened the door. "Mr. Johnstone? Customer fur ye..." With one last look at Jas, he walked back to his car doors.

Leaning against the Portacabin, Jas waited.

Jimmy.

Jimmy Mygo.

Jas tensed.

One of the Rottweilers gave a low growl, then whimpered.

Where Liam was top dog in the Johnstone pack, Jimmy was the dirt you scraped from your shoe. If there was a vulnerable face around – male or female – Jimmy laughed in it, fucked it, then cut it up. At twenty, having spent more time in Longriggend Borstal than out, Jimmy was the black sheep of a thoroughly ebony flock. No pretence of respectability, Jimmy sported his peccadilloes with pride. He ran the girls, a group of terrified prostitutes including, until two years ago, Marie McGhee...and now presumably the boys. There were stories of how Jimmy broke-in his stable of whores, told by the few who'd escaped, fled to new identities, new lives: Jimmy believed in a thorough road-test for all his rides.

Jas tensed again and closed his eyes.
Jo Hunter's face appeared.
Completely, frighteningly sane, Jimmy was a walking lobby for capital punishment. Bad to the bone, he gave new meaning to the concept of antisocial behaviour.
A creak from the Portacabin door.
Beneath shades, Jas opened his eyes.
A red-faced figure, sweating in the obligatory fawn-coloured coat: Arthur Daley's alter ego. The dogs began to bark ecstatically. A cellular telephone in one hand. The other was extended. Liam Johnstone gave the impression of healthy affluence, of a slightly old-fashioned respectability straight from Burton's window.
Jas stared.
The outstretched hand remained. "Good afternoon, sir..."
The polish and veneer extended further than gleaming cars. Carefully-modulated tones. Not the gravel voice on the answering-machine. But Liam wouldn't involve himself directly: always the showman, the whip-cracker. Someone else would turn the cartwheels.
"...let me show you our facilities, the complete valetting package for the busy executive..."
The hand of friendship transformed to one of salesmanship.
Jas looked into the bluff, hearty face, into the dead pupils.
If eyes were the windows of the soul, Liam's venetians were well-and-truly down. Jas had met Liam many times.
"I do a clean-up service myself..." Jas matched the accent. "Rubbish should be put firmly in its place, don't you agree Mr. Johnstone?"
A flicker, then the blinds were back down. "I didn't catch your name, Mr...?" Smooth as baby-oil, tough as raw meat.
"How's Jimmy doing?" Jas leant against the thick, mesh fence. Above, a merciless sun glanced off his shades.
Liam scrutinised his face. Thoughtful. "Jimmy? Can't say I know the name. Now..." Business-like. "..our rates are highly competitive, Mr...?"
Jas removed the shades.
Stare. Aggression leaking from behind the blinds. "Ah ken you..." Veneer chipping to reveal cheap formica. Voice raised. "Michael? Get oot here!"
"Wan mair piece a trash aff the streets, eh Liam?" Jas grabbed the hairy lapels. Pushing the bulky form back against the mesh fence, Jas held him there, minty breath on his face.
"Michael! Noo!"
The dogs began to growl.
Jas maintained his grip. Liam's face was inches from his own. He inhaled fear, a musky undernote beneath Hugo Boss.
There was no sound from the Portacabin.
Sledgehammer Man had merged with his scrapheap, hear-no-

evil, see-no-evil.

Releasing the lapels, Jas patted the luxurious fabric. "Ah don't think Michael heard ye, Liam. Gie it another go..." He seized the man's testicles and squeezed hard.

Liam's falsetto shriek pierced the air. He dropped the cellular telephone and clutched at his genitals.

"Well, well..." A drawling voice. "...Detective Anderson! Long time no see..."

Liam crumpled to the ground, retching.

Jas focused on the tall, thin designer suit making its way slowly down the Portacabin steps. Versace wore Michael Johnstone like a hair-shirt, penance for high-priced pretensions. Dark hair greased back in a pony-tail. Bad teeth. You can take the man out of Provanmill...

"Whit've ye done tae Liam?" Mild curiosity, not concern.

Stepping over the writhing body, Jas met Michael at the bottom of the stairs. he mounted the first step.

"Far enough, Jas..." Sloppy vowels, the glint of a blade.

Jas stopped. Michael's eyes said he was somewhere in lunar space, but the knife would be used instinctively.

The head shook slowly. "Jas, Jas...ye're losin' it, man..." Mock-regret. "...getta grip. This'll no solve onythin'..."

"Stay aff ma back, Michael. Ah've nae argument wi' you or Liam..."

"Whit makes ye think we'd bother wi' the likes o' you, Jas Anderson? Nae need. The polis'll handle it fur us..." Laugh. "...is that no whit we pay oor taxes fur?" Glassy eyes shone in glazed sunshine. "Aggravated assault, Jas..." A tutting sound. "...whit ye did tae poor Jimmy wizney very nice, wis it?" Emotionless.

Jas leant on the stair-rail.

"Ye could dae time fur that, Jas, no' jist..." Laugh. "...disciplinary proceedings. By the way, Neil sends his regards. Ye ken how close he an' Jimmy ur. He tried tae phone ye but ye wurney in. Sez he'll keep a bunk warm fur ye in the Bar-L..." Leer.

On the ground, Liam was fumbling with the cellular telephone. Breathy, still-strangled, gasping words. "Ah'm callin' the polis, Anderson. They'll huv ye inside so fast..."

"Leave it, Liam. Jas wis jist goin' – is that no' right?"

"Stay aff ma back! Wan mair BMW in ma patch an'..."

"Whit ye oan aboot?" Liam was on his feet now, massaging his damaged groin. "Somewan nicked yer cor, Anderson? Well, dinny bother lookin' here. We're clean..." He hobbled towards the dogs

"Ye've been warned, Liam. Ah don't want ony trouble."

On the stairs, Michael laughed again, low and detached. "Yer whole life's trouble, Jas! Noo, awa' back home an' gie that wee cracker in yer bed wan fae me..."

A red, raw emotion surged in his head. With one swift movement Jas knocked the knife from Michael's hand and seized the unshaven neck. "Stay away." The words were even. Beneath his palm, an adam's apple bobbed.

Michael gurgled, clawing at Jas's knuckles with bitten-down fingernails.

Jas let go, and walked from the yard.

Michael's voice hissed after him. "Widney dirty oor hands, Anderson...yer ain lot'll git ye..."

He strolled along stifling Argyle Street and up Wellington Street towards Pitt Street. Divisional Headquarters.

The paint on the Johnstones' new venture was still tacky, and underneath they were the same as ever: cold, hard and ruthless. Had one of Liam's trained seals been behind the wheel of the white BMW, the job would've been done properly. If the brothers were after Jas, he wouldn't have got out of that breaker's yard alive.

But at least the phone-calls had been explained...

Jas looked at his watch: 2.50 pm. Could Neil Johnstone have organised the murder attempt from his prison cell?

Pushing open the door of Divisional Headquarters, Jas approached the desk. "DS Anderson to see Doctor..." He pulled out the card and read. "...Mawhinny. Three o'clock."

The duty sergeant nodded, lifted a telephone and directed him to a row of seats.

Jas sat.

"Warm, isn't it?" English accent.

The room was a claustrophobic cube in the basement. Jas dragged his eyes from the wall opposite. The small, cell-like chamber tried to look like a consulting room and failed. Dr. Mawhinny, with his talk of things meteorological, tried to sound friendly and failed.

Jas knew why he was here. This man could see into his soul...if Jas let him.

He looked at Dr, Mawhinny, who lounged back in his chair on the other side of the room. "Summer often is." His eyes glanced over this wrist-watch: twenty minutes had passed.

A laugh. Uncomfortable, forced joviality. "Not Glaswegian summers, I gather. This is my first, and I must say I'm quite impressed. Almost puts London in the shade..."

Jas looked at the wall, then the psychiatrist.

Dr. Mawhinny produced a packet of cigarettes and shook them at Jas.

Jas declined.

"Mind if I do?"

Jas shook his head.

"Odd things happen when the mercury shoots above, say, eighty degrees..." Mawhinny lit a cigarette.

Jas placed the accent. Oxford. Donnish. He looked at Dr. Mawhinny's shiny, hairless head. Wisps peeked perkily from his ears. The man wasn't in good physical shape. Baggy formless trousers strained over a too-tight belt. Unintentionally unstructured, his tweed sports-jacket hung limply from narrow shoulders. Beneath the table there were sure to be white socks in black shoes.

"...especially in countries unused to such temperatures. You Scots..."

Eyes now on the Mawhinny features, Jas examined his examiner. Insipid brown eyes sat above a broad nose, which bore down on a weak mouth.

"...most Celtic races, in fact, much as they bemoan their cold, damp climate actually thrive in it..."

Late forties, having only recently tumbled from his ivory tower, theorist becoming realist, academic becoming practitioner.

"...even in tropical climates there's a danger-zone. Below this lies the norm; above, it's too hot to do anything. In between are about three degrees wherein tempers fray, blood pressures rise...the irritability factor surfaces."

In the Heat of the Night, Cat on a Hot Tin Roof, Jane Fonda and men called Bubba. Jas smiled at the wall.

"Everyone is affected, those in stressful occupations to a greater extent. People react to ordinary situations..." Cough. "...in extraordinary ways..." Pause. Sigh.

Jas stared at the wall, just above the skirting-board. It was in need of a coat of paint.

Scraping of chair-legs.

Jas looked up. Mawhinny was on his feet. Jas watched as he approached a filing cabinet, opened it, rummaged then withdrew a file. Returning to his chair, Mawhinny sat down, smiled.

Jas stared at the thin lips.

Throat clearing the phlegm of too many cigarettes. "Is there anything you'd like to talk about, DS Anderson – may I call you James?"

"No."

"To which question?"

"To both."

Sigh, then another cigarette. "This isn't helping anyone, DS Anderson." Exasperation. "I know why I'm here. As part of the internal investigation into your alleged assault on Mr. Johnstone, I'm obliged to assess your...er..."

Jas bent down and rubbed his ankle. The sock was warm with blood.

"...state of mind. Do you understand what that means, DS Anderson? Do you know why you're here?"

Jas straightened, nodded.

Pleased. "Good. Now...a bit of background would be helpful. Do you like your job?"

"I don't need to like it. Do you like yours?"

"Well...I get satisfaction from helping people..."

"So do I."

Pause. Rustling of papers. "Do you see that as the main objective of your work?"

"Yes."

"Were you helping someone when you assaulted Mr. Johnstone?"

"He's beyond help."

Surprise. "That's not what I mean. Do you see your assault on Mr. Johnstone as a means of helping someone else – his alleged victim, perhaps?"

"He's beyond help."

Papers rustling. Pause. Comprehension. "Ah, yes. Joseph Hunter." Pause. "I don't envy you your job. Would you like to talk about it?"

Jas looked at the wall. "No."

Sniff. "Well, there's plenty of time for that." Pause. "I see from your record..." More rustlings. "...that you joined the police force at nineteen. "Pause. "Good group of 'Highers'. Shame to waste them. I'm sure you could study for a degree, maybe part-time. There are many schemes on offer, these days. A couple of years' leave of absence..." Pause. "Does that appeal to you, DS Anderson?"

Jas looked from the wall to Mawhinny, then back to the wall.

"Well...perhaps not. Now..." Pause. The squeaking of PVC upholstery. "...I need to know a bit about you."

Jas looked at his watch: thirty minutes had passed.

"Are your parents alive?"

Jas nodded.

"How's your relationship with them?"

"Ah see them about twice a year." They had never met Leigh, never wanted to.

"Your childhood was happy?"

"I've no complaints."

"Now...siblings?"

"Three brothers and a sister."

"Ah, yes..." Another cigarette.

Jas tensed.

"Your older brother works in London – casino manager. Your sister is also involved in...er, the entertainment industry?"

"Babs sings." Dougie was a lost cause.

"The others?"

It was all in the file. "Alec's a physics teacher, David's on the dole..."

"And how do they feel about you – your career?"

"I don't ask them." Jas looked at Mawhinny. His career they could live with. His lifestyle?

A long pause. Sigh, then: "You're not making this any easier, DS Anderson. Tell me about yourself, in your own words..."

"What do you want to know?" Jas cracked his fingers. The sound echoed.

Mawhinny jumped, then laughed. Nervous. "More about you, James..."

"It's Jas."

"Unusual contraction. I've not heard that one before. As in freeform?"

"As in James with the 'm-e' omitted..."

Interest. "Is that how you see yourself, Jas? A James with no middle, a man with no..."

"Ah don't see myself..." The emptiness... Jas pushed the insight aside. "...not without a mirror." He looked at the amorphous pink face. Mawhinny's brown eyes glowed hazel. Jas shrugged.

"And who would that mirror be, Jas – your wife, girlfriend? Family? Colleagues?"

Jas sighed. Even to this highly-educated, presumed reasonably-intelligent man it was inconceivable that a Glasgow cop might be gay. "The one on my bedroom wall."

Snort, then sigh. "Come on, Jas. Don't play games. You're a bright guy..." Mawhinny flicked through the file in frustration.

"I'm not playing games." Jas looked at Mawhinny.

Sweat beaded the man's face.

Jas smiled.

Mawhinny scowled. "Have it your own way, DS Anderson." He picked up a pen and began to write. "I need to understand why you attacked Mr. Johnstone, and to do that I need to understand you..."

Jas watched the flabby hand produce neat script.

Mawhinny looked up. "Clear enough so far?" Barely-concealed sarcasm.

Jas nodded.

"And to do that you must answer some questions. How do you feel about that?" Jas shrugged. "Give me straight questions, I'll give you straight answers." Straight...straight...

"That's better." Mawhinny recommenced writing. "Now..."

Jas closed his eyes.

"You freely admit the attack on Mr. Johnstone?"

Jas nodded. Jo Hunter's face quivered.

"Why did you attack Mr. Johnstone? Can you explain to me how you felt at the time, how you feel about it now?"

Jas opened his eyes, blinked. "Question one: because he was askin' fur it. As for questions two and three: I can, but I don't think

I will." He glanced at his watch. Minute hand on twelve.

The hour was up.

Jas rose. "Will you want to see me again?"

Mawhinny remained seated, closing the file. The face was tired. He lit a cigarette. "Tomorrow at the same time?"

Jas nodded. "Goodbye, doctor."

"Think about what we've said, Jas..."

Jas left the room.

Six

AS HE WALKED along Sauchiehall Street, Jas surveyed the empty pavements. Too hot for shopping. Too hot for most things. Glasgow city centre was unnaturally quiet. The pedestrian precinct shimmered in stultifying heat. He crossed Rose Street.

Ahead, a small figure emerged from an ice-cream parlour, holding a large cone. Over-sized leather jacket. Long dark hair. Sweat pants. Large black trainers.

Jas quickened his pace, drawing parallel.

She stiffened, turned then grinned. "Wanna licka ma pokey-hat, mister?" Marie extended the dripping confection. The scar twitched.

Jas stuck a finger into the melting ice-cream, withdrew then sucked it. He scowled, saccharine stinging his tongue.

Marie laughed. "Ye're sweet enough, Big Man." Elbowing her voluminous shoulder-bag aside, she took his arm. "Whit you dain' way up here?"

He told he about Mawhinney.

She giggled at the name, then shook her head. "Ah widney like to git inside that skull o' yours, Jas...."

"What brings you oot fae under yer rock?" He looked at the pale, untanned face.

She slapped him playfully. "Business." Marie tapped her nose.

"Dain' hame visits?"

She laughed.

They walked on. Outside Marks and Spencer Marie stopped. She turned to Jas. "Goat tae get somethin' fur ma tea, Jas – comin' in?"

The air-conditioning beckoned like a lover. Jas loosened his tie. "Sure..."

They walked through double swing-doors and up stairs.

Marie seized a basket, steering Jas towards the 'Cook/Chill' section. "Ye survived the Johnstones, ah see. Whit happened?" She scrutinized the sell-by date of two chicken tikkas.

Jas told her, including the two BMW encounters.

She returned one of the chicken tikkas to the refrigerated unit, placing the other in the basket. "Aye, sounds like Neil right enough. A wee toe-rag, that one..." She moved on.

Pilau rice dropped into the basket.

"Git yer number changed..."

Fresh raspberries and a carton of cream joined the main course.

"...Neil's aw' talk. That'll shut him up..." Marie lifted a bottle of wine, examined the label then arranged it and two identical bottles carefully to one side of her other purchases.

Jas took the basket from her.

"Ye're still left with the car, though. Neil's no' that organised..." Marie led the way to the check-out. They joined the 'Five-items-and-under' queue. "...an' onyway, hit an' run's not the Johnstones' style." She fingered the scar. "Huv ye annoyed onywan else recently, Big Man?"

Three shoppers in front, two behind.

"Not that ah know...." A tap on his shoulder, tentative. Jas turned.

Middle-aged woman in pastels. "Excuse me, but I think you'll find there are six items in your basket." Frowning, Kelvinside. "This queue is for five items and under."

Behind, mumbles of agreement and support.

Marie spun round. "Ye want tae make somethin' o' it, missus?" The scar twinkled, looking for a fight.

Kelvinside paled under heavy tan foundation and stepped back.

Marie stepped forward.

Kelvinside searched for back-up but, sensing trouble, her supporters had decamped to a newly-opened check-out.

Jas placed the basket on the conveyor belt and loaded out five items. He retained one bottle of wine behind a separate 'Next customer' bar.

Marie reached into the pocket of her leather jacket.

Kelvinside blanched.

Marie laughed and produced a large wad of notes. She turned back to the conveyor belt, giving the check-out girl two of many twenties.

"Would you like a carrier, madam?"

Marie opened her shoulder bag and carefully packed her shopping. "Naw thanks, hen. Ah want tae dae ma bit fur the environment."

Jas grinned.

Marie pulled at his sleeve. "Come oan – ah want this lot home afore it thaws..."

Lifting the wine he paid for it, then handed the bottle to Marie. They left the store.

Outside, Marie thrust a fiver into his hand then hailed a taxi. "Can ah drap ye onywhere?"

Jas shook his head. "Ah like the walk..."

The taxi drew up.

"Ah canny tempt ye back fur...coffee, ah suppose?"

"Why wid ya want tae dae that, Marie?"

Uncharacteristic blush. "Ye ken ah like ye, Jas...eyewis did..."

He laughed. "Ye're no' ma type, Marie – no' ken that by noo?"

The taxi sounded its horn, impatient.

Marie opened the door and leant in. "Cool yer jets, fuck-face!" She turned back to Jas. "Ye said...if ah ever needed ta talk..."

He sighed. "No' noo, eh Marie? Sorry...ah've problems o' ma ain tae sort oot." He pushed the long black hair back from the sweaty pale face. "Another time?"

She shrugged, tossing the shoulder-bag into the back of the taxi. "Queen Elizabeth Square, pal," she barked to the driver. To Jas: "Ah'll keep ma ear tae the ground aboot yer BMW. Look efter yersel...ah'll be in touch." Marie got into the taxi.

It sped off.

Jas began the two-mile walk to Eastercraigs.

Passing the large E-shaped Royal Infirmary which squatted on the edge of Townhead Interchange, he paused. Jas clenched and examined his right fist. The three small cuts which made up Jimmy Mygo's one attempt at self-defence were healing. Only a little redness remained. Jas walked on: too late for a tetanus-booster anyway...

The flat smelled of lemon beeswax and Lacoste. Locking the door, Jas removed jacket and tie. The shirt clung to his body like a desperate child. He removed it, chest glistening.

Sounds of water running.

Jas moved through to the kitchen. "Someone's been busy..."

Leigh stood in front of the sink, washing dishes. "I did some shopping too," he replied, without turning. He wore jeans and bare feet. A single droplet of sweat trickled down his naked spine.

Jas's groin throbbed.

"Chicken, a salad – that okay?" Leigh dried his hands and made to turn.

Jas approached from behind. He placed one hand on the broad back, pressing. With the other, he undid Leigh's narrow leather belt...

The Game.

The Game.

After Mawhinney, after more lies.

...unfastened the button-fly, dragging faded denim down over smooth, flawless flesh.

Facing the sink unit, arms braced, Leigh arched his back.

Hands on the slim waist, Jas ground his groin against Leigh's firm buttocks. The friction of the fabric teased his penis.

Jas groaned.

Leigh's head dropped forward, face obliterated by a cascade of sun-bleached blond hair. Other blond hair etched a golden triangle on the small of his back.

Jas bent, licking the soft down. His penis was iron. In the pit of his stomach, something tensed: not yet...

Leigh was panting now.

Jas drew back and sat on one of the wicker kitchen chairs. Slowly he unlaced his heavy boots, then pulled off socks.

The sound of Leigh's breath filled the airless room.

"The jeans," Jas ordered.

Obediently, Leigh scrambled out of tight denim. The task completed, he spread his legs, arms once again braced.

Lifting an apple from the table, Jas began to eat. Biting into the hard fruit, his teeth penetrated the outer skin, shattering the surface tension. Beneath, the flesh was fragile, moist. Jas plunged in, tearing, bruising. Taste exploded on his tongue. He savoured the sensation. Mouth full, Jas chewed slowly, then swallowed.

His erection was uncomfortable.

Leigh groaned.

Jas took a second bite. Different textures vied for attention. Sweet skin and bitter tissue. He looked at Leigh, watching, eating.

"Jas. Please...don't make me wait."

Closing his eyes, Jas focused on the task in hand. The apple was masticated pulp, dissolving into liquid in his mouth. Leigh's moans filled his ears. Jas continued to eat.

"Please, Jas..."

Wiping his mouth, he stood up and tossed the shredded apple core into the bin. Slowly he began to undo his belt. Standing by the honey-coloured body, he could see Leigh's paler prick curving upwards. His eyes swept the tanned body.

Every muscle was rigid, hard, pulsating.

Jas exhaled. "Leigh. Turn round."

Leigh moved to face him, raised his head. Eyes closed, sweat sparkled on long lashes. Lips parted, chest heaving, his arms now hung limply by his sides.

Jas's prick strained painfully against metal zip.

Power. Power in a powerless world.

Jas stared. "Come to me, Leigh."

Leigh opened his eyes and walked forward. With the leather belt, Jas secured eager wrists behind Leigh's back.

Pupils were dilated. Leigh smiled.

Jas punished with hard lips. From his groin, sharp arrows of pain coursed through his body, skewering their target. Forcing the head back, Jas continued the kiss, breaking the fragile pink skin. He tasted blood.

Leigh cried out.

Jas drew back, sweat soaking his hair. With the side of his hand he carefully blotted the cut. Seizing Leigh's bound wrists he pushed him backwards, through to the bedroom...

An hour later, Jas lay on his back, one hand behind his neck. A head rested heavily on his thigh. Jas traced Leigh's face, running fingers up through hair matted with sweat and rapidly drying spunk. Despite the electric fan which whirred mechanically in a corner, the room was a sauna. His mouth was dry. The scent of Lacoste merged with a saltier odour.

He gazed up at the mirror. Dr. Mawhinney's clumsy words returned to him. Jas looked at the reflected image.

Two men, two bodies. Jas extended long white limbs and stretched. He stared. Cropped fair hair above a square-jawed face. Body hair darker, spreading over chest and arms. A bluebird tattoo nestled amidst thick pubic hair. Jas peered at his face. Deep-set eyes looked quizzically back at him from beneath heavy brows. Slightly crooked nose, broken once, years ago. Large mouth. Blunt chin. No oil-painting. Jas smiled.

Leigh was the real mirror. Leigh defined him. His life with Leigh was the real life.

DS Jas Anderson was a lie.

A song seeped into his mind: "'I'll be your mirror, reflect what you are/In case you don't know...'"

Leigh mumbled something and nuzzled Jas's balls.

Jas hooked hands under Leigh's arms and dragged him up beside him. "What?" He caressed the split lip.

"'I'll be the wind the rain and the sunshine/The light in your door, to show that you're home...'" Leigh repeated. He grinned, stroked Jas's wet hair. "Didn't know you were a Nico fan...or is it Sartre?"

Jas laughed and sat up. There was a small blood-stain beneath where Leigh's body had lain. He frowned. "Come on, time for a shower..."

Leigh yawned languidly. "Later...I'm too comfortable."

Swinging his legs over the side of the bed, Jas got up. His thighs trembled. "Now..."

"Oh...all right, but only if it's warm..."

"Jist fur you, ah'll make an exception, this time!" Jas went ahead into the bathroom, where he took a small bottle of antiseptic from the medicine cabinet. He switched on the shower and stepped in, quickly washing while he waited for the water to heat up.

Leigh strolled through the doorway.

"In ye get..." Jas opened the door to the perspex cubicle and stepped out.

Leigh yawned again, obeyed. He stood smiling, submitting under gentle jets as Jas soaped a soft sponge and began to wash.

He paid particular attention to the delicate, easily damaged skin, crouching to examine the fragile tissue surrounding Leigh's arsehole.

"I must make chicken salad more often," Leigh murmured, pushing wet hair out of his eyes.

There was a tiny tear in the anal opening. Jas washed then dabbed the area with antiseptic. "Ah must be more careful."

Leigh winced slightly then relaxed. "How was your visit to Dr. Freud?"

"Nae problem..." He closed his eyes and lied. Jo's face swam towards him. Jas clenched his fists. A hand ruffled his hair:

"You sounded him out, then?"

Jas opened his eyes and stood up. He watched water course over Leigh's smiling face. "Naw...no' yet. Ah'll dae it the morra."

Tomorrow...and tomorrow..and tomorrow.

"Yeah..." Exaggerated scepticism flashed across the wet face.

Jas scowled. "Ah said ah'll dae it! Don't...nag me."

The scowl mirrored. "I don't mean to – I just want you to be happy and..."

"Ah ken..ah didney mean tae..."

"Forget it!" "Slidy fingers tugged playfully at his earlobe. Turning off the shower, Leigh shook himself, dog-like. "Don't know about you, but I'm starving. Let's eat." He padded through to the lounge, leaving large wet footprints on the polished maple floor.

The flat was quiet. Leigh had left for the lab. Jas sat alone in the lounge. Jo Hunter...

He stood up and walked to the window, it was open, as were all eight windows. No breeze, no air. The sound of children's voices drifted across from Alexandra Park. Jas closed the window, then the other seven. As he lifted his jacket, the telephone rang. The number had been changed that afternoon. He waited for the answering-machine to pick up. It obliged. After the usual preamble, a female voice:

"Jas? It's Ann. I'm off duty. Give me a ring back at..."

DC Ann McLeod. Late twenties. His partner for two years. Promotion had passed her by...so often.

A woman in a man's world.

Ann was okay...one of the few people he could've come out to. One of the few people who knew only too well what it was like to be different from the cop-norm.

She survived.

Could he? Jas lifted the receiver. "Hi Ann. How did ye git this number...?"

Fifteen minutes later he was on his way to the Royal. His thoughts were elsewhere.

Jimmy Mygo had regained consciousness and would be interviewed tomorrow.

Seven

JAS SAT ON one of the plastic seats in Pitt Street's reception area, gazing at a 'Stop Smoking Now' poster. Outside, the sun blazed behind a thick layer of cloud, its presence still felt. The mercury tipped eighty, hotter than ever. The main door to Divisional Headquarters stood agape, propped open by two fire extinguishers. Hatless, lifeless, the desk sergeant stood breathless in the airless hall. Two weeks of stifling, suffocating heat. The weather had to break before something else did.

Jas shifted on the hot plastic.

He was early for Wednesday's three o'clock appointment. On returning to the flat last night, he found it empty. When he had awoken this morning, Leigh was still absent. A hastily scribbled note on the kitchen table confirmed he had been and gone: 'Last day of the summer term. Back at five. After this, I'm all yours...'

Jas smiled. Following a two-hour workout at the gym, he'd showered, shaved then caught a bus: too hot to walk. No phonecalls, no BMWs.

Maybe it was over.

A voice at his side: "DS Anderson?"

Jas turned as Large sat down beside him. DS Clark was nowhere to be seen. "Inspector McNeil."

Large withdrew a packet of cigarettes.

Jas eyed the 'No Smoking' signs, then Large.

Large returned the packet to his pocket. "Thought I might catch you here. Phoned your home, but got no answer..."

So much for unlisted numbers. Jas sighed. "I have an appointment with..."

Large interrupted. "I know. I've cleared this with Dr. Mawhinney." He stood up. "A word..." He walked towards the stairs. Jas followed.

They strode along one corridor, then another. Eventually, Large paused, holding open a door. Jas walked into a room identical to Mawhinney's basement cell in shape. It was less sparsely furnished, a small PC and a large desk. The desk bore the remains of two prepacked sandwiches.

Large sat, motioned for Jas to do likewise.

Jas stood.

Large swept the sandwich wrappers into one drawer and produced a file from another. He looked up. "In the light of our chat the other night, do you wish to alter your statement concerning the alleged assault on Mr. Johnstone, DS Anderson?"

Jas shook his head. Maybe Leigh was right: maybe being pushed was easier than jumping.

Large sighed, looked down. He withdrew a loose sheet of paper from the file. "DS Clark has just returned from the hospital, where he intended to interview Mr. Johnstone. Were you aware he had regained consciousness?"

Jas remained silent.

"Well, he has – last night, but has now apparently discharged himself. The ward sister informed DS Clark that Johnstone left the hospital at noon today..."

"How did he manage that?"

Large scowled. "With his injuries, Christ only knows, but he has and that's what matters!" He drummed on the desk with nicotine-stained fingers. "This is developing into a rather complicated situation: we have a serious assault, but no victim." He lifted a sheaf of papers. "We also have statements from the officers who attended the scene, attesting to antagonistic behaviour towards yourself, DS Anderson, from Mr. Johnstone. And then there's the knife." Large opened another drawer and produced an evidence bag. "Traces of your blood have been found on the blade..."

There was certainly enough of it around that night. Jas rubbed bruised knuckles. The cuts were red, puffy smudges.

"There's also Johnstone's history of violence..."

Jas fingered the fabric of his navy linen suit.

Pause. "This is off-the-record, you undersatnd."

Jas nodded.

"You don't need to asnwer, you know that."

Jas stared.

"Have you had any contact with Mr. Johnstone, or his family, since the alleged assault?"

He could at least be honest about that. "Saw Liam and Michael yesterday..."

"What the fuck did you do that for?" Large thumped the desk with his fist.

Jas shrugged. The phone-calls and the BMW were his business. "Tae send Jimmy a 'get-well-soon'message..."

Large stood up and walked to the window. "Did they make any threats?"

'Yer ain lot'll git ye...' Jas shook his head.

"Did you make any threats to them?"

"Nothin' that wid cause Jimmy tae discharge himself..." Jas joined Large at the window.

Large looked at Jas. "Do yourself a favour, mate. Think about that night again. Maybe you got a few things wrong. You'd just finished a week on nights, right? You were tired..."

Jas stared at smudgy glass. They weren't going to make this easy...but why should they, why should the coward's way out be the easy way out? "It's all in ma statement, Inspector."

Large laughed harshly. "In all my years with CIB I've never seen anything like this! Use your head, son! Christ...!" He gripped Jas's arm.

Jas pulled away.

"Cards-on-the-table time, mate. There's really no complaint here to investigate. You weren't thinking straight, that night. Mawhinney's report will back you up. It was a stress-related incident. Now Johnstone's gone to ground: as the victim and only real witness to the attack, CIB can't proceed without him. He'll not press charges – even if we had the manpower necessary to track him down. Apply for compassionate leave, get some time off." Large walked back to the desk and sat down.

Jas watched.

"Look: you could be back at work in a fortnight, with only a verbal warning against you – no disciplinary proceedings..."

"Whit aboot Mawhinney?"

"Oh, that will continue, on a weekly basis, to iron out any wrinkles..."

Jas glanced out the window. Traffic thundered across the unsound Kingston Bridge. Two weeks in LA with Leigh. Sun, sand and...?

"If you've had enough of the streets, maybe think about a transfer." Large smiled. "We're always looking for exceptional officers in CIB."

Who guards the guards?

More guards...

Jas walked to the door. "Ah don't want to keep the doctor waitin'..."

Sigh. "You're a good officer, DS Anderson. Use that brain of yours. Talk to Mawhinney – get everything off your chest..."

Jas opened the door. "Thanks fur the advice, Inspector McNeil." He walked from the room, closing the door behind him.

Mawhinney was waiting outside.

Jas walked on. Mawhinney scrambled to keep up. "Get things sorted out?"

He continued to walk. At the end of the corridor, Jas paused and turned. "Same room as yesterday?"

Weary nod.

They descended to the basement...

"Tell me about your work." Desperation. Mawhinney pulled at his ear-hair. Fifteen minutes of silence had passed.

"Not much tae tell." Jas smiled. "You surely ken whit the duties of a DS involve..."

"Don't be clever!" Irritated. "You know what I mean..."

"Oh, ah'm not clever, doctor. You're the clever one. Ah'm just a humble cop." A cowardly, lying cop.

Mawhinney stood up. "Tell me about the Jo Hunter case..."

Jas closed his eyes. The red tattoo was a beating drum. "You've read the notes. Why ask me tae go through whit you already ken?"

"Just tell me." Mawhinney's voice behind him.

Jas stared straight ahead. Five minutes passed.

Rustlings. Then: "Okay, I'll tell you..."

Mawhinney sat down, eyes on another file. "Joseph Hunter was twelve at the time. According to his attackers' confession, which I gather was disallowed at the trial, he was abducted at 4 pm the previous evening, on his way home from school. The blue van was later identified by a classmate and her mother, traced back to one of Mr. Johnstone's associates. Three men were involved, two in their forties, and a younger man – twenty, I see. The van was driven straight to the disused iron works in Shettleston. They remained in the van until it got dark."

Jas tried to close his ears, couldn't. He was back there, on that night, three months ago.

"The boy was beaten, sodomised and..." Intake of breath. "...further sexually assaulted over a five-hour period. He was forced to perform oral sex on two of his attackers, then penetrated anally with a car-jack, and a two-by-four section of timber. The latter acts probably took place outside, on the waste ground, from the copious amounts of blood found. The medical report states the boy was undoubtedly unconscious by this time. Emergency surgery was carried out, to save his life. However, he's been comatose for twelve weeks now – since the attack, in fact. At the trial, without a statement of accusation from the victim himself, the police had to rely on forensic and largely circumstantial evidence. While the other two men confessed, Mr. Johnstone maintained, on the advice of his solicitor, that he was there under duress. The evidence you gave, Jas, was discounted by the judge, as were the confessions. The defence claimed their clients had found the boy's body, and were attempting to resuscitate him when you arrived..."

"Liars."

"They have alibis, Jas, claim the van was stolen, even reported it so later that night..."

"Ah saw whit ah saw..."

Sigh. "You claim Mr. Johnstone was attempting oral intercourse with the boy when you arrived. He maintains he was carrying out mouth-to-mouth resuscitation..."

"Tryin' tae clear the airway with his prick, wiz he?"

"You think I don't understand, Jas..." Pause. "Believe me, I do. I know why you attacked Mr. Johnstone..."

"So why dae ye need me?" Jas laced his fingers, unlaced them then repeated the sequence.

Sigh. "We've been through all that. For my report to your superiors, I must be sure this was an isolated incident. I don't condone what you did, Jas, but I don't criticise either. That's not my job." Pause. "And, as a police officer, it can't be yours – hasn't been, until recently – not from what I read in your record."

Jas rubbed his knuckles.

Rustlings. He looked up.

Mawhinney closed one file and picked up another. "Ever considered stress-management, Jas...?"

Maybe aromatherapy?

"...help you cope with your work?"

"Ah get by."

"I wouldn't call beating a man to half to death the actions of someone...'getting by.'" Mawhinney looked at Jas.

Jas looked back.

"And your attitude in these sessions bears out this impression. You're tense, Jas." Cigarette packet produced, extended, then: "Sorry, you don't smoke, do you?"

Jas laced, then unlaced his fingers.

"How long's it been?" Cigarette lit. Laugh. "I can spot a reformed smoker at one hundred paces."

"Four months."

"I admire your will-power, Jas. I couldn't cope without them. Do you miss the nicotine?"

"Ma bank-balance doesn't."

"Heavy consumption?"

"Sixty a day."

A patina of admiration. "Can't have been easy. Do you like a drink, Jas?"

"Gave that up three years ago. It's a mug's game."

Sigh. "A man with no vices. Jas Anderson: a man with no..."

"Look: can we git oan wi' this?" Too close...too close. Jas shifted in the moist, plastic seat.

"Do I make you nervous, Jas?"

You make me sick. "No."

Curious. "I must admit you don't look uneasy. Most of the people I see feel a little uncomfortable the first couple of times. Talking to a stranger's never easy, especially in these circumstances."

Jas shrugged. Talking to strangers was easy.

"But you do seem tense. You need to relax more – we all do. I'm a golfing buff. What do you do for fun?"

I work out and I gag my lover. "I work out."

"Ah..." Understanding. "...the natural high. You look in good shape, physically. But how about emotionally. All those free-floating endorphins are just as much of an escape as nicotine or alcohol. Do you socialise much, Jas? Are you in a relationship at the moment?"

Jas stared at Mawhinney. A chance? His chance to come clean? He frowned.

Mawhinney looked away. Nervous, then impatient. "I'm not prying, Jas. Given the type of work you do, you must have balance in your life, understanding and support from those close to you. Some officers chose not to discuss work with their spouses. Others find it helps. Either way, if you don't get a complete release from your job – off-duty – the strain will start to show. Work hard, play hard – that's the secret..."

Support...Leigh.

Understanding...Leigh.

Balance...balance? Leigh's body tied to the bed. Jas scowled.

"Do you use the police gym for your workouts?"

Jas shook his head. "Local sports centre. They've got better facilities."

Mawhinney began to write again. "Good idea, mixing with the community. Lifts barriers, builds bridges. Play any sports?"

"Chess."

Nervous laugh. "I mean team sports: football, rugby, tennis – that sort of thing?"

"Just chess."

Sigh. "Says in your file you were on the division rugby squad, until recently. Why did you quit?"

Jas stared. Contact sports had become...uncomfortable. Anyway, he'd rather be with Leigh, thrust his face into another guy's arse for the right reasons. "I couldn't concentrate. My game was suffering." A half-lie...progress?

Mawhinney scribbled, then stopped. "That's not what I hear..."

Jas looked at his watch. It had stopped.

"Oh, you were very good.."

"Chess is more ma...thing now."

Sigh. "Okay, we'll leave the rugby...for now." More scribbling. "If you're into chess, I'm sure there's a club you could join, competitions. I'm sure you could..."

"Chess isn't about competitions."

"So what is it about, Jas?" More scribbling.

Mind-to-mind combat. Outwitting your opponent. Keeping

four moves ahead, anticipating his actions, setting traps, leading him where you want him to go. "Chess is most satisfying when ye ken yer opponent.."

"Who do you play with?"

Three attempts to teach Leigh the basic moves had progressed into another type of lesson. "Gary Kasparov."

Mawhinney stared.

"Chess computer. Level twenty-four. Ah've no' won yet."

"And how do you feel about that, Jas?"

He shrugged. "It's a challenge. Ah'm workin' on it."

Mawhinney put his pencil down. "Chess is a very logical game, very rigidly structured. Some people find it frustrating. Don't you feel confined by the format?"

"The computer does: ah don't." The Game: the more formal the rules, the more scope for imagination...

Things were coming together in his mind.

The emptiness...and how to fill it. Really fill it.

Jas cracked his fingers. "Do you play, doctor?"

Mawhinney smiled. "Used to. Maybe we could have a game, sometime..."

"Ah don't think so."

Laugh. "Afraid I'd beat you?"

Jas sighed. "Afraid ye wouldn't."

Balance...

Mawhinney scribbled on. "What do you mean by that?"

Jas stared at the wall above Mawhinney's head.

Mawhinney looked up. Jas shrugged. He knew what he wanted to do.

"Did Mr. Johnstone beat you in court, Jas? Is that why you attacked him?"

"He beat the system."

"But you represent, uphold the 'system'. In outsmarting the courts..."

"He didn't..." Jas clenched his fists. The guy was good...very good. "...his brief did."

"So why did you attack Mr. Johnstone?"

"It's all in ma statement."

Mawhinney sighed. "It's a violent world, Jas. I don't need to tell you that incidents like the assault on Joseph Hunter are not so...unusual. You've surely seen as bad, if not worse, in the course of your twelve years..."

... decapitated torso of a three-year-old girl found in swing-park.

... massive RTA at Townhead Interchange.

... the 'Baudelaire' rapist. Created his own orifices in the stomachs of dead prostitutes.

"...so why choose now to take the law into your own hands?"

Jas stared. "Ah don't know." He knew.

He also now knew what was missing – really missing – in his life.

Pause. Mawhinney scratched his head. Another pause, then a change of subject. "Do you have children, Jas?"

"Ye know ah don't!"

"I know you're not married, Jas. That's not the same thing. You may be supporting numerous offspring all over the country, for all we know."

"Ah don't, an' ah'm not."

"You like children Jas?"

"Aye, but ah couldn't eat a whole one!"

Angry. "Don't be flip, sergeant! It doesn't suit you. Do you plan to have children?"

Jas closed his eyes. He didn't want – or need – anything, anyone else. "No."

"Choice, or do you or your partner have a fertility problem?"

Jas laughed, opened his eyes and shook his head. "There's no room in ma life fur kids."

Mawhinney scribbled. "Must be a crowded life, Jas. Your work, chess with a computer, the gym." Pause. "Where would you find the time?"

Jas closed his eyes.

Sigh. "Sorry. You're making this very difficult for me, DS Anderson..."

"Is yer job usually easy?" Jas opened his eyes.

Laugh. "I like to think I can put my...er, people at their ease, Jas, get them to open up. Usually, after an out-of-character incident, such as your attack on Mr. Johnstone, the officer concerned has got whatever was bothering him out of his system. The tension has been released, the man concerned is contrite, aware of what he has done..."

Jas stared.

"...but I'm failing with you, Jas. I sense whatever motivated the attack on Mr. Johnstone has not been exorcised from within you. I think I can help..."

No one could help. The solution lay in himself.

"Is there some problem, Jas, something at home?"

Jas smiled, shook his head. A year ago there had been a problem. Loneliness had helped him do the job, stay numb. Now, with Leigh...

"Are you in a relationship at the moment? Is this...?"

"That's none o' your business!" The familiar words came before he could stop them.

"It is, if it affects your work, your ability to do your job." Low voice. Feigned understanding. "Is the lady concerned married? To another police officer, perhaps?"

Jas sighed. Another assumption. "Ah don't make a habit of

fuckin' other people's wives."

Disappointed. "A problem at work, then? I've talked to some of your colleagues..."

Jas frowned.

Mawhinney smiled. "Oh, don't worry. Only good things. You all stick together, don't you? One of the few perks of the job, I believe. Police solidarity, the type of camaraderie civilians such as myself find it hard to either understand or penetrate..."

Jas watched the psychiatrist watch him.

"...according to everyone I've talked to, Jas, you're a good man to have around. Your DI – Moira Campbell, is it?"

Jas nodded.

Mawhinney leafed. "Nothing but praise. However, she wants a clean bill of health from me, before you're reinstated." He looked at Jas.

"Do ye huv the time?" Find me unfit for duty and get it over with.

Mawhinney looked at his watch. "There's still a few minutes left."

Jas laced then unlaced fingers, watching as Mawhinney flicked back to another file. He closed his eyes.

"Appalling business, this Joseph Hunter case..." Pause. "I asked you about children for a reason, Jas. Was it the...sexual nature of the assault that...got to you?"

A tattoo was beating on his closed eyelids.

Not sexual...

Not sexual...

Sigh. "You're not alone there, Jas – the idea of male same-sex congress can be disturbing for many men..." Pause. "...myself included. Your abhorrence is perfectly understandable. Homosexuality – let alone paedophilia – is a condition to be pitied, disgusting though you may find its...practitioners."

Jas's eyelids shot open. Chair legs scraped on concrete. He stood up, glaring at the flabby, pathetic excuse for a man and his flabby, pathetic excuse for insight. "Whit Jimmy did tae that boy wis nothin' tae dae wi'...sex, nothin' tae..."

"Not sex as you know it, perhaps..."

'...as you know it...'

'...as you know it...'

'...as you know it...' Jas clenched his fists. "Nothin' tae dae wi' sex full stop!" He glowered at Mawhinney.

Mawhinney stood up, brow creased. "Ah..." Arm outstretched. "...sit down, Jas..." Lowering motion.

'...as you know it...'

Jas stared at a point above the wispy head and saw Leigh and himself...naked...entwined...

"Please sit down, Jas – I think we're getting somewhere at last."

Jas stared...and saw Leigh...and himself....laughing, playing... He sat down.

Mawhinney did likewise, then began to scribble.

Jas watched the neat handwriting form upside-down, then smiled.

Mawhinney talked while he scribbled. "It's a...reaction many...police officers experience, Jas, and it's nothing to be ashamed of." Pale eyes raised. "A form of..." Smile. "...well, 'homosexual panic' is the technical phrase, but we can talk more about that on your next visit." Head lowered, more scribbling.

Jas's smile waned into a frown. This guy was so wide of the mark he was in a different world.

Mawhinney wittered on.

Jas thought of Leigh, of holidays, of a new job, a new start, of going to LA and never coming back.

He thought of what he really wanted, needed in his life, and of the one person who could supply it.

He thought of tethers, restaints...of freeing Leigh and freeing himself, filling the emptiness in the most obvious way.

Jas smiled.

"...do you understand, DS Anderson?"

Jas nodded.

"Good! That's settled, then. Your statement will still stand, but I'll add a rider to it. The Johnstone incident was a one-off, a stress-related reaction. It was an unpremeditated response to over-work and exceptional circumstances..."

The night of the attack, Jas had followed Jimmy Mygo for two hours.

Scraping of chair-legs. Mawhinney beaming, hand extended. "I'll recommend some compassionate leave, DS Anderson. You and your lady-friend take a holiday, spend some time together. I think our heat wave's about to break, anyway. Give me a ring when you get back: we'll arrange another appointment..." The pale, extended hand flapped weakly, a flag of surrender.

Jas turned towards the door. "Goodbye, Dr. Mawhinney

Surprised. "This has helped?"

Jas grinned. "More than ye'll ever know."

Eight

UNDER A HEAVY sky, Jas strolled down Queen Street. There was no sun, no breeze, no air: only pink, murky clouds the consistency of used cotton-wool. Pressing down on the earth, they did a good job of soaking up any moisture. Occasionally a golden shard struggled though, illuminating the scene. The streets were dry bones.

The world seemed different.

He was different.

Jas carried his jacket like an older, outer skin. In the inside pocket two documents crouched. One was a copy of his own statement, conveniently amended by Dr. Mawhinney: the charges had been dropped.

The other document was a formal, written warning, a copy of which DI Campbell would attach to his record. One black mark in the greying world of his life as a cop.

He could recommence duties in a fortnight's time.

Jas smiled and quickened his pace.

Outside a branch of 'Holidays Direct', he paused and examined the cards on display. One drew his eyes:

Flight only. Prestwick to Los Angeles. £268.

Departure date was tomorrow, returning in thirteen days. Thrusting a hand into his trouser pocket, Jas located and fingered a credit-card. Two weeks of sun, sand and...

He pushed open the door.

Leigh was asleep on the lounge floor when Jas entered the flat. Blond hair, secured in a pony-tail, draped over a tanned shoulder. He wore white tennis shorts and lay prone, one arm tucked beneath his head. On the CD player, 'Blur' blurred softly. The TV silently strobed Wimbledon's men's semi-final.

Dumping his jacket on a chair, Jas turned the music and the TV off. He knelt beside the long, lithe body. Leigh's skin was the colour of maple, blending chameleon-like into the polished floor. Broad shoulders tapered to a narrow waist, framed by tight, white cotton. Jas stroked one sinewy thigh and smiled.

Muscle twitched beneath his fingers.

Leigh moaned and turned over. The gold nipple-rings twinkled, catching stray rays of muted sun. He remained asleep.

Jas watched as the flawless, hairless chest rose and fell in even breaths. Leigh's lips were parted, his forehead damp with sweat.

This guy had taught him The Game, taught him how to use the tensions to give pleasure to them both.

This guy deserved...openness.

Tonight The Game would be...different.

Ignoring the hardening in his trousers, he fanned his lover awake with two airline tickets.

Leigh mumbled, eyes still closed.

Jas leant over and brushed Leigh's lips with his own, then stood up, nudged the prostrate from with the toe of a heavy boot. "Come oan, sleepin' beauty!"

Leigh's eyes slowly opened.

Jas continued to wave the tickets.

Lightning-like, Leigh focused on Jas's fingers. A hand darted up, tried to snatch the tickets.

Jas laughed, drawing the airline-folders above his head. Leigh sat up, blinking rapidly. "What's that?"

Jas backed away. "Come an' see..." He wafted the tickets.

Fluidly, Leigh rose from the floor, padding towards him. "We going somewhere?"

Jas nodded.

Leigh made another grab for the tickets.

Jas winked.

Leigh's eyes sparkled. "A film? A show? The all-dayer in the park?"

Jas laughed. "Ah'm a bit auld fur all-dayers...."

Leigh knelt at his feet.

Jas could see the outline of excitement in the tight tennis-shorts. He held the envelopes tantalisingly just out of reach.

Leigh grinned.

Jas laughed, tossing the tickets at Leigh. "Ah'm away fur a shower..."

Under the cold water, he rubbed at his body roughtly, enjoying the sensation. Skin tingled pink, his balls contracted. Jas ran a hand along the length of his hardening prick...

Not yet.

Later. Tonight was different. Special.

Jas made himself wait...the way he'd made Leigh wait.

The cold shower cleansed, purged, purified with frozen fire. He closed his eyes: Jo was faint. Jas turned up the water-pressure.

Mawhinney elbowed his way in. Had 'a problem at home' given rise to a 'problem at work'?

Leigh...?

Leigh wasn't the problem. He was the solution, countermanding years of self-imposed isolation and denial.

BL: Before Leigh.

Urges, tensions vying for release. No need for long-term relationships...numerous, anonymous men had been only too pleased to oblige on a casual basis. Parks, deserted beaches, toilets...Jas smiled. The smell of piss mixed with Domestos could still get him hard. He gazed up into the shower-head as glacial spikes pricked his face.

A lifetime of dark, faceless bodies, his hands pressing faceless heads into his groin, holding faceless backs hard against damp, tiled walls...His hands...holding others at arm's length...

A hot shiver of memory shot through the shower's icy blast.

Eighteen months ago. Glasgow's necropolis. Another purely physical attraction, a series of satisfying, sweaty encounters in derelict mausoleums.

Not in darkness. Not hidden away in shabby corners, beside constantly running urinals. In sunshine. In daylight, with bright hot puddles of sun illuminating Leigh's naked back.

Jas rubbed his face vigorously: Leigh knew him better than he knew himself.

Leigh was sussed.

Leigh had invented The Game.

The Game had become Jas's life.

He turned his face away from the shower.

Mawhinney nudged him: 'work hard, play hard'.

Sexual static charged his body. Leigh...living with Leigh, eating with Leigh, sleeping with Leigh, fucking Leigh...

Trusting Leigh?

Jas shook droplets from his hair, dug fingernails into flesh. Turning the presure-control to 'Full', he bent rigid under cauterising water. Numbness seeped through skin, through flesh and sinew to bone and marrow.

Most cops still on the streets were either hollow men or virtually psychotic.

Jas was hollow no longer.

Leigh knew him better than he knew himself. Tonight Leigh would know him in a different way.

A heavy longing gave way to anticipation.

Jas smiled.

The shower-door swung open. Leigh's head appeared, eyes shining with pleasure. Taking one step forward, he saw Jas's rosy skin. A tentative hand through the icy water, swiftly withdrawn. He grinned, leaning lazily against the cubicle. "So does this mean you've reached a decision?"

Jas rubbed water from soaking hair. "You gonney phone they friends o' yours?"

Leigh nodded. "Already done it! Julian'll meet us at LAX. John says we can stay as long as we like. They're off to Sacramento for a week, so we'll have the place to ourselves." Excitement and frustration painted the strong face. "Now tell me what you've decided!"

Jas grinned.

Leigh whooped, eyes fixed on Jas's body. "You won't regret it!" He stepped into the shower, gasped at the temperature and threw his arms around Jas's neck. "Maybe we can think about a more permanent move, eh? Get away from Glasgow, start again..."

Gently, Jas disentangled himself. "Aye, maybe. Now..." He laughed. "...where's ma tea?"

Leigh grinned. "I suppose the least I can do is feed you!"

Jas stared at the wet white cotton which outlined Leigh's prick, a second, almost transparent skin.

Heart thumping, he pushed Leigh in the direction of the kitchen.

Leigh sat patiently on the other side of the table while Jas ate. "Good session with Dr. Freud?"

Jas crunched on crisp salad. "Ye could say that."

"So what happened about the assault charges?"

Jas chewed the steak methodically then swallowed. "Dropped."

Leigh leant an elbow on the table. "Those two guys who came here looking for you, they were...?"

"That's all over, Leigh." He grinned.

Leigh sighed. "Well, I'm glad. Jimmy Mygo got off with what he did – why shouldn't you?"

Because two wrongs don't make a... Jas scowled and pushed his plate away. "Maybe ye're right." He glanced around. "Ony juice?"

Leigh swiftly removed the plate, opened the fridge and took out a carton of orange-juice. He poured a glass, placing it on the table.

Jas downed it in one, stood up. Clean jeans and an Everlast T-shirt stuck to his sweating skin. He looked at Leigh.

The wet tennis-shorts were almost dry.

"Jas..." Leigh touched his shoulder. "...I want to pay my half of the holiday..."

Jas laughed. "Oan your wages?" He stroked Leigh's collarbones, moving down to finger a nipple-ring.

Tonight would be different.

Tonight would be trust.

Tonight would be...

Jas sobered, feeling himself start to harden.

It didn't go unnoticed. "Will I go and get things ready?" The voice was low.

"Aye..."

Leigh smiled and walked from the kitchen.

Jas followed.

Wild new thoughts raced through his brain. Jas watched as Leigh produced the familiar props they'd used to prop up the life he had outside this flat.

He didn't need them anymore.

Tonight...

Jas walked to where Leigh was fumbling with the handcuffs. An unfamiliar sensation coursed through his body.

"Okay?" The voice was low, husky.

Jas took the steel bracelets from Leigh and clipped each to the bedhead's brass bars. He stared deep into confused blue eyes. "Ye wanna...fuck me, Leigh?" The alien words articulated an emotion he'd never let himself feel.

Trust.

He knew every inch of Leigh's beautiful body, had used it, controlled it for months.

Now it would use and control him.

He wanted to open himself completely.

Leigh was staring at him. A smile twitched the full lips. "You...sure?"

Jas nodded. Words wouldn't come...didn't need to. He flinched as Leigh traced a pulsating muscle on the side of his neck.

Lower, another muscle pulsed. Jas stood very still, then raised arms as Leigh's hands tugged at the hem of the Everlast, pulling it up over shaking shoulders, then head.

Two sets of eyes surveyed two very different chests: one hard and white, coated in a mat of thick dark hair, the other bronzed, smooth, punctuated by shining gold rings in erect brown nipples.

Jas shivered despite the oppressive warmth of the bedroom. Leigh took his face in his hands, kissing him gently on the mouth.

A different kiss...

Not a hard kiss...

The only hardness tonight was their pricks.

Jas's heart hammered louder, filling his ears. He remained motionless, transfixed by Leigh's lips.

The softer the caresses, the more he wanted Leigh's hardness inside.

Leigh's hot tongue in his mouth. Lost in sensation, Jas moaned as strong fingers moved to the waistband of his jeans, deftly undoing belt, then unzipping. Then pulling.

Tight denim slid slowly to the floor. Jas was naked beneath. Mouth glued to Leigh's, he raised one, then two knees, stepping from the jeans.

Then the mouth pulled away. Leigh stroked Jas's forehead with the back of his fingers. The other hand roamed over stomach. "I love your body, Jas – you've never really let me...touch you..."

Touch...

Trust...

The thought did strange things to his mind. He felt the heat of Leigh's hot gaze on his hotter flesh. Every nerve ending tingled with longing as he walked towards the bed.

His arena. Their arena. The arena where the hunter was now to become prey.

The vulnerability sent shocks of pleasure through his whole body.

"You'll never know how long I've wanted to..." Leigh's words tailed off, the sentence unfinished.

Jas swept a tangle of gags and restraints onto the floor then sat on the side of the bed. He looked up at Leigh. "Ah never gave ye the chance, did ah?" Prick brushed navel.

A gentle smiled lit up the handsome face. "Do I have Dr. Freud to thank for this?"

Jas watched as Leigh slowly unzipped the shorts then walked towards him. "No' really...it wiz..."

The assumptions...new assumptions, just as damning as the old...and maybe more accurate. Mawhinney's assumptions that... not only was Jas straight, he was panicking over some imagined threat. H e watched Leigh fumble with the tennis-shorts.

The whole world was assumptions, threats...

The BMW and the phone calls crept into his mind...but didn't stay.

Leigh pulled off shorts, freeing the long, elegant prick.

Then a firm hand pushed him back onto the bed. The other began to fondle his nipples. Jas swung legs over onto the duvet, then raised arms and seized the metal bars of the bedhead. His heart began to hammer.

A handcuff rattled.

A muscle twisted deep in his arse. Jas sighed and stretched himself out. It had been a long time...too long. Fifteen years...

He stared at the ceiling. He'd been young...too young. The physical pain had been almost unbearable...

Fifteen years. Fifteen years since he'd let a guy fuck him. Now the word made him shudder with anticipation.

For so long the fucker, the controller.

Now?

He wanted Leigh inside him like he'd never wanted anything else.

A tongue traced the outline of his jaw.

Jas inhaled and tensed.

Leigh's wet tongue slid down under chin to neck, licking dark stubble.

Jas tightened fingers around metal bars.

The tongue began to play amidst chest-hair, moving between nipples.

A hot, liquid feeling in his stomach almost eclipsed the lightning which flashed up and down the length of his prick. Jas closed his eyes and felt himself start to dissolve...

The tongue flicked down onto stomach, then thighs, teasingly avoiding the groin area.

Jas's back arched reflexively as a blond ponytail brushed his prick.

Leigh continued the wet journey of discovery.

The bed-head's metal bars were slick in his grasp as Leigh's tongue paused...then lips touched the inside of his thigh in a soft kiss.

Jas groaned. A warm droplet of pre-cum moistened the head of his prick.

Then the hands...

Following in the wake of his mouth, Leigh's hands began to massage stomach, knead the hard muscle. Gentle at first, strong fingers roughened in their touch.

Another set of muscles inside Jas was now spasming uncontrollably.

Leigh's hands parted thighs, fingers searching for the dark opening.

Jas raised knees and lifted his arse, allowing access. Two sighs split the silence as a tentative index finger edged in.

His balls clenched unexpectedly. Jas inhaled and bit back a cry. His legs began to shake convulsively.

One hand caressing a hairy thigh, Leigh's finger continued to explore.

Pounding in his head. It had been so long...too long. Jas opened his eyes and stared at the top of a shining blond head. Breath escaped his lips in short, sharp pants.

Then the finger removed.

Disappointment filled his brain. It was soon dispelled. "Turn over."

Jas looked at the handsome face. Then obeyed. In a quick movement he flipped over onto knees and buried his face in a pillow.

It smelled of sweat, Lacoste...Leigh.

A sigh from behind. Then more words. "You're beautiful, Jas..."

A wet finger traced the length of his spine, pausing at the base. Jas felt his arsehole contract again.

The moist digit continued downwards.

Jas clenched his teeth, moved knees further apart and began to undulate.

Two hands spread the cheeks of his arse.

Jas inhaled deeply.

Open...open and vulnerable.

Paradoxically, the openness was the key to the emptiness.

Openness would fill the void.

Somewhere in the distance, an animal moaned.

The Jas-animal.

The taming of the Jas-animal.

He felt the warm air of the still room flow up into him. Then pressure against his thighs, the hot pressure of other thighs.

Then the finger again, this time slick with KY. Kneading, stretching, relaxing, moistening...opening.

Then the lubricated head of Leigh's prick leant against his arsehole...

Muscle tensed...then relaxed a little. Then more.

Then the first half-inch of Leigh's slick prick.

Jas let go the pillow and grabbed at the edge of the mattress. His right hand brushed a small, cold object: the gun. He pushed it away and gripped the metal bed-frame.

His prick shivered as Leigh edged deeper inside, filling him, filling long-forgotten muscles that took Leigh's length into his body. Prick slapped off stomach.

Leigh withdrew, then thrust again.

Jas mumbled soundless words pillow-deep. The impact of Leigh's thrusts deadened everything...deadened the physical pain, the pain of fifteen lonely years – the pain of everything – with the pleasure of this...He had no mind, nothing of his own. All he had was Leigh's.

Hands were gripping his waist.

Nothing else mattered. Only this...

Behind, Leigh changed position and thrust from a different angle.

Jas screamed into the pillow as the head of Leigh's prick slammed deep inside him.

Nothing else mattered.

Only this...

Only now...

One of Leigh's hands seized the back of his neck, pushing face further into pillow.

Breathy words: "Oh, Jas..."

Leigh was grinding against him, now, long languid movements which pierced Jas's heart. Then strong arms wrapped themselves around his chest, raising his trembling body from the sweat-soaked bed. Warm nipple-rings scraped the skin of his back as he leant against Leigh's chest, sinking into the thrusts, then raising himself onto knees...then squatting back onto Leigh's prick.

A hot mouth on his neck, teeth gripping flesh.

Leigh relaxed back onto his heels, pulling Jas onto his lap.

The strong prick thrust ever upwards as Leigh manoeuvred, then stretched out tan thighs. Then paused.

Jas closed his eyes, mind a soaking morass of Leigh and Leigh-induced ecstasy.

One hand still on Jas's waist, Leigh pressed the palm of the other against Jas's sweating knuckles, opening the clenched fist, twining the fingers with his own.

He groaned as Leigh began to guide his hand over chest and down to groin. Sparkles exploded on his eyelids as Jas felt his own palm stroking and caressing his own prick.

Intensity of sensation threatened to overwhelm him.

The thought was picked up...

Leigh clasped both hands to Jas's chest.

Then movement...different movement.

He opened his eyes as Leigh, without withdrawing, fluidly manipulated Jas around to face him. He tensed inside as he drew up trembling legs, holding Leigh's prick in place, then stared into liquid blue eyes.

Leigh stared back, face contorted with tension. "Oh, Jas..."

Legs brushing each other's waists, they both leant forward into a kiss.

Jas felt his swollen prick brush Leigh's hard stomach as a hot mouth sucked on his. Then he was on his back, legs over Leigh's shoulders, hands flailing for the bed-bars. And missing.

Twining Jas's fingers with his own, Leigh pressed his arms against the mattress, holding him there. He began to thrust again – harder, faster.

Jas felt an explosion of pleasure deep inside his body as Leigh jabbed the prostate gland. Shimmers of sensation pulsed in his guts. He found himself smiling.

Sweat dripped from Leigh's shining face, trickled down and dropped onto Jas's face. Lips already parted in exertion twitched into a reflective smile...or something beyond a smile.

Jas's prick was impossibly hard, ossifying against stomach as Leigh's body dipped over his with each down-stroke. He felt the familiar tingling of incipient orgasm deep in his balls as his guts turned to mush.

Leigh's strokes were sharp, stabbing jabs, erasing the emptiness, erasing the...

In two, quick jutting movements Leigh came. Floods of warm liquid filled the final emptiness.

Leigh's mouth gasped against his neck as Jas felt the hot shower of his own spunk splatter against his face...

Sometime later, he felt Leigh withdraw.

A big part of Jas went with the softening prick. He closed his eyes, lips frozen in a grin.

There would be other times...a lifetime of other times.

A warm mouth kissed his neck.

Thighs trembling, calves cramping, Jas eased legs onto the bed and opened his eyes.

Leigh was gazing down at him, breathing heavily, grinning. "You were worth the wait!"

Jas stared until his heart returned to normal, then blinked as Leigh reached over to lick a trail of spunk from his cheek. As he opened his mouth to respond, Leigh closed it with his own.

Two tongues danced in a sea of semen and saliva.

When Jas pulled away he knew he'd found what he'd been looking for.

Leigh laughed. "You look well and truly fucked!"

"Ah feel it!" Jas slowly swung cotton-wool legs over the side of the bed. An unfamiliar lightness filled the space left by Leigh's prick. He smiled. "C'moan...ah'll wash ye."

Leigh moved away. "What's the sudden obsession? I like...to

feel you in me when you're gone." He leant over and kissed Jas's chest. "Sometimes, when you leave for work, I lie here for hours, smelling you, feeling your spunk ooze out of me..."

For the first time, he knew the feeling. Jas laughed, stood up. "We can still dae that, but..."

Leigh put a finger on Jas's lips. "I know. Hygiene..." He turned.

Jas scanned the flawless body. The small cut had not bled again. He lowered his head, kissed the puckered skin then stood up. "You hungry?"

Leigh nodded. "Fuckin' ravenous...want what's left of the chicken?"

Jas shook his head. "Maybe later. Things tae dae."

"Not...?"

Jas scowled. "Jist one last time. We'll be away fur a while. Ah need tae explain tae Jo..."

"It's over, let it go..." Leigh knelt on the bed, wrapping his arms around Jas's waist.

He nodded. "Ah ken that now..."

Together they walked to the shower.

"Will you be long?" Dressed in jeans, Leigh sat at the table eating a sandwich. He held it out.

Jas took a bite, chewed slowly. "Naw...an hour or so. Whit you gonny be dain'?"

"Well..." Leigh stretched and yawned. "...I thought I'd have a little snooze, then start packing. Want me to do yours?"

Jas nodded. "You ken whit sorta stuff tae take."

Leigh grabbed an apple and walked from the kitchen.

Jas watched the lithe body saunter away.

The same lithe body which had so recently covered, filled his own. His sore prick twitched.

Jas smiled as he moved to the washing machine. Rifling through clean laundry, he located jeans, socks and a sweatshirt. His docs were in the bedroom.

Leigh lay on the bed, propped up on two pillows. The unused harness lay beside him, the unwanted handcuffs still dangled from the bedhead. He grinned. "I've got the lab Camcorder home for the holidays. Fancy taking it with us?"

Jas sat beside him, pulling on the heavy boots. "Wid they let the results back through customs?" He laughed.

Leigh ran a finger down Jas's chest. "With your build, we could make our fortunes in the hardcore market..."

Jas kissed the finger, took it into his mouth and nibbled the nail. He closed his eyes, felt the warm, slim digit brush teeth and tongue, then run itself along the outside of his teeth. Then the finger was removed. Jas felt arms around him:

"Yours, Jas...only yours – remember?"

His stomach flipped over. "Leigh..."

"Don't go..stay with me..."

Jas felt himself pulled down onto the bed. He fumbled for Leigh, drew the body to him. In his arms, Leigh was completely trusting, completely relaxed.

They both were.

Balance...balance...

"Leigh..."

Three words. Why were they so hard to say?

"Mmm?" Leigh nuzzled his ear.

"Nothing." Jas eased away and walked to the wardrobe. The biker's jacket.

"You'll be too hot."

Jas smiled, dropping the leather onto the bed. He lifted keys from the bedside table. "Back soon."

Nine

AS HE WALKED down Cathedral Street towards the Royal Infirmary, distant rumbling heralded a break in the weather. Nearly ten, but the temperature remained high. Jas shrugged and grinned. A new strength rippled through muscle, dwarfing the effect of countless workouts.

Strength that came from...another's strength. Leigh's strength. Strength that came from...inside. Strength that would see him through anything.

A warm, unfamiliar contentment filled his heart.

Something slipped into place. Leigh. Two weeks of sun, sex and...another decision.

It was over.

The double-life was over.

The emptiness was gone, gone like a bad dream.

The bad dream that had been his life.

Grinning widely at two bemused drunks, he walked through the hospital entrance.

At the door to Intensive Care, a hand on his shoulder:

"A word, Sergeant Anderson..."

Jas followed the black nurse into her office. He smiled, held up a hand. "Look: ah ken ah'm a bit later than usual, Sister, but ah'm aff on holiday the morra. Two weeks..." He noticed her expression. "Whit's wrang?"

She shook her head, pointing to a chart on the desk.

Jas picked it up. A consent form. He looked back at the nurse.

Beneath the hardened exterior her face crumpled. "The results of the test are through..." She glanced over his shoulder. "The doctors think it would be best for the family if..."

Jas stood up and walked through to the ward.

He was different, but Jo...?

...looked the same as ever. Small, freckled face framed by soft ginger hair. Jas took a pale hand. "Hi, pal..." The nurse at his elbow, whispering:

"Virtually no cerebral activity. The brain is undamaged, physically, but has ceased to function. Keeping him here like this is only prolonging the agony for everyone and..." Professional realism. "...we need the bed..."

Jas squeezed the tiny hand. "When?"

"Maybe tomorrow, maybe the day after. Ah can't really say. But it will be soon...want to say goodbye?"

No. Jas nodded.

"Ah'll leave you two then, for a while..."

At midnight a hand touched his arm. Whisper. "Come on, Sergeant Anderson. Go home. It's over..."

Jas released Jo's fingers and walked from the ward, down four flights of stone stairs and out into the night. Above, thunder growled. Beside the entrance to 'Accident and Emergency' he stopped.

'It's over...'

A lot was over.

Spitting rain speckled his face.

His double life would be over.

It was all over for Jo. Thirteen years of life, gone 'tomorrow, maybe the day after...' The flick of a switch.

Jas thrust hands deep into jeans pockets and walked towards the necropolis. He crossed the Bridge of Sighs in gloom. The rain was heavier now, spotting his face like wounds. 'It's over...'

Jas walked.

Lightning tore the heavens apart, searing into thirsty earth. Grass dampened beneath his feet.

Jas walked.

Lights from the Ladywell Brewery twinkled in the distance, outclassed by other, more natural illumination.

Pausing by a dead tree, Jas sat down on an overturned headstone. He read the inscription:

'Why seek ye the living among the dead? He is not here.'

He is in the Royal, in a child's bed, awaiting death.

Jas sat, rain filling his eyes, soaking his sweatshirt, washing over his body. He lowered his head.

Another crack, but not lightning.

Another leak, but not water.

Jas stood up and walked on.

At the top of the necropolis, by the John Knox monument, he paused again. The city spread its legs before him, beckoning. Jas turned away and sat down.

'It's over...'

Over for Jo. Over for Jas. Time to cut loose...

Time to unite two lives.

Jo wouldn't die in vain.

Jas took his pain, used it.

Jo's pain had made him feel.

His pain would give him strength.

Leigh had done the rest...

Leigh.

Jas grabbed a handful of warm, wet earth.

Three little words...

They'd never passed his lips.

He'd say them tonight...

Eventually, the thunder ceased.

Jas relaxed.

Slowly, the lightning faded.

Leigh's face strobed before his eyes.

The rain eased off.

Jas stood up, clothes heavy with water.

LA. Leigh. He could do nothing here. He climbed down the steep hill, through the hole in the fence and out onto Wishart Street.

On Alexandra Parade he glanced at his watch: 2.14 am.

Leigh would be worried.

Jas smiled. For the first time in his life he felt...complete. Two halves were uniting, creating more than the whole. A warm sensation spread through his wet body.

Leigh was filling the vast hole, rushing in, healing.

A lightness swam in his head. He was high...without alcohol he was high. Jas quickened his pace.

Leigh was the only thing he'd ever needed.

Why had it taken him so long to...?

Ahead, he could see flashes. More lightning? Jas turned into Eastercraigs.

Two police cars and an ambulance. The door to his block was wedged ajar. Jas walked faster, then ran. Past two uniforms, a gaggle of neighbours, upstairs. Police radios squawked, voices were low. The front door was open. A strong hand on his arm:

"Are you the owner of this flat, sir?"

Jas ignored the question, thrusting the hand away.

It regripped, accompanied him into the hallway and through to the bedroom.

Ten

BRIGHT, BLINDING light. Flashes, then red. More flashes. Murmured words. Jas blinked, rubbing rain from his eyes. He blinked again.

The bedroom was full of people. Men. Uniforms and suits. Jas looked around. "Leigh?"

The grip on his arm. "Are you the householder, sir?" Low, detached, procedural.

"Aye, where's...?"

"Yer name, sir."

"Whit's happpened? Where's...?"

Patient. "Your name, sir?"

"Jas... James Anderson." He looked at the hand on his arm. "DS Anderson. Ah'm wi' London Road. Whit're you dain' here?"

A crowd around the bed. More camera flashes. Voices. A smell. Coppery, salty. Familiar...

Jas wrenched his arm away. "Where's Leigh?" He moved towards the crowd around the bed.

"Chief?" Patient again, but not to Jas.

More voices. One raised above the others, angry. "Get a holda him, Williams..."

"Come and sit doon here, si..." Patient again. Two pairs of hands on his arms.

Jas shrugged them off, continued towards the bed. He breathed in the smell, pushing through the huddle. "Whit's...?"

A voice across him. "Sorry, chief, we couldney..."

Leigh.

Jas stepped by the bed.

The huddle fell silent, broke to embrace him.

Leigh lay on his side. The harness. Two handcuffs dangled from the bed-head. Jeans, bare broad back and...

Jas's heart hesitated, then quickened.

Blood...on the sheets, the pillows, the harness, the wall-mirror stippled with tiny red dots. Jas looked up into the reflection. Leigh's soft blond hair was a molten mass of crimson and grey mucus.

"Christ! Leigh..." Jas swayed.

Someone behind steadied him.

He moved to the other side of the bed. His progress was unimpeded. Blood dripped from Leigh's fingers, pooling on the polished floor. His eyes travelled up the hand, the arm and shoulder to the handsome face. There was no face, only a wet, purple mass.

A twist deep inside. "No..." Jas stretched out a hand. Rain dripped from his arm onto Leigh's tanned back.

"Git him oota here, willya?" Angry.

A voice in his ear. "Let's sit doon, sir..." The first voice, patient. A hand on his shoulder now. Williams?

Jas pulled away, skin warm and cold by turns. Sweat and rain cooled to a lukewarm cocktail. Water dripped into his eyes. Pounding, which began in his heart, spread through his body. There was noise in his ears, fizzing, then a high-pitched whine. Jas stared.

Where Leigh's blue eyes had been was now mush. Nose gone the same way. High slavic cheekbones pulverised into sand, gritty beneath shards of tanned skin. One lip lung limply over splintered, bloody teeth.

Jas's breath was coming in short, shallow pants. He knew he was going into shock. He tried to focus his eyes elsewhere.

On the bedside table, an apple lay untouched.

A different smell now. Damp serge. Jas looked up.

Two constables, hatless, wet-haired, impartial faces. One took his arm. "Ye got ony whisky in the house, Mr. Anderson?"

Jas shook his head. "Leigh..."

"Tea, then? A nice hot drink. Let's go intae the kitchen, Mr. Anderson..."

"Leigh..." Jas buried his face in his hands. "Oh Christ..." He felt himself moving, one foot then the other. He stopped, rooted. "Where's Leigh?"

"Get him oota here!" The angry voice again.

Williams: "We're tryin', DI Monroe..."

Jas moved his eyes. Tall man, thin, weedy. A suit.

Cold eyes scanned his face. "Do you know this man, Mr. Anderson?"

"Leigh..." Nothing else would come.

Weedy scowled, then turned to the unifroms. "Git him calmed doon. Then git his statement, boys..."

Jas was propelled into the kitchen.

A mug was pressed into his hands. "Drink it sir, ye'll feel better." Soft voice. Leigh's voice?

Jas lifted and drank the hot, sweet liquid. It burned his mouth then hit his stomach like lava. He retched.

A hand on his shoulder. "Easy...easy..." Soft, soothing.

Jas wiped bile from his lips. Someone handed him a tea-towel. He used it, looked up.

Concerned blue eyes. Leigh's eyes?

No. Leigh was dead. The world was unreal. Jas exhaled. "Got a...?"

PC Williams fumbled in his pockets, produced a Kensitas packet. He passed it to Jas.

Three months...he put a cigarette to his lips.

Williams struck a match.

Jas cupped shaking hands around it, lighting the cigarette. He inhaled, coughed, inhaled again.

The soft voice, above his head. "Hiv a look fur an ashtray, Malkie..."

Jas smiled. "Ah don't smoke – wanted tae throw aw' the ashtrays oot when..."

Williams sat beside him, placing a saucer between them. "Given up, eh?"

Jas nodded, drawing smoke deep into his lungs.

The sound of another match. "Ah've tried eight times. Canny live withoot them..."

Jas smoked the cigarette. Then:

"Dae ye feel up tae a few questions, Mr. Anderson?"

Jas nodded. "Leigh. Whit...?"

"Hold on..." Rustlings. A notebook produced. "Ah'm PC Williams, by the way. Baird Street." Friendly, concerned... not long in the job.

Jas stared at the clock: twenty-five to three.

"Ye want a towel or somethin', Mr. Anderson? Yer soakin'."

"Whit happened in there?"

"DI Monroe'll talk tae ye later, Mr. Anderson. He's wi' the..." Regretting the words. "...duty pathologist. Ah jist goat here, coupla minutes before yerself." Reassuring smile.

Jas took in the words, but... "Whit happened?"

Sigh. "Ah really don't know, sir. The officers who took the call..."

"When?"

PC Williams consulted his notebook. "Came in er...1.15 am."

The necropolis. The rain. Sitting in smug self-congratulation under John Knox. Jas lowered his head to the table, pressing a hot cheek against cool wood. Why hadn't he come straight home?

A hand on his shoulder. "You okay, Mr. Anderson? Wid ye like another cuppa tea?"

Jas raised his head, shook it.

A voice behind, older, bored. Malkie? "Git oan wi' it, Gavin!"

"Er...right. Yer name is James Anderson?"

Jas nodded.

"...and this is your flat – 2B, Seven Eastercraigs, Dennistoun?"

"Aye."

"Age?"

"Thirty-three."

Stupid procedural questions. He gave it.

"Occupation?"

"DS with London Road – ah telt ye that already..."

"Sorry, sir. You know the drill..." Apologetic.

Jas nodded.

Throat clearing. "The dead man...?"

Agony gripped his heart. Jas swallowed. "Leigh..."

Pause. Expectant. "Go on, sir..."
Jas clenched his fists. "Leigh Nicols."
Shuffling. "Ye shared the flat wi' Mr. Nicols?"
Jas nodded. Shared everything...
"Age?"
"Twenty-four."
"An' yer relationship tae Mr. Nicols, sir?"
What could he say but the truth? Finally. "We were..."
The door opened. Jas turned his head. Weedy plus two uniforms. One held the handcuffs, the other carried the harness. "Can you explain these, DS Anderson?" Ice formed on the words.
Jas stared.
Weedy continued, solemn-faced. "Yer wee game get oota hand?"
Jas stood up. The empty mug shattered on the floor.
Williams: "Mr. Anderson says he shared the flat wi' Mr. Nicols, sir an'..."
"Shared his fuckin' bed wi' him tae, nae doubt!" Weedy laughed, a hard grating sound.
Confusion in Williams' eyes. "But...?"
Jas watched the young face take in his brawny form. He shrugged, then scowled at Weedy. "So fuckin' what?" Twelve years of lies, and Leigh, gave him strength.
Weedy grinned. "A DS, ye claim? Who's yer guv'nor?"
"DI Moira Campbell." Jas glowered. "Whit's wrang, pal? Ye don't believe me?"
Weedy shook his head, disgust painting his face. "So it's come tae this..." Laugh. "...they must be desperate doon at London Road, workin' wi' the likes o' you..."
An explosion in his head. Fingernails into palms.
Weedy turned to Soft-voice. "Whit's his alibi?"
Williams looked at Jas, then his notebook. "Ah've no' got tae that yet..."
Alibi: the word was a slap on the face. Jas brushed it away, turned. "Ah need a shower..."
Weedy laughed. "Ye're not on, DS Anderson..." The title was spat. "...git they claes aff!"
A uniform produced a large polythene bag.
Jas's mind slowly cleared. The phone calls, the BMW, Jimmy Mygo out of hospital. He began to strip.
Weedy continued. "There's a boay in there wi' his face blown aff. The doctor sez..." Pause.
Jas peeled off the wet sweatshirt, sat down and began to undo boots. A latex-sheathed hand appeared, waiting. Jas wriggled out of soaking jeans. Naked beneath, he stood up.
Five pairs of eyes stared.
Jas wanted to stare back.

An unfamiliar blush spread over his rapidly-drying cheeks.

The latex-sheathed hand gathered up his wet clothes, placing them in the bag.

Weedy walked to a pile of unwashed laundry, threw Jas a T-shirt and jeans. The T-shirt was Leigh's Lacoste polo-shirt. It would be too tight. Jas pulled it on anyway, then the jeans.

Weedy stared talking again. "The doctor sez...anal intercourse had taken place within the last twenty-four hours. Signs of bruisin' and tearin'..." He laughed. "That boay's face wiz nothin' compared tae the state o' his arse! Ye could drive a truck up there..."

Behind Jas, PC Williams moved to the sink and vomited.

"Ye make me sick, DS Anderson, ya dirty bastard!"

Leigh...

Legs buckling, Jas sat down hard. Leigh...He opened his mouth. "Jimmy Mygo." A whisper.

Laugh. "Is that another o' yer bum-chums, Anderson?" Weedy slapped PC Williams' shoulder. "Get him intae the van an' doon tae London Road." Voice in his ear. "Jist tae help wi' oor enquiries, ye understand, DS Anderson." Weedy took the handcuffs, swung them back and forth. "Nae need fur these, ah take it?"

Jas stared as gleaming metal oscillated in the kitchen's dull light. "Whit happened in there? Did ye get ony prints...?"

Weedy laughed. "Done oors ago, Anderson. We've been waitin' fur ye tae reappear..."

Jas felt himself dragged to his feet. In front, Weedy pushed the kitchen door open.

As they passed the bedroom, Jas could see bare brown feet disappearing into a body bag. The room was an abattoir. He shivered. "Let me git ma boots an' ma jaicket, will ye?" He pointed to the bed.

Just one last look. To say goodbye.

Two goodbyes in one night.

Both thanks to Jimmy Mygo.

Weedy. "Git him some shoes, son..."

A uniform brushed past, returning with buckled biker's boots. He held them out like a challenge.

Jas accepted, tried to put the boots on standing up. Eventually, he succeeded. "Ma jaicket..." Arm twisted savagely up his back.

Weedy's sneer. "Evidence."

Jas looked. The black leather biker's jacket was splattered with brain.

Outside, the sky was dark. Rain resoaked Jas's body as the van door was unlocked. He shivered.

Pushed into the back, Jas sat on the floor, alone. No accompanying officer accompanied. PC Williams' quizzical eyes glanced once, before he locked the door. Something tight pressed onto his chest.

Leigh's T-shirt?

In the back of the dark van darker shudders racked Jas's body as a black veil descended over his brain.

The reception area of London Road police station was empty. Jas sat on a hard, plastic seat, looked at his watch. 3.30 am. Thursday mornings were always slow. At the desk, Weedy was talking to Chic Currie, the duty sergeant.

Jas looked at his hands, laced then unlaced his fingers. He knew what would happen now. A formal statement, details about Leigh: his job, colleagues, his activities the night he died. His stomach knotted, unknotted then knotted again...

"Over here, Anderson!" Weedy's voice.

Jas got up and walked to the desk. He tried to smile. "Chic."

Sergeant Currie looked away. "Name."

"Chic?"

An elbow in his ribs. Weedy's. "Jist answer the man!"

Jas shrugged. "He kens ma name..."

Sergeant Currie wrote, then paused. "Empty yer pockets, please."

Jas stared at Chic.

Chic looked away.

"Fur Christ's sake, whit is aw' this?"

Weedy: "Jist dae it, Anderson..."

Jas sank hands deep into denim. A bunch of keys, some loose change, a handkerchief. He laid them on the counter.

Sergeant Currie looked at Weedy, then produced a pair of thin rubber gloves from a drawer. Putting them on, he gingerly lifted each item in turn, gave a verbal description, wrote it down, then placed the keys, change and handkerchief in a brown envelope. "Sign fur them, please." He held out a pen, but didn't look up.

Jas signed.

Sergeant Currie sighed. "Interview Room Three's empty, sir..."

Weedy grabbed his arm. "Come on, Anderson. Let's git this ower wi'..." He pushed from behind.

Jas was marched along a corridor. Through an open door, a pale face appeared. Messy dark curls. DS Ann McLeod smiled. "Jas? What are you doin' here at..." She looked at Weedy, sobered. "What's happened?"

Weedy scowled. "This fuckin' fairy's..."

"This fuckin' fairy's gonny tear yer fuckin' heid aff!" Jas spun round, grabbing Weedy by the lapels. A female hand on his shoulder, pulling:

"Jas, come on. Take it easy...."

He let go.

Weedy seized an arm, twisting it up Jas's back. "Assaultin' a senior officer, Anderson. Naughty, naughty..." Flip words, breathless tone. Weedy was out of condition. He pushed Jas onwards.

A voice after them. "Want me to get the duty solicitor, Jas?"

Before he could answer, Weedy laughed. "Ah'll see tae that, hen." To Jas: "Ye've nothin' tae hide, huv ye Anderson?" He twisted the arm higher. "It's aw' oot in the open now..."

Two uniforms appeared ahead. Weedy hurled Jas towards them. "Take him in, boays. An' keep yer distance..."

Jas was pushed into Interview Room Three.

"Let's go through it again, DS Anderson..."

A stranger. He had said his name, but Jas had forgotten it. Beside the stranger, Ann, looking solemn. He wondered vaguely how she'd wangled that.

"You've formally identified the body as that of Mr. Leigh Nicols?"

Half an hour earlier. A short car journey to the Royal. Cold, fluorescent light. The smell of formaldehyde and disinfectant. Leigh naked on a stainless-steel autopsy tray. Beautiful Leigh, flawless Leigh beautiful and flawless no longer...

Breath caught in Jas's throat. He nodded.

"For the tape, please, DS Anderson."

Procedural, by-the-book. Jas tensed. "Yes."

"Thank you. Now..." Rustlings, papers flicking.

Jas's statement.

"...you and Mr. Nicols were, er...friends. Is that right? You lived together as...?"

Lovers...he'd never said the word aloud. It stuck in his throat even now, a final denial of everything Leigh was...had been. A whisper escaped dry lips. "Aye, ah lived with him..."

"Answer the question please, DS Anderson – and speak up."

Ann to the stranger. "I think we all know what the arrangement was, sir."

Throat clearing. "Yes, DS McLeod." Uncomfortable. "I think we do..."

Pause. Jas looked at Ann. She smiled consolingly.

Deep breath. "Now, last night at approximately 8 pm you and Mr. Nicols engaged in anal intercourse..."

Jas closed his eyes. He could still feel Leigh's prick deep inside, still sense Leigh's spunk in his arse.

"...as part of a sado-masochistic sex game involving the use of physical restraints on Mr. Nicols, which you say was 'routine'..."

"No!" The word rang round the small room.

Surprised voice. "But you told us earlier..."

"That wis whit we...usually did." Jas opened his eyes. He wouldn't – couldn't – deny Leigh any longer. He blinked. "Last night...Leigh fucked me." He stared at the disbelieving face, watched as narrow, uncomprehending eyes flicked over his body.

Jas sighed. He knew the score: fucking, he could probably get away with. Being fucked – submitting to the prick of another man – was completely alien to this smart-suited, sober-faced detective. A smile twitched his lips.

Passivity...this man would never know the strength, the joy of passivity.

The sober face creased into a frown of distaste. Throat-clearing. "Well...er, right, DS Anderson. Let's get on with it." Narrow eyes lowered to statement-sheet. "After...this had taken place, you say you washed, dressed and went to visit...er...Joseph Hunter." He glanced at Ann. "DS McLeod phoned the Royal, and Sister Duncan confirms your presence there. You arrived about 10 pm and left just after midnight..."

Jas tried to focus on the face. It floated before his eyes. Mid-forties, soft, flabby... He shivered.

Sigh. "As far as we know, DS Anderson, you were the last person to see the dead man alive. We need to get this straight. You understand that, DS Anderson?"

Jas stared. Straight...there was nothing straight about...

"Do you understand, DS Anderson?" Irritation.

Jas stared.

Ann: "Make an effort, Jas..."

An effort, an effort... He stood up.

"Sit down, Anderson!" Angry.

Jas sat.

"Now stay there!" Sigh. "So...you left the hospital at about midnight. Tell me again what you did between then and arriving back at your flat, at 2.16 am."

"Went fur a walk." Explanations dragged from somewhere at the back of his mind.

"Where?"

"The necropolis. The big cemetery doon from the Royal."

"I see..." Unconvinced. "Did you meet or talk to anyone, in the course of this walk?"

A new assumption...the promiscuous assumption. Jas shook his head. "Ah wisney cruisin', if that's whit ye..."

"Then why did you go for this walk, DS Anderson? It poured last night, not the best time for a..."

"Needed to think."

Ann bent her head to the stranger. Whispers.

He nodded slowly. "I wasn't aware of Joseph Hunter's ...condition, DS Anderson. Must have been a shock to you. I can understand you might want to clear your head. But why did you not go home and...?"

A knock at the door. Ann rose, opened it. A WPC held out a piece of folded paper. Ann took it, read it, then turned. "Sir?"

He rose, walked to the door, read the note, came back. "Interview suspended at..." He looked at his watch. "...5.45 am." He switched off the tape-recorder. "Don't talk to him, DS McLeod." The stranger left the room.

Jas stared at Ann.

The explanation. "They've found the weapon." The pale face was stony. She sat on the corner of the desk, staring. "Look. The tape's off. Tell me, Jas. Did you do it? Did you kill...?"

Jas shook his head.

Ann exhaled. "The truth?"

Jas nodded. Something hot and heavy filled his head. "Jimmy Mygo. Leigh had been fucked recently...an' no' by me."

She sighed. Long pause, then: "It's possible. He's out of hospital. You know Jimmy: he always pays his debts. But..." Pause. She shook her head. "Why kill him?"

The chink in his armour. Fuck Leigh, fuck-up him. Kill Leigh, kill... "Ah've got tae find him, Ann..."

Angry. "Let us take it from here, Jas. You've done enough damage. If you hadn't taken things into your own hands with Jimmy..." Pause. Sigh. "Sorry – I didn't mean..."

"Naw, ye're right, Ann..." A cold claw clutched at his soul. "...if ah hudney gied Jimmy a doin'..."

"Don't, Jas..." A soft, female hand on rough, sweating fingers. "...it won't do you any good..."

The door opened. Ann withdrew her hand and stood up.

The stranger was back. "Do you own a gun, DS Anderson?"

Jas sighed. Leigh was dead.

"Do you, DS Anderson?"

Jimmy Mygo...Jas sighed. "Put the tape back oan..."

"Well, that'll do for now, DS Anderson..."

Jas had stopped speaking.

"...your account of events will be checked. That gun should've been handed in..." Frown. "...pity the only other person who can verify how you came by the weapon – apart from the boy, who'll probably refuse to speak to us – was Mr. Nicols. The gun was in your flat. How it found its way there is immaterial." Throat clearing. "We'll certainly look into the information you've given us regarding Mr. Johnstone, the BMW and the threating phone calls you've been receiving. In the mean time, go home and stay there. SOCO has finished. We'll need to talk to you again, no doubt, when the forensic results come through."

Jas stared.

Ann's voice. "Come on. It's the end of my shift. I'll give you a lift..."

Jas rubbed his face. He was back in Reception. The brown envelope was in front of him. Taking the money, keys and handkerchief, he stuffed them back in his pockets. The too-tight T-shirt hurt his chest.

Chic's voice. "Sign here, please."

Jas signed, then turned. The reception area was crowded now. Shift changeover. He focused on the far wall. Ann pulled his arm. "Let's go..."

Jas began to walk.

Whispers, sniggers filled his ears. Someone bumped hard against him.

A high-pitched falsetto. "Oops! Sorry, dear..."

Bitter laughter, whistles. A growl. "Fuckin' poof!"

Jas walked on.

Shouts now. "Queer bastard, ya dirty..."

"Come on, boys.." Ann moved in front of him. Placating. "...let us through..."

A body darted forward. Uniformed, young, angry. "You bled in the squad-room, Anderson. Christ knows whit diseases yer carryin'...

Another voice. "We shouldney huv tae work wi'...

"Grow up, ya stupid fucks!"

The hall fell silent: Ann never swore.

Jas looked around. In the background, Weedy grinned, made an obscene gesture. Beside him, Chic Currie stared past Jas into middle distance. A group of about ten uniforms stood directly in front of of Jas. A sea of navy serge.

Mixed ages, one attitude. Loathing seeped from every pore.

He recognised most of them, had worked with at least five. Good guys, fair guys, some married, some not. All police officers.

All straight.

All hating.

Despite – or maybe because of – all his years in the force, it didn't come as a surprise.

Weedy's voice. "All right, boys...let the ladies through.

The serge sea parted. Ann pulled him out into the rain.

Eleven

THE CAR stopped.

Jas looked at his watch: 6.15am.

Ann switched off the engine, lit a cigarette.

Jas opened a window.

Rain poured in.

He shut the window.

Sigh. "How you feeling?" Harsh laugh. "Stupid question..."

Jas stared through the windscreen.

"I wish you'd told me you're gay. You and Leigh were together...?"

"Eighteen months..." Too short.

The tip of a cigarette glowed in the murk. "That's too bad..." Sigh, then business-like. "I've known you..."

Jas rubbed his face.

"...what, four years now? No skin off my nose if you like guys..."

Jas reached for the door-handle.

A hand on his arm. "No. Wait. I need to say this. Back there, in the station..." Another cigarette. "...that's not on. I partnered you for two years, Jas, my best two years so far in the job." Softly. "I'm with Kit Marshal now – know him? Thought I could handle that type." Sad smile. "He's not half the cop you are. I'm considering a transfer. The guy's got more hands than an octopus..." Inhaling slowly. "You never gave me any hassle. Oh, I know why, now, but it doesn't make any difference. You treated me like an equal, didn't try to get me into bed, then make me feel like some frigid schoolgirl when I turned you down. We had some good times Jas, eh?"

Pause.

"Jas?" Light pressure on his arm.

"Aye, we had some guid times, Ann..."

Sigh. "Sorry, didn't mean to go on. You don't need this right now..." The hand removed.

He opened the door.

"Get some sleep. Is there someone I can phone for you, a friend, your family?"

Few friends, and his family...? On the wet pavement outside Seven Eastercraigs Jas shook his wet head. "Thanks anyway, Ann. Ah'm okay..."

Scowl. "You don't look okay!" Softening. "Take an aspirin, and a hot drink.."

He walked towards the door, fumbled for keys.

Raised voice from the car. "Sure you don't want to come back to my place? We could talk, I could..."

"Go home, Ann." He glanced at his watch: 6.55am.

Sigh. Engine starting.

Jas opened the door to the building and paused. On the ground floor another door closed softly. Nosy neighbours.

"Jas?" Ann again.

He turned.

Pink face faint in half-light. "Remember: we'll sort it out." Solemn now. "Don't try anything on your own. You'll only make matters worse."

Could they be worse? Jas smiled weakly, raised a hand. "Ah don't think ah'll be doin' anything for a while. 'Bye, Ann..." He watched as the Ford Fiesta reversed and moved off in the direction of Kennyhill Square. Turning, he walked into the building.

The door to the second-floor flat was locked. He opened it, paused, inhaled deeply. An odour, faintly medical, warm and comforting. "Lei...?" A syllable cut short. He closed eyes, mouth and door.

Silence.

Eyes blinked open. On the hall table, where Leigh's keys usually sat, a printed card.

Jas sat his own keys beside it.

In the lounge, he stripped off the Lacoste T-shirt, and boots, then crouched on the floor.

The numbness.

The old numbness.

He need it...now!

Jas began to exercise.

After fifty-six press-ups he halted.

Sit-ups next...thirty...forty...fifty...sixty...

He counted in his head, and when he lost count he stopped.

His mouth was dry.

Burpees...

At seventy-five, sweat coursing from his chest onto the floor, Jas rested. He lay on his side, breathing slowly and heavily. Heartbeat pounded in his chest, echoing round his head, filling it.

Numbing it?

Nowhere near.

Skull thumping with Leigh, Jas moved through to the shower. He switched it on. The water didn't feel cold. He checked the temperature-control: it read zero. Jas stood rigid, bracing himself, waiting for the chill. It didn't come. His skin glowed red under the icy jets. He continued to wait.

After ten minutes he switched the shower off. Water ran from hair into eyes, from eyes down onto burning cheeks. Salty droplets joined the other water. Jas shivered and reached for a towel.

In the kitchen, he finished the orange juice, tossing the empty carton into the bin. On the table lay a saucer containing two cigarette ends and a small quantity of ash. Jas emptied the saucer into the bin, washed it, dried it and replaced it in a cupboard.

He looked at the pile of laundry, grabbed an armful and began to load the washing machine.

Two pairs of jeans, jogging trousers, jockstrap and three sweaty T- shirts; an assortment of socks and underpants.

Jas walked to the lounge, returning with jeans and the Lacoste T-shirt, which smelled of Leigh's aftershave and his own sweat. Jas pulled the jeans on, thrusting the T-shirt into the washing machine. He walked through to the bedroom.

Darkness.

Jas opened the venetians. Outside, dawn was struggling through a leaden sky. Rain beaded the windows, warm tears on cool glass.

He turned away, wanting those tears, wanting the release.

Tears were a luxury.

Revenge was a necessity.

The bed gaped at him, empty and naked. Coverless duvet and pillows lay in a heap on the floor. Contrary to Weedy's words, the biker's jacket was still there.

He walked to the bedside table. Greyish streaks of fingerprint powder smeared its surface. The apple had been dusted too. Apart from that, there was little mess.

Jas looked around for something to wash and, finding nothing, returned to the kitchen. Dumping washing powder into the drawer he programmed the machine for a full cycle, switched it on then sat down at the table.

A cigarette, a drink, a...

Leigh.

Walking back through to the lounge he began to exercise again.

Press-ups only, this time.

With each rise and fall of his body, the pain in his heart was slowly eclipsed by the pain in his wrists, arms, shoulders and neck. A rhythm was established, syncronising itself with the pounding in his head.

Up...down.

One...two.

One...two.

One...two.

One long line from head two heels.

Torso held rigid, Jas continued.

Gradually, grey crept into his mind.

He scowled, clenching his teeth.

It wasn't enough.

Muscle in his upper arms began to twitch spasmodically, breaking the rhythm.

Jas moved more slowly, reasserting a balance.

With each dip he paused three inches above the polished, maple floor.

One...two.

One...two.

The pressure behind his eyes increased, spreading outwards, dulling the grey to black.

In the raised-arm position he paused, closed his eyes.

Sensation imploded, sealing the pain of Leigh in a numb, black hole.

Nothing.

Jas lowered his body to the cool wood, stretched trembling arms on the polished surface.

The limbs continued to pulse with a life of their own. Blood vessels danced on his eyelids, then faded.

Nothing.

Less than nothing.

Sweat pooled around him. Warm denim stuck to wet legs.

Jas rolled over.

With one hand he unzipped jeans, peeled them over throbbing thighs, calves and bare feet.

Perspiration dripping from soaking hair, jas walked through to the bedroom and reclosed the venetians.

He shook the duvet free from under the biker's jacket, tossing it onto the bed.

A pillow tumbled to one side.

He picked it up, fingers contacting with stiffness. In the half-light he peered at the cotton. A dark, Asia-shaped stain marred one side. Jas raised it to his face, sniffed.

Something for the machine he'd missed.

Holding the blood-stained pillow, he sat on the bed. The smell which permeated the flat was strongest here. Jas shivered, dragging the duvet around his shoulders. He sat motionless for several seconds, gripping two corners of the duvet, then lay down on the bed, rolling his body into a foetal ball. He held onto the pillow.

Above his head, blood still spotted the mirror.

Cocooned in pulsating, strained muscle, He plunged into black...

...black gave way to grey, then blue, yellow, white, daylight, Duke Street. Sun blazed overhead.

Leigh stood about forty yards away. He was wearing the harness and jockstrap. Gold nipple-rings twinkled.

Jas began to walk.

Leigh held out his arms.

Jas raised the gun.

Leigh bent down, hands behind back, head lowered.

Jas walked on. He stopped inches from the kneeling figure. He could smell Lacoste. Gripping the blond ponytail, he dragged the head back. His hand brushed soft skin.

Leigh smiled. "Yours...only yours..."

He slipped the barrel of the gun into Leigh's mouth, closed his eyes and squeezed the trigger.

No report, only the sound of tissue splitting. Warm flesh hit his face, running down hot cheeks into his mouth. He ran a tongue over his lips, tasting Leigh's warm blood. Opening eyes, he looked down. One hand still held the blond ponytail. Jas raised his hand.

Shards of skin and scalp clung to the shining hair.

Leigh's lips parted in a crimson gash. "Jas...?" A smashed tooth dropped from his mouth. Bloody saliva smeared the ruined chin, dribbling onto the tanned neck.

Jas closed his eyes.

Hands clutched at his knees.

He felt a warm mushiness pressed against his thighs, pushed it away.

Leigh fell to the ground and laughed. A grating sound.

Not Leigh.

Jas opened his eyes.

Propped up on one elbow, Jimmy Mygo leered at him, sodden T-shirt dark with gore.

A dull buzzing filled his head. Smothering heat pressed down on him. There was something wet and bitter in his mouth, choking, suffocating. Jas flailed his arms, fighting his way out from beneath layers of padded duvet which swathed his body like a shroud.

In the distance, a muffled hiss: "Jas? Come on..." Male voice. Familiar...and unfamiliar.

He sat up, eyelids soldered together. "Leigh?" Jas reached out an arm and patted the bed, searching.

Only cold, slightly damp fabric.

No Leigh.

Jas rubbed his eyes.

Leigh was dead.

The voice: "Jas? I've spoken to DS McLeod. I know what happened. Come on, answer!"

Impatient.

Not Leigh's voice.

He disentangled himself from the duvet and sat up.

Darkness.

He opened his eyes: more darkness.

The clock read 19.45: he'd slept nearly twelve hours.

Jas stretched. His legs quivered.

An amplified sigh echoed in the hallway. Then the voice returned, clearer now. "Look! Ring me back on..." Pause.

Jas stood up.

His knees buckled.

He sat down again.

"...894-5717, extension..."

Focusing his mind, he stood up a second time and walked slowly through to the hall. He lifted the telephone receiver and spoke into it.

Nothing.

He tried again. "Jas Anderson." The words were hoarse and detached.

Cool voice rippling with tension: "Andrew Clark, Jas. Sorry to wake you – I know you must be..."

"Whit dae ye want, pal?" His head was full of feathers, stuffing his brain.

"Are you okay? You sound a bit..."

"Aye, ah'm fine." He shook his head. "Still half asleep, that's all..."

"Right. Listen. I haven't got long. Just tell me one thing. Last night: that was straight up, wasn't it? You had nothing to do with that...man's death, did you?"

A flash of nightmare seared his eyes. Leigh. The gun. "Ah didn't shoot him, if that's whit ye..."

"Don't argue the finer points with me, Jas..." Irritated. "...we haven't got time. You didn't pull the trigger – even accidentally?"

"No." He sat down on the floor.

"That's all I need to know. We're trying to find Jimmy Mygo, but no luck so far. He's gone to ground." Sigh. "To tell the truth, I don't think we'll be looking much longer – at least, not for reasons that'll do you any good." Pause. "The rest of forensics are through, along with the early autopsy results..."

Jas tensed.

Long pause.

"Why you dain' this, Clark?" Jas pulled the telephone onto the floor. The answering machine began to whine. He disconnected it.

Lowered voice. "You helped Ricky when I was too...stupid to do anything for my own son. This is the least I can do...hold on – someone's coming in..."

He was phoning from the station. Jas wound the telephone flex around his left hand.

Fast whisper. "Look: the handgun you took from that kid showed a variety of smudged prints, which isn't surprising, given its illegal history. One set was clear enough to identify, though: yours. Suicide's been ruled out. The doctor says no way – angle of entry's all wrong."

Jas tightened the flex.

Sigh. "I can't do much with your alibi for last night, you realise that. Sure you don't remember passing anyone, on your way into the necropolis?"

"Ah didney go there fur the social life!" He laughed.

"I don't think you realise how bad this looks. Things are all very circumstantial at the moment, but they're not going to stay that way for long."

Jas unwound the flex, ran his fingers through its coils and began to wrap again.

Muffled: "Yes, sir – I'll be right with you." Whisper. "You still there?"

The skin above the flex turned white. "Ah'm here."

The flex cut into muscle.

Muffled. "Right, sir." Whisper. "I'll phone you back." The line buzzzed, disconnected.

Jas held the receiver close to his ear then unwound the flex. The receiver dropped, clanging of tubular metal. The floor was cold beneath his naked flesh. He stood up, replaced the receiver. Almost immediately, it rang. Jas picked it up.

Voice normal pitch, still urgent: "Listen carefully, Jas. Some DI from Baird Street's whipping your division up into a frenzy. Says you got carried away during whatever...game you were playing at the time, shot...Mr. Nicols, then tried to blame Jimmy Mygo...

Jas closed his eyes.

In the background, DS Clark talked on. "There's some guy with hairy ears and a name like a horse appeared. Psychiatrist. Says he talked to you. What the hell did you say to him? I got a look at his report. Couldn't make much sense of it – psycho-babble and jargon, for the most part – but the words 'paranoid, withdrawn, highly-volatile individual' jumped out at me." Sigh. "Seems your...orientation is regarded, in certain quarters, as some sort of personal slight." Angry now. "Don't know if it's the fact you're gay, your particular...er, kink, or just that they had their noses rubbed in it, last night..."

Last night.

"...or the fact that you didn't tell them years ago."

Jas began to punch the floor with a fist.

"Anyway, your friend's death suits a lot of people, confirms what they think about – what's the phrase? – alternative lifestyles. I've tried sticking up for you – Christ! I even told half the canteen about Ricky – but they won't listen to me. Say I don't understand..."

You don't. You can't.

"...but I know this. You're a good cop, Jas. Okay, what you did to the Mygo character wasn't on, but worse happens in custody every day, and no one blinks an eye..."

Cover-ups.

"...you were prepared to carry the can for what you did. Fair enough. You're gay. Fair enough. But you're not some kind of...animal..."

An animal.

The Jas-animal.

The untamed Jas-animal.

He punched the floor, harder now.

"...a disease-carrying animal. Look: I know the score. Ricky made sure I read the literature. But this lot? Gay equals AIDS. They're running around like blue-arsed flies, demanding HIV tests and God knows what else! It's really shaken them up..." Pause. "As far as your friend..."

"Leigh! His name wis Leigh!" Words spat, taking the rhythm of the punches.

"Sorry." The voice strained to understand. "As far as Leigh's death goes, DI Monroe knows a good brief would get any charges against you dropped, so we've been told to resurrect the Jimmy Mygo case. My boss is waving your account of events." Angry. "You're about to be hung by your own words. The psychiatrist is claiming something about repressed sexuality and instability." Pause. "New statements have been taken. PCs Forsyth and Lambie have withdrawn their claim that Jimmy Mygo attacked you. The Stanley knife's gone missing. I don't know how they've managed it..."

"The cover-up uncovered."

"What?"

"Nothing."

"All this because you..." Hollow laugh. "...what is it about cops and gays?"

Jas frowned. You tell 'em: you're one and the father of another.

"Listen: you've got a couple of hours at best. Monroe's arranging a warrant for your arrest, on the attempted murder of Jimmy Mygo – and he'll get it! He's taking over the case, and he'd brought in the big guns: some brass from Stewart Street is here now – Assistant Chief Commissioner Sloan, no less. I think they intend to hold you on suspicion, until they can make something stick..."

Jas slammed his fist into the floor, drawing blood from already-damaged knuckles.

"If I were you, I wouldn't hang around there. Get out. I don't know where you can go, and I don't want to..." Sigh. "I never thought I'd say this to anyone, let alone another cop, but I can't guarantee you'd get a fair hearing down here. You've seen what some of the boys can do to 'uncooperative' suspects – and that's when they've no feelings on the matter one way or the other! I'll do what I can here, but I can't promise anything..."

"But..."

"Just go, man! get out of there!"

The connection was broken, the receiver dangled lifelessly. Jas sat on the floor, sucking bleeding knuckles. Mawhinney's words:

'The type of camaraderie few civilians can understand...'

The sea of blue was closing ranks.
His ain lot would hold his head under until he drowned.
Jimmy Mygo: Leigh's killer, Jas's victim.
Find him before the cops do.
He walked into the bedroom and began to pack. Clothes swam before his eyes. He stuffed them into a holdall. Kneeling beside the loose floorboard, he prised it up and removed the handcuff box.
Two airline tickets stared at him. Departure time eleven hours ago.
Two weeks of sun, sand and...
He was out.
Out and vulnerable.
Out and...alone.
He crushed the two tickets, replacing the box with stiff, unwieldy fingers. It wouldn't fit back in. He scowled, removed the box and stretched a hand into the space, searching around for the obstruction.
A book.
Jas withdrew his hand.
Leigh's filofax. Jas sighed. Addresses, phone-numbers. Leigh's family, the friends in LA.
Informing the relatives.
One of the first things a cop was taught.
One of the hardest skills to master.
One of the worse duties to carry out.
He thrust the filofax into the holdall, dressed then walked to the lounge.
No longer dark.
The room was chaos. Books, cushions, videos, CD boxes splayed on the floor.
Cops were clumsy searchers. Jas shrugged. What had they expected to find?
He moved to a large vase, extracting cash-card from inside, then sat on the sofa.
Find Jimmy Mygo.
Andrew Clark's words: '...gone to ground.'
Who'd know where? Who knew everything, everyone's whereabouts?
In the bedroom, Jas lifted the biker's jacket. His hands slid over the leather, smearing grey brain-mucus over black.
He shivered. Taking keys, he noticed a small business-card. He picked up the white rectangle and stared: 'Andrew Clark.' Two telephone numbers, one Edinburgh, one a mobile phone.
He slipped the card into jeans' pocket, opened then relocked the front door.
At the rear of the building, garden and wall.
Jas vaulted it easily.

Rain was still falling as he walked towards the Gorbals.

Twelve

GREY DAY suppurated into night as he walked down Abercromby Street. His legs were lead. Rain drove onto hair, into his face. No one in sight.

At the intersection with the Gallowgate, Jas paused. Road clear.

He stepped off the pavement.

The white car appeared from nowhere, screeching wheels on wet tarmac. Jas threw the holdall at the windscreen. It bounced off onto the road.

The BMW stopped, reversed, then came at him again.

Jas threw himself at the bonnet, hands tearing at the polished surface, searching for a grip and a face behind the wheel.

The driver looked away.

Jas scrabbled at a wing-mirror. Hands clammy, slippery. "Ya bastard! Whit's wrang? Wan death no' enough fur ye?" He clutched the aerial. It broke off.

The car pulled back, swerved sideways. Jas slid from the bonnet into the gutter. The white BMW sped off towards Shettleston.

Jas strained at the disappearing number-plate.

R B blank, blank blank blank? Stored for later. He stood up. A pain pierced his side. Ignoring it, he walked into the middle of the road and picked up the holdall.

Fuckin' Jimmy Mygo. First Leigh, then...

Jas clenched his fists. "You're dead, scum." He walked on.

Ahead, Hutchisontown leered up through distillery steam and a haze of smirry rain from the other side of the Clyde. At its feet, four nine-foot pigeon coops dominated a patch of waste ground, blackened aluminium standing-stones. Beyond, a police car sloped across McNeil Street. Light flashing, siren silent.

Gorbals police station was nearby.

Jas darted behind one of the structures.

A flutter, then animated cooing.

The patrol car stopped, reversed, then headed back along Ballator Street.

Birds quietened. Jas walked on.

Queen Elizabeth Square shone glossy with puddles. A lamentation of youths huddled crow-like in a doorway, picking over carrion. Jas approached. The gathering scattered.

Jas stopped. On the ground, a leather money-pouch, ripped

open. 'Royal Bank of Scotland' emblazoned one side. Empty. Like he was, without...

Eyes following running figures, Jas shrugged, moved on. He began to climb the stairs to the flats above.

Rain dissolving new graffiti: 'Dalmarnock Posse. Legalise car-crime'.

Streaky, impermanent. Unlike the message.

He continued. Passing fifteen open landings, warm wet air brushed his face.

Rain was the norm in Glasgow, the last two weeks an aberration.

Things grew in the rain. Mainly weeds.

Sweating, Jas readjusted the bag on his shoulder, jogging the last flight to the sixteenth floor. He passed no one.

On the landing, petrol fumes. He scanned six doors.

The door to Flat Six, as on his last visit, was ajar. Charred paint blistered the surface.

The tally-man, the weeping woman, the kid...

The gun.

Jas pushed the door wider with his foot. "Onywan at hame?"

Silence.

Old habits die hard. Twelve years of police training took him in. The smell of petrol was stronger now. Melted nylon carpet scrunched under the biker's boots. He walked along an unlit hallway, glancing into rooms, all empty.

More emptiness in an empty world.

At the end of the hall, another door. Closed.

Bedroom?

He pushed the door open. Cheap curtains stopped two inches short of the sill. Dark. Body-smells. In the corner, a heap. Jas walked towards it, crouched down.

From the heap, an arm, thrown free of stained sleeping-bag. A pale limb. One single puncture mark.

Jas nudged the heap with one boot.

No response.

He peeled back the dirty fabric.

A face. Male. Open, blank eyes, lips crusted with blood and vomit.

The kid.

Jas shivered and turned away. Eyes acclimatising to the gloom, he looked around. A syringe lay a few feet away, beside it a fragment of blackened foil. A candle-stub lurked by matches. Crumpled clingfilm licked clean.

Jas scowled. Maybe if he hadn't taken the gun five days ago there would be two bodies less in Glasgow.

Where was the mother?

Efficiently, Jas scanned the dim interior.

Only the kid.

He debated reporting the death. No-one should die this way.

Leigh...

He shook his head, shrugged off the blue and walked from the burnt-out flat. The kid was well out of it. Heroin OD: a relatively painless way to go.

Like the young, old habits die hard...but they do die.

Outside Marie's flat, a security gate had been erected over the heavy, solid-core door. Ornate, wrought-iron swirls. Jas thrust his fist through a rococo oval and knocked.

No answer.

He looked at his watch: 20.14. Nights were Marie's busy times. She could be out, or otherwise engaged.

Jas knocked again, struck the metal gate with a boot. It absorbed the kick, vibrating softly.

No answer.

He crouched, leaned back against the fence.

Jimmy Mygo was up and about. He needed to know where Jimmy was hiding. He needed Marie.

Jas closed his eyes, gave the gate one last thump. Head thumped back. Even if she heard, Marie wouldn't answer. She had to be careful. There was no way to let her know it was safe...

After ten minutes, he stood up. Head clearer. With one bleeding knuckle he rapped softly three times, paused, then rapped once. He waited.

Minutes passed.

Three raps back.

He rapped once.

Bolts unbolted, chains unchained. The clicking of two four-lever mortice locks. The door opened. Cheerful. "Yer a wee bit early, son, ah'm no' quite..." The words died.

The gate stood between them. Jas looked through an iron spiral. The hallway was unlit. A small shape. "Marie?"

The figure stood two feet back from the gate, then stepped forward slowly. Hair shrouding face, black reflective body: PVC all-in-one. Suspicious. "Whit dae you want?"

She stressed the third word. Her caution brought him comfort. The comfort of the familiar.

"Can ah come in?" He picked up the holdall, gripped the gate. "Ah need tae..."

"Get oota here, ya mad bastard!" Marie stepped back. Disgust...more disgust.

"Whit ye on aboot?" He dropped the bag.

"Whit dae ye want w' me, Big Man?" Sarcasm. "A shoulder tae cry on? Somewan else tae love wi' yer fists?" Voice hard.

"Ah need a favour, Marie..."

"Ye're all the same." Shouting, now. "Polis..." Voice harder. The scar twitched. "There's mair psychos in Strathclyde Police than the Bar-L." Hurt. "Ah thought you were different, Jas." Angry. "Jist shows how wrang ye can be..." She turned, pushing the door.

Jas blocked it with a hand.

She turned back. "Git oota ma life, ya..."

In the gloom, he cuaght a glimpse of bruised flesh around one eye. He scowled, staring at the shiny jumpsuit. "Ah wis under the impression you doled oot the punishment these days, Marie. Wan o' yer punters fancy a shot at the rough-stuff?"

Harsh laugh. "Ye're hardly in a position tae pass judgement, Jas Anderson!"

Leigh...

Sweat dribbled into his eyes. Jas reached into his pocket.

Marie moved behind the door. "Pull a gun oan me, pal, an' ye'll no' live tae regret it!"

Reailsation. Marie was all-seeing, all-knowing. Super-snout.

Jas removed his hand from the pocket, wiping face with a wet handkerchief. "Ah don't know whit you've heard, Marie, or who ye heard it from. But ah'll only say this wance: ah didney kill Leigh..." Fists clenched. "...ah'm finished in the force, ah ken that. But ah'm no' stoppin' 'til ah finish Jimmy Mygo tae." He grabbed the bars between them. "That bastard'll wish ah'd killed him the first time..."

The door edged back. Silently, Marie produced a key and unlocked the gate. It swung inwards. She stepped aside.

"Thanks." He walked into the flat.

She locked the gate.

In the gloomy lounge, more furniture had appeared. Two black leather sofas, CD player, a small glass-topped table. Expensive. Something to protect. Hence the gate?

He walked to the window.

Venetians now, too. Jas opened the slats. Parallel lines of fading light split the room. Voice at his side:

"Lea' them shut, eh?" She wrestled the cord from his hand. "Ah'm no' long up..."

The room plunged back into grey.

A flare, then match lit cigarette. Marie smoked.

Jas sat down hard. He liked this room. It smelled of the outside world, of life...hard life. The odour deepened the numbness.

Marie perched on the table, swinging a black, liquid leg. Turning, he looked up at her. She looked back through narrow eye-slits, silently smoking. Eventually, she exhaled noisily, stubbing out the cigarette in a small ashtray. "Ah'm sorry aboot Pretty-boy, Jas." A hand on his arm. "Jimmy always pays his debts. But the polis?"

Angry. "Bastards..." Squeeze. "...never mind that hauf Baird Street CID's cheatin' oan their wives, using tarts oan the side fur their ain wee kinks."

Jas flinched, looked away. Leigh was no...kink. What he had felt last night was no...kink. What he felt for Leigh had to go...so that he could live.

...so that Jimmy Mygo could die.

Jas pulled the numbness more tightly around himself.

Marie's fingers tightened, then the hand removed. Shuffling. "Ah ken ah shouldney be surprised, though. Been a snout fur near enough three years noo, seen things..." She tapped her nose. "...but ah thought the polis'd be straight wi' wan o' thur ain..." Low laugh. "Maybe straight's no' the best word..."

He clenched his fists.

"Ye want tae talk aboot Pretty-boy? Git it oota yer system?" Smile. "Ah'm a guid listener, Jas. Ye git tae dae a lotta listenin' in ma line o' work..." Soft, trying to be nice.

Safe in the numbness, as smile twitched his mouth at the thought. "Whit ye want tae hear? That ma wife disney understand me?"

Leigh had understood everything.

Marie laughed. "Glad tae see ye've no' lost yer sense o' humour, Big Man!" She sat down. "But ah'm here fur ye, if ye need tae talk, eh? Like you wur here fur me..." The scar twitched.

He hadn't been there for Marie. She'd testified as part of the case against Neil Johnstone: he'd abandoned her to the brothers' tender mercies. Jas shook his head.

Marie nodded. "Huv it yer ain way." Laugh. "You an' me, Jas. We're survivors, eh? We dinney need onywan..."

Leigh. The thought cut into his heart. He bled inside. Jas seized the name, pushing it away. Marie was right.

"Ah'm forgettin' ma manners. Take aff yer jaicket. Want a coffee or somethin' stronger...sorry. Still aff the booze?"

Jas nodded. "Nothin fur me. Ah'm no' stayin'. Jist tell me where ah can find Jimmy."

Sigh. "He's a hard man tae track doon, Jas. Ah'll need time..."

"Hours?" He stood up. "Days?" The room swam.

A steadying arm. "Ye're no' lookin' well..."

He scowled. "How long?" Pressure on his arm. He sat down.

"Ah canny say..."

Jas fumbled for the holdall. "Ah'll be aff, then..."

"An' where wid ye go, tell me, wi' six divisions after ye?" Marie stood up, arms akimbo. Angry head-shake. "Ye widney last a minute oot there noo. Stay here, Jas – at least 'til ah kin find whit rock Jimmy's crawled under..." Laugh. "..an' crawl's the word. 'Suspected brain damage', ye say?" More laughter. "He widney ken the difference!"

Jas clenched his fists.

A high trilling sound.

Marie glanced towards the bedroom. "Ma mobile, Jas. Ah'll no' be a minute..." She left the lounge and walked to the bedroom, closed the door.

Jas waited a few seconds then got up, moved to the bedroom door and stopped. After another few seconds he walked through to the kitchen, filled a pint glass with water and drank it.

Marie reappeared, opened the fridge door and removed a bottle of wine. She poured one glass, drank it. "A punter – tae cancel." Explanation where none was necessary. "Business is always slow towards the Fair. "Flip. "Family holidays..." Flip. She poured another glass.

Jas refilled his with water. He looked out the window at the leaden skyline. "Marie?"

"Right!" Casual avoidance of the unasked question. "Ah need tae git ready. Are ye sure ye dinny want somethin' tae eat?"

Outside, heavy clouds massed. Jas stared. The glass quivered between his fingers. "Ye telt me only wan guy had yer mobile number – the guy ye got it frae. That wis him, wasn't it? The wan ye're snoutin' fur..." He turned.

The glass shattered, showering the area with water. Tiny slivers arrowed the air.

Scream. "Christ, man!" Hand to face. A small cut on cheek, a baby brother for the scar.

"That wis him, wasn't it? tell me, Marie." Blood trickled from fingers onto laminated worktop.

The words a rush. "Aye, that wis him, Jas. Ah wisney lyin' tae ye, man – honest! Is he no' a punter tae, though? He gies me money, just like the rest..."

"Aye, but it's whit he gies ye the money fur that worries me..." Jas turned on the cold tap, thrusting his hand under the flow. Pink spirals circled the sink, vortexing ever tighter.

Marie was paler than pale. "Listen Jas. Ye're a mate, ye ken that. Ah widney grass up a mate, wid ah?"

The water stung, then numbed. A comfortable state.

Jas frowned. "But wid ye, Marie? That's whit ah need tae know. Ah need to be sure."

Marie picked a thin sliver of glass from her cheek. Fingers shaking, she laid it on the worktop. "Ah didney tell him nuthin'..."

Jas turned off the tap. His hand still bled. "Ah want tae believe ye, Marie..."

On her cheek, a single red droplet. Relaxing. "Blood brothers, eh Jas? Like the wains..."

Jas rubbed damaged with undamaged hand.

Marie smeared the chin cut.

Hands clenched in a blood bond. Tiny fingers embraced in a giant grip.

"Swear, Marie..."

Reluctant. "Ye ken ah widney blab on ye, but onyway: ah swear ah'll no' turn ye over tae ma guy fur money, Jas. Okay?"

He nodded, exerting finger-pressure. Marie yelped.

Three knocks at the door, one long. "Fuck!" Irritated. Hand pulled free. "That'll be ma nine o'clock punter. Let him in, will ye?" Flustered. "Ah need tae git things ready..." She left the kitchen.

Jas remained at the sink.

Shout from the bathroom. "Go on, Big Man. Ye're okay – only ma clients ken the knock."

Wrapping hand in a dish-towel, Jas walked to the door and gave the answering tap, waiting for the appropriate response, then opened.

A tiny oriental man, neatly dressed.

Another shout from the bedroom. "Is that Mister Lee?"

Lee. Leigh...the name was everywhere.

Worried eyes, then acceptance. The elfin figure bowed. "Madam is at home?" Polished, unaccented words.

Jas opened the door wider. "Aye, pal. Madam's at hame. In ye come..."

In the kitchen, he found a First Aid box and bathed the cuts. The small flat was silent, except for the occasional moan from the bedroom. Jas sat down.

Quiet. Thought unavoidable.

He stood up, walked to the window. Leigh.

He walked to the fridge. Leigh.

He walked to the far wall. Leigh.

He walked to the table. Leigh.

Jas didn't kill Leigh. But he would kill Jimmy Mygo.

He walked back to the window, heart pounding. The leather jacket itched against his skin. He removed it, then the sweatshirt.

The kitchen was cramped. Jas pushed the table against a wall, crouched.

One...two.

One...two.

One...two.

Jas closed his eyes. Slowly, grey filled his mind...

Time passed.

Voice above him. "Is this the..floor-show, Big Man?" Laugh.

Jas paused, opened his eyes.

A pair of spike-heeled boots inches from his face.

He jumped to his feet. "Where's Mister...the punter?"

Marie laid the mobile phone on the table and lit a cigarette. "Him? Ach, he's in the wardrobe. He'll be there a good hauf an hour yet..."

Jas wiped sweat from his forehead, pulled on the sweatshirt, sat down. "Ye got a shower ah can use?"

"Help yersel'."

He looked at Marie. The make-up made her ugly, hard. The blackened eye obliterated, pupils shone neon. The scar blinked on whitened skin.

A mask, to show not hide. What you see is what you get. Masks were... useful.

Jas looked away, began to unbuckle boots.

"By the way, ah made a coupla calls while you were workin' oot. Didney want tae disturb ye..."

"And?"

"Nae sign o' Jimmy since he left the hospital. He's no' bin back tae his lassies, an' ah thought that'd be the first place he'd run. Everywan kens whit happened, Jas. Jimmy had it comin'. But Pretty-boy didney deserve..." Pause. "Ony sign o' the cor, recently – the BMW?"

"A wee encounter oan ma way here...got part o' the number..."

"The cor disney make sense, Jas." Marie sat down. "Jimmy may be daft, but he's no' stupid. It's no' his style, tryin' tae run folks over wi' cors." She fingered the scar. "This is Jimmy's style..."

...like shooting a guy point-blank was Jimmy's style.

Jas blinked. "Forget the BMW, then. Jist find me Jimmy."

Frown. Soft voice. "Ah'm no' tryin' tae tell ye yer business, Jas, but wid ye no' be better aff keepin' oot the way, at least 'til...?"

"Ye ever see a man wi'...his face blown aff, Marie?" He unbuckled boots.

Weedy's words: 'Ye could drive a truck up there...'

Jas closed his eyes. "Christ knows whit Jimmy did tae Leigh afore he finally put him oota his misery." Pain filled his chest. He opened his eyes and looked up. "Ah need tae find him – ye ken that."

Sigh. Face heavy with sympathy.

Jas tensed. He wanted her help, not her pity.

"Sure, Big Man. Ah'll try again in the mornin'..."

A shiver swept his body.

Time. Too much time. Time for Jimmy Mygo to leave Glasgow, get far away.

How far could he get with concussion and post-op shock?

His mind cleared. Police resources: they wanted Jimmy as much as he did. Only the reasons differed.

Marie had eyes in Glasgow.

Jas thrust hand into pocket. Slick fingers found Andrew Clark's card.

CIB had eyes all over the country.

Jas looked at his watch: 22.15, then at Marie. "Can ah borra yer mobile?"

Shrug. Nod towards the table. "Be ma guest." Smile. "Mind an lea' yer 50 p, though..." She poured more wine.

He lifted the phone and walked through to the bathroom.

Waiting for lukewarm water to cool down, he stripped. His body burned achingly. Lifting the mobile phone from the floor, Jas sat on a pink, fluffy toilet-seat cover and looked around. Small room, freshly decorated. Recently-installed power shower, cheap green waterproof curtain. Newly-tiled walls. A large mirror. Underneath, a row of bottles.

He picked one up. Heavy.

Jas read the inscription: 'Oscar'. Opened, and sniffed. Expensive, cloying, sweet. He grinned: everything Marie wasn't. He replaced the bottle with the rest of the range, then punched out Andrew Clark's number on the handset.

It rang out. He disconnected, peered at the card. The other number was Edinburgh. DS Clark had phoned from Glasgow.

Jas punched in London Road's number and waited.

It was ringing...then answered.

Jas modulated his accent.

Polite reply. No, DS Clark was out. Was there a message? Could he ring him back?

Jas scanned the mobile for a number: nothing. Too risky anyway. "No, thank you. I'll call again."

The voice bade him goodnight.

Jas severed the connection, placed the phone on the floor and stepped into the shower. Under sub-zero jets a plan formed. Marie. Andrew Clark. Both owed him something. Friends...of a sort. Between the two, Jimmy couldn't escape him. Jas smiled.

A tingle played on his spine. Throat on fire.

A soft knock. "Jas?" Tentative.

He switched off the shower. "Aye, Marie?"

The door opened. "That's Mister Lee away hame. Ah've a taxi booked." Grin. "West End joab. Guid tipper." Broader grin. "Lock up behind me, Jas. Ah'll be back aboot two. Try an' git some sleep." Concern. "Ye're still no' lookin' yersel'. Use the bed – it's mair comfy than they fuckin' leather sofas." Hand pointing to the medicine-cabinet. "There's some Atavan in there, if ye need it..." She turned.

He followed her to the door, dripping.

Marie wobbled in spike heels, catching one in the hem of a long, leather coat. She paused, faced him. A hand on his cheek. "Be guid, Big Man. Ah'll seeya later..."

He locked the gate then closed, double-bolted and chained the door.

Thirteen

FROM THE black leather sofa, Jas stared at the artexed ceiling. Tiny plaster stalactites stared back, pricking his retinas. Beneath, his naked body adhered to tanned hide. Two sticky skins sweat-cemented uncomfortably into one. He got up, walked to the bag and rummaged for jogging pants. His hand brushed more leather.

Leigh's filofax. Jas withdrew it from the holdall and sat down hard.

The two guys in LA. Leigh's parents. They should be told.

He gritted his teeth and opened the leather folder. A package of documents slid out onto the floor. He bent down. Letters, secured by an elastic band. Rough fingers fondled the papers. No envelopes. He removed the band, and the top letter.

You don't read other people's mail.

Jas unfolded the paper. London address. Dated 18th June. Three years ago.

'My one and only...how I count the hours 'til we are together again...'

Jas refolded the paper and replaced the band. Fingers trembled.

He had a life before Leigh. Leigh had a life before Jas.

Beautiful body cold in the morgue: Leigh had no life, now.

Jas clenched his fists, shivering. He had no life, now.

Jimmy Mygo would have no life, soon.

He stretched out on the sofa and closed his eyes. Leigh's face and Jimmy's merged into one. In the distance, a shadow-face, freckled and pale: Jo Hunter.

Leather beneath naked spine...

...he sat in the drivers' seat of a car, a powerful engine vibrating up through his body.

Beyond the windscreen, he could see a figure. A man, naked. Lean, tall, blond hair ponytailed. The figure held something aloft, waved it.

Jas peered. The figure grinned, beckoning.

Jas released the hand-brake. The car moved forward.

Leigh waved again.

Jas gripped the steering-wheel, knuckles whitening. The car continued forward, gaining speed.

Leigh's mouth was moving.

Jas wound down the window.

'Come and see, Jas...'

He pressed his foot down hard on the accelerator. The car hurtled towards the figure.

Jas closed his eyes.

The car was doing sixty at least. He felt wind in his face.

Opening his eyes, he saw the distnace between himself and Leigh had not changed. The accelerator hit the floor. Centrifugal force threw Jas back in his seat.

Leigh was still waving. 'Come and see...'

Taking one hand from the steering-wheel, he opened the glove compartment. It lay snuggled between and AA map and two Mars-bar wrappers. Jas lifted the hand-gun, felt its weight. He opened the car door, got out and began to walk.

Yards...miles. Minutes...hours.

Leigh stood smiling, waving a love-letter.

Jas raised the gun.

Behind, the shrill scream of tyres.

Jas turned.

Yards away, the white BMW revved its engine. Behind the steering wheel, Jimmy Mygo grinned, one elbow protruding from the open window.

The car lurched forward, then stopped.

Jas looked down.

Leigh lay at his feet, blood pouring from a huge wound where his face had been. Crouching, Jas took the body in his arms and stood up. Leigh was still breathing, his chest fluttered helplessly. Jas pressed his face to what was left of Leigh's.

Ahead, the sound of spinning wheels.

Holding Leigh tight against his body, Jas tossed the gun away. He faced the oncoming car and Jimmy Mygo's crazy face.

A lisping whisper from Leigh: 'Yourth...only yourth...'

Jas repeated the words over and over as the white BMW smashed into him, crushing, splintering bone and tissue into liquid. Leigh's skin melted with his own, tangled in a lovers' knot of mangled muscle. The same blood mingled, coursing from fractured veins.

In his head: 'Yours...only yours."

Hands tried to part them, pull him away from Leigh.

"No..."

His own voice echoed in his head.

"Jas?"

Hands on his shoulders, pulling, shaking.

"No..."

He fought harder, pushing the hands away. "No..." He found a neck and squeezed it hard.

A sharp sound, then stinging on his face.

Jas opened his eyes. Thunder in his ears.

The scar twitched. Marie leant over him, face frozen with fear. "Christ, Big Man! Ah thought ye wur gonny kill me..."

He loosened his grip on her throat, shook his head. "Marie..."

Hands tucked a blanket around his sweating body. His cheek still stung.

"Sorry aboot the slap, Jas." Relief. "Ye dinney ken yer ain strength..."

"Whit time is it?" He pushed the blanket off and sat up, eyes focusing in the gloom.

Marie wore men's striped pyjamas and bleary eyes. "Nearly seven. Ye woke me wi' aw' yer shouting! Why did ye no' take a coupla Atavan?"

He wanted numbness....not brain-death.

Jas stood up. Andrew Clark. "Where's yer mobile?"

"Sit doon a minute – ah've somethin' tae tell ye..."

"Jimmy?" The name filled his head.

Sigh. "Aye, it's aboot Jimmy, but it's no' whit ye want tae hear, Big Man..." Marie produced cigarettes, lit one. "Jimmy didney kill Pretty-boy..."

The cigarettes lay on the other sofa. He looked at the packet.

"...ah wis talkin' tae wan o' his lassies – ken Elaine? Well, she sez – an' she disney owe him onythin' – Jimmy wiz over in Shawlands Wednesday night. He's still there." Grin. "Elaine sez he's in an awfy state. Holed up wi' some auld pal..."

"Jist cos he didney pull the trigger..."

"Jas, he's bin semi-unconscious since he left hospital! Staggered intae a taxi, gave the address then passed oot. Hisney stirred since. The pal's in a panic, scared Jimmy's gonny dee oan him..."

"Where in Shawlands?"

"Ye no' hear whit ah'm sayin', Jas?" Exasperation. "The only thing Jimmy's bin plannin' the last coupla days is his ain funeral!"

He clenched his fists. A pain shot down his arm. He ignored it. Not Jimmy...not Jimmy...not Jimmy...

'Yer ain lot'll git ye, Anderson...'

"Liam and Michael." His heart hamered.

Quizzical look.

He told Marie about the breaker's yard, the unveiled threat.

Thoughtful. "Aye..that's a possibility."

They sat in silence.

Jas's heart slowly returned to normal.

Throat clearing. "You okay noo? Ah mean, ah'll stay wi' ye, Jas, if ye wanna talk, or anythin'..." The blanket repositioned.

He laughed. "Away ye go, Marie. Ah need tae think." The blanket prickled against his hot skin. She was tucking him in like a wain. He sighed, surrendering to the gesture.

Like he'd surrendered to Leigh? The two responses were miles, lifetimes apart.

Marie hovered over him. "Ah'll seeya later then, Jas – aye?"
Her hot breath was slightly sour. Lips brushed his forehead.
He laughed at the gesture. "Ye're gettin' soft, Marie – away an' git yer beauty sleep!"
She winked then padded from the room.
Pushing off the blanket, he lay on his back.
Not Jimmy.
He rubbed his face. Cool for the first time in days.
Liam: cold, calculating Liam with the camel-coat facade.
Michael: 'Gie that wee cracker in yer bed wan fae me...'
Jas clenched his fists.
The thought came from nowhere. The door to Seven Eastercraigs hadn't been forced. Leigh had let his killer into the flat.
Michael liked his boys pretty and passive.
Michael could be very persuasive.
Michael played rough.
Weedy's words: 'Ye could drive a truck up...' An image of Leigh with no face, fist-fucked into oblivion. A scream circled silently in his head, escaped in a low sigh.
He closed his eyes.
Think.
Jimmy was out of the picture. Michael or Liam were now in the spotlight.
Think...think...
Who phoned the police, reported the crime?
Andrew Clark would know...
Jas reached for the mobile.
DS Clark was off-duty, a different polite voice informed him. Any message?
Jas declined and rang off. He scowled.
Procedure. Leigh was dead in Jas's bed, killed by a gun bearing Jas's fingerprints. He needed an alibi. Surely someone – a neighbour? – had seen Jas leave the Eastercraigs flat that night?
Surely someone had seen Leigh's killer either enter or leave the flat?
He got up, walked to the kitchen. He drank some water then glanced at his watch: 7.20. He could be in Dennistoun by eight. Risky but necessary.
Back in the lounge, he dressed quickly. No time for work-outs or showers.
Shrugging on a jacket, Jas left.

Outside, rain coated slick pavement, slapping beneath biker's boots. Mind blank, he tried to remembered his neighbours' names as he crossed the suspension bridge to Glasgow Green.
Nods in the Close, Christmas cards at Christmas, whose turn

to cut the grass in the back court. Faces: no names.

Top floor, left. Two women. Nurses?

Top floor, right. Old woman with yappy dog.

First floor, left. Jas and Leigh.

First floor, right. Wee greying man, very keen on neighbourhood watch schemes.

Ground floor, left. Couple with a baby.

Ground floor, right. Miss Dunlop. Eighties.

A name!

Jas quickened his pace, striding through early morning murk.

At 7.55 he stood in Alexandra Park, peering through iron rails at the red sandstone block which made up Eastercraigs. No police cars, no unmarked cars, as far as he could tell. No plain-clothed surveillants. Where would they be looking for him? Evidently not here. Jas pushed a loose paling aside.

He moved towards Number Seven. Using his keys, he opened the communal door and walked the few yards to the bottom flat.

Fort Dunlop. Jas smiled.

A year earlier, when a door-entry system had been suggested, Miss Dunlop was its most vocal opponent. A veteran lace-curtian twitcher, she enjoyed the comings and goings inherent in tenement life, still minded the sense of community from the old East End of the fifties. Two break-ins and a mugging changed that mind.

Jas knew Morag Dunlop now lived behind a constantly-locked door. But the curtain-twitching went on.

He pressed the bell. It jangled distantly. Jas pressed his ear to the hardwood door.

Slow footsteps, then: "Yes?" Polite, faint.

"Police, Miss Dunlop. Can we have a word?" He hated the pretence, but had no idea what the papers were printing now.

"Put your identification through the letter-box, please."

He'd taught her that himself. Jas crouched. "It's me, Miss Dunlop. DS Anderson from upstairs." He pushed the flap open.

Eyes peered back. "Why didn't you say so, son..." The door opened.

Jas walked in.

The flat smelled of naphtha and tobacco. Mis Dunlop wore an ancient dressing-gown and lethal, ill-fitting slippers. But she didn't shuffle, instead laboured purposefully ahead to the kitchen-cum-living room. "Sit down, Sergeant Anderson."

The nicotined face stared at him. Jas sat awkwardly in a small armchair. "How're ye keeping?"

She smiled toothlessly. "Thanks for the thought, Sergeant Anderson, but as you can see, I'm fine now."

Jas looked blank.

Miss Dunlop sat down in the armchair opposite and coughed.

"Just a wee bout of the emphysema. They didn't keep me in long..." She reached for a handkerchief, then a cigarette.

His mind cleared. Miss Dunlop had been taken to the Royal last week. She wasn't here the night Leigh died. Jas stood up. This was a dangerous waste of time.

"And how's yourself, Sergeant Anderson? You're not looking too well, if you don't mind me saying so."

Miss Dunlop's rounded, West End vowels echoed in his head.

She drew on the cigarette and coughed again. "The weather, I expect. Too damp. After all that sun, too. And how's your lodger?"

Jas froze.

"It's about time that grass was cut again, so tell Mr. Nicols he can drop in, the first dry day, for the key." Smile. "I know you're very busy, Sergeant Anderson..."

She didn't know.

"...but now that Mr. Nicols is on holiday from the university he'll have plenty of time..." Coughing interrupted.

"Can I get you anything, Miss Dunlop? Water?"

Shake of head. "Thanks anyway, son." Hoarse, breathless. The tiny chest heaved. Panting.

Why doesn't she know? Jas moved forward. "I'm going awway for a while, Miss Dunlop, so..."

"On holiday? That's nice. I suppose Mr. Nicols watches the flat for you. Can't be too careful these days..." Cough.

He turned towards the door. "Look after yourself, Miss Dunlop."

Smile. "Nice young man, Mr. Nicols. He must work very hard up at the university. I don't sleep well, Sergeant Anderson. Is it shift work he's on, like yourself?"

"Don't get up, Miss Dunlop. I'll let myself out..."

"I know your routine, Sergeant Anderson." Proudly. "I see you come in every morning about eight, when you're on nights..."

No time. No time. Politeness made him pause.

"...now, Mr. Nicols, he's in about three-ish. I don't usually see him, but I hear the car. Not heard it for a while, though. Always used to stop at the top of the street..."

Jas smiled, remembering. Leigh and his taxis. Would never walk anywhere.

"...lovely big white car. Mr. Nicols must have important friends up at the university. You don't see many BMWs in this part of town."

Jas stiffened.

The car following Leigh.

Reminiscent. "My brother owned a similar model, when we all lived in Kersland Street – just after the war, you know, Sergeant Anderson. Tommy's pride and joy, it was..."

"Miss Dunlop?" His voice was a croak.

"Sorry, Sergeant Anderson?" Confusion, then smile. "I'm holding you back. Have a nice holiday." She stood up, swayed, then sat down again.

No time for pretence. "Miss Dunlop, how often did you see the big car?"

"Oh, not often. Once or twice a week, then less, recently." Worried. "Is anything wrong?"

Jas shook his head. "Nothing at all, Miss Dunlop. Just a wee problem with noise pollution. Did you see the car's driver at all – or the registration number?"

Cough, then head-shake. "As I said, the BMW always stops at the far end. My eyesight isn't what it was, Sergeant Anderson." Sigh. "So like Tommy's car." Regretful. "He sold it, you know, to pay gambling debts..."

Jas patted her hand. "Look after yourslef, Miss Dunlop." I'll see you again soon..."

He let himself out of the flat, brain a jumble. Slipping from the building, he walked quickly back to Alexandra Park. Rain overflowed from a brimming sky. Under a large chestnut tree, he paused.

Why was Miss Dunlop unaware of Leigh's death? Even if she hadn't been at home that night, people still talked to each other in Dennistoun. Someone would've told her. Did any of his neighbours know? If not, why not?

For some reason, Leigh's death had not become public knowledge. Jas knew press blackouts were common, while enquiries were on-going. But usually for specific reasons – to avoid panic amongst civilians, or discourage copy-cat crimes.

Neither applied here.

Understanding. No need. The police had their suspect, their evidence. Beneath his feet, a grateful earth soaked up moisture.

His stomach churned.

The white BMW. Leigh followed by the white BMW. The same white BMW which had tried to kill Jas three times? Undoubtedly.

Had the driver killed Leigh? Possibly.

Jas slumped against the tree-trunk, mind racing backwards. Raindrops ran from hair onto face. BMWs, car-valetting. Michael Johnstone's predatory face filled his eyes.

Leigh: beautiful, innocent Leigh.

Over a year ago. 'Squires' bar, late on a Friday night.

Leigh's whisper: 'Think you've got an admirer, Jas...'

Michael Johnstone's leer, directed at Leigh, not him. Dilated pupils scanning the hard buttocks, the strong legs.

'Gie that wee cracker in yer bed wan fae me, Anderson...'

Two birds with one stone. Sex and revenge. Fuck Leigh, blow him away. The ultimate set-up. An image of Michael Johnstone's skinny body hurting Leigh swam before Jas's eyes. Two ponytails, one dark and greasy, the other blond and shining. Two bodies...

Jas slamed his fist against chestnut bark.

Three small boys in wellies and raincoats glanced over, then backed away.

After the ritual exchange of cryptic knocks, Marie opened the door. "Christ! Ah wiz worried aboot ye! Where've ye been?" The scar twitched.

He walked past her into the dim lounge and took off jacket, biker's boots and sodden jogging pants. Leaning back on the leather, one question: "Dis Michael Johnstone own a BMW?"

"Jas!" Exasperation. "Ah've telt ye, no!" Quizzical look. "But ah suppose he could get his hands oan wan, if he hud tae..." A cigarette was lit.

Jas detailed Miss Dunlop's information. He frowned. "Somewan wiz followin' Leigh, knew his shifts. Michael kens all the right buttons tae press...kens whit the idea o' him wi' Leigh wis dae tae me..." Fists clenched, then unclenched. "But why kill him?"

Marie sat down, shook her head. "Icin' oan the cake, Jas. Michael's a wicked bastard."

He closed his eyes, then opened them.

Marie blew a smoke ring. "But as far as entry no' bein' forced, Jas, Pretty-boy widney open the door tae jist onywan, at that time o' the mornin', least of aw' Michael Johnstone – wid he?"

Jas scowled. "Cut the pretty-boay, Marie – eh?" His voice rang then died in the cube-like room. "Leigh wis...more than that..." He shivered. Tightening in his chest. Suddenly he couldn't breathe... A hand on his shoulder:

"Sorry, Big Man...didney mean tae..."

Jas shrugged on the numbness and inhaled deeply. He had to act...and to act, he had to think.

Marie's hand fell away. "Ah'm nippin' oot, Jas...see whit ah kin find oot fur ye – eh?"

He tried to concentrate. Ring Andrew Clark. Find the owner of the white BMW. He walked into the bedroom. In the distance, a door slammed. The mobile phone lay amidst a pile of underwear. Jas seized it, punching in a memorised number. He counted ten rings, then heard a voice:

"Yes?"

"Andrew? It's Jas Anderson. Look: ah need a favour. Ah want ye ta..."

"Slow down, man." Sigh. "I've been taken off the investigation." Wry laugh. "ACC Sloan doubts my impartiality...for reasons best known to himself!"

Jas cracked the fingers of his left hand, impatient. "Ah need ye tae..."

"There's something you should know. The PM report's through."
"There's more? Did Leigh..?"
"I've got a copy here..." Soft voice.
"Okay, read it."
"I'm not sure I..."
"Get oan wi' it, pal!"
Silence. Rustling. Then: "Oaky, here we go..."
Jas sat down on the bed.
"...this is the body of a twenty-four-year-old male Caucasian. Blood group O. Contents of stomach reveal a small quantity of semi-digested food, mainly chicken. Death occured at approximately 1.15am, 7th July, due to cerebral haemorrhage. Cause of death, gunshot wound to the face, fired at closed range. Bullet lodged in cerebellum suggests shot was fired approximately two inches from victim's lower jaw, entering the brain at a forty-five degree angle. Calibre of bullet is consistent with the handgun found at the crime-scene..." Pause.
"Whit is it? Whit's wrang?"
"I shouldn't really be telling you all this over the telephone..."
"Get on wi' it!" Jas laughed. What did it matter, now?
Sigh. "Okay. Rectal examination shows heavy keratinisation, plus some evidence of tissue scarring..."
The tiny cut. Jas shivered. Leigh...
"...this, plus traces of semen in the anal tract would suggest the victim was a practising homosexual." Voice lowered. "Christ, Jas...I'm sorry..."
"Go on." Something in the voice prickled his spine, cutting through the memory of Leigh's spunk deep inside his own body.
Throat clearing. "Analysis of blood sample shows a lymphocyte count of 950, T-cell ration correspondingly low at 190." Pause. "Do you want me to go on?"
No. "Let's hear the rest."
"Incubation of blood sample indicates presence of cytome...cytomgl..."
"Cytomeglarovirus, pal. CMV." Jas closed his eyes.
"Chest X-ray clear, no indication of lung infections other than CMV, no internal KS or thrush..."
"Thanks, pal. That'll dae. Ah git the picture..."
"I'm sorry, Jas. Is there anything I can do? What was the favour you wanted?"
"It's no' important, now. Ah'll be in touch." He severed the connection.

Fourteen

A DOOR slammed in the distance...another opened.

Voice beside him. "Well, that's that!"

Jas stared at Marie.

Sigh. "Ah asked around 'boot the rest o' the Johnstone rubbish. Liam wiz at the dogs, doon at Shawfield, last night: Jimmy wisney mentioned. Michael wiz wi' some new kid he'd taken a fancy tae, at Club X. He didney even ken Jimmy wiz oota hospital – or so ah hear."

The buttons on the mobile blurred into one. His voice was a shadow. "Whit aboot Neil?"

Head shake. "He's aw' mooth...an' he's still safe in the Bar-L. Naw, the big cor disney make sense. Ye've bin fitted up, man...an' the polis are helpin'..."

He heard the words but, like the BMW, they didn't make sense.

A hand shook his shoulder. "Are ye listenin', man?" Frustration. "The Johnstones wantin' ye inside, on their territory, them steein' ye up fur murder: that makes sense. So why try to kill you as well?" Sounds of a cigarette lighting. "Much mair fun tae let justice take its course, an' deal wi' you in Barlinnie..."

"Leigh was HIV-positive." His fingers tightened around the handset as he clutched at the last straw. Blackness enveloped him.

Cold against his lips...then dribbling down his chin. He coughed. Alcohol vapour stung his eyes open. He stared, then pushed the glass away. Marie sat on the bed, holding a Smirnoff bottle. "Whit's this fur?"

Solemn-faced. "Medicinal, ah think." Shrug. "If you dinney want it..." She tossed the glass back in one, then stood up. "Right, Big Man. the Johnstones can wait." Hands on hips. "We've got tae git you tested, eh? When wur ye last done?"

Jas stared. "March." The date inscribed on his heart. For Leigh's sake: as the passive partner, Leigh's risk was higher than his own. NHS. Three counselling sessions, then the first test. Then the waiting.

Negative.

Three months of waiting. Three months of condomed sex. A third skin between his and Leigh's.

Second test.

More waiting.

Negative.

Hand on his shoulder. "An' Pretty...er, Leigh?"

He scowled. "Same time. Negative tae...false-negative." Inaccurate tests. Fuckin' waste of time!

Sigh. "Well, ye need tae test again."

He stood up. "Whit's the point? Ah don't fuckin' care..."

Angry. "Whit kind o' attitude's that?"

He looked at the tiny figure. "It's ma attitude, Marie, an' it's ma body." An explosion in his head. "Knowin' disney dae ony guid." Pity, regret, longing and anger cooled on hot skin. "Leigh didney jist have the virus, Marie. He wiz developin' full-blown AIDS. CMV, T-count shot tae fuck..." He closed his eyes.

Selfishness made him think of himself...of two nights ago...of the traces of Leigh's spunk still deep in his arse. He pushed the thoughts away and remembered Leigh...

Pneumonia or KS would be next. The beautiful body wasting away, ravaged by ugly brown sarcoma. Pretty-boy pretty no longer.

Firm. "Christ, Jas! Ye've got tae test, then..." Angry. "That dirty wee..."

"Dae you ken nothing, Marie?" He grabbed her shoulders, pulling her down onto the bed. Jas stared into fearful eyes. He knew he was shouting. "Even if ye can trust the tests, wan infected partner Christ knows how long ago: that's aw' it takes. Fuck!" He shook thin shoulders. His stomach churned. "Leigh wiz ill, Marie. He wiz ill an' he didney ken..." Knuckles shone white.

Hard breathing. "Well, at least he deed quick, Jas." Rubbing one shoulder. Insistent again. "But ye've got tae test, man. Even if ye're positive, there's treatments, these days..."

He laughed. "Whit: AZT? It's a race tae see whit kills ye first wi' that wan – the disease or the drug!" He clenched his fists. "Same wi' Septrin an' Dapsone...mair toxic than the fuckin' virus..."

Sigh. "They're makin' progress aw' the time, man..."

"Oh, yeah! Ye kid paint yer body wi' developing fluid. They're sayin' that stimulates the T-cells. An if aw' that fails, there's always positive thinkin' an' vitamin fuckin' C..." He snarled, shook his head. "Naw thanks, Marie. Ah eat well, ah feel great...

So had Leigh.

"...ah'll take ma chances..."

So had Leigh.

They both had.

Marie rubbed sore shoulders. "Aw' the same, Jas, ye canny go aroon' wi' this hangin over ye. Ye ken the odds. It might no' be as bad as ye think. Ah've bin dain' smack fur eight years, noo, sharin' needles 'til eighteen months ago. There's bin mair punters up me than the Blackpool Tower! Ah'm clean..." Head down. "It's the luck o' the draw, Jas – ye said so yersel'."

Luck...that's what it came down to. One prick was all it took.

An urgent, frustrated sigh. "Test, Jas. Ye could huv as long as ten years. Ten years wi' somewan else..." Pause.

There would be no one else. Only Leigh.

Sigh. "If no' fur yersel', dae it fur...me. Ye're wan o' ma best mates – ma ainly mate, these days. 'Member? We're survivors..." Soft. "...blood brothers. Test, Jas."

He shivered.

Marie draped an arm around his neck. "Ah can arrange it. No' much o' a wait, none o' that counselling shite. Ah ken a doctor at the Western. Results in a coupla days..."

He stood up. "If it'll shut ye up, Marie...noo tell me whit else ye found oot aboot Michael Johnstone, eh?"

Sigh, then: "He wiz nowhere near the East End two nights ago – ah double-checked. " Hard grin. "There wiz a kid over at the Southern General gettin' his arse stitched, early Wednesday mornin'. Guess who wiz sittin' in the car-park, snortin' coke while some doctor repaired his damage?"

Jas frowned.

Vodka poured, drunk. "Both him an' Liam've got alibis as lang as yer airm, man..."

His brain began to function.

'Widney dirty oor hands, Anderson...'

He shrugged. "Disney mean they didney arrange it."

Grudging admittance. "Aye...that's true, ah suppose..."

Jas rubbed a sweating face.

Liam or Michael's hired help...who?

Glasgow was filled with men eager to obey orders. Some wore serge, others designer suits. Still others were gray, faceless guys in cheap jeans with habits – or kids – to support. Killing didn't pay much, but it did pay. The Johnstones would be spoilt for a choice of penny-assassin.

Jas stood up, swayed. Strength returned to his legs. Purpose. Intent. Liam and/or Michael were in this somewhere...

From the bed, Marie smiled. "That's it, Big Man. Away yew go an' huv a shower. Ah'll gie the doctor a ring..."

He walked through to the lounge. From one of the leather sofas, Leigh's filofax winked at him. Jas picked up the leather folder, caressing the binding...

...the way Leigh had caressed his body, his soul.

With an incubation period of three months to ten years, AIDS had been pipped at the post by a single gun-shot.

Jimmy was out of the picture.

Michael could well have arranged Leigh's death.

Find the BMW, find whoever Michael hired.

He sat the filofax on the table, stripped of the T-shirt and began to exercise. The press-ups came easy.

So did the thoughts...of Leigh dying...of hospices...the smell of pot-pourri air-fresheners and death. Places where houseplants flourished and people died...slowly, painfully. Thoughts of dementia...of Leigh's clever brain decaying into mush...

The grey mush on the bedroom mirror, the life, the bedroom he'd shared with Leigh for the past fourteen months.

Sweat stung his eyes.

The bedroom in which Leigh had died...quickly.

At least, he hoped it had been quickly.

The BMW...

...whoever had been responsible for Leigh's death would die very, very slowly.

He stood up, arms quivering. "Marie? Gie's that phone!" He walked through to the kitchen.

She sat on a bar-stool, scribbling on a note-pad. Smile. "That's you fixed up, Big Man. Bit mair difficult than ah thought. But the doctor owes me a favour. Four this afternoon – okay."

He snatched the mobile phone and began to punch.

"Got that, Andrew? White BMW. Canny be that many o' them. Sorry ah don't know the whole reg..."

By his side, Marie was eating. She held out a piece-and-sausage to him.

The smell of cooking food. Vomit rose in his gullet. Jas shook his head at the sandwich.

She shrugged, continued to eat.

"Okay...thanks. Gie's a ring back...Marie? Whit's this number?"

Lowered eyes. "Ye ken ah canny tell ye, Jas. Ma guy widney like it..."

"Aw' fur fuck's sake!"

Apologetic repeat. "He widney like it..."

"Andrew? Ah'll call ye back. How long d'ye think it'll take? Okay. Five it is." He hung up, turned to Marie. "Whit is it wi' this new guy yer snoutin' fur? Why aw' the cloak-an'-dagger stuff?"

Eyes avoided his. "Part o' the deal, Jas. Mind when ah wiz snoutin' fur you we had oor wee arrangements? Well, this guy's the same. Ah'm no' even meant tae be usin' it fur personal calls. It's fur him tae always git me..."

"It's a fuckin' nuisance, Marie..."

"Ah'm sorry." Hurt. "But huv ah no' been useful tae ye in other ways, Jas? Ye can stay here as lang as ye like. Ah'll help aw' ah can..."

"Aye, Marie..." An arm around her shoulder. "...ye're a guid mate."

She punched his arm, playfully. "Away intae the shower, man. Ye smell like a badger's arse..."

He stood up.

"Can ah no' git ye somethin' tae eat fur comin' oot? Ye must be hungry..."

"Ah'll eat later..." He walked to the bathroom.

Icy water refused to cool his skin. The longer he stood under the faucet, the hotter he became. Jas rubbed his face. He needed a shave. There was no time for that, no time for anything. He hoped Andrew could trace the BMW. A vein pulsed in his forehead, beating in time with his heart.

He turned off the shower, grabbed a towel and walked back to the lounge.

Marie was reading a magazine. She looked up, throat clearing: "Ah've booked ye a taxi fur hauf past three, Big Man. Ah ken ye like tae walk, but it's too risky. It'll pick ye up ootside here an' wait fur ye at the hospital. Want me tae come wi' ye? Ah ken whit it's like..."

He shook his head. "Ah'll dae this alone, Marie..." Alone...like Leigh had been alone... He lifted his watch from the table: 3.15. From the sports bag he plucked underwear, jeans, T-shirt and began to dress.

The drive to the far end of Argyle Street was swift, his mind elsewhere. Leigh dying was almost worse than Leigh dead. Images of pain stabbed his blurring brain, joined with visions of Leigh: happy, healthy, body vibrant with life. Outside, Glasgow sloped past in the rain.

As he walked through the Western Infirmary's Accident and Emergency department, a tall blond boy caught his eye. He was reading a poster, holding a blood-soaked towel against one cheek. Dirty hair fell over a dirty face.

Leigh's face? Jas shrugged and walked on.

The doctor was young, Asian and nervous.

One prick's all it takes... Latex-sheathed hands slid a thin needle under skin, withdrew it then gave him a number. Come back in three days. Miss McGhee said he'd been counselled, knew the drill.

Jas stared at the young face, at the old eyes. Leigh's eyes?

The doctor turned away.

Jas left.

In 'Accident and Emergency', long denim-clad legs now stood in front of the poster. Leigh's legs? Jas brushed against the slender body.

"Watch whur ye're goin', pal!" Blonde girl, sores around mouth. Junkie's face.

Jas turned away and walked out to the waiting taxi.

On the journey to the Gorbals, he stared at the back of the driver's neck. Not Leigh's neck.

"Okay, son. Here we are..." The taxi pulled up.

Time was moving too fast. Traffic was never this light. Jas fumbled in his pocket for change.

The driver turned, laughed. Big florid face. Shaking head. "Pit yer money away, son. It aw' goes on Marie's account." Grin.

Jas opened the door and got out.

"Gie the lady ma regards, son..." The taxi drew off.

He stood in the drizzle, below Hutchie E's mocking gaze.

One more rat into the trap.

Rain trickled from his eyes. He walked towards the stairs.

Marie unlocked the door. pale. Concern. "Everythin' okay, Jas?"

He nodded.

She closed and relocked the door.

Together they walked to the lounge. On the sofa lay the letters and the filofax, plus a pile of newspapers.

He swept them onto the floor and sat down. His watch read 4.30.

Marie began to talk. Jumpy. The scar twitched with St. Vitus' Dance.

Jas removed jacket, T-shirt and moved to the floor. Slowly, with each press-up, he relaxed. Muscle trembled, throat burned. With each lift of his arms he counted inside, blocking the pain, blocking thoughts.

Marie talked on, words running into one.

Jas stood up and walked through to the kitchen. Marie followed. He drank two pints of water and watched as she withdrew a self-sealing cellophane bag from under the sink. Three sterile syringes sat beside a small, white package. She laid the bag on the kitchen table and pulled off a training-shoe.

He returtned to the lounge. Sit-ups. After a while Marie came into the room. After another while he stopped. "Whit time is it?"

She looked at him, pupils a pin-prick. Lazy laugh. "Time you gied aw' that a rest, Big Man. Ma furnishings'll no' stand it..."

He looked down. His back felt rough. Friction burns. A pool of sweat glistened with blood on the nylon carpet. "These flats aways wur a bit damp. Whit time is it?"

"Just oan five. Phone yer pal an' ah'll make us somethin' tae eat..."

"No' fur me."

Angry. "Ye'll eat whit's put doon tae ye, Big Man!"

Jas laughed. "Ye're no' ma mother, Marie!"

Detached sadness. "If ah wiz, they'd huv taken ye away fae me years ago..."

It was everywhere. Leigh had his, Marie had her own pain. "That's in yer ain hands, naebody else's. " He eyed the bare toes. "Git aff the junk an' ye'll see them again..."

Hard face. "Keep yer nose oot, Jas Anderson!" Softening. "Sorry, ah..."

"Ah ken, Marie, an' yer right." He stood up. "None o' ma business..." He walked through to the bedroom and the mobile.

Andrew answered on the second ring. "You didn't give me much to go on, but we've got a name. Can I ask why you want this information, Jas?"

He laughed. "Ye can ask...but ah can't tell ya. Not yet, anyway."

Sigh. "If you know something about Leigh's death, something the police should know.."

"As soon as ah've got ony information, it'll be ma pleasure tae wipe that smug grin aff Monroe's face. How's the search fur Jimmy Mygo?"

"Nothing so far." Sigh. "I've never seen so much manpower devoted to digging up dirt on an officer, Jas. Your parents have been contacted, and someone's gone to London to talk to your brother..."

Jas clenched his fists.

"...ACC Sloan's handling the investigation personally, now. Some of the boys have given up leave to find you. "Sigh. "If half the energy devoted to this was chanelled into real police-work, Glasgow would have no crime problem..."

A stab in the dark. "Who...reported Leigh's death?"

Pause. "Anonymous call...probably one of your neighbours heard the shot..."

Jas knew otherwise. If Miss Dunlop didn't know...no one knew. "Why the press blackout?"

"Monroe and Sloan think it's best. They can't risk media interest."

Jas frowned. Which headline would be bigger: 'Death of Man in Flat' or 'Gay Cop Sought by Strathclyde Police'?

"Anyway...I hope this is straight up. Your BMW..."

He tensed.

"...belongs to Richard Beatie."

Beatie...Beatie. The name was familiar. R B Blank / Blank Blank 3. Personalised number-plate.

Andrew Clark read off the complete registration number. "It's parked in town at the moment – I checked. Want his home address?"

"If ye've got it..."

"4A Clarence Drive. Telephone number 394-6793. I've got his Chambers' number too, if you're interested. "He read out a 552 number and an address in George Street.

Jas knew it, had been there many times. "Thanks..."

"Sorry I can't help more..."

"Ah'll be in touch..."

"Tell me one thing, at least." Pause. "Where does the Deputy

Procurator Fiscal fit into all this?"

Jas scowled. "That's whit ah want tae know!" He severed the connection.

Back in the lounge, Marie was slumped in a stupor, eyes unfocused. He shook her shoulder.

No response.

He shrugged. Everyone had their own oblivion. No one's living was easy...

He glanced at the mobile, then his watch: 5.15. The PF's office usually knocked off early on a Friday. He'd give it 'til the half hour, then phone the Clarence Drive number. Jas sat down opposite Marie.

Not Jimmy. Not Michael. Hardly 'hired help'.

Richard Beatie: a mistake?

Three attempts at murder were no mistake.

Why was one of Strathclyde's top legal figures trying to kill him?

Had he succeeded in killing Leigh?

It made no sense...no sense...nonsense.

Marie mumbled formless vowels. An arm slipped from the leather couch and dangled, brushing Leigh's filofax.

Jas had trodden on a lot of toes in his time, but never those shod in advocate's shoes.

The pain returned, shocking in its intensity: the pain of loss. He lifted the love letters, shuffled them aimlessly in his hands. Others had loved in the past, loved and lost. Jas's pain was neither new or unusual. He wanted to know more about Leigh, know the things Leigh would never have the chance to tell him. Jas began to read...

Fifteen minutes later, five sheets of paper sat in a neat pile. Three names, all London addresses, all written over two years ago.

Leigh's past. For some reason it helped...a little. But did nothing to solve the part Richard Beatie played in his own and Leigh's present.

Opposite, Marie mumbled. "Jas...whit...?" The mouth was slack.

He cleared his mind, punched Richard Beatie's home phone number into the mobile.

Answering-machine. Male voice. Youngish. Well-spoken. 'You have reached 0141-394-6793. I'm not available to take your call at the moment. If this is a business matter, please ring the office. If not, leave a message after the tone. Thank you.'

Jas disconnected.

One word flitted on the periphery of his brain: why?

There was only one way to find out.

Fifteen

SIX THIRTY IN RAIN-SOAKED Hyndland, red sandstone tenements lined quite streets. Tenements: the great leveller. Same material as Dennistoun, same age – maybe even same architect. But each two-bedroomed flat here cost at least £10,000 more than he'd paid for the Eastercraigs flat, and these were probably smaller.

Bigger on prestige, though. Their owners hoped high prices would help blot out Partick to the south, Maryhill to the north. Jas smiled. Glasgow was like that. Much as you tried, the layout never let you forget what you shared the city with.

He peered into a shop window. No metal shutters here: the residents' association wouldn't approve. Security grills would make Hyndland seem more like Glasgow and less like their precious 'West End': an oasis of genteel living in a desert of discontent. Inside the shop, £900 suits lounged unprotected on wooden hangers. At the back of the shop, a mirrored wall.

In dull half-light, Jas focused on the reflection of 4 Clarence Drive.

Half an hour earlier he'd rung the bell labelled: R. Beatie. No answer. No BMW parked outside.

He shivered, skin prickling under heavy leather. Too hot to keep on, too cold to take off. As a concession, Jas unzipped the biker's jacket and turned up the collar. He continued to focus.

A feral, unknown face eyed him suspiciously. White, sweating skin half-hidden by three days' growth. Dilated blue pupils under heavy eyebrows. Short, dirty blond hair, wild and angry. Hulking black leather.

Jas whipped round. The figure was gone.

He turned back to the mirror, smiled. Doppelganger smiled back.

No linen suit, no detective's protective shell. What was left?

Jas Anderson...a man.

A man whose lover had died.

A man whose lover had been dying anyway.

A man whose love for his lover had never been expressed.

A man whose lover had been stalked, killed by the driver of a white BMW with personalised plates?

...a white BMW belonging to Richard Beatie.

Why?

He rubbed his face.

Behind, a flash of white. Jas narrowed his eyes and stared into the mirror. Big car, BMW, registration RB1 873, pulled up outside number 4.

Aerial missing.

Jas tensed, feeling the metal friction burn on his right palm.

No screaming wheels this time. A smooth, silent halt.

Jas watched.

A man appeared from the driver's side. Late thirties, grey-suited. Expensive – like the area. Dark hair expertly cut. Tanned, handsome face. Classic good looks.

The man was smiling. A briefcase under one arm.

Jas scowled.

Richard Beatie. Deputy Procurator Fiscal. Second-in-command within Strathclyde's Department of Public Prosecution. Jas had worked with the PF's office on many occasions, but never with Beatie.

He watched as the dark-haired man set the car alarm, watched as he covered the ground between car and tenement in long, easy strides. He looked fit, for an advocate. Squash, probably, or £2,000-a-year health clubs. Foreign holidays: the tan was real. Jas waited until Beatie was inside the flat, then crossed the road.

No controlled-entry system here. He walked through the close and up two flights of stairs. State-of-the-art security system, though.

Outisde 'Flat E' he paused.

Why?

Why had Richard Beatie been following Leigh?

Why had Richard Beatie killed Leigh?

Why had Richard Beatie tried to kill Jas three times?

He pressed the bell. No chains, bolts or bars, the door opened quickly. "If it's about..." The smiling face hardened, eyes cold fire. "What can I do for you, Mr...?" Beautiful vowels to match the beautiful car. A polished leather brogue wedged in place behind the half-open door.

"Anderson...James Anderson. I'd like a word, Mr. Beatie." Calm, collected.

The door swumg open. "I knew you'd show up, eventually. Come in..." Easy, unperturbed recognition.

Something in the man...in his manner, in the eyes...

Something Jas recognised in himself.

Something they shared.

Something told him Richard Beatie was gay.

Jas walked into the hall and through to a large lounge. The decor was Laura Ashley-meets-Dickens. Fussy. Dark floral wall coverings made the space seem smaller, oppressive. Heavy navy-blue curtains drapped two oriel windows. Custom-built bookcases dominated two walls, floor to ceiling. The room brimmed. A table, two bureaux. In a corner, conspicuous, a PC sat on a black-ash desk, a visitor from another era. It jarred with three mock-Victorian sofas, antimacassars and all. On every surface, knicknacks snapped at each other, vying for attention.

The clutter pressed in on Jas.

From behind: "Please sit down, Mr. Anderson." Smooth, polite, unruffled. Nothing to hide, or something hidden well?

Jas walked to the window. "Thanks you, I'll stand." He looked out onto slick Clarence Drive. Two smartly-dressed women scuttled by, arm in arm, under a large umbrella. "I think we both know why I'm here." Police tricks. He turned.

Richard Beatie stared into his eyes.

Jas stared back.

Beatie looked away. "Glad you've seen sense at last. There's no reason why this shouldn't be settled in a civilised manner. We're all adults, after all..."

The man talked in riddles, was everything Jas expected from an advocate: professional, unemotional. Words as body armour.

Jas decided on the direct approach. "Why are you trying to kill me?"

Smile. "I had no intention of harming you. I merely hoped to frighten you off..." Open, confident.

Jas scowled, irritation itching. "As you can see, it didn't work. Of course, I'm aware of who you are, and your position. But I've never met you...before today. Why don't you tell me what this is all about?"

Laugh. Beatie sat down on a horsehair sofa. Long, elegant legs stretched out, crossed at ankles. "Let's not play games. You may be able to frighten Jason, but you don't scare me."

Jason? Jason?

Despite the veneer, Jas could see a hint of nervousness in the small, brown eyes. He shivered, concentrated. "I'm not here to talk about any Jason..."

"You're pathetic, Anderson." A crack in the body armour. Beatie got up. "What do you want – money?" Sigh. "I'll write you a cheque. Name the amount. Just get out of our lives. Let Jason come to me..."

His head buzzed with confusion. Rage rose in his throat, primitive and guttural. "Ah'm no' here tae talk aboot ony Jason, Beatie! It's Leigh ah'm interested in – Leigh Nicols – an' yon lovely big cor parked ootside. Ken whit attempted murder is?"

Beatie paled beneath the tan, exposing white vulnerability. "I don't know any Leigh...don't know what you're talking about. I presumed..." Throat clearing. Trying to stay calm. "Jason was right: this is a waste of time. Please leave. I don't think either of us want the police here..."

"The polis are already here, Beatie..." Jas grinned.

The advocate shrank back against a wall.

Jas walked past him, lifting a small china figurine from a bureau. "...an' they're no' leavin' 'til they find oot why ye've been tryin' tae kill me." Rough hands stroked the delicate porcelain. He turned. "Want tae try again, Beatie, man tae man? Nae cor this time..." A sharp crack. Jas fingered the decapitated shepherd's head, then dropped it.

"Get out of my home, you...animal...out of our lives. Let Jason go!" Brave words from shaking lips.

Jas laughed. "Who's this Jason?"

Beatie stepped forward. "You make me sick, Anderson." Fear sweating from every pore. The unrufflable ruffled. "Just leave us alone..." Pleading.

Jas laid the headless figurine on a table, hands trembling. He looked at Richard Beatie's white, frightened face. What did the man fear? "Let wan o' us speak English. You seem to know me, and you evidently knew Leigh Nicols, and where he worked." Beneath the heavy leather jacket, dampness trickled down his back. "Your car was seen outside our flat on several occasions: I have witnesses. I also have witnesses to three attempts on my life. Leigh's already dead and now you're..."

"Jason's dead?" Beatie's eyes dulled over.

Jas struck the table. A collection of tiny glass animals tinkled. "No' Jason – ah don't ken ony Jason! Leigh: twenty-four, blond, ponytail..." The rest stuck in his throat.

Eyes never leaving Jas, Beatie edged along the wall to a small desk, lifted then held out a photograph.

Jas took it. Something died inside him, as he stared at the image of Beatie, relaxed and smiling again, in rugby shirt and sweatpants. One arm was draped around a smaller figure, blond hair hidden under a leather cap Jas had never seen before, a faded denim jacket and denim shorts. He wore Raybans...Jas's Raybans. Leigh grinned out of the photograph. Jas handed it back.

Beatie's voice was low. "That's Jason..." The eyes smiled.

Jas scowled. "That's Leigh..."

'Yours...only yours.'

His mind exploded, little bits of Leigh sticking to his skull. He lurched towards Beatie, pinning him to the wall with one hand. With the other, Jas hit him. The photograph slipped to the floor, crunching under a heavy boot. He seized Richard Beatie's smooth throat. "Why?"

Beatie made a choking sound.

Jas saw tears were mixing with the blood which dribbled from a split lip. He lowered his fist.

Beatie sank to the floor. "How did he die...was it quick?"

"Somewan blew his fuckin' face aff, but ah suppose ye could say it wiz quick!" He looked at the heap of a man.

Beatie sniffed, unhearing. "I was with him when he got the

results. He was so brave...but frightened. I wanted to look after him, wanted him to stay with me. I've read all the books, knew what to expect. All that mattered was that Jason..."

Jas leant over and hit him again. For Leigh, for the lies, for knowing about the HIV when he hadn't.

Beatie grimaced through the pain. "You're a selfish bastard, Anderson. You must have known Jason didn't love you..."

Leigh. Leigh. Leigh. Lies...

"...but you weren't big enough to let him go to someone who did. I begged him to leave you, but he was scared." Angry. "What did you do to him, Anderson?" Elegant fingers grasped the leather jacket. "What sick game are you playing now? Jason's not dead..."

'Game...games...' The Game? Shaking free of the advocate's strong grip Jas pushed Beatie's head back. Lies...all lies. "Tell me..." He knew Leigh was dead, knew it didn't matter anymore, but had to know. "...how long?" He didn't want to hear, but made himself listen.

Gurgling words. "A year, only a...oh Christ!" Beatie wrenched away. "I can't believe he's..."

"Oh, believe it!" Jas grabbed the dark hair with one hand and hit the handsome face with the other. "He's dead, all right. Now tell me when you met him." He glowered into already bruising eyes.

Beatie had aged ten years in ten minutes. The expensive grey suit crumpled around him. So did the body armour. He wiped his face and began to speak. But not to Jas. The dark eyes focused on the shattered picture-frame at his feet: "A year ago. Club X on a Saturday night. He was so beautiful. I had to have him. Oh, I know it was only sex at first, but later..." Words dissolved.

Jas shook him.

Teeth rattled. "...I'd never met anyone like Jason. So gentle, so open, so..." Eyes pleaded with the photograph, then looked at Jas with loathing. "I didn't find out about...you until later. It hurt, at first, that I had to share him, but it didn't really matter." Scowl. "You had Jason during the day, but he was mine at night...all mine." Sigh. "He used to call you 'my keeper', know that? He wouldn't tell me your name, or anything about you..." Low voice. "...but I could work out the sort of set-up you had. I knew you lived in Dennistoun somwhere...didn't want to know any more." Angry. "Not then..."

Jas let go and sat down on the floor. Thought flooded in. Leigh and Beatie. No...

Head lowered, Beatie was engrossed in his final summation. "Okay, so I couldn't have Jason completely, but I was grateful for anything, any time with him at all..."

Jas was beginning to numb. Lies...Leigh's lies. More lies. "When did Ja...Leigh test positive?" He closed his eyes.

'Yours...only yours.'

Beatie sniffed. "Two months ago. He wasn't feeling well. Little things: night sweats, sore throat, off his food. We thought it was 'flu, but nothing would shift it. I made him test..." Sobbing. "...we got the results last week. I was negative..."

Jas opened his eyes.

Tears ran down Beatie's handsome cheeks. "Oh, God! He was so scared." Angry. "More of you than the bloody disease! When he eventually found the courage to tell you about us, about the symptoms, why would you not let him go? You didn't care about Jason, you bastard! Why did you want to hurt him, keep him..." Silent crying.

Jas stood up. Beatie's questions bounced off his brain.

I didn't know...

I didn't know...

I didn't know...

What would I have done, had I known?

Sniff. "I wanted to have it out with you, face to face, Anderson, but Jason wouldn't let me. Said you were mad, unpredictable, that you'd never give him up..."

"The car?" Rationality began to edge in.

Nod. "God help me, I wanted you dead! If you were out of the way, Jason would be free. I knew you did some sort of shift-work, but a cop...?" Disbelief. "I hung about one night last week, after I'd dropped Jason off, saw you come in late, watched you go into the same flat he'd gone into. Into his bed..." Veins stood out on the tanned throat. "That doesn't matter now, I suppose..." Sobbing. "...nothing matters now..." Beatie looked up. His face was red, blotchy. "Get out of here, Anderson! Jason's dead – you can't hurt him or me any more..." He tried to get up.

Jas kicked him.

Beatie moaned and slumped back to the floor.

Sweat poured into Jas's eyes. Beatie and Leigh. Leigh's body...He kicked the prostrate form again.

Beatie gurgled. Croaking words. "Trying to control me the way you controlled Jason, Anderson?"

Jas stepped back, blinking. The Game?

Pain made Beatie brave. He clutched his stomach. "Couldn't live with him, couldn't live without him, Anderson. Is that how it was?" Slowly, the trembling man found his feet. Blood poured from the split lip, dribbling down over the strong chin. "I know your type. It's pathetic, Anderson. You're not out, my friend, are you? What are you frightened of – that I'll tell your big, butch police colleagues exactly what they share the locker-room with, dear?"

The epithet struck home. Jas stared at the headless shepherd and flinched.

Beatie gained confidence. "All that anger, Anderson..." Laugh.

"You didn't even know your lover's name!" Goading. "How does that make you feel? Does it hurt?"

Jas switched his stare to the advocate.

Beatie's eyes were wild. "Jason hated you. Anything else he ever felt for you died a long time ago. He told me that. We laughed at you, Anderson..."

Jas clenched his fists.

"...after we'd made love, we laughed at you..." A hollow parody circled around the room.

Leigh. Leigh. Leigh. Lies. Jas turned and walked unsteadily towards the door, his own body armour in tatters.

"That's right, you bastard! Walk away. You can't face it, can you? You're a joke, Anderson! Christ knows what Jason ever saw in you..." The laugh became a choking sound.

Jas paused, heart ice. "Did you..." He made himself say the words. "...were you wi'...Leigh two days ago?" He turned.

Sad eyes. "Yes...in the afternoon. We made love for three hours..." Eyes to a doorway. "...through there, on my bed..."

Wednesday night...giving himself to Leigh...giving himself to a stranger...a stranger still hot from another man's arms. Jas pushed the image away. "Where wur ye early Thursday morning?"

"What business is it of..."

"Leigh died at approximately 1.30am that morning, Beatie..." The numbness helped him remain rational. "Ah ken where ah wiz at that time: dae you?"

"You...bastard! How can you suggest...?"

"Where wur ye?" Fists tightened. "The polis'll want tae know."

Beatie picked up the shattered photograph and began to stroke it. Low voice. "I was at a Law Society dinner. City Chambers." Angry. "Jason was with you, that night, Anderson... not me! He was going to try to reason with you, one last time." Cracked lips moving, no sounds. He looked up. "Now get out of my home."

Jas couldn't move. He stared around the room where Leigh and Beatie had sat together, laughed together...loved together. He stared at the man with whom he had shared Leigh.

Rage flashed across bruising eyes. "Get out!"

Jas turned away from Richard Beatie's grief-stricken face and slowly walked from the room.

Sixteen

THE JOURNEY from Hyndland to the Gorbals was a tunnel leading from black into blacker. One minute he was standing on the corner of Clarence Drive and Hyndland Road, the next he was watching the rear view of a cab speed off into murky night. Cancer ate into his soul.

Leigh and Beatie...

The filofax...the love letters...

This was no old love.

This was now.

No BMW following Leigh...but dropping Leigh off outside *his* flat!

Leigh hopping from Beatie's bed into Jas's...

Three agonies melted into one, swelling to fill his heart: Leigh's death. Leigh's illness. Leigh's lies...

Pain became anger. Anger became hate.

He glanced at his wristwatch, shivering – 9.30pm – then coughed and spat on the ground.

He needed sleep. He needed food. He needed...to be someone else.

Jas walked towards Hutchie E.

After an eternity of open landings, stairs which stretched for ever and faces that leered from shadows, he reached the sixteenth floor.

Marie was waiting behind the security gate, eyes a pale yellow light in the evening gloom. "Ah wiz watchin' fur ye, Big Man. Did yer polis-pal...?"

Jas pushed at the gate, gripping iron swirls with slick fingers.

An unlocking sound. The gate swung open.

"Christ! Whit's up wi'...?"

He walked past her into the flat. Her voice dogged his heels: "Well? Who owns the big cor? Did ye find oot?"

In the lounge, the filofax lay on the sofa like a tart, its covers sprawling open. Jas picked up the leather wallet; letters tumbled free.

Marie talked on.

Jas didn't hear. He began to read...

Fifteen minutes later he was sitting on the sofa. The lounge was empty. Jas fingered the last love letter, dated February this year. Notepaper watermarked 'Kensington Park Hotel, London'.

My beautiful little animal,
The conference is almost over. I'll soon be back with you again in Glasgow. These four days have been hell. The time passes so slowly without you in my arms. The thought of our last night together keeps me going. I think of you beneath me. I hope you've been a good boy while I've been away. You know what bad boys get...

Jas re-read the letter three times, forcing himself to dwell on the scribe's descriptions of Leigh's body.

Another's hands. Another's lips. Another's prick.

Jas clenched his fists, the final words of the letter etched on his brain:

...counting the minutes til I can fuck you again
All my love,
G.

Pain became anger. Anger became hate.

'Yours...only yours...'

He slammed a fist into black leather. Leigh's face...lying, betraying ...face. He punched until soft leather slid with sweat. He punched because Leigh was dead, murdered...and because that should be more important.

He punched because he was being fitted up for the murder.

He punched because it was all he could do.

When his arm hurt too much to punch any more, he stood up and walked from the lounge.

In the kitchen, the half-empty Smirnoff bottle lay by the kettle. Jas reached over, unscrewing the top with shaking hands. He drank.

Liquid fire seared his throat, landing in his stomach like paraffin. He retched. More burning, in his mouth now.

A hand on his arm. Worried. "Tell me, Big Man? Whit happened? Whit's made ye so...?"

He wiped bile from his lips and took a second swig. This time the vodka stayed down.

The bottle shuddered in his grip as Marie pulled at it: "That'll no' solve onythin', Jas..."

He pushed her aside. Four years of abstinence made him angry. "Aw' back tae yer smack, ya fuckin' junkie, an' lea' me alone!"

The bottle slipped from his hands, shattering on the bare concrete floor. He looked down. Little droplets splashed down the sweatshirt and pooled at his feet.

Marie was tugging his arm. "Come on, Big Man. Let's git you cleaned up..."

He sat down on a bar stool, staring straight ahead as she knelt before him, unbuckling boots, peeling off damp clothes. When he was naked, she pushed him through to the shower.

Under warm water Marie washed vomit and Beatie's blood from his body, but not his mind. Leigh's face, smiling from the framed photograph, refused to leave. It clung to his eyes tauntingly, teasingly: 'Yours...only yours...'

Prick throbbed between iron thighs. He thought of other men, other bodies eager for his.

Leigh's face blinded him.

He shuddered.

Marie washed his back...like Leigh once had.

Beatie...other men thrusting between the tight buttocks.

Prick still hard.

He focused on Leigh underneath Beatie's athletic body...

His erection wilted.

Jas sighed.

Marie turned off the shower.

'Yours...only yours.'

Beatie... 'G'... How many others?

Small, deft hands patted his body with too-soft towelling.

A scream grew in his throat. "Leave it, will ya!" He looked down into frightened eyes.

Low voice. "No' this time, Jas. Ah need tae ken whit happened..." She gently dried his face. "...ah want tae help."

He pushed the towel away and walked from the bathroom. At the bedroom door he paused. Marie's rumpled sheets beckoned.

A voice behind. "That's right, Jas. Have a wee lie-doon..."

Pressure on one shoulder. It was as far as she could reach.

Jas walked into the dark room and sat on the bed.

Marie sat beside him. "Ye've got tae talk tae someone, sometime, Big Man. Talkin' helps..."

He looked at the tiny figure. Inside, his stomach spasmed.

Talking. Tell someone.

Marie was strong, stronger than he was. But could she contain the black anger which filled his body, threatening to eclipse the light?

Jas talked. The words were small and insignificant, compared to the acts.

But it was the words which hurt.

Behind measured, factual information a torrent of unanswered, unanswerable questions.

Why had Leigh kept the HIV results from him, but told Beatie?

Leigh knew The Game better than Jas. If he had wanted to go

to Beatie, Jas would have let him – reluctantly – but would have let him nonetheless.

He coughed, wiped his mouth with a hot arm.

Why hadn't Leigh told him? Leigh had known Jas better than he knew himself. But Jas apparently hadn't known Leigh at all.

Was Richard Beatie 'G'?

He stopped talking.

Marie squeezed his hand. Silent, urging.

A phone-call would establish whether Beatie had been present at the Law Society dinner on Wednesday night, as he claimed. But his movements afterwards could be harder to verify.

Jas rubbed his forehead. He knew Beatie hadn't killed Leigh – Jason, as Beatie knew him: there was too much love in those eyes, love Jas had wanted to beat out of the man.

"Go on...git it aw' oot..."

Torture by thought continued: Why had Leigh wanted Beatie? Why had he used a ficticious name? Why hadn't Jas been enough for him?

Leigh and Beatie, laughing at him...

He stared into Marie's eyes.

Leigh's eyes? Betraying eyes. Laughing eyes. Lying eyes.

The biggest hurt of all: Leigh lying to him and about him. Jas swallowed hard. "Why wid he dae that, Marie?"

She stroked his arm. "Ah've nae answer fur ye, Big Man..."

Where could he get answers, about a man he had never really known?

His Leigh.

Beatie's Leigh.

G's Leigh.

The university's Leigh?

Marie lit a cigarette.

The mobile lay on the bed. Jas picked it up. Work numbers had been exchanged a year ago, only to be used in an emergency. Leigh's work number committed to memory, never dialled. He punched in digits: even during holidays, the chemistry labs would be manned. Research went on.

A woman's voice answered. Older. A smoker's rasp.

If his neighbours hadn't known of Leigh's death, if Richard Beatie hadn't, would the workmates?

Lies. More lies. "Good evening. I wonder if you can help me. I'm calling on behalf of Leigh Nicols. He left research material behind in the lab, last week, and I was wondering... Nicols. Leigh. L-E-I-G-H...One of your assistants...what about Jason Nicols?... Are you sure?" He watched as Marie blew grey smoke away from his face. "Sorry to have bothered you. My mistake." He disconnected.

My big fuckin' mistake.

Marie's eyes were on him.

The thoughts came before he could stop them, his whole body on fire. How wrong could he be? No 'yours, only yours', no job at Glasgow Uni: they had never heard of Leigh Nicols.

He wished he had never heard of Leigh Nicols. But he wouldn't carry the can for his death.

He looked at Marie. She knew better than to ask.

Leigh had lied about at least two other lovers, about his job. What else had he lied about?

The past eighteen months dissolved. Laughing with Leigh, living with Leigh, fucking with Leigh.

Trusting Leigh.

He could still remember the feel of Leigh's hard prick deep inside his body...

'Yours...only yours.'

Lies. Lies. Lies...

Marie: "Let it go, Jas. He's no' worth it. Ye've enough tae worry ye..."

He shook his head, tried to dislodge the squatting thoughts. An uninvited guest, Leigh refused to leave. The handsome face danced before his eyes. Jas gripped a pillow between sweating fingers.

Feel the words. Mean the words.

"Ye're right, Marie. Only two things matter noo: he's deed, an' the polis want tae fit me up. Ah've got tae know who kilt him, an' findin' oot who wis fuckin' him is as guid a startin'-place as any..." He closed his eyes.

"Three things."

He opened his eyes. "Whit?"

Soft. "Three things, Jas...ye forgot aboot the test. Leigh wis dyin' before that bullet ever hit him..."

Feel the words. Mean the words. He spat. "Fuck that!" He wiped lips on the back of hand. "Ah never want tae hear that wee bastard's name again, Marie – okay? Aw' that's important is ah find who killed Lei...him..."

Leigh. Leigh. Leigh. Lies.

Marie stood up and left the room, returning seconds later with the Smirnoff bottle. She sat down. "An' how dae ye plan oan dain' that?"

As the drank, he told her.

Two hours later he lay on his back. Bits of Leigh's life – the other Leigh – littered his chest. He brushed the love letters away. Through vodka fuzz, the artexed ceiling swayed soothingly. Marie's voice in the distance:

"So, whit ye're sayin' is that his death could've had nothin' tae dae wi' you, Jas, or the Johnstones..."

His voice didn't sound like his. "Aye. There wiz me, Beatie, this 'G' –Christ knows how many others..."

The games Leigh had been playing were far riskier than anything he and Jas had ever got up to.

"Ye met him – whit, two years ago?"

"Aboot that. Transferred up fae London tae dae research at Glasgow Uni..."

Giggle. "The first lie, eh Jas?"

The first of many.

"Ken whit ah think, Big Man? He jist couldney help himsel'..." She talked on.

Jas closed his eyes. Blackness sucked him down. He opened them again quickly.

Marie's mouth was moving, a new Smirnoff bottle clutched in one hand. "Some folks are like that, Jas. Wan's never enough..." The mouth continued to move.

The monogamy was Leigh's idea. Jas had been wary of commitment, of the restrictions. Leigh had talked him round.

There had been no one else for almost two years.

How many others had Leigh fucked in those two years... twenty-four months...one hundred and four weeks...seven hundred and twenty-eight days...seventeen thousand four hundred and seventy-two hours...one million forty-eight thousand three hundred and twenty minutes?

How many times had Leigh fucked other men?

How many times had Leigh lied?

How many times had Jas believed him?

He stared at Marie's wallpaper. Blue, with a faint, darker pattern. Blue, like his linen suit. Blue, like denim. Blue, like Leigh's eyes. Blue, like Leigh's lifeless lips in the morgue... A tap on his arm.

Marie held out the bottle.

He shook his head. "Ah've had enough..."

More than enough.

She smiled, moving closer. Slurring. "Better?"

He nodded.

Her face was very close now. The scar twitched. "Whit aboot somethin' tae eat, Big Man? Ye must be hungry..."

He wasn't.

She answered for him. "Chicken okay? Gie me fifteen minutes...an' git some claes on..."

He looked down at his pale, naked body.

"...ye'll frighten the punters!" She slapped his thigh and stood up, unsteadily.

His mouth edged towards a smile. "Aye, aw' right..."

She swayed from the bed to the door.

"...an' Marie?"

She paused.

"Thanks."

She turned, shrugged. "Whit ur mates fur!"

Later, in the kitchen, he ate the Marks and Spencer chill/cook Satay Chicken. Cardboard in his mouth. Each time he paused to chew, Marie's eyes were on him, ready to scold. He continued to eat, and with each mouthful the emptiness grew. Finally, he pushed the plate away.

Pleased. "That's guid, Big Man. Ye need tae keep yer strength up." The plate was removed. "Noo, ye can huv a wee creamy caramel thing if ye like, or ah think there's some choc'late biscuits somewhere..."

Jas laughed. His lover was dead, he was wanted in connection with the murder and she was offering him wee creamy caramel things. He stood up. "Lemme make a phone call before ah decide..."

Quizzical. "Aboot the assistant PF?"

He nodded. "Accordin' tae polis-logic, if Beatie wiz fuckin' that wee liar, that on its own gies him as much o' a motive fur murder as me. An' then there's 'G'..."

"Yer pal...whit's his name?...will he no' git intae trouble...?"

Jas picked up the mobile. "Andrew can pass it oan...say it wiz an anonymous tip-aff." He punched in the number, glancing at the wall-clock: 11.30 pm.

Another polite voice put him through to DS Clark.

"Andy? Ah've got some news fur ye..."

Hiss. "You stupid prick! What did you think you were doing?"

"Whit...?"

Angry. "You've just made matters worse by interfering! Why didn't you tell me about Leigh and Richard Beatie?"

"Cos ah didney know masel' until..."

"You've really done it now! Beatie's been in – I've just typed up his statement. Why did you hit him? Why did you go to his home in the first place?"

Satay chicken churned in his stomach. "Ah needed tae..."

"What?" Sarcastic. "Sign your own death-warrant? Two queens bitching over a pretty boy – that's what Monroe and Sloan are saying now...only, one of the queens got a bit carried away, killed the object of the dispute then beat up his rival..."

"Ah only hit him a coupla times, ah wiz angry..."

Snide. "Let's just be grateful you weren't as angry as when you shot Leigh in the face!"

Jas clenched, then unclenched his fists. "Ah didney kill him, Andy. Ye ken that..."

"I believe you..." Softening. Reluctant. "God knows why, but I do. But what were you thinking of, attacking Beatie like that? You've just given yourself a rock-solid motive for killing Leigh:

jealousy. Beatie's statement reads like bad film noir, Jas. He's painted you as some psychotically possessive basket-case who would rather kill Leigh than let him go..."

"An' whit wid you call cruisin' round Glasgow in a BMW, tryin' tae run me over: normal behaviour?"

"There's only your word that happened at all. And, believe me: your word doesn't count for much around here, at the moment."

Faced with smooth, educated Beatie, or himself, whose version would he believe? "Is Beatie's motive no' as strong as mine, accordin' tae that bastard Monroe? We were both....involved wi' Leigh."

Silence cracked down the line. Then: "His alibi's unbreakable, Jas, and frankly, I'd say he didn't have the bottle to kill."

'Unlike you.' Jas closed his eyes.

"Wednesday night, he was at a dinner in the the City Chambers. Afterwards, he went on to a club with colleagues – it all checks out. There's a string of witnesses as long as your arm who'll corroborate this."

"Fuck!"

"His interpretation of the...relationship between you and Leigh fits Monroe and Sloan's mould, Jas – and it confirms the psychiatrist's opinion of your state of mind." Pause. "It gets worse, man. Beatie's going to the press – he's been told about the Jimmy Mygo incident – no doubt screaming about the calibre of officers we're recruiting these days, brutality, cover-ups...the whole thing. That's really put the wind up Sloan. He's had to call a press conference tomorrow, in time for the Sunday papers." Sigh. "Three warrants are outstanding, now: you're wanted in connection with the murder of Jason aka Leigh Nicols, the attempted murder of Jimmy Mygo – who still hasn't turned up – and the aggravated assault of Richard Beatie."

Jas opened his eyes, shivered.

"I don't know where you are, and I don't want to, but I suggest you keep a very low profile until I've got something to go on. The trouble is, Sloan's got all the evidence he needs..."

"He hisney got me..."

"It's just a matter of time, Jas: you know that." Exasperation. "I'll do all I can, but there's not much hope the way things stand at the moment: you've no alibi that stands up, we've got the weapon with your fingerprints clearly shown, and a motive that suits these bastards down to the ground. I need another diection to move in, someone else with reason to kill Leigh." Soft voice. "Maybe his other friends could help...?"

"Hold on..." Jas walked through to the bedroom and lifted the filofax: why hadn't he thought of it before? Flicking through the blank pages, Jas narrowed his eyes.

"Have you talked to any of his friends? His family?"

He didn't know how.

Sigh. "Workmates?"

More blank pages. Where was Leigh when he said he was working? With Beatie? The deputy PF had said that Jason was with Jas at nights...

With 'G'?

Jas frowned: he had lived with a man for two years and knew nothing about him.

Frustration. "Come on! There must be something..."

The friends in LA. Julian and...? Jas flicked faster. White, wordless pages flew past. "Sorry..."

Angry. "Quite the enigma, your Leigh..."

Not his Leigh. Not anymore.

"You shared your life with the man." Probing, procedural. "Did he ever mention anyone to you – even in passing? Do you know anything about this guy, anything I can follow up?"

A bundle of love letters, someone called 'G', a lot of anger...? Jas frowned. A cop from Edinburgh with a gay son knew as much about Leigh as he did. "Nothin' that wid help..."

The answers lay in the past.

How much could Andrew Clark do, desk-bound in Glasgow? Jas needed to find out more about Leigh, before he could find out about 'G'.

Everything pointed south.

"Oh well..." Philosophical. "I can ask around the pubs and clubs, see if anyone there knows anything..."

He'd get nothing, even if there was something to get. Too many closet doors still too tightly shut...and he was polis.

"...you have any photographs of Leigh I could borrow? If he was using one false name, there may be others." Thoughtful. "I mean, I could get my hands on one of the PM shots, but..." Tactful.

There wasn't much of a face to identify. Jas remembered his wallet. "Ah'll post wan tae ye, but ah don't ken whit guid it'll dae..."

"It'll be a start, Jas..."

It'll be a dead end.

Concern. "Listen: are you somewhere safe? I mean, are you alone?"

"Ah'm wi' a mate..."

"Can he be trusted, Jas? I mean..."

"He's a she..." He looked at Marie, who had finished washing dishes and was now loading cutlery into a drawer. "...an' yeah – ah trust her..."

He had to trust someone.

"Well, I hope you know what you're doing. Stay where you are. Don't go out. It's probably best I don't have your number, but ring me on the mobile – say, tomorrow? I'll run Leigh through the

computer, see what it can come up with."
"Thanks, Andy.."
Embarrassed. "Nothing to thank me for yet. Save it for later..."
His mind was with the wallet-photograph, with the face of a stranger.
Firm. "One last thing: don't try to leave Glasgow. The airport's under surveillance, as are the stations and the buses..."
"Ah'll ring ye the morra." Jas disconnected and turned to Marie. "Can ye lay yer hands on a cor?"

Seventeen

"HOW LANG will ye be?" Marie watched as he buckled the bikers' boots.
"As lang as it takes." He lifted the love letters. "Three London addresses, wan hotel. It's the only place tae start, Marie..." Jas stuffed the letters into an inside pocket. "Ah canny dae onythin' up here onway. Ma face'll be in every paper..."
She laughed. "Ma life wi' a star! Ah could sell ma story tae the *Record* – ah can see the headlines no..."
He tensed.
She noticed. "Only jokin', Big Man. Ye ken ah widney..."
"Ah ken."
She mock-slapped his shoulder.
"You sure this cor's reliable?"
Marie perched on a sofa arm. "Nae problem, Jas. The boays dae a run every weekend. Easier than drivin' yersel', safer than the train. Ye'll huv tae make yer ain way back up, but, they..."
"Ah don't wanna ken whit they're carryin', Marie.."
Frown. "Ah wisney gonney tell ye, onyway..."
He laughed. The thought of action invigorated: the thought of finding 'G'...?
She fussed around him, patting his jacket. "They'll no' ask your name, so don't you ask theirs. Git some sleep oan the way doon. Ye should be there by aboot seven the morra mornin', the roads'll be quiet."
Jas looked at his watch: just after 1 am. He wondered what Dougie's shifts were like, these days.
Her eyes took in the movement. "An' ye'll go straight tae yer brother's place? Ye no' wanna phone him, tell him ye're comin'?"
Douglas Anderson, thirty-nine, married with two kids. Jas had never met the wife, never seen the kids. His mother made sure he saw the wedding photograph, though, every Christmas for eight

years.

Dougie and Jas had been close. Once. His brother now managed the Park Lane Sporting Club in London's West End. The last time they'd spoken... But that was years ago.

Maybe Dougie had mellowed.

Maybe pigs might fly.

Technically, Jas had been suspended from Strathclyde Police. The pig had flown. Anything was possible...

Marie left the room.

He punched Dougie's number into the mobile.

Five hundred miles away, the phone rang in his brother's Barons Court house. Then an answering machine. An unfamiliar voice. Ten years of southern comforts and elocution classes had modulated Dougie's warm, Ayrshire vowels into a sloppy sub-Sloan slur, consonants clipped to nothing:

'This is the home of Douglas and Phillipa Anderson. We're not available to take your call at the moment, but please leave a message after the tone. Thank you.'

Douglas Anderson. The family man. The big wheel in casino circles. His big brother.

Douglas Anderson: the stranger.

Jas began to leave a message. "Dougie, it's me. Ah need a favour..."

Click, then receiver lifted. "What do you want?" Voice calm. Only a hint of anger.

"It's bin a lang time, Dougie..."

Mirthless laugh. "Not long enough!"

Nothing had changed. Unbroken hate tingled up the phone line. Jas sighed. "Dougie, ah need somewhere tae stay."

Irate. "I hope you don't think..."

"Come oan, Dougie, ah..."

"Don't call me that." Taut. "We're not kids anymore..."

"Jist this wance, Dougie. Two nights at the maist. Ye ken ah widney ask if there wiz ony other way."

Sponge-like, Dougie soaked up the accent. The years had disappeared, but not the animosity. "Ah don't want you onywhere near ma hame..."

"Ah'm comin' onyway, Dougie." He clenched his fists. "Wid ye rather ah turned up at yer work?"

"Ye widney dare..."

"Ye've done well fur yersel', Dougie...ye've got a lot tae lose. Whit wid yer posh friends think o' yer wee brother from Glasgow...?"

The threat hung suspended between them, across the border, across the years, across the family ties.

Exhale. "Okay, ye can come – but ainly two nights – an' ah'm dain' this fur ma mother, no' you. She's worried sick aboot ye..."

He didn't need the guilt, not now. "Thanks, Dougie. Ah'll be there 'boot seven the morra mornin'." He severed the connection and went to find Marie.

She was in the kitchen, making sandwiches. She didn't look up from her task. "It's nice ye've got family, Jas. Ye kin always count oan family.." She struggled with cling-film, then swore.

A tightening in his guts. "Aye..ye can always count on family, Marie."

Leigh had been his family...

She turned, thrusting a parcel at him. "In case ye're hungry oan the way doon."

He took the squashy, inexpertly-wrapped bundle. "Ye're spoiling me, Marie!"

Outside, the sound of a car-horn.

She moved to the window, slit eyes through venetian slits. "That's the boays, Jas. Blue Escort over by the far wall. Git goin'..."

In the hall, he paused. "If ah had yer mobile number, ah could..."

Head down. "Here..." From a pocket, a set of four keys. "In case ah'm no' in when ye git back." She thrust them into his hand, then began to unbolt the door. Outside the flat, she seized his arm. "Guid luck, Big Man. Ah hope ye find whit ye're lookin' fur..." On tiptoes, she kissed his cheek.

"Ye're gettin' soft, Marie..." He inhaled the cloying perfume and coughed on it.

She pulled away, grinning. "Ye're right, Big Man! Noo, away doon. The boays dinney like tae be kept waitin'." She closed the security gate and smiled through iron spirals.

He walked down to the car.

The only six words which would be spoken in six hours. "We'll drap ye in Hammersmith, pal."

In the shabby blue Escort, Jas passed Marie's sandwiches to a bullet-headed teenager in a Fila T-shirt. The driver shifted into gear, looked barely old enough to be doing so legally. In the back, beside a battered holdall, Jas sat silently, Leigh's face a faded image.

Just outside Carlisle, he remembered Andy Clark's request. He removed his wallet. Inside, warrant card: that could be useful. Also cash-line card and thirty pounds in cash. Underneath, a folded photograph, taken a year ago in the garden of Seven Eastercraigs, by a neighbour. Himself: frowning at the camera's unwanted attention, bare-chested, pushing an ancient lawn-mower. He smiled at the memory. At his side, Leigh: grinning in shorts, blond hair falling into eyes...

Jas tore the photograph in half, opened the car window and tossed his image into darkness.

The car's speed increased as it joined the M6. Predictably, so did the temperature. His sweatshirt lived up to its name, so he took it off. The jacket's nylon lining itched against his skin, but was slightly cooler.

Around Manchester, he fell into a dreamless sleep.

Around Luton, the sound of low-flying aircraft woke him up.

Fila T-shirt was eating the sandwiches. Banana sandwiches. The scent of the blackening fruit filled the car.

Jas thought of family picnics, decades ago...of himself at eight, Dougie fourteen. Two boys, one tall for his age, awkward, the other stocky and muscular. Same dirty blond hair, same crooked smile. Wrestling on the beach, football: so alike, inseparable despite the age difference. They did everything together.

Close. The Andersons were a close family.

Eight years later, the age difference grew. Jas was sixteen before he knew another closeness.

Kenny Forsyth: best mate at school.

Wrestling on the beach...more than wrestling.

Dougie's confused eyes. His brother had never forgiven him, refused to forget. Made excuses not to share a room with him. Two months later, Dougie left home.

His mother: "James..." To this day, she wouldn't call him 'Jas'. "Dougie's just..." Uncomfortable. "...uncomfortable, he'll come round. Give him time..."

Jas gave time. Dougie took it, twisted it, threw it back in his face. Declined to visit when Jas was there, refused to talk to him on the phone. Finally, three years later, the showdown.

At nineteen, Jas joined Strathclyde Police. His mother was pleased, so was his father – as far as Jas could tell. Chris and David made siren-noises whenever he came into the room.

Dougie was overjoyed, came home to visit. The evening was etched on Jas's brain. Proud of the serge, he shook Dougie's hand then embraced him. Old times. Just two boys wrestling on the beach. Talking, joking, drinking, the closeness back. Then the rub:

"So? Got a girlfriend yet, Jas? The ladies like a man in uniform." Wink.

Jas had smiled, winked back: "So do I..."

His mother's frightened face.

Dougie's embarrassment masked by violence.

More wrestling...bloody faces.

Sitting in Kilmarnock Infirmary's Casualty department, his mother sobbing beside him.

Dougie was always good with his fists.

As the car slowed to a roundabout, Jas smiled, then frowned: in his brother's eyes, he gave 'bent cop' a whole new meaning.

Minutes later, under Hammersmith flyover, the car stopped: 7.25am. Grabbing the sweatshirt, Jas got out into bright London sunshine, limbs stiff from sitting.

Fila T-Shirt gave a sullen, silent salute before the car turned back towards the motorway.

Across the road, in a newsagent's, Jas asked directions to Margravine Road.

As he walked past Hammersmith police station, having just left a car which was carrying a large amount of money in a shabby holdall which would be exchanged somewhere in Kilburn for a large amount of cocaine, Jas paused. The training died hard...

He smiled.

...but it did die. He walked on.

London was sunny, pleasantly so. Cool breezes fanned his sweating face. The alien accent was soothing. He could be a foreigner, a tourist... anything in London. The anonymity pleased him. The capital was more than big enough for him.

Jas had visited London three times. Once, aged eight, on a family holiday: he remembered the Changing of the Guard.

Once at seventeen: he remembered the Guards, one in particular.

The last time had been four years ago: he remembered little, had been drinking heavily.

This time would be different. He wasn't here for pleasure. Catching sight of himself in a shop window, Jas paused, stared.

No police-shell.

No Leigh-shell.

No job...no lover...no friends...

Jas scowled at his reflection. What was left – another shell? Shells within shells, men within men.

Inviolate beneath it all...

...Jas blinked and walked on.

As the newsagent had directed, he turned left into a row of neat, white-painted houses. Dolls' houses. Ahead dirty white marble headstones peaked over a well-cut hedge.

From his mother, he knew Dougie's terraced abode backed onto a cemetery. Jas looked for number thirty-three. A few minutes later, he found it.

An affluent, prosperous-looking green Volvo estate sat in front of a neatly clipped box hedge. Behind, a white, two-storey building, large square windows on the ground floor. Rose garden. A child's bicycle lay abandoned in the porch area.

Last Christmas, his mother had never tired of telling him about this house, how well Dougie was doing, how happy he was with his wife, how beautiful the children were. The underlying message was transparent: 'Why don't you want these things too?'

Jas slung the sweatshirt over one shoulder and pushed open the gate.

Despite everything, he did hope Dougie was happy.

His brother didn't open the door: a small, overweight man in a Paisley-patterned dressing-gown did. Tired eyes peered: "Yes? Can I...?" The brow furrowed in recognition.

The voice on the answering machine.

"Hello, Dougie." Jas stepped forward, extended a hand. His body filled the small, tiled porch.

His brother shrank back. "Christ! You've changed, Jas..." Too surprised to deny him.

Jas scanned the short, balding figure. When they were kids, Dougie had been the fit one, the muscular one, the sand-kicker. For years, Jas had looked up to Dougie, wanted to be Dougie. He grinned down at his brother. "So huv you, Dougie!" The hand remained outstretched.

Dougie nervously tightened the dressing-gown cord around a non-existent waist.

Jas eyed the loose folds of flesh beneath the satin. "Ah've grown up an' you've grown out – eh, Dougie?"

Almost a smile, then memory took over. "I suppose you'd better come in – ma mother would never forgive me if I turned you away..."

'Ma mother': the convention. As if the mother who loved Jas could not be the same mother who loved Dougie.

He replaced his hand in his pocket and stepped into the hallway.

Dougie led the way into a long lounge, which seemed to be two rooms knocked into one. The wide, square windows looked out curtainlessly onto the rose garden. A comfortably, easy room. Habitatty, ethnic. Untidy, family clutter: a lived-in living-room. Not Dougie's taste. Jas looked at home-made shelves bursting with books, turned and raised one eyebrow at his brother. "Ah see ye've gone native."

When they'd shared a bedroom, Dougie's half had been army-organised.

Hiss. "Keep your voice down. Pippa and the kids are upstairs..."

"Ma nephew and niece..." Jas smiled. "...the wans ah've never seen." A framed photograph on the upright piano caught his eyes.

Dougie closed the living-room door.

Jas lifted the small portrait. It showed a good-looking woman sitting on a cane chair. Older than the bride in his mother's album, but still striking. One her lap, a toddler. By her side, a little girl. "Ye're a lucky man, Dougie..."

Behind, a cold voice crackling with violence. "Stay clear of them! If I catch you anywhere near my son..."

"For fuck's sake, Dougie!" Jas spun round, fists clenched. He stared into his brother's eyes. "Whit dae ye think ah am?"

Fear momentarily replaced loathing, then dissolved. "Keep your voice down."

Jas scowled. He needed Dougie, for the moment. "Sorry..." He replaced the photograph on the piano and sat down.

Dougie moved away, reluctant to breathe the same air. "What's this all about? I had some jumped-up wee nyaff from the police at the door, couple of days ago, asking if you'd been in touch. They asked ma mother the same thing. Wouldn't tell either of us what it's all about..." Worried, despite the hate.

For whose skin?

But at least they were talking.

"Better ye don't know, Dougie..." Jas tried to blot Leigh's bloody face from his mind. Moisture trickled between his pecs. "Ah've done nothin' that need concern you." He wiped his chest with the damp sweatshirt. "Whit huv ye telt yer family?"

His brother turned away. "Nothing."

"They don't ken ah'm stayin' here?"

"I don't want them involved wi' the likes o'..."

A soft tap at the door. Woman's voice, southern accent: "Douglas?"

Jas laughed softly, got up. "Well, they're aboot tae be!"

Dougie's face was a mask.

Jas walked to the door and opened it.

Dark eyes stared into his. Bride's eyes. "Doug...oh, I'm sorry, I didn't know you were busy..." Aristocratic face, strain showing around the eyes, as she took in his appearance. Surprise, annoyance then confusion flittered across the fine features. She looked questioningly beyond Jas, to Dougie.

The ball was in his court, and he knew it. Low voice, barely controlled. "Pippa, this is my...brother..." The word formed with difficulty, delivered like a curse. Dougie stalked past his wife into the hall.

She stared after him.

Jas stared at her back, a strong back in a man's shirt. "Sorry if we woke ye. I'm James..."

Behind them, Dougie's feet on the stairs.

She turned.

He extended a hand again.

She acknowledged the gesture coolly, then grasped his hand in an equally cool grip. "Ah...you're the...?"

"Ah'm the queer!" Jas felt himself under scrutiny. He held her smooth fingers.

Amused. "I was going to say policeman! You don't look like one."

Jas grinned. "Poof or polis, Mrs. Anderson?"

She laughed but didn't answer. "Call me Pippa." Eyes on his naked chest. "Sit down, James..."

He released her hand, moving to a chair. A door closed upstairs. "Dougie has bin kind enough tae offer me your sofa for a few nights..."

"Your mother calls him that." She laughed softly at the diminutive, then sat down, frowning. "Douglas didn't tell me you were coming..." Inconvenienced?

"He didn't know 'til last night."

"Ah..." Thoughtful nod. "I'll make up the spare room."

Jas sat forward in his chair and examined his brother's wife. Late thirties, about Dougie's age. Short, well-cut sandy hair framed an oval face. Arty-looking, evidently responsible for the decor. Jas knew from his mother's monologues Phillipa Anderson had been a teacher, had given it up for Dougie and the kids. He wondered what his brother had given up for her. "If ye're sure it's no trouble, Mrs..."

"Pippa, please." Abstractedly, she began to pick up toys from around her feet, placing them beside her on the sofa. "It's no trouble." Intelligent eyes inspected his face, weighing him up. Low voice. "To be honest, I didn't know quite what to expect from you, James Anderson. Douglas hasn't told me much, but your mother..!" Eyebrows raised.

Jas smiled in understanding. Mrs. Anderson, senior: his own personal PR agency. He stood up.

Voices on the stairs. "Mummy! Mummy!"

Jas turned. A small figure shot towards him, colliding with his legs. Jas gently seized pyjama-clad shoulders.

"William!" Mock-admonishing. The school teacher in her.

Jas smiled.

"What have I told you about running? You'll hurt yourself!" To Jas. "I'm sorry, he's a little boisterous..."

"What's your name?" The boy was looking up into Jas's face, eyes wide.

Jas bent down, ruffled the child's sandy hair. "I'm James." Mock whisper. "But you can call me Jas."

Solemnly, the child held out a hand. "That's a funny name. I'm William. I'm five. Pleased to meet you, Jas."

"Likewise, William." He clasped minature fingers.

Proud. "And this..." Pippa pushed an older girl forward. "...is Alison. Say hello to James, Ally. He's a policeman, up in Glasgow."

Sulky seven, wearing identical pyjamas. Eyes from Jas to her mother. "I want to call him Jas, mummy – like William. Can I?"

He knelt beside her. "If I can call you Ally, you can call me Jas – okay?"

She smiled. "Okay, Jas."

He saw his sister Christine in the the smile.

Pippa moved forward and gathered the children to her. "Now,

you two: back upstairs and get dressed."

He watched as Ally reluctantly left the room. William hung back, hugging the door frame: "Are you Taggart, Jas? You talk like him!"

He laughed, deepening his accent. "Ah dinney look like him, though, ah hope?"

William squealed with delight. "Do more, Jas!" The child burst back into the room, running towards outstretched arms.

Jas swept the young boy up over his head. "Ya wee rascal!"

William grabbed a handful of Jas's hair and pulled.

Jas yelled, then laughed again.

Pippa stood up, disentagling fingers from locks, scolding softly.

Looking put-out, William pouted at Jas. "Can we play later? You be Taggart and I'll be a bank robber?"

He grinned. "Guid boays don't rob banks, William..." He glanced at Pippa.

Nod. "Later, maybe..." She shooed her son from the room. To Jas, warmer now. "Coffee? Something to eat?"

He shook his head. "Coffee wid be great. Ah don't eat much in the mornings..."

Why did women always want to feed him?

"James?" Hesitant.

He caught her eyes, grinned. "You can call me Jas tae, if ye like.."

Curious. "Unusual nickname – as in 'freeform'?"

Remembering what he'd left behind in Glasgow, a shiver swept his body. He sat down, rubbed his face with both hands.

"You okay?" Concern.

"Tired, that's all."

Sigh. "I'll make that coffee..." Tactful. "...though perhaps a wash first..."

Jas stood up, his own sweat sour in his nostrils. "Thanks."

She nodded. "Bathroom's first right at the top of the stairs." Smile. "Don't let William pester you. I'll be in the kitchen..."

Several cups of coffee later, Pippa Anderson leaned back in her chair and frowned. "I'm sorry, Jas. I had no idea you two were...how long has it been?"

"Twelve years..." His sweatshirt churning in the washing-machine, Jas wore a white polo shirt he presumed belonged to Dougie. It was too tight. He stared at his cup.

"Douglas never talks about you, never suggests a visit to Glasgow." Curious. "I knew you'd had some sort of big argument – your mother told me how Douglas broke your nose, years ago."

He rubbed at a distorted section of bone, then looked at the interested, open face.

Embarrassed. "I just presumed Douglas didn't like your being a policeman." Sigh. "I'll talk to him, Jas, see if I can patch things up between you." Angry. "You're the children's uncle, for God's sake!"

He scowled, appreciating the gesture but knowing Dougie wouldn't.

She read his expression correctly. "Well, maybe a little exposure to each other will do more good than talk..." She poured more coffee. "What brings you to London, anyway – police business?"

"Ye could say that, but it's more a personal matter,"

She didn't pry, took him on trust.

It made a change.

Pippa stood up. "Well, if you need anything..."

Behind him, in the biker's jacket, the love letters stirred in an inside pocket. He smiled. "Ah need an 'A to Z' an' the use o' yer telephone..."

Eighteen

HE REPLACED the telephone. The Margravine Road house was silent. Dougie had said little before taking the kids swimming, half an hour ago. Pippa had left soon after: once a week voluntary work at a nearby hospice.

Jas had almost told her about Leigh, about the test...about the rest.

But all that was his problem.

Leigh was dead: nothing he had done with Richard Beatie or 'G' could hurt any more.

This wasn't about Leigh.

This was about Jas...and a murder charge.

Before she left, Pippa had given him a bunch of keys: "Come and go as you like. Dinner's at eight, if you're free." Concern. "You all right? You look a little..."

He'd smiled, pushed her away with empty reassurances.

Pippa had returend the smile. "I hope you and Douglas will be able to spend some time together – do him good to rediscover his roots." She had acknowledged her own cliche with a laugh.

He knew what she meant.

But it was up to Dougie...Jas had more important things to worry about. He looked at the telephone, then stared at the letter in his hand:

18 Lyttone Grove, Putney. Leslie Edwards.

Edwards' letter to Leigh was three years old...start at the beginning...

On the phone, Mr. Edwards had been deep-voiced, cagey, becoming cagier when Jas had used the police-mask. But he had eventually agreed to speak to him at 10.30 am.

Jas looked at his watch – 9.25 – then the map. Putney: not far from here. Maybe he could walk. He needed the exercise. Jas sighed. Saturdays were good. If luck was with him, he should be able to talk to Leigh's three ex-lovers sometime today.

The second letter: 'All my love, Harry' – just Harry. Address: 6 Northbank Road, Walthamstow. Date and telephone number.

Jas switched his eyes to the Underground map. Walthamstow ...Walthamstow. It eventually appeared. The other end of London.

Maybe this wasn't going to be as easy as he'd thought. He sighed, dialled the number.

A woman's voice: Harry was at work. Who was speaking?

Jas said he'd call back later.

Third letter. Leon Marshall: 22 Ormonde Gardens, Chelsea. Headed notepaper. Impressive address.

He grabbed a pencil from the 'Postman Pat' pencil holder beside the phone, rolling it between rough fingers. He'd do Chelsea and Putney this morning, Walthamstow this evening or tomorrow, whenever Harry got in from work.

Opening the phone book, Jas ran the pencil down the M section until he rached 'Marshall: L'. He dialled.

The phone was answered after four rings.

"Mr. Leon Marshall?"

Sleepy voice: "Yes?" Older, cultured.

Jas gave him the police-spiel.

Marshall sounded charming. Of course he wouldn't mind if DS Anderson called for a chat. He was glad something was finally being done about those kids and their golf balls. They were a menace.

Jas didn't contradict him. An appointment was made for noon.

High noon.

Lifting his jacket, he set off for Putney.

On Platform 2, multicoloured snakes writhed before him. Eyes narrowing, he located Putney on the Underground map. There were two: Bridge and East. Where was Lyttone Grove?

A train pulled noisily into the station. Westbound. Jas knew they all went through Earl's Court. He got on.

Busy – even at ten on a Saturday morning.

As the train moved off, Jas lurched with it, grasping at a ball-like thing which dangled from the arched ceiling. Sweat already soaked Dougie's polo shirt.

Why was he always so fuckin' hot? He scowled and surveyed his fellow passengers.

People said Londoners were cold, distant. The passengers on

this train lived up to their reputation. Eyes lowered, to a man – or woman.

On Glasgow buses and tube, gazes were met, returned, challenged.

He was homesick already. Jas sighed and sweated some more, before thumbing through the 'A to Z'. Bridge or East? He looked up, panning the compartment. He caught the straying eyes of a West Indian woman with a pram and two small children. He smiled.

The woman looked away, began to fuss unnecessarily over her brood.

Jas looked down.

A small, dark-skinned man clutched another ball-like thing beside him. Jas cleared his throat and talked softly.

The man listened, made a helpless gesture: a tourist, equally ignorant. But he took the 'A to Z' from Jas, nimble fingers flicking easily. After a few minutes he paused, looked up: East Putney for Lyttone Grove. The man closed the 'A to Z', turned to the Underground map on the back: Wimbledon train from Earl's Court.

Jas thanked him, raised his eyes and met dozens of other pairs, which immediately scrambled elsewhere. He scowled: he had done the unthinkable, talked to a stranger on a train. He was a curiosity...on every level.

The train stopped.

The tourist smiled and got off.

At Earl's Court Jas got off. People scurried everywhere, ants in a panic. Someone bumped against him, swore, glanced up then apologised.

Jas walked on. Eventually, he found the right platform. Eventually, a Wimbledon train came.

He got on, sat down and stared out the window. Four stations passed. More sunshine than he'd expected from the Underground. At the fifth, he rose, 'A to Z' slick in his hand.

The ticket collector was black and beaming. And helpful. Called him 'man'. Lyttone Grove wasn't far. Complicated set of directions.

Having taken in none of them, Jas thanked him. Moments later, he hailed a taxi.

He was getting lazy.

18 Lyttone Grove was a terraced house similar to Dougie's. Unlike Dougie's, it was split into two flats. Jas pressed the bell marked 'L.Edwards'. He smoothed down his hair. It rebelled against the movement.

Pippa's words: 'You don't look like a policeman...'

He hoped a shower and a shave had helped.

The door to the lower flat opened. A big man, older than Jas, not as tall. Military bearing. Fortysomething. Crew-cut, receding hairline. Moustache, heavy black eyebrows. Cloney. Suspicious.

Jas fingered the warrant card in his pocket, produced it with a flourish. "Mr. Edwards? I phoned earlier. DS Anderson ..." The ID flicked open, then flicked shut.

Edwards barely glanced at it.

From the same pocket, three-year-old words rushed from the love letters into his brain, pursued by images of Leigh and Leslie Edwards.

The man spoke.

Jas re-focused on Leigh's ex-lover.

"What's this about?" Deep, resonant voice.

"Inside, I think..." Jas nodded beyond to the hallway.

Reluctantly, Edwards ushered him into the flat.

Tiny room, sparsely furnished. Batchelor pad. Unlived-in, very masculine environment. Over the back of one chair, a grey uniform. Jas eyed it, then Edwards. "Forces?"

Edwards shook his head. "Security guard..."

"Ex-army?"

Nod, then impatient. "Look. What do you want?"

What did he want? To know more about Leigh... Jas produced the torn photograph, held it out wordlessly. Edwards took it.

Jas watched his face. A flicker of recognition, then nothing. Eyes down.

"Do you know this man, Mr. Edwards?"

Denial.

"Your memory isn't too good, is it? I've just shown you a photograph of Mr. Leigh Nicols. You had an affair with this man four years ago..."

Bristling. "What business is it of yours?"

"Leigh Nicols is dead, Mr. Edwards..." Jas flinched, recognising himself in this man...more of himself than he'd seen in Richard Beatie. The police-mask was slipping, revealing the man beneath. He tensed. "That makes it police business. Killed four days ago, a single gunshot to the face."

Ex-army.

Jas scowled. "Do you own a revolver, Mr. Edwards?"

The man stared at the torn photograph, ignoring the question. "Jason. Christ!" The facade crumbling. "Haven't seen him in years. Where...how did you...?"

"Jason Nicols – using the name Leigh – has been living in Glasgow for the past two years. Certain letters from you to the dead man have been found. We need to explore all avenues, Mr. Edwards: this is a murder inquiry – you understand?" Jas watched the craggy face crumple. He pulled the police-mask back in place. "You last saw Mr. Nicols...?"

Edwards steadied himself against a wall. "Three years ago..." Then panic. It sat uneasily with ex-army bulk. "Listen. I can't afford to be dragged into all this." Eyes narrowing. "My job could be on the line here. I don't want any trouble..."

You and me both. But Jas had trouble... "Just tell me what you know about Leigh or Jason Nicols, Mr. Edwards. That's all I'm interested in." He looked at the man.

Edwards met his gaze, addressed the man behind the mask. "You know how it is..."

Jas clenched his fists: the mask was transparent with this man. "Tell me anyway."

Leslie Edwards began to speak. A different voice, the voice of a man still hurting: "I know – knew – very little about Jason. We met..." Distant eyes, remembering eyes. "...in the Pitstop, Earl's Court – you know it?"

Jas didn't, but nodded.

"I was on the last night of two weeks' leave, back from Germany. Jason was so...different." Smile. "Oh, the sex was..."

"I'm not interested in all that, Mr. Edwards. When did you last see Leigh – Jason?" Jas continued to clench his fists until the knuckle-skin gleamed transparent.

Sigh. "Three years ago, in Maida Vale – his crummy flat. We went back there...about eleven. It was a Wednesday night...out last night together." Regretful. "When I woke up next morning he was gone. Thought maybe he'd been called away somewhere, at short notice, but I was kidding myself. There was no note, nothing. All his stuff was gone too." Pain in the eyes. "Couple of days later, I went back to Maida Vale – place was boarded up. I think squatters have got it, now..."

"Why did he leave? Did you have an argument?"

Distant. "We never argued. Jason was everything I ever wanted. Things were good between us..." Edwards looked to Jas for understanding.

Jas looked away.

"...or so I thought."

"Someone else?"

"No idea. He certainly didn't mention anyone. I wouldn't have minded sharing Jason – or, rather, I would have, but if it was the only way I could continue to see him..."

Jas frowned. It was all so familiar. "Go on..."

Inhale. Edwards sat down. "Nothing more to tell. I've no idea why he left. He was going to move in here – this flat was empty, most of the year."

"Did Leigh...Jason mention any other friends or family?"

Headshake.

"Did he mention Glasgow?"

Headshake.

Jas sighed. "Is there anything else you can tell me, anything which might trace his movements?"

Sad smile. "I hired a private detective to do exactly that. No sign of Jason anywhere." Worried again. "I won't need to come to Glasgow, to identify the body, will I? I couldn't bear that..." Edwards covered his face with large hands.

The cold room, Leigh on a stainless steel autopsy tray. Jas scowled. "No...that's been taken care of..."

Thirty minutes later, he was walking back to Putney East station.

Nothing.

Jas paused, sat on a wall. Leslie Edwards: desolate, even after three years. The same emotion Jas had seen in Richard Beatie's eyes painted the man's face. Something churned inside him.

Jas kicked his heels against brickwork.

He'd take a look at the address in Maida Vale, visit Earl's Court later. But after three years, it was a long shot. And anyway, Edwards had been motivated to look long and hard: Leigh had left a big hole in the man's life.

Jas got up. Next stop, Chelsea.

He was getting the hang of the tube. Outside Sloane Square station, he glanced at his watch: 11.30am. The sun was high in the sky. Jas removed the biker's jacket, stripped off Dougie's too-tight polo shirt and tied it around his waist. He put the jacket back on and began to walk down the Kings Road towards Ormonde Gardens.

Parallel with Chelsea barracks, two blond boys swished towards him, swinging Armani shoulder-bags. Jas stopped, met their stares. They nudged each other, giggling like kids. He remembered Leslie Edwards, scowled and walked on. The scent of Lacoste made his eyes water. Leigh's smell...

In a concrete square, he sat down on a bench, opened the 'A to Z' and began to flick.

A voice above him: "Are you looking for something?" London vowels filled his ears.

Leigh's vowels. Not Leigh's voice.

He looked up.

One of the blonds. Very handsome, very confident. Heavy eye contact. Wide smile. Very pushy.

What the hell! Jas smiled back. "Somewhere called... Ormonde Gardens?"

Blondie moved closer. "Oh, you're Scottish?"

Wide blue eyes. Not Leigh's eyes.

Jas nodded. "Ormonde...?"

"On holiday?" Blondie perched on the arm of the bench, easy in baggy linen jeans and jacket.

This was getting boring. Jas stood up. "Dae ye ken Ormonde

Gardens or no'?" He scowled, rubbing sweat from his chest.

Blondie's wide blue eyes widened further. "Yeah..." Glance back over shoulder.

Jas followed the line of vision to where the other blond stood, holding both Armani bags and grinning.

"We can show you, if you like..." Ambiguous, testing.

Jas reached into the biker's jacket and produced his warrant card.

Blondie's eyes were huge pools. "A policeman? A Scottish policeman, too! You're not from Glasgow, by any chance...?"

Two Taggart comparisons in one day were two too many. Jas got up and began to walk away.

Blondie was still talking. "We've got a couple of friends in Glasgow – Donald and..." To his friend. "...Alex? What's that Scottish guy's name, the one with the..." Gesturing. "...tit-rings?"

Jas paused, turned back. A chance? Leigh's photograph dug into his skin. He showed it to Blondie. "Dae ye know this guy?"

Blondie's friend appeared. Two tanned faces stared at a third, then two shaking heads. "Sorry..."

"Thanks anyway." Jas stared to move away.

Blondie's voice behind, still helpful. "What about Ormonde Gardens? We can..."

"Ah'll find it masel'..." Jas smiled.

Persistent. "It's no trouble..."

Jas laughed, continued to walk away.

Maybe Londoners weren't so cold after all.

A few streets down, he found Ormonde Gardens. Very smart. Flats, but not tenements. Selling the whole Eastercraigs block would maybe buy one floor in this leafy, tree-lined road. Number 22 was at the far end. Zipping up his jacket, Jas strode towards the home of Leon Marshall.

At the entrance, a doorman, officious in shabby braid.

Jas produced the warrant card.

Again, it was hardly glanced at.

He followed the doorman inside and waited while an intercom was buzzed. Mumbled words. Looking round the cool, marble interior, Jas untied the polo shirt from his waist. Drying sweat stiffened the white fabric.

Eyes on him.

Jas looked back at the doorman and smiled. "Ah'm no' used tae yer weather yet!"

Suspicion. "What police station did you say you were from?"

Jas tensed.

Behind, a lift pinged. Then a voice: "Thank you, Frank. Ah. Sergeant Anderson. You're a little early..."

Jas turned. A small, elegant figure smiled at him fron the lift. Dapper. Relaxed. Frail – early sixties.

Leigh and Jas.

Leigh and Beatie.

Leigh and Edwards.

Leigh and...Leon Marshall?

Jas walked towards the open lift.

The small man talked constantly on the way up. Jas gathered there was some problem with kids from south of the river and golf clubs. At the third floor, the lift stopped. As the doors slid apart, Leon Marshall stood back, ushering Jas ahead.

"Second on the left, sergeant. It's open..."

Jas walked along thick carpet, past pastel walls and through the doorway.

Leon Marshall followed slowly behind him.

The Ormonde Gardens flat could not have been more different from Leslie Edwards's sparse, cramped accommodation.

Leon Marshall evidently had money and knew how to spend it. Tasteful...very tasteful. Polished beechwood floor, French windows, small balcony beyond. Off-white everywhere: walls, leather sofas, small pale wooden coffee table, laptop PC. A fan hummed where a fire should have sat. Above, a large ornate mirror. On the mantel sat a bulky bronze: two men embracing. Rich ore jarred in the light, bright room.

Jas caught his own reflection, then Leon Marshall's brown eyes.

"Now...some iced tea, I think..." The voice in the mirror. "...or maybe something stronger?"

Jas turned, regarded the man. The posture said elderly, the walk said elderly. The face was more accurate. Mid forties, very smooth, very soft. The man looked at Jas.

Jas looked away. "Tea's fine..."

Polite smile. "Please make yourself comfortable, Sergeant Anderson. Take off your jacket, if you like. You look rather hot..." Leon walked from the room.

Jas's throat burned. An image of Leigh in this flat, with this man, buzzed in his brain. He smiled; couldn't even think straight.

The small man reappeared in the doorway, holding a tray. He padded over, geisha-like steps, setting a tall glass on the table before Jas. "About those blasted Battersea brats..."

"I'm afraid there's been a misunderstanding, Mr Marshall..." Jas produced Leigh's photograph.

The man stood a few inches away. Quizzical.

"...I'm here in connection with a different matter." He held out the photograph. "Do you know this man?"

Leon Marshall moved forward, took the photograph.

Jas watched his face.

Curiosity, then shock: "You've found him?" The tone brightening.

"Do you know this man, Mr, Marshall?"

The neat hand shook slightly, eyes staring at Leigh's face. Shock to joy, pleasure brimming from tired eyes. Leon Marshall turned to the French windows. Breathless voice: "Billy! They've found Jason..."

From the balcony, a shadow rose. Jas watched as a very large man in swimming trunks lumbered into the room. Overdeveloped muscle pulsed in huge arms, biceps and triceps gleaming in the noon sun. A show body, probably worse than useless. Impressive nonetheless. Jas stared as the Incredible Bulk moved surprisingly swiftly into the room. Above a tree-trunk neck, the face was angry.

Nineteen

BILLY THE BULK made straight for Leon Marshall, over whom he towered like a benevolent giant. "Who the fuck's this?" He eyed Jas.

Low voice, trembling with anticipation. "Says he's a policeman, Billy. He's here about Jason."

Jas stared at shining muscle, then produced the warrant card and held it out. "DS Anderson..."

The Bulk snatched the card, scrutinised then handed it back. "So?" Less antagonistic.

Either Billy couldn't read or didn't care: Jas was well out of his area of jurisdiction, here. "I'm following up a death in Glasgow – Wednesday night. Leigh Nicols..." He looked at Leon. "...you knew him as Jason, I believe?"

Leon Marshall sat down. "Dead?" Tears formed behind crinkled eyes. "Jason's dead?" A deflated balloon, air leaked from parted lips.

The Bulk patted a slim shoulder. Soft voice. "Hey, what do you care? He was..."

"Jason was part of my life, Billy..." Words hardly audible. "...you don't understand..."

Jas leant against the mantel, his presence ignored.

The Bulk stiffened. "Oh, I understand fine! You spent a small fortune on that little tart and how did he repay you? Took the money and ran..."

"Christ, Billy!" Louder. "Jason's dead. I can't think about all that now." To Jas. "How did he die – was it..." Tension framed the mouth, blocking the obvious.

"Gunshot wound to the face, Mr. Marshall..."

Unbelieving. "Someone shot him?" Leon stared past Jas to the far wall.

The Bulk's gruff laugh. "So your precious Jason played his little game once too often? He had it coming!"

Games...more games.

Jas tensed. "A man is dead, Mr. Marshall. All the police have are a few letters from yourself..."

"You wrote to him?" The Incredulous Bulk, to Leon. "How could you be so...?"

Marshall reddened. Laboured breathing. "Billy...my inhaler...please..." Pink face straining for air.

The Bulk walked swiftly to a small cabinet on the other side of the room.

Jas leant over and loosened Marshall's top shirt button. Harsh, gulping sounds came from a goldfish mouth. "Take it easy..."

The Bulk returned, handed Leon a small blue cylinder.

The panting man grabbed at it gratefully, puffing into desperate lungs.

The Bulk sat attentive on the sofa, a hand on Marshall's shoulder.

Jas watched as the slight man's chest began to rise and fall more evenly. Slowly, the breathing returned to normal. The Bulk's eyes never left the frail body. Eventually, Marshall's eyelids fluttered, then closed, the breath shallow, but steady.

Whispered order: "Out here." The Bulk gestured to the French windows. "Give him some time..."

Jas followed the large form out onto the balcony. "Will he be okay?"

The Bulk sat down on a floral sunlounger and frowned. White, untanned lines streaked the broad forehead. "Leon's not well. He mustn't get upset. I can tell you anything about... Jason Nicols you need to know." Antagonism swelled in the hot air, the name delivered with undisguised loathing.

Jas moved to the wrought-iron railings and looked down. Ormonde Gardens was quiet. No kids in sight. He sighed: from the looks of him, low-flying golf balls were the least of Leon Marshall's problems. He turned back to the muscular figure. "Right, Mr..."

The Bulk snorted. "No names, Mr. Policeman – and I'm not making a formal statement, so you can forget that. Leon doesn't need all this, and neither do I..."

"Makes no difference to me..." Jas shrugged. "...I'm here, how shall we say, unofficially?"

The Bulk laughed mirthlessly. "Thought as much! Can I ask your interest in Leon and this Jason-character?"

Jas flinched. "Ye can ask...Now, Jason..."

"Little toe-rag!" Veins pulsed against the Bulk's neck.

"You knew Jason Nicols?"

"Only met him a couple of times, but knew the type. Leon's a sitting duck for boys like Jason. Loves the pretty ones, but it's not just sex – not these days, anyway. Makes him feel good – young, attractive company."

Jealousy talking? Jas looked at the Bulk: he and Leigh were poles apart. But there was something in the way Billy watched the smaller, frailer Leon ...something less than sex...or perhaps more. "Mr. Marshall lived with Jason before you?"

Another snort. "Jason didn't live here, and neither do I, Mr. Policeman – at least, not in the way you mean. I'm Leon's brother..."

Judge not...

The Bulk picked up a towel and rubbed his face. He sighed. Slow, reluctant: "I suppose you might as well know. A little over three years ago, Leon tested positive. I moved down from Nottingham, when I found out – as a nurse and his only relative, I felt I owed him that much." Angry eyes tiny pinpricks in the huge face. "So, I get off the train at Euston – what's there to meet me? Leon and this little..." Thin mouth twisting.

"Jason?"

Nod. "It's disgusting. A guy like Leon – a clever investment banker and HIV-positive...a couple of months' hand-holding and the occasional blow-job, get the will changed, then into a hospice with the loved one at the first sign of any symptoms. Would've set the little bastard up for life..."

Jas sighed. "You had a word with Jason?"

Head shake. "Never got him alone – and if I had, it would have been more than 'a word' that heartless leech got from me!"

Jas looked at the hard, muscular body: means.

The Bulk went on, low, menacing voice. "Couple of days after I arrived, Jason was off – looking for another living corpse to suck dry! Leon was heartbroken." Concern. "I tried to tell him what Jason had been up to, but he'd have none of it, the old fool! Had me trudging round London, trying to find his precious little gold-digger..."

Jas looked at the angry, protective eyes: motive.

Opportunity? "Mr...er, Billy: where were you last Wednesday night?"

The Bulk scowled. "Nowhere near Glasgow, if that's what you're thinking, Mr. Policeman, or whatever you are." Softer, regretful. "I was where I've been almost every night for the past three months. Here, with Leon." Angry laugh. "He's lasted much longer than I would have expected. If Jason Nicols had hung around for the payoff, he'd have had a long wait..."

Leigh's waiting days were over. Jas clenched his fists: his own may have only started. "Any idea why Jason left when he did?"

"Leon said I'd frightened him off, that Jason couldn't...be himself, with a straight around." Scowl. The Bulk stretched out on the sunlounger. "That's a laugh! I doubt if Jason – or whatever name he used – was ever himself. It was all an act." Voice lowered. "I wouldn't be surprised if he had more than one poor sucker on the go at once. Oh, there's no doubt I was cramping his style, and I'm glad he left when he did." Fists tightening into hard balls. "If he hadn't, or if I'd found out where he'd gone..."

More threats, more anger. If Leigh made a habit of befriending dying men, how many other well-built, well-adjusted, irate relatives and friends were out there? How many would have...?

"You knew him, didn't you?"

Jas stared.

Nodding. "Thought you were one of Leon's old Territorials pals when I first saw you. "Thoughtful. "But there's something else – I can see it on your face, Mr. Policeman. The same look Leon..."

"I'm here to find out who killed Leigh..." The police-mask was slippng. Jas unzipped the bikers' jacket. "...aka Jason Nicols, and why – nothing more. Did Leon mention where he and Jason had met?"

Shrug. "Some bar in Earl's Court – can't remember the name..."

"The Pitstop ring any bells?"

Pause. "Could be it. I can ask Leon..."

"Did Jason mention any family, or friends?"

Head shake. Growling voice. "An orphan – at least, that's what he told Leon. Christ! His sort make me sick!"

Leigh...the actor, the game player par excellence. "Does...did Leon have an address for Jason?"

Shrug. Calmer. "Some dump in Maida Vale. He went round there, Leon cried like a baby when no one knew where his beloved Jason had moved to..."

"Billy? Billy?" Weak voice from the lounge.

The Bulk was on his feet in seconds. "Coming." To Jas: "Stay here." He walked through the French windows.

Jas took off the biker's jacket, wiped his sweating chest with the Bulk's beach towel. He leant against the raiking. His throat still burned, yearning for the iced tea.

A sound from the lounge reached his ears. Moving to the French windows, he watched Bulky Billy Marshall gently lift his brother in two huge arms and carry him from the room.

Jas sighed. He had no place here. Leigh's tracks were faint. Pulling on the jacket, he walked from the balcony through the lounge and into the hall.

At the door, a voice behind him. Jas turned.

The Bulk, clad in black sweatpants, worry lines around the eyes. A slip of paper clutched in a meaty hand. He thrust it at Jas. "The address of Nicols's flat, though what good it'll do..."

"Thanks." He took the fragment, scanned the broad face then glanced towards a closed door. "I'm sorry about your brother..."

The Bulk followed his eyes, then scowled. "Leon gets by...we both do..." He moved closer.

Jas looked up, feeling hot breath on his hotter forehead. He stared into the eyes of a frightened man. "Thanks for talking to me..." He opened the front door and left the flat.

Outside, Jas walked slowly back onto the Kings Road. He found a cafe and sat down at a pavement table. Heat and exhaust fumes prickled on hot skin. No one came to take his order.

He closed his eyes and saw Leon Marshall in his brother's muscular arms. He remembered Richard Beatie's offer to nurse Leigh.

Despite The Bulk's accusations, there were motivations other than money.

Jas opened his eyes. He removed the four love letters from his jacket pocket and spread them over the gingham table-top. He stared.

The more he discovered about Leigh's past, the more sense his death made.

His Leigh, the man he'd shared his bed – his life – with, for the last eighteen months, was fading like a wet dream. Jas clenched his fists and stared at Leigh's paper-trail.

From the dates on the leters, he knew that three years ago, Leigh was simultaneously: being fucked by Leslie Edwards – albeit spasmodically, due to the man's postings abroad; caring for or exploiting Leon Marshall – depending on how generously you interpreted it; and somehow involved with Harry from Walthamstow. All the while living in some grotty Maida Vale bedsit.

Jas smiled. If nothing else, you had to admire the guy's energy!

Leon Marshall's soft moans sobered his mood. Having fun was one thing. Cold, calculating exploitation of a dying man was quite another.

He flicked through the letters, scrutinising dates.

Leigh had known Leslie Edwards for approximately six months, then left.

Leigh had known Leon Marshall for a shorter time, but made an equally big impression, before leaving in a similar fashion.

What about Harry?

Jas got up, located a pay phone inside the cafe. He punched in the E17 number.

No answer.

He returned to the table and his present problem.

Had Billy Marshall scared Leigh off the London scene completely, forcing him onto pastures new in Glasgow; or was there another reason Leigh had moved north?

Had Leigh been running a similar scam in Glasgow?

Jas scowled. If so, things had backfired considerably. Somewhere along the line, Leigh had picked up the virus himself.

People swirled around the pavement table. A waiter finally appeared. Jas ordered iced tea. When it came, he drank swiftly and ordered another.

His mind slowly cleared. He looked at the scrap of paper Billy the Bulk had thrust at him: 18 Warlock Road. Same address that Edwards had given for Leigh. His watch read 2.15pm. After paying for the drinks, Jas made his way towards Sloane Square.

Half an hour later, he stood on the southbound platform at Warwick Avenue station.

Nothing. More nothing. The information from both Edwards and Leon Marshall's brother had been slightly out-of-date. 18 Warlock Road had been reclaimed from squatters sometime in the last year, and converted into owner-occupied flats.

Jas got the same anwers as Leigh's other ex-lovers, but from different mouths. Not surprisingly, none of the present tenants knew anything about Leigh/Jason Nicols.

He scowled and sat down beside two youths in football colours, who immediately moved away. This was turning out to be a complete waste of time.

A train arrived. Jas got on. The compartment heaved with bodies. At Picadilly Circus he got off, waited on a crowded platform for a Picadilly Line train.

It came, announcing 'Heathrow' on the destination board.

The airport. LA. Leigh...

He shrugged and got on.

It was approaching five o'clock as Jas walked out of Barons Court tube. Across the road, the cemetery caught his eye. He was actually looking for a phone box. Jas strolled through the gates.

Greying stone angles welcomed him with open wings and sorrowful faces. Under a particularly sombre seraph, he sat down.

He liked cemeteries.

He could think in cemeteries.

He had walked in Glasgow's necropolis the night he had last seen Jo Hunter and Leigh.

He had met Leigh in the necropolis, two years ago...

In this warm, empty, alien cemetery, unchecked memory flooded back...

The layout of Glasgow's necropolis made it ideal running terrain. Jas did three circuits each day. That day he pushed himself, did four. Pausing at a huge, crumbling mausoleum, breathing heavily: he still smoked, then. Gazing at Glasgow's skyline while his heartbeat gradually slowed. Removing sweatshirt to cool down. A voice at his side:

"Got a light, mate?"

Surprise. The necropolis was his domain...his and the glue-sniffers. Jas had looked round.

Clear blue eyes, smiling at him, not the eyes of an addict. Jas withdrew a light from sweatpants, sparked and held it out.

The man cupped smooth fingers around Jas's hand as he lowered a cigarette towards the flame.

Electricity. Even then...

No names.

Shining blond hair. Shorts, leather jacket in summer. Nipple-rings gleaming on hairless chest.

Jas read the singals, led the way.

Two men.

Two bodies.

So much life amomgst the dead...

...a car-horn roused him. Jas rubbed his face. The memory faded, erased by the movement.

Another car-horn, then children's happy voices.

He stood up and began to walk back to Margravine Road.

The Volvo was still absent, so he used the keys Pippa had given him. A voice as he opened the door:

"Douglas? Is that..." Pippa's face appeared at the far end of the hall. Disappointment hurriedly masked. "Oh, it's you, Jas. Come on through..."

"Jas! Jas!"

Tiny hands grabbed at his knees. He bent down and lifted his nephew with one hand, tucking the wriggling body under an arm.

Squeals. "Jas! You're all hot..."

He walked through to the kitchen.

Pippa stood at the cooker, stirring. "William!" Automatic, not scolding. "Let Jas sit down..." She turned. "Want a...?" Pause. Smile. "You do look warm! There's wine in the fridge..." She turned back to the stirring.

Spicy, aromatic odours wafted up.

Jas walked to the sink, filled and drank a glass of water. It hit his stomach like a brick.

William squirmed playfully: "Don't you like wine, Jas? Daddy lets me have a little, sometimes..."

He gently lowered the child to a standing position, then sat down on a stripped pine chair.

William scrambled onto his knee.

Pippa, cheerful. "Have a good day?"

Good day...a dead lover who preyed on dying men? Jas sighed. "Ah found things out..."

Saucepan lid on saucepan. Pippa sat down opposite. Eyes on his chest: "What happened to the shirt?"

Jas looked down at gleaming skin, then back at his brother's wife. "Must've left it on a train. Sorry..."

William giggled. "I left my gloves on a train and Mummy..."

Embarrassed laugh. "Don't worry about it, Jas. Douglas won't miss it. Now..." Schoolteacher voice. "...what about a shower before dinner? Your sweatshirt's dry..." She reached round, plucking the 'Lonsdale' from a pile of clean washing.

Jas took it, eased William off his lap and stood up. "Thanks..."

Tugging at his leg. Pouting. "You said we could play, Jas..."

He ruffled the sandy hair. "Later. Let me git cleaned up first..." Jas headed for the shower.

Under cold water, he soaped his body, his mind on Harry from Walthamstow. The only lover not to use a surname, the only one to include a phone number. A woman had answered: sister, wife...given Leon Marshall's condition, nurse?

Jas rubbed his face. No, the woman had said Harry was at work, evidently still able to hold down a job.

The date on the letter was most recent: January two years back.

Six months before Jas met Leigh.

Maybe Harry knew why Leigh had left London.

Maybe Harry could tell him about 'G'...

...Jas turned off the shower. His body glowed scarlet, his mind cooled.

Leslie Edwards was the past. Leon Marshall was the past. Harry was the past.

'G' and Jas overlapped. Pulling on jeans, he walked downstairs.

The lounge was empty. He cleared his throat. "Pippa?" The name felt strange. "Okay if I use yer phone?"

Distant voice. "Help yourself..."

He dialled the Walthamstow number. Woman again. Irritated. Harry's shift didn't end until midnight. Who was calling?

Jas took a chance. An old friend from Glasgow. Down for the weekend. When was the best time to catch Harry?

The woman softened. Any time tomorrow morning.

He thanked her, rang off.

Pippa appeared in the doorway. "Dinner in about half an hour – okay?"

He nodded, rubbing hair with a towel. "Where's Dougie?"

Offhand frown: "Haven't seen him all day. He dropped the kids off with a neighbour about noon..." The words tailed away.

Jas scowled.

She caught the expression. Laugh. "Don't worry – he'll be back..."

Jas dried bare feet. He wasn't worried, didn't need the Dougie-problem. He needed to exercise.

"Come through to the kitchen, if you like..." Wanting to talk.

He didn't need her problems, either. A small solution presented itself:

"Jas! Can we play now?" Five-year-old William Anderson pulling at the leg of his jeans.

He grinned. "No cops an' robbers though – eh?" He looked up. Pippa was gone.

William sat on the floor, expectant.

"Count fur me, eh?" Jas knelt beside the boy, began the press-ups.

A small, clear voice began to count. At thirty-nine, it stopped.

"Whit's happened?"

"Don't know any more."

Jas moved onto his back, clasped hands behind neck.

William sensed a game. He clambered onto Jas's thighs and seized two belt-loops. With each sit-up, the boy flattened himself against the taut stomach, in a parallel movement.

Jas laughed.

William counted.

At thirty-nine, Jas unclasped his hands and grinned. "Ye're doin' guid, boay..."

William giggled and tried to tickle.

Jas tickled back, more effectively.

William shrieked with pleasure, attempted escape.

Jas grabbed a leg and continued to tickle.

William threw himself forward onto Jas, began to pull his hair.

Jas mock-frowned. "Ye fight dirty, ya wee..." He tickled harder.

The play brought Pippa through from the kitchen. She stood in the doorway, laughing, as William wrestled with Jas. "Watch out for the feet, Jas! He's got a kick like a mule..."

In one easy movement, Jas flipped William onto his back, pinned him there with one arm. "Dae ye give in?"

"Never!" William wriggled free from the loose arm, pushed Jas aside, then climbed onto his chest.

"Ah surrender! Ye've won, William..."

The sound of a door slamming.

Pippa, laughing: "That'll be Ally." Raised voice. "In here. Did you manage to...?"

"Get away from my son!" The hot room cooled with icy words.

"Daddy! Come and wrestle. I've beaten Jas..."

He tried to sit up but the boy was too heavy.

"What's wrong, Daddy?" Confused.

Pippa: "Doulas, where have you been? I was worried..."

Dougie moved forward. Eyes bored into his. "William, go to your room..."

"Why, Daddy?" He grasped Jas's ears.

Jas lifted the boy and sat him on the sofa.

Annoyed. "Daddy, I was winning..."

Jas stood up, glaring at his brother. "Maybe if ye spent a bit mair time wi' yer family, Dougie..."

The fist came before he could block it. Pain flared in his cheekbone. In the background, Pippa's angry voice. William began to cry.

Jas rubbed the smarting bone then turned away. Anger and frustration smouldered inside him, twelve years of anger and frustration. But this wasn't the time...

Behind, Pippa was soothing her son.

...and it certainly wasn't the place. He looked into his brother's hating eyes. "Ye're a fool, Dougie. But it's your hoose. Ah'll go..."

Pippa. "You're not going anywhere, Jas!" Furious. "If anyone's leaving, he is..." Cold look to her husband.

Dougie rubbed reddening knuckles against a thigh. He glowered at Jas.

Jas glanced at William, at the tear-stained, five-year-old face. Eyes steel, he stared back at his brother – the despoiler, the poisoner of young minds.

Dougie flinched.

Jas strode past him into the hall. Upstairs, he collected jacket, boots and the newly-washed sweatshirt from the bathroom. Passing an open door, he glanced in. The guest bedroom.

He would never be a guest in this house.

He shrugged and walked downstairs. From behind the closed lounge door, angry voices. At the foot of the stairs, a small figure, sobbing. Jas paused, sat down behind William.

The boy turned, eyes wide. "Why doesn't Daddy like you, Uncle Jas?"

The title turned a knife in his guts. Jas ruffled damp, sandy hair, words caught in his throat. He had no answer – at least, none a five-year-old would understand. He smiled. "Tell Mummy I said thanks..." Jas handed the house-keys to William. "...and give her these..."

The boy threw his arms around Jas's neck.

Jas hugged the tiny body tightly, then gently disentangled himself. He sat the keys on the hall table and stood up.

The raised voices continued.

He pushed them away: not his problem. As he opened the front door, Wiiliam's voice behind him:

"I don't care what Daddy says. You're nice. Would you like to see my hamster?"

Jas smiled. "Maybe next time. Guidbye, William."

"Goodbye, Uncle Jas."

Twenty

JAS RUBBED his cheek as he wandered up Earl's Court Road. Fuckin' Dougie had done it again...

The only man ever to get the better of him...at least with his fists.

But bruises and broken noses healed.

Leigh...

Jas shrugged off the name and turned into a side street, surveying a row of pubs. In the distance, a chequered flag waved limply.

He walked towards it.

The Pitstop...

Inside, the pub was oak-panelled, traditional-looking, the racing theme apparently ending with the name. A murmur of conversation rose up to meet him: no background music. Jas looked around. A group of older men were talking at a corner table. Well-dressed in understated Ralph Lauren. One glanced over as the door swung closed behind Jas, then looked away.

He walked into the pub. His eyes were drawn to a muscular figure, lounging against a central support. Stocky. Longish dark hair fell over strong features. Shoulders moved in time to unheard music. A Walkman hid both ears. Jas's eyes travelled down the swaying body. Tight denim encased tighter thighs. Even at this distance, he could see the outline of the man's half-hard cock. Jas grinned and walked on.

Behind the horseshoe bar, a tall blond boy polished smearless glasses. As Jas approached, he looked up and smiled. "I'd like to see the other guy..." Eyes on Jas, then the bruise.

Leigh's eyes, wide and guileless. Jas scowled, resenting the overture. "Double vodka."

The barman blushed, looked away. "Coming up..." He retreated to the optics.

Jas regretted his curtness. When the barman returned, he managed a smile and a shrug. "It's a sore point..."

The barman brightened. "You're Scottish?" He placed a thick, stubby glass in front of Jas.

"Glasgow. Doon fur the weekend." He swallowed the drink in one, held out the empty glass and a fiver. "Another."

The barman talked while he poured. "Don't know Glasgow. Been to Edinburgh, though..."

Jas took the drink, sipping this time. He watched the talking boy. Early twenties, cropped platinum hair, black eyebrows. A dark, downy shadow on the upper lip. White T-shirt outlining firm, as yet undeveloped, muscle.

"Your first time in the capital?" The boy leant one bony elbow on the bar.

Jas shook his head. Leigh's photograph burned in his inside pocket. "Ah'm lookin' fur somewan." He finished the vodka.

Mock-shy smile. "Will I do?"

Jas laughed, fumbled in his pocket. "Ah'm lookin' fur somewan in particular." He held out the photograph. "Ah'm telt he used tae come in here..."

The boy took the photograph, examined it. "He's very handsome ...what's his name?"

"Leigh Nicols...middle name Jason. Mean onythin'?"

The boy shook his head, then looked at Jas. "I don't recognise him, but I only started working here last week..."

"Gary?" A voice from further down the bar. "Any chance of some service?"

The boy returned the photograph, raised jet eyebrows in exaggerated, smiling annoyance. "Back in a minute." He padded off down the bar.

Jas watched him go then turned to examine his fellow drinkers. The Pitstop was filling up. A tall guy in leather was feeding money into a juke-box. Blur's last single drifted over, bringing with it memories he wanted to forget. Jas hefted his empty glass and turned back to the bar.

A voice at his side. "Get you another?" Soft, mellow tones.

Jas looked round. One of the Lauren set. About Leon Marshall's age. Healthier-looking. Jas fingered Leigh's photograph. Free drinks and information. He had nothing to lose. "Ah'll huv a vodka..."

One eyebrow raised. "You're Scottish?"

Jas grinned and extended the photograph.

And so it went on...

Two hours and countless vodkas later, Jas was back at the now-crowded bar. He had asked, shown to the photograph of Leigh to at least twenty men of all ages. No face had admitted any sign of recognition. When he mentioned other names, two older guys recalled Leon Marshall, but hadn't seen him for years.

They had exchanged knowing glances with Jas.

No one appeared to know Leslie Edwards, let alone the pretty blond boy he'd picked up here three years ago.

Almost everyone knew a Harry, but not one from Walthamstow.

Jas sighed and motioned to a barman. Blond Gary seemed to have disappeared. He ordered another vodka.

Familiar voice at his shoulder, shouting over the noise. "Let me get this...." A hand on his arm.

Jas turned.

Blond Gary smiled. "No luck finding your friend?"

Jas shook his head. "Three years is a lang time..."

The boy was pushed by others seeking the relief-barman's attention. Bracing hands against Jas's chest, he tried to steady himself, failed and fell forward.

Instinctively, Jas caught him, thin bare arms under sweating hands. He closed his eyes, feeling another's body against his. Platinum stubble brushed his face, the smell of clean hair and cheap soap filled his head.

The boy remained in his arms. "Sorry, er...what did you say your name was?" Low words, hot breath against his neck.

"Ah didn't, but it's Jas..."

The boy moved back, settling in against the bar. "That's unusual. As in...?"

"Don't say it!"

The boy laughed. "I'm Gary." He tried to hold out a hand, but it was crushed in the crowd.

"I know." Bees in his ears.

A voice above the buzz. "Who's the vodka?"

Jas turned his head. "Over here! And a...?" Head turned back to Gary.

"Orange juice..."

Jas smiled. "Wise man..."

Gary produced some coins.

Jas waved them away. "Let me..."

The boy smiled. "Thanks." Embarrassed. "Money's a bit tight – they don't pay much here."

"Bet the tips are guid, though..." Jas watched as the boy reddened and chewed nervously on a bottom lip:

"I get by..." A hand over the luminous, silver crop. The blush increasing.

Jas grinned through a vodka haze. "Yer shift over?"

"Yeah..." More comfortable. "...I'm a student. This is only a summer job. What line you in?"

"Ah'm wi' Strathclyde Police. CID."

Panic in the blue eyes.

"Ah'm oan holiday..."

Relief. "Your friend – was he...?"

The words melted before Jas could grasp them. Around him, wisps of conversation blended with thumping techno from the jukebox, merging with his thumping heart. He looked at Gary's moving lips.

"...someone special?"

Not Leigh's lips.

Lies...

He smiled, watching the boyish face. "Naw...no-wan special..."

The drinks arrived. Jas paid and took them, handing the orange juice to Gary.

They drank wordlessly in a crush of sweating bodies.

Someone knocked Jas's elbow. Vodka spilled down the Lonsdale, soaking through to evaporate on hot flesh. He drank what was left in the glass swiftly. He wanted out of here. He looked at Gary. He wanted...

From beneath hooded eyes, a glance then smile. Words redundant. He turned and pushed forward.

Jas took a step, then stopped, blinking. Faces swam before him. A surprisingly strong grip on his wrist:

"We'll get a taxi..."

He followed the blond head out of the Pitstop into the night.

Gary gave an address Jas didn't catch. In the back of the black cab, a hand on his crotch, stroking with soft fingers. Jas threw back his head and closed his eyes.

Leigh's fingers for so long.

But not any more...

Jas rubbed a rough hand over the bristling crop, then pushed the head downwards.

Low voice: "Hold on, we're almost there..."

Then a wet mouth on his own dry lips. Gary tasted of citrus and peppermint. He pulled away reluctantly as the cab pulled up.

Jas opened his eyes, fumbled in a pocket. Finding notes, he tried to pay with something, couldn't see the denomination.

The driver looked puzzled.

Gary laughed and opened the passenger door, taking the money from him.

Jas watched as the driver rolled down his window, accepting what he could now see was a £5 note. He laughed. "In Glasgow ye pay afore ye git oot..." A drunken, slurred voice.

His own.

Outside the cab, his head cleared slightly in cool night air. Gary pulled him towards the shadowed outline of a building. Jas followed up three flights of steep stairs, waited while keys jangled, then walked into a disinfectant-smelling room.

Hot, airless.

Gary switched on a single spotlight then moved through a doorway in the far wall. Kitchen?

Jas took off the biker's jacket and sat down on a narrow bed, illuminated by the beam of light. Sweat beaded on his forehead. He found himself craving a cigarette. Christ, he was nervous!

It had been Leigh for so long...

Shout from the kitchen: "You okay through there?"

Jas removed the Lonsdale. "Aye, fine." He began to unbuckle the biker's boots.

Husky voice at his side, then more jangling: "Keep them on..."

He raised his head. An Aryan vision knelt before him. The white T-shirt and baggy jeans exchanged for studded collar, heavy leather harness and a tiny G-string which barely contained Gary's excitement. A halo shone around the lowered, cropped head. In one hand, cuffs dangled. The other gripped two nipple-clamps. Jas stared.

Soft, supplicatory: "What do you want me to be?"

Jas stood up, groin throbbing. He clenched his fists, looking down at the pale skin.

Not Leigh's skin.

Leigh was dead.

Leigh was a lying, conniving little bastard.

Anger pulsed up from the bruise, into his temples.

Anger at Leigh.

Anger at Dougie.

Anger at himself...

Jas seized the studded dog-collar, wrenching the boy to his feet.

Long lashes fluttered on pale skin. Breath quickened.

In one swift movement, Jas grabbed the handcuffs, spun the figure around and secured both wrists behind the narrow back. With one knee he pushed Gary down onto the bed and held him there. His prick was hardening. Rage beat a tattoo in his guts.

Rage at Leigh.

Rage at Jimmy Mygo.

Rage at the world...

Breathing heavily, Jas flipped the body over, gazing at the hairless chest. No nipple-rings. Gary's eyes still, closed.

He gave the innocent face a back-handed slap.

The eyes shot open.

He found himself staring into limpid blue pools, pupils the size of footballs.

Gary smiled, licking his lips. "Don't make me wait, Jas..." A pink handprint decorated one cheek.

Another slap, harder this time. The pressure in his balls was growing. "Whit are ye?"

Gary stared up at him, then lowered his eyes. "Whatever you want me to be..."

Jas clenched his fists, kneeing the figure back over into a prone position. "Whit are ye, Leigh?"

The reply was muffled, inaudible.

With slick fingers, Jas stared to undo the fly of his jeans, then paused. His right fist pulsed.

Mumbles from the pillow.

Jas closed his eyes. Leigh's face danced before him, joined by

Richard Beatie's, Leon Marshall's, Leslie Edwards's. Leigh's voice echoed in his tired brain: 'Yours...only yours...'

His brother's venomous hiss: 'Get away from my son...'

Liam Johnstone's taunt: 'Yer ain lot'll git ye, Anderson...'

Michael Johnstone's leer: 'Gie that wee cracker in yer bed wan fae me...'

Snaking words joined into one thick boa, wrapping around him. His throat burned under the pressure. Jas seized a thin, white neck and began to squeeze. "Leigh..." Metal studs dug into his palm.

The taunts grew louder.

Jas looked down at hard white buttocks, separated by a thin black leather thong. He ripped off the G-string. "Leigh..." His brain was a mass of sound.

Movement beneath him.

Jas released Gary's neck and spread two mounds of muscle. Another voice joined the cacophany of hate, rising to a scream as he pressed an open palm on the back of a cropped, blond head. One, two...then three sweating fingers forced their way into warm, moist flesh.

"No..." Distant, muffled.

Eyes closed, he pushed faces away. They laughed and moved closer, crowding onto his eye-lids. Heat from the single spotlight scorched his left cheek. Dougie's parting gift pulsed on the other. Through gritted teeth, Jas continued to push with his right fist, blocking out the noise in his ears.

"No...."

He edged between sinewy thighs. Thumb slid under index-finger as tensed muscle fought the intrusion. The open palm of his other hand slid on smooth, sweating neck-skin.

"No..."

A different voice. Jas shook his head violently.

Like so much morning mist, the voices dissolved. In their place, a single word repeated, then sobbing.

Jas opened his eyes, withdrew his knuckles.

Gary reeled over, scrambled clumsily to his feet. The blue eyes heaved with fear as he backed away, hands still restrained behind back. A torn leather G-string slipped to the floor. Jas looked at Gary.

Not Leigh...

Eyes scanning for the handcuff keys. Under the spotlight, he found them. With trembling fingers, Jas moved towards the terrified, tear-streaked face.

Gary inhaled and backed further away.

Jas sighed, held up two open hands in apology. "S'okay. Lemme..." Quickly, he reached over and undid the braclets.

The boy rubbed his wrists, then the back of his neck. Shaking voice. "Get out!" Rabbit eyes.

Jas sat down on the bed. Everything was hot and spinning. "Are ye okay, Gary? Ah didney mean tae..."

"Get out!" Gary edged to the door, opened it.

Jas lowered his head and rubbed his temples. "Ah'm sorry."

The boy lifted the biker's jacket and sweatshirt from the bed, tossing them out into the hallway.

Jas looked up at the movement. "Did ah hurt ye?"

Fear became anger. "I'm not into the heavy stuff. Christ! It's just a game! I thought..." Sniff.

A game...game.

Monroe's acid: 'Yer wee game git oota hand, Anderson?'

Jas rose. "Ur ye bleeding? Let me..."

Shriek. "Keep away from me!" More sobbing, then softening. "Just leave – okay?"

Jas walked unsteadily towards the open door. He turned. "Look, Gary. Ah'm sorry. It wizney meant tae happen..."

"Please leave." Quiet. "This was obviously a mistake..."

Jas looked into frightened eyes, then walked from the room.

Outside, the streets were quiet. He slipped the sweatshirt and jacket back on and began to walk. He had no idea how long he walked or in which direction. A few other drunks swerved to avoid him, cursing in low, resentful tones.

He walked on.

The beginnings of a hangover crept up on him: head achy, legs lead, breath sour. Hot sweat cooled on an icy body. Ignoring the drumbeat in his temples, Jas walked on 'til he saw green. He strode towards it, glancing at his watch. Digits flashed in more green. Raising wrist to face, he made out 2am. Then a fence, secreted within a thick hedge. Jas scrambled over it, tearing jeans on a vicious iron spike. Lumbering through a thicket of trees, he walked on until the sounds of cars and the gleam of street lights faded. He sat down beside a prickly-looking bush.

Within seconds, he was asleep.

Something made him start. A loud, booming sound, rhythmic. Eyes flashing open, light poured in. Jas groaned, tried to stand up. He wobbled and sat down again. He looked around. Marble and granite obelisks shone in dappled sunshine.

The booming continued, from beyond the trees.

Somehow he always ended up in cemeteries. This one looked well-kept and prosperous.

As his ears focused, the booming became tolling, ringing.

This cemetery had a church – a functioning one.

Jas glanced at his watch: 6.50. Early mass.

The bell rang on.

He got up and walked slowly to the trees. Through branches, he caught the outline of a red brick, domed building. A few people were making their way through a distant gate towards the structure. Pausing at a table-shaped marble monument, Jas watched them, then closed his eyes and sat down.

The remnants of a dream meandered through his mind.

Leigh...with cropped blond hair, minus nipple-rings. A seedy bedsit. Warlock Road? One spotlight...

Throat clearing above him: "I'm sorry, my friend, but you can't stay here..." Apologetic.

Jas opened his eyes.

A cassocked figure. Young, worried-looking.

Jas smiled. "Where is here?"

Cassock took a step back, looked more worried.

Jas laughed. "It's no' a philosophical question, Father! Ah got lost last night, woke up...?"

"Brompton Oratory." Weak smile. "You're in the grounds of Brompton Oratory. Private property, I'm afraid..."

"Thanks, Father." Jas stood up. "That's all ah needed to know." He made his way past the bemused rector to the iron gates.

At the tube station, Jas found a cafe. He drank three cups of black coffee. In the cramped toilet, he surveyed himself in a cracked mirror. Blood-shot doppelganger eyes blinked back from above the bruised cheekbone, which was now yellowing. Filling the dirty hand-basin with cold water, he submerged his head twice, then dried his face and hair with paper towels. Jas consulted the mirror a second time: much the same. He brushed down jeans and returned to his table.

After another coffee, he pulled out the 'A to Z' and a letter. He looked at his watch: 8.30am.

Thrusting money at the waitress, he walked out into a London Sunday morning and what Harry could tell him about Leigh.

Twenty-One

JAS STARED at the monolith of 6 Northbank Road, Walthamstow.

Tower block.

Harry's letter gave no surname or flat number.

On the fourteenth floor, after trying eight Hs – most of whom had been black – he was losing patience. Jas scowled at another neat, freshly-painted door, on which a small brass plate proclaimed 'H. Roberts'.

He knocked for the ninth time. It was 9.45am.

Seconds later, the door swung open. White, slightly-built man, early forties. Soft, gentle baby face framed by receding sandy hair. Navy shell-suit. "Yes?"

Jas leant against the door-frame. "Harry? I'm a friend of Jason's..."

The phrase had done nothing for eight previous Harries. This time, a response.

Baby-Face glanced warily over one shoulder into the flat, then moved forward, closing the door behind himself. Back to Jas: "I don't know any Jason." Feigned nonchalance, door handle in hand.

The letter to Leigh pulsed in his pocket, words committed to memory:

> My only one,
>
> I know I won't see you until next week, and it hurts so much. I don't know if I can last without you, without your sweet mouth, your sweet cock teasing me...

Jas took a step towards the slight figure. "Let's not play games, Harry. I need some information."

Baby-faced bluster. "Don't know what you're talking about. I..." Behind, the door opened.

Baby-face fell backwards, flapping for balance.

A woman in a loud, floral dressing-gown steadied him. Thirtysomething. Dark hair. Tired-looking face. Pushing past Harry, she studied the doormat sullenly, then: "Bring the papers in when that bloody kid finally gets around to delivering them, will you Harry?" Inquisitive glance at Jas.

Baby-faced panic. "Yes, Miriam...no problem."

Miriam paused, frowning, waiting...to be introduced?

Jas stared.

Baby-face found baby-voice. "Work-stuff, Miriam. I'll be in soon."

With a shrug, Miriam backed into the flat.

Harry reclosed the door in her wake.

Silence.

Jas took it, broke it. "Good-looking woman..."

"Cut the crap! Leave her out of this..." Baby-face all grown up.

Jas shrugged. "I'm not here to cause any trouble, Harry. What you do is your affair." Noise on concrete steps. Jas turned. Folded bundle thrown at his feet. Back view of a young, baseball-capped boy. Jas lifted the news-paper and handed it to Harry. "I'm trying to trace Jason Nicols. I'm aware of your relationship with him. Jason left London a little over two years ago. Any idea why?"

Angry Baby-face. "No..."

"Come on, Harry..." Jas sighed.

"It was all a long time ago. I don't want to talk about it – okay? Now, please go..."

Jas tutted. "Ah can't do that, Harry, not until ah find out more about Jason..."

"That...!" Baby-rage. "If he's sent you down here..." Baby-splutter closed baby-mouth.

Jas edged forward. Leigh cold on an autopsy tray flashed before his eyes. "Jason didn't send me, Harry. He doesn't know I'm here. Tell me what you know about..."

"What's your interest in him, anyway?" Baby-faced curiosity cut him off.

Jas took a chance. "Nothing to what your wife's will be, if she finds out. Still fielding for both sides, Harry?"

Pale, baby-faced fear. "You don't understand..."

He did understand...only too well. two lives, never meeting. Double strain, double lies...

Baby-face crumbled wordlessly.

Empathy stirred in Jas. He couldn't afford the emotion. Staring at the baby-faced shell, he scowled. "Okay, Harry. Let's start at the beginning. You met Jason Nicols...?"

Compliant sigh, the baby-puff knocked out of him. "On the Tube. I was on my way home from work..."

"Your work is...?"

Scowl. "Customs and Excise. Heathrow. Jason picked me up..."

"When was this?"

"Two, two and a half years ago..."

The letter from Harry to Leigh read very differently from the way the man sounded now. Another abandoned lover, or was there more? "The relationship lasted...?"

Shrug. "Six months." Worried. "Why do you want to know...?"

"My business, Harry. Just like what you do is yours." He stared at the man, then the door behind him. From inside, sounds of a radio. "Why did Jason end the relationship?"

The warning was enough. "He met someone...special." Eyes

narrowing.

"Name?"

Head shake. "No idea..."

"Know where I can find this...someone special, Harry?"

Scowl. "No, and I don't want to..." Avoiding eyes.

Jas frowned. "Ye're a bad liar, Harry." He began to crack his fingers. "Ah don't like liars..."

Leigh lied.

Harry flinched. "Okay, okay! Jason went up north with him."

"Where, exactly?"

"Just north – somewhere in Scotland, it seems. Jason's not here any more and that's all that matters."

Jas smiled. "That's better, Harry. See whit ye can dae when ye put yer mind tae it! Keepin' tabs on Jason, were ye? Didney like the idea o' sharin' him?"

"No, it isn't that...or it wasn't, back then." Ashamed. "I followed him – I'm on shift work, you see. Jason used to be... accommodating, fit in with my schedules. Then he said he could only see me during the day, said he'd got a job. I didn't believe him..." Anger tinged with shame. "Christ, I was jealous! I followed him from the Warnock Road bedsit one night, to see where he...worked – turned out to be a hotel up west..."

"The Kensington Park Hotel?"

"Could've been..." Pause. "Yes, the big one at Hyde Park. Anyway, I saw Jason go into the foyer, saw exactly what kind of work he was doing! He met the same guy three nights in a row..."

"Did you get a look at this other guy?"

Head shake. "Grey hair and a suit – that's all I took in. Jason came clean, when I confronted him later – I'll say that much for him! – said the guy was Scottish, that it was the...real thing, and he'd asked Jason to, you know, move up there with him..." The baby-face was near to exploding.

Jas clenched his fists. "Did he tell you anything else about this guy?"

"No...at first I thought he was a tourist, then what with Jason only meeting him at night, I presumed he was down on business – a conference, sales rep or something like that..."

"When was all this, exactly?"

Thoughtful, then: "January...yes, January."

Six months before Jas met Leigh.

"And Jason left London...?"

Angry. "Same month...and good riddance!" Hate ballooned from the pink baby-face.

Jas studied the contorted features. Behind the loathing, baby-blue eyes, something else was lurking. He removed Harry's letter to Leigh from his pocket, held it out. "This is your property..."

Harry took it, read it. Shock. "How did you...?"

"Where was the letter sent?"

"Warnock Road – the bedsit." Baby-face twisted. "How did you get this?"

Jas frowned. "Ever hear from Jason again, more recently...or see him?"

Baby-stiff. "No. Now tell me..."

"Ever been to Glasgow, Harry?"

Laugh. "Why would I want to do that? What's in Glasgow?"

A dead body. Jas closed the gap between himself and Harry, towering over the baby-body. "Are ye sure Jason didney contact you again?" He scowled.

Baby-face gasped. "No, no. I never heard from him. Did Jason send you? Please tell me..."

"Jason's dead, Harry." There was definitely something else here, something behind the baby-mask. He watched the baby-face closely.

Something – relief? – edged into the eyes.

Jas seized it. "Tell me the rest, Harry."

"Nothing to tell, not now..." Baby-fingers calmly tore the love-letter into tiny pieces. Harry stepped forward and tossed the fragments over the fourteenth-floor balcony.

Scraps of a dead relationship scattered in the wind. Jas watched the remnants of a man's love flutter helplessly to the ground.

When he turned back, Harry was gone. Jas pounded on the front door until the neighbours appeared.

He scowled.

The neighbours disappeared.

He kicked the door. "Thanks fur yer time, Harry..." Jas walked slowly towards the stairs.

On the train into Central London, he found a corner seat and looked at the floor. Three ex-lovers.

Leslie Edwards. Security guard, in the army when Leigh met him. Abandoned early one morning, three years ago. Still smarting.

Leon Marshall. Investment banker and part-time major in the TA. Abandoned equally suddenly, six months later. Despite Billy's best efforts, still smarting.

Harry Roberts. Customs officer. Bi...or closeted. Abandoned two years ago. Harry seemed to be relieved when he discovered Leigh was dead. Seething, not smarting.

The letter from 'G', dated February this year, had been sent from the same hotel where Leigh had met the man whom he left London with, two years earlier.

Coincidence? Jas frowned. His brain lurched in sync with the tube train.

Grey hair, suit...businessman?

Hotel records. If not a name, then dates of conferences.

The train slowed.

He stood up, getting out at Oxford Circus. On sunny Regent Street, he shivered and hailed a taxi. Three drove by, then one stopped. To the driver: "Kensington Park Hotel." Might as well arrive in style.

The cab moved off. In the back seat, Jas fumbled with the police-mask, rehearsing more lies.

The driver locked eyes with him, in the rear-view mirror: "Heavy night, man?" Young, black, grinning.

Jas scowled. "Ah look that bad?"

Easy laugh. "'Pends who you wanna impress, man..."

He needed to impress a receptionist enough to see guest records.

Eyes in the mirror, peering. "Don't I know you?"

Jas tucked sweatshirt into jeans, ran a hand through sticky hair. Outside, London flicked by, unreal as a comic-book. "Don't think so. Ever bin to Glasgow?"

"Nope. Manchester, once." Studied gaze. "You famous?"

Jas laughed.

The driver grinned. "That's it. You're in movies – right? I know the voice..."

"Ah'm no one, pal..." Jas rubbed his face. It was rough beneath rough fingers. He rehearsed more lies.

"Don't dis me, man. I know that face..." Eyes back on the road. "It'll come to me." Sigh. "You stayin' at The Park?"

"No' exactly..."

"Dropped a coupla suits off there, last night. Maybe that's where I..."

"Look, pal..." Jas leant forward. "You dinney ken me: ah dinny ken you. Let's lea' it at that, okay?"

Huffy. "Sure, man, sure..."

Silence descended.

Jas stared out the window as the cab pulled up in front of a tall, glassy structure. Bright sunshine glanced off chrome spars. Beneath, four broad concrete steps led up past an avenue of neat bay trees to a large entrance. On the bottom step, a doorman lurked. Jas sighed.

The taxi slowed to a halt. Jas got out.

"Four-fifty, man..."

Jas produced a fiver. "Keep the change..." He thrust the note through the rolled-down window.

Grinning. "Thanks..."

He stared to walk away.

"Man?"

Jas paused, turned.

A pen and paper thrust through the open window; "For when I place that face..."

He walked the few steps back to the cab, wrote: 'Jim Taggart' on a note-pad, then held it out.

Beaming. "All-right, man!"

Jas waved and walked towards the entrance.

The interior of the Kensington Park Hotel: air-conditioned cool, crowded. No one gave him a second glance as he walked up to a long, fake-marble reception counter. Behind, figures of both sexes in identical white-shirt, blue-crested-tie uniforms efficiently answered phones and dealt with guests.

Jas propped himself against the counter and waited. Lifting a leaflet, he debated joining American Express. To his left, a Japanese guy was arguing with a harassed-looking man, who wore a badge in bold blue letters proclaiming him Assistant Manager. To his right, two middle-aged women in tweeds were inquiring tentatively about the vegetarian menu. Jas replaced the leaflet and stared straight ahead. Left hand into pocket, fingering warrant card. Eventually:

"Sorry to keep you, sir. How can I help?" Pre-rehearsed, tinkling.

Jas lowered his stare.

Young girl. Late teens. The blue tie askew, pink cheeks flushed. Light brown hair, neatly secured behind neck. Name-badge read 'Angie Berger'. White teeth bared in professional smile.

He produced the warrant card and a practised smile of his own. "Good morning, Ms. Berger. DS Anderson – Hammersmith Police. I'd like a word with the manager."

Glance at the warrant card, then eyes back to Jas. Grin, raised eyebrows, then sigh. "Mr. Simpson's not here at the moment and..." Head sideways at the Japanese man. "...Mr. Nathan's busy. Can I help?" Genuine, not pre-rehearsed.

He returned the grin. "I'm inquiring about a man who stayed with you in January two years back and again in February this year."

Worried look.

He smoothed it away with the police-lies. "No big deal, Ms. Berger. Car theft. We just need to establish whether the gentleman did in fact stay here when he claims he did. If I could have a look at your records for those two months..."

'G' and Leigh nudged their way into his thougts.

'G' and Leigh together, in a room floors above. Jas frowned, closed his eyes.

Relieved laugh. "No problem, DS Anderson..."

Jas opened his eyes.

Angie Berger turned to a VDU screen and began to tap. Then chatter. "You're Scottish, aren't you?"

He looked at the Japanese guy, caught the Assistant Manager's eye, looked away. "Yes, Glasgow..."

Angie Berger continued to tap, head down. "Friend of mine did her training in Glasgow, at the Albany. Nice place – not as big as The Park, of course." Pause, head still down. "Awful about that murder up there, last week. A policeman, too..." Chatty, unconcerned.

He tensed. "A policeman was murdered?"

More taps. "No...a policeman killed someone. Thought you would've known..."

Jas gripped the smooth counter, blinking. He stared at the floor.

Obliging: "Now, Detective Anderson. I've got the months on-screen. Do you know the days, or even the week this man stayed with us...?"

"What's the problem, Ange?" Another voice, man.

Jas looked up.

Assistant manager. Professional smile.

Angie, natural smile: "No problem, Mr. Nathan." Turning from the screen, gesturing. "This is Detective Anderson..."

Jas extended the warrant card.

Nathan took it, examined the card, then Jas. Frown.

Angie talked on, hushed tones. "It's about a car theft, Mr. Nathan. DS Anderson wants to..."

"You're a long way from home, officer..." The Assistant Manager coolly fingered the card. "...what can we do for Strathclyde Police?" Suspicious eyes bored into him.

Angie, confused. "I thought you said Hammersmith...?"

"Good morning, Mr. Nathan." The police-mask felt insecure. Jas tried to smile. It froze, half-formed. "I'm inquiring about a guest who stayed with you in February..."

"Excuse us a moment, DS Anderson..." Cold, distant. Still holding the warrant card, Mr. Nathan took Angie by the arm and pulled her away from the screen. He touched the keyboard, briefly. They huddled, his hand still on her arm. Whispering. Glances over shoulders.

Jas frowned. He leaned over the counter towards the VDU.

'G'.

He had to know.

A cursor winked on an otherwise blank screen.

He looked at the Angie/Assistant Manager huddle, straining to hear.

Nothing.

He drummed fingers on the smooth, polished surface of the reception desk, then turned and scanned the foyer. A few feet away, a burly man in jeans and T-shirt was reading a tabloid, face hidden. Jas stared at the front page.

A familiar head-shot stared back. Two years youngers, shorter hair, face expressionless in the photographer's flash.

The same face as on his warrant card.

The warrant card still held by the Assistant Manager. Instinct prickled on his spine: the press conference, Andy Clark's words: 'Sloan's issuing a statement in time for the Sunday papers...'

Including the nationals, apparently.

He focused on a headline, strobing cheap ink on cheaper paper: 'Cop Sought in Brutal Slaying.'

He walked quickly out through the hotel doors.

Shimmering sunshine hurt his eyes. Jas slowed his pace, strolling out of the driveway and onto what looked like a main road.

No one followed.

He walked past a large park. Children played, families wandered carelessly amidst dappled sunlight. He tore his eyes from them and scowled.

Fuckin' warrant card. Using it was a mistake.

Jas sighed and walked on. 'G' had eluded him. For the moment...

At Hyde Park Corner station, he bought a paper from a gnarled, hatted vendor. On the first train to appear, he digested words. They didn't make appetising fare, but probably sold well.

Jas stared at his photograph, then stuffed the newspaper down the side of a seat. London was no longer anonymous, nor useful. No more letters, no more lovers.

'G' and Leigh had moved north.

Jas clenched his fists. So would he...

Glasgow. Marie.

He remembered the small figure making sandwiches, washing his tired body, drying his hair. He remembered her flat, her voice: 'Look efter yersel', Big Man...'

As the train pulled away from another station, he knew he needed help. Between Marie's street nose and Andy Clark's access to the police computer, 'G' could not escape him.

Jas had dates, a physical description of sorts, and a letter. He glanced at a smeary wristwatch: 1.46. Homesickness washed over him in waves.

How frequently were shuttles to Glasgow?

He closed his eyes and dozed to Heathrow. Images of Leigh and a faceless grey man waltzed on his eyelids.

An hour later, he wandered through Terminal Three in search of British Midland: an hour after that, in Terminal One, he found it.

A freckly redhead coolly informed him the first available seat was on the 20.30 flight. Reluctantly, using his last eighty pounds, Jas booked, giving the name Jason Nicols.

Four hours to kill. Had staff at The Kensington Park Hotel called the police yet? Undoubtedly.

At a cashline machine, he emptied his account. He knew the

transaction would be registered, could be traced. But who was to say he'd returned to Glasgow? Britain was a big place.

In a gift shop, the stink of his own sweat strong in his nostrils, Jas bought an XL 'I ♥ London' T-shirt and a black baseball cap bearing no legend.

In the toilet, he stripped off the Lonsdale sweatshirt and binned it, then washed face, hair and torso with evil-smelling soap. He was attempting to dry himself under an automatic hot-air stream when the door opened.

Jas glanced up. A business-suit glanced away and entered one of the cubicles.

Turning the 'I ♥ London' T-shirt inside out, Jas struggled into it. It was too short. He tucked the hem into jeans and peered in the mirror.

Skin on cheekbone yellow and puffy.

Still DS James Anderson.

He pulled on the baseball cap, then the biker's jacket. He looked back at the mirror.

DS James Anderson was gone.

Jas scowled. A surprisingly youthful, pink face scowled back.

Jas left the toilet, bought a book and a coffee and settled down to wait.

Twenty-Two

THE EIGHT-THIRTY shuttle to Glasgow was too busy, too cold and the seats were too small. Cramped in the corner by a tiny window, Jas changed position for the nineteenth time and tried to get comfortable. He pulled the biker's jacket more tightly around his body. The T-shirt had come loose from the jeans again. He tightened his belt another notch and tucked it back in. As he changed position for the twentieth time, the jersey snaked free. He sighed and gave up. On the pull-down table in front of him, congealing chicken. His stomach contracted and he looked away.

His fellow-passengers seemed engrossed in cellophane-wrapped business reports. Businessmen to a man.

Was this how 'G' travelled?

Jas closed heavy eyelids and tried to sleep. His mind heaved with unanswered questions.

Leigh's three ex-lovers were unrelated points on a map. It was trite to think of types, but none conformed to any. What had attracted Leigh to them, what linked them...apart from Leigh?

Leon Marshall was well-off: the other two weren't.

Leslie Edwards was butch: the other two weren't.
Harry Roberts was married: the other two...
"Something to drink, sir?"
Eyes blinking open, Jas stared at the steward. Late twenties, good muscle-tone under the British Midland cabin-crew garb...Something clicked.
Uniforms.
Leslie Edwards – security guard, ex-army.
Leon Marshall – major in the TA.
Harry Roberts – customs officer.
The steward met his stare, misinterpreting its intensity, and smiled. Low voice. "Can I get you anything, sir?"
Jas looked away. "Vodka."
Uniforms: a link.
"Straight?"
Jas winced at the remark and shook his head. Alcohol was a bad idea. His brain was fuzzy enough. "Make that an orange-juice..."
The steward reached over, placing a small bottle and a plastic glass on the pull-down table. He looked at the chicken-mess, then Jas. "Finished?"
Jas smiled. "Aye. Take it away..."
The steward removed the meal and moved off, glancing back only once.
Drinking from the bottle, a new picture formed in his head.
Uniforms...Leigh liked uniforms. A common enough fantasy.
But Leigh had never mentioned it. Jas clenched his fists.
Richard Beatie.
'G'...
Leigh had never mentioned a lot of things...
Another potential piece in the puzzle. 'G' could be uniformed...
Jas looked out the tiny window. Below, Paisley's dirty underskirts flared up through dusk and cloud wisps, grey on darker grey.
"Ladies and gentlemen, we are now approaching Glasgow Airport. Please fasten your seat-belts and extinguish all cigarettes..." The steward's practised tones.
Jas gulped the last of the orange-juice, closed his eyes and fastened his seat-belt. As the plane began its descent, citrus burned in his throat. Blindly, he located a sick-bag and used it.
When he opened his eyes, the plane was stationary.

Thirty minutes later, he sat in a taxi. He looked at his watch: almost ten. The driver burbled on about a murder and a nation-wide manhunt.
Jas pulled the baseball cap further down and tried to think.
Andy Clark and the police computer could gain remote access to the Kensington Park Hotel's records. That would give him names...but

how many?

There were two dates.

Only one name should surface.

But then what?

There was nothing to suggest 'G' had anything to do with Leigh's death.

Jas scowled.

There was nothing to suggest he hadn't...

Hutchie 'E' was larger than life, as the taxi pulled into Queen Elizabeth Square. Jas paid the driver with an English £20 note and got out, patting a side zip pocket. Marie's keys were still there. Breathing in yeasty, distillery air, tinged with chemical fumes, he walked towards the flats.

It wasn't raining, but had been until recently. Fresh, oily puddles squeaked beneath the biker's boots as he crossed cracked tarmac and began to climb stairs. An unfamiliar sensation pattered in the pit of his stomach, a parody of another.

Anticipation?

The same feeling he'd known, returning to Eastercraigs after a hard shift.

Returning from the Blue to the blond.

Returning to home ground, to Leigh...

Relief.

Jas scowled and continued to climb.

Keys in hand, he paused for breath outside Flat 5 on the 16th floor. Out of courtesy, he reached through the security gate and knocked once.

No answer.

He remembered the code, used it.

No answer.

Hand shaking, he inserted a key. As he undid the final lock, a chain was unchained inside.

Tension in his stomach began to ebb away.

After London, after Dougie, after two days in a foreign land it was good to be...where?

Home?

He frowned: this wasn't his home, never would be. But Marie was the nearest thing to a friend he had left...

As the door opened, he stepped forward.

Hair pulled back in a tight knot, full make-up, long leather coat over tiny body. In the dark hallway, she moved back, allowing him entry.

He walked towards the lounge.

Marie closed the door and followed.

More darkness. Despite the bravado, he wondered if the scar

ever bothered her. The woman never used a light if she could help it. In the dim room, he sat down and looked around.

Leather sofas, soundless TV picture, overflowing ashtray, empty vodka bottle, closed venetians.

He smiled. Safety in the familiar. He leant back.

Marie sat down.

He peered at her through the gloom. "So? How's it goin'?"

Shrug of thin shoulders. "Ye're back, then..."

He laughed. "Looks like it, eh?"

She stood up and walked to the window, opened the blinds an inch, then closed them.

He took off his jacket, then the cap and T-shirt. His scalp itched. "How's things been up here?" He scratched.

Another shrug. "Okay."

"Ony chance o' a shower, Marie?"

She turned, looked at him. Curious. "Whit happened tae yer face?"

Jas touched the bruised cheek-bone and grinned. "Ma brother's way o' tryin' tae kill the fatted calf. It's nothing'..." Eyes focusing in the darkness, he noticed a purplish bruise on her cheek, just above the scar. "Who've you been annoyin'?"

She perched on the small table and lit a cigarette. In the quivering flame of a match, two yellow, red-rimmed eyes met his, then looked away. She sniffed.

Jas got up and moved to the table. "Whit's happened?"

Junkies never cry.

Lowered head. Quiet voice. "Nothin', Big Man. It's no' bin wan o' ma best weekends, that's aw'..." Half-laugh, then rushed words, head up. "Noo, how did ye get oan in London? Wiz yer brother pleased tae see ye?" Wandering around the room.

Jas followed with his eyes, frowning. Something was...different. He shivered. Maybe he was different. Maybe talking to guys, other guys in the same position as himself had...what? His body stank. "Ah'll tell ye aw' aboot it after ah've washed – deal?" He began to unbuckle biker's boots. His stomach grumbled, empty like his mind was empty. "Christ, ah could eat a horse!" Standing, he unzipped jeans and pulled them off. Tired muscle trembled naked in his thighs.

At his side: "You lost weight, Big Man? Ye look..."

"Didney eat much in London...." Jas rubbed his face. "...ye ken ah canny stomach foreign food!"

A weak smile shimmered on the pale face. "Listen, Jas – want a fish supper? Ah've got tae go oot onyway..." Uncertain. "Ah've got tae..." Voice quivering.

The shakes?

He didn't care. Couldn't care.

"Want tae come with me? Ye look like ye could dae wi' some

fresh air after the flight..." Nervous.

Jas laughed. "Ah want a shower an' a sleep, Marie. Oan ye go..."

Jaundiced eyes met his. "Dae ye understand, Jas? Ah dinny want tae..."

"Christ!" She wasn't making sense. "Ah've seen ye shoot up before – whit's the big deal?"

Marie seized his hand, squeezed it hard, then walked to the door. "Ah'll no be long, Jas..."

"Make that a coupla fish suppers, eh?"

No response.

Seconds later, the door banged shut.

In the silent flat, he began to exercise.

After twenty minutes his arms gave way, buckling beneath him. His body was stiff and sore. He managed forty sit-ups before stomach-cramps set in. He lay on his back until the pain subsided then walked through to the kitchen.

No glasses.

He looked through overhead cupboards then under the sink. At the back, behind an economy-sized Domestos bottle lay a broken syringe. Jas shrugged: Marie was running low. He drank from the tap, wiped his mouth and headed for the shower.

Under soothing hot water, behind the cheap green curtain he soaped aching limbs. Fuck! He was getting soft: taxis, a disaster of a work-out, warm showers...

Tomorrow would be different. After a good meal and a sleep he'd be back on top.

On top of 'G'.

Glowing under lather, Jas washed his hair. As he rubbed at matted tufts with rough fingers, waves of tension washed from his body in a tide of suds. He closed his eyes.

Leigh was a distant pinprick, stabbing vainly at his heart. More important matters concerned Jas now. His photograph was in the newspapers, no doubt on TV too. It was a miracle he had made it from the airport unspotted. He knew he couldn't leave this flat, not until 'G' was more than an anonymous initial.

Andy Clark could arrange that. Jas knew he should phone now, get things moving. But the warm, comfortable shower weakened him.

Like Leigh's lies had weakened him...

Through the running water, he heard the front door open, then close. He smiled.

Marie hadn't been long. He wondered vaguely where she scored, these days. Obviously somewhere close. Shampoo ran into his eyes, stinging sharply.

He blinked, tilting his face upwards to meet the flow.

The stinging continued. "Marie? Geez a towel, eh?" He rubbed at smarting eyes with a soapy hand.

Something hard and heavy hit the back of his skull.

Sparks shone before stinging eyelids, then faded to grey. No pain. Only surprise. Jas staggered forward, clutching at the shower-curtain. As the rail collapsed, wet fabric draped around him, sheathing his body in slippery, clammy PVC.

Another blow, glancing off shoulder.

This time pain, shuddering down his spine. He fell back against the cubicle wall, clawing at fabric. He opened his eyes. A green, fishy pattern swam amongst tiny stars. "Marie?"

More pain. Head again. A black hole opened up before him. He pushed it away and tried to stand up. The PVC shower-curtain clung to him. "What the fuck...?"

"The junkie slag'll no' help ye now, ya bastard!" Low voice, gruff. Not Marie's.

The cubicle shook as something heavy connected with its frame.

Another voice. "Fuck! Git a hold o' him, Angus. Ah canny see whit ah'm dain'."

On the shower floor, Jas shook his head, thrashing in the PVC shroud. Three blows rained down. Twisting, he managed to deflect the last two with one arm. With the other, he finally found a rent in the curtain and widened it.

Legs...three sets. Work boots. Something wooden.

The baseball bat was raised by a brawny, brown-encased arm, poised above his head.

Jas's ear sang a strange song, behind which snatches of angry conversation came and went like a chorus.

As the baseball bat fell, he darted forward and pushed at a pair of legs. A muffled crack echoed in the confined space. Jas watched as a man's skull contacted heavily with the bathroom wall. Thrusting the shower-curtain away, he surveyed the scene.

Three men. One on the floor, face down, the others standing over him, mumbling. Inches away, the baseball bat.

Three large men. Black heads. Two shouting, shaking. The one on the floor silent, motionless.

As he clambered from the shower-cubicle, the two turned.

Ski-masks. Holes for eyes and mouth.

Jas lurched for the bat, but the larger of the men was quicker. The bat was snatched and held firmly.

Through the fog in his head, Jas scanned for a weapon.

The one with the bat growled. "Come oan, then, tough guy. Let's see ya take oan somewan yer ain size..." Moving slowly, like a fighter.

Jas circled, naked, vulnerable. Pain pulsed down one arm. He had to get out, or...

Baseball-Bat moved towards the door, closing it with a foot and a hollow laugh.

Jas backed away into a low shelf. Bottles tinkled. He reached behind, searching. His hand brushed plastic, spare toilet-rolls then something more solid.

From the side, a gloved hand seized his neck, pushing his head back.

From the floor, moaning.

Baseball-Bat glanced down. "Ya bastard!" He moved quickly for a big man, then stopped.

As pressure on his windpipe increased, Jas elbowed Gloved-Hand hard in the ribs.

A grunt.

Eyes never leaving Baseball-Bat, Jas threw one fist back into Gloved-Hand's face.

Crunch, then another grunt, muffled now. The gloved hand slid from his neck.

Fumbling, Jas grabbed a stocky bottle from the shelf, smashing it off the wall.

A sweet, sickly odour filled the cramped space.

Jas grinned, glancing at the broken perfume flagon in his right hand. Between them, he and Oscar de la Renta couldn't fail. He waved the stub of heavy glass before Baseball-Bat's masked face. "Git oota here, pal, before we both dae somethin' we'll regret..."

"Oh, ye'll regret it aw' right..."

Something hit the side of his head. A fist. Jas swayed, punch-drunk, then turned.

Gloved-Hand was back in action.

Jas raised the remnants of 'Oscar'. Vision blurring badly, his arm seemed to move in slow motion. He blinked rapidly, trying to speed it up. In a series of freeze-frames, he watched the shard of glass circle away from Baseball-Bat, unimpeded, and rip diagonally up through Gloved-Hand's ski-mask. Tight black wool parted like lips, bisected.

He brought his hand down, slashing again.

The man's scream ricocheted off the walls to join the singing in Jas's ears. He watched as two gloved hands attempted to cover the jagged cut, from which blood was pouring onto a green, ex-army jacket. A new, coppery smell tinged with fresh sweat mingled with the overpowering stench of perfume. Jas coughed and spat.

A thud on his shoulder.

Adrenalin pounded through Jas's veins as he swung round quickly enough to grab the bat, wrenching it free of a hand dotted with red hairs. Bloody 'Oscar' slipped from his fingers.

Somewhere on the floor behind, Gloved-Hand was still screaming.

Breathing heavily, Jas gripped the bat with both hands and prodded the man in the chest. "Whit did ah ever dae tae you, pal?"

The big man's green eyes darted from Jas to his two accomplices and back again. Hoarse, surprised voice. "Said it'd be easy..."

Jas hit him in the stomach. "Who said it'd be easy?" As the large head lolled forward, Jas reached over and pulled off the ski-mask.

A shock of ginger hair topped a freckled face.

Jas stared. A familiar face. "Ah ken you, pal..." His own voice died in the bathroom, like words under water. The small space was silent now, apart from the sound of laboured, wheezing breath. Jas lowered the furry toilet-seat and sat down before he fell down.

Freckled face and ginger fringe. Intensive Care. The oil-rigs. Jas looked up at spiky red stubble.

Low voice. "Get oan wi' it..."

Jas sighed, seized a handful of hair and yanked the head sideways.

The pink, panting face strained with anger and frustration. Felix Hunter's eyes were dead, stagnant puddles. "Ye kilt ma wee brother, pal. Ye may as well kill me..."

Still holding the baseball bat, Jas stood up, his body smeared with blood, sweat and expensive scent. He stared at the crouching, defeated figure. "Ah don't know who ye think ah am, pal, but ah want tae."

Felix Hunter massaged his stomach.

Jas scowled. "How did ye ken ah wis here?"

Loathing. "Got a phone-call at hame, an oor ago. Said they wur polis, that wan o' the bastards that..." Crumpled mouth unable to speak the word. "...that hurt Jo wis livin' here wi' some tart..." Eyes hard, hating. "You were at the trial, pal, ah recognised ye straight away."

Jas sighed. "Ye're right – ah wis at the trial. But ah'm a cop – ah found Jo, ah wis giein' evidence against Jimmy and his mates, Felix..."

"Oh Christ!" The man fell silent.

Jas stared. "This phone-call...did ye git a name?"

Head shake. Low voice. "Look, pal. Ah'm sorry fur aw' this, it's jist..." The freckled face twisted.

A boy was dead.

Two boys were dead.

Jas understood.

A moan.

Jas looked down at the floor. Another of his would-be assailants was coming round. A few feet away, Gloved-Hand had stopped screaming and was now pressing a fluffy towel against his ruined face. Jas stood up. "There's a mobile phone aroon' here somewhere, if ye want tae call an ambulance..."

Felix Hunter straightened up and moved towards the prostrate figure. Crouching, he grabbed an arm and heaved the other large man to his feet. "Come oan, Angus. Let's git oota here..."

Jas frowned with cracked lips and rubbed the back of his head. It felt strange, alien. He watched through fuzzy vision as Felix Hunter moved past him, half-carrying, half-dragging Angus. The bathroom was on wheels under his bare feet. Jas followed the pair through the doorway, leant against a wall.

Gloved-Hand brushed against him, mumbled, then staggered into the hall.

Jas focused his rolling mind. Staring at the pulsing remains of Marie's bathroom, he called after the three casualties: "How did yous get in here?" On top of a blood-splattered bathroom, he wasn't looking forward to explaining to Marie how her precious security had been breached, kicked in by three misinformed men. He walked out into the hall.

Felix had stopped just in front of the wrought-iron gate. His companions were nowhere in sight. He looked at Jas, sighed. "Yer door wis open, pal – jist like the guy said it would be. Nae hard feelings, eh?" A hand extended in the gloomy hallway.

Jas stared.

The hand dropped. Quiet words. "Ah'd watch ma back if ah wis you, pal. Somewan oot there disney like ye..." Felix walked away, closing the door, then the gate behind himself.

Jas continued to stare at the solid-core door. Then he turned and walked unsteadily back to the lounge. Rage throbbed in his head, blocking pain.

Automatically, he moved through to the bedroom, opened the wardrobe: empty. He opened a small chest of drawers: empty.

No clothes, no works under the sink. Nothing.

Marie was gone. She did not intend to return. When she had left, Felix and the boys had arrived. Why?

He sat on the rumpled bed and rubbed his face. Why?

Sound rang in his ears.

Why had Marie betrayed him?

In the distance, a different, shriller ringing.

He shook his head. Pain scissored through his skull. Jas clenched his fists. Slowly, the dull ringing subsided, replaced by the high-pitched buzz...from beneath the bed.

He stretched under and located the mobile phone. Pressing the *Answer* button, he held the receiver close to his ear.

Educated, soft tones leaked from the phone: "Well? Is he dead? Is Jas Anderson dead?"

He continued to hold the receiver for several seconds, then laid it down.

Only one person knew this number.

The guy Marie snouted for.

Another cop.

Twenty-Three

IN THE SHAMBLES of a bathroom, bloody shattered glass dug into his bare feet. He ran cold water into the hand-basin. A dull humming had replaced the ringing in his head. Jas gripped cool enamel and closed his eyes.

A rapid tattoo was beating inside him.

He turned off the tap, leant over and plunged his aching head into icy water. Shuddering under the shock, his mind numbed. After twenty seconds, he surfaced gasping, then straightened, shaking thought away in droplets. A black world swayed violently. Jas raised his head and opened his eyes.

An image mocked him from the mirror. He stared, full-faced the challenger. A death-mask: whitened, tight skin over throbbing skull.

He patted his face with a fluffy green towel then sat down on the toilet seat.

The hum in his head was almost tuneful.

Training took over. Tentatively, he began to examine the contours of his skull, shaking fingers starting at forehead and working back. Two inches above his neck, a large soft section. He prodded, then gasped as fissures of agony cracked his spine. More slowly, he continued the self-examination. A couple of lumps, some swelling, nothing serious.

Painstakingly, he rotated his head slowly left, then right. The room shimmered, then stabilised. No stiffness yet, but it would come.

He stretched out his right arm and looked at it through narrowed eyes. The hand trembled. Adrenalin: an old friend. He made a fist, stared at the knuckles, then relaxed.

He raised his left arm. A pale digit wavered before his eyes. Moving finger towards nose, it connected with an eyebrow.

A shiver crept over his scalp, thousands of tiny insects scurrying through his hair. The wave spread down his neck until his whole body shook.

He gripped naked thighs. A light prickling replaced shaking. Someone walked over his grave.

Jas scowled. Someone had tried to dig his grave then push him in.

A cop.

The cop Marie snouted for.

If the police knew his whereabouts...he had to get out of here.

In the lounge, he dressed in slow motion, limbs moving through mud. Marie's TV strobed on oblivious, as he fastened a now-cracked watch to his wrist, then buckled biker's boots.

'G'.

Andy Clark.

On plywood legs Jas walked to the bedroom, punched in London Road police then cancelled the call.

Andy's words: 'Phone me at home...'

He punched another seven digits, waited, counted fourteen rings before disconnecting. He scanned the empty room then stared at the mobile phone.

Marie...

A fist tightened.

She'd sold him out, grassed him up.

Never trust a fuckin' junkie!

He'd deal with her later.

Jas grabbed the baseball cap, thrust the mobile into a pocket then walked from the dim flat down sixteen unlit flights of stairs into blurry dark.

It was almost midnight. He was alone...but he was alive.

The boots were iron-clad, pounding the wet pavement. He walked up Abercromby Street. Occasionally, when the leather jacket made contact, tiny tinkles played up and down his right arm. The soft, pulpy section of his skull pulsed, a new heart to replace the old, broken one. Jas walked on.

He'd worry when it didn't hurt...

In the early hours of Monday morning, he made his way slowly towards his destination. Turning left onto Duke Street, the dark shadow of Monteith's mausoleum loomed up at him in the distance, over the aluminium storage cylinders of Ladywell Brewery. As he approached the entrance, a group of overalled workers breezed through the opening gates. Gruff voices talking, laughing. Shift changeover.

Life went on.

He crossed to avoid them. On the other side of the road he slowed, hearing an engine. It passed. He saw it was a police car, no siren.

Almost parallel now, he watched the car draw up beside the crowd of men. A white-shirted uniform got out, calling to the workers. They paused and one of their number approached the uniform.

Jas's feet dragged. Unheard words exchanged. The large drayman shook his head. The uniform shrugged, turned.

Jas lowered head and quickened pace.

The sound of a slamming door, engine revving. Then the shriek of tyres.

He focused his eyes on Monteith's mausoleum, which was just visible over a group of trees. He walked on, more slowly. Speed attracted attention.

The workers' voices rang in his brain, the only sounds in the still night. At traffic lights, he paused. Red man. The filter from John Knox Street was on. No cars came. Sounds of braking at his side. Then: "'Scuse me, pal..."

A tightening in his guts. Jas began to cross the road.

Car door opened, then closed. Footsteps. "Hey, pal?"

Jas froze, then turned.

White-shirted uniform.

Jas stepped backwards onto the pavement. Leigh, Marie and a faceless grey man draped the approaching figure. He tensed. Too late to run, too late for anything...

"Ye've no' seen a wee dug, ah suppose?" Sheepish grin.

Jas found a voice, not his own. "Whit sorta wee dug?"

The uniform stopped, inches away. Young guy, darkish hair. A stranger. Not 'D' division. "Jack Russell – a wee white thing, wan black eye...?"

Jas sighed. He began to shake his head then thought the better of it. "There wiz a wee dug back there..." He pointed down towards a patch of waste ground. "It wiz white, but ah didney notice ony black eye – bin in a fight, hiz it?" Stomach muscles spasming uncontrollably.

Laugh. "Thanks, pal. A wuman in Coocadens is affy worried aboot it, though how it got away doon here..."

"Nae problem..." He turned to walk away. A glimpse of white car beyond white shirt dazzled him. Motion-sickness spun his head like a top. Jas clutched at the traffic lights.

Distant. "You okay, pal?" Concerned voice.

Jas tried to raise his head, failed. He dry-retched.

"You feelin' okay?" Concerned voice closer now.

Jas wiped stinging lips and straightened up. "A bad pint, ah think ...either that, or the curry."

Understanding grin. "Aye...well, mind how ye go, pal. Guid night..."

Jas released the traffic lights, raised a hand in salute and reeled off up John Knox Street. The parody of drunkenness came too easily. He needed to sleep. The car sped off behind him.

Further up the hill, a smile of relief threatened his lips. Either the cop didn't read station memoranda, or Jas must really look like shit. Not a glimmer of recognition on the man's face. He turned down into Wishart Street. A hundred or so yards ahead, the hole in the fence which would get him off the streets. That time he'd been lucky, but luck wasn't something he'd had a lot of, recently.

Luck was unreliable.

If he was to stay in the open long enough to track down 'G', he'd need more than luck. He'd need sleep...and a plan.

The sound of a car engine.

Jas flattened his body against iron railings, jarring his right arm. Hot needles of agony coursed through his veins.

The car drove past, unheeding. He massaged the damaged limb, found the hole and climbed in.

Long, wet, uncut grass and dark trees welcomed him like a mother: familiar, unquestioning, sheltering. He knew the necropolis well, knew the best places, the secret places.

An ancient gravel path rimmed the perimeter. Under slants of amber street-light, Jas relaxed and began to climb. Ahead, tombstones appeared, jogging memory.

Memories of jogging...

He frowned in the increasing darkness. Necropolis. Necro polis: dead policemen.

He passed the outline of a huge column, topped by a draped urn, and remembered long-gone tobacco barons. A change underfoot: smooth tarmac. He turned left, his footsteps the only sound. Climbing a steep bank, Jas plunged deep into the heart of the dead city. Darkness enfolded him. Grass slithered under his feet. Balance deserting him, he slipped and fell heavily on his left side. He lay panting in the undergrowth, lungs bursting.

Rustlings. Jas tensed. He wasn't alone...

A small brown rabbit bounded from a nearby bush, stared at him with black, trusting eyes before loping off into the distance. Jas smiled, found his feet and continued.

On a rough, pebbled pathway he wandered past rows of glistening granite sarcophagi, up into an avenue of tall obelisks and celtic crosses. He'd had a theory, years ago: headstones as phallic symbols, in inverse proportion. The bigger the splash, the more insecure the incumbent. He glanced up at the towering John Knox monument.

The cool air was clearing his head. A thought burst in before he could stop it. A couple of yards away, Leigh's favourite.

He strolled over. Lights from the hospital filtered through trees. Two mock-verdigrised, cast-iron angels, complete with wings, flanked an imposing headstone. Naked, boyish chests, muscular thighs topped by discreetly draped fabric. Far-from-innocent eyes gazed into each other's faces, wing-tips touching across a name-plaque. Leigh was convinced the sculptor must have been gay.

Jas scowled and walked on. What did it matter? They were both dead now...

Finally, his own favourite. A simple grave. White granite. No fuss, no huge expense, no eulogy. Just a name, two dates and five words: 'Artist, animal lover and mountaineer.'

What you were, not what you did, lived on.

He traced the faded inscription then turned away.

Down a steep, heavily-mossed flight of stone steps, he found what he was looking for: 'their' mausoleum.

Most of the structures in the necropolis were crumbling and damp, destroyed by glue-sniffers and the elements.

Whether due to its position, or the almost impenetrable path which led to it, 'their' mausoleum had survived intact for a century and a half. Leigh had said the architecture was Byzantine-revival. Jas scowled.

Leigh had said a lot of things...

Reaching through spiny bramble briars, he located a rusting, iron door. He pushed, climbed into musty-smelling blackness.

Still water-tight, at least.

Still theirs?

He stared, then blinked rapidly, eyes narrowing in the velvet pitch. Memory, which had been dripping from a crack, now poured through a wide breach.

He had fucked Leigh in this crypt every Sunday for a month. Jas shivered, sat down on the cold, stone floor. The same stone floor where he had lain naked, smoking and watching Leigh dress.

The same stone floor on which they had talked for hours.

The same stone floor on which the lies had started...

Jas scowled. He was wrong to come here, too much of the past...

When there was an uncertain present and a non-existent future, what was left but the past...?

He took off the baseball cap and jacket. The mobile clattered on flagstone, shattering the quiet and chasing Leigh's shadow away. Jas picked up the phone and punched in numbers.

Andy still wasn't home.

He frowned and cancelled the call.

Impotence churned in his stomach. He could do nothing on his own. He needed help.

He'd needed Leigh...

He'd needed Marie...

He needed Andy.

Tomorrow...

He laid himself out on the cold stone, draping the biker's jacket over his chest. He closed his eyes.

Lids fluttered, refusing to stay shut. Adrenalin kept sleep at bay. From outside, little sounds seeped into the echoing tomb, magnified and distorted. Jas knew a couple of homeless kids who had tried camping out here. They'd left after two nights, spooked by the noises. He sighed and tried to relax.

The rustlings were more soothing than the silence.

In silence, the hum inside his head grew. Jas listened to the tiny, external scraps of sound. He moved onto his side, pulling his legs up. He repositioned the jacket. He considered working out, but couldn't face it.

As he concentrated on the activity of his unseen companions, his body began to unwind. He heard rhythms in the scratchings, a code of half-repeated messages. They filled his ears...then faded...

On the periphery of his brain, something stirred.

The guy Marie snouted for...

If the police knew his whereabouts, why hadn't he been arrested? Why had Felix Hunter been sent?

A black pit opened up in front of him, pulling him down and away from questions, beatings, lies...Pulling him to sleep...

Two years ago.

Watching Leigh undress.

Watching Leigh turn to face him. The blond hair shorter then, flopping lazily over one eye...his body slick with sweat. Leigh sprawled across him, face buried in Jas's groin. The sensation of warm nipples, tipped with cool metal, brushing his naked thighs.

Fingers twined around soft blond hair, massaging the scalp. A frisson of pleasure spread up from groin over stomach. Leigh pulling away to watch Jas's orgasm...

Then another vision, more recent. His body helpless under Leigh's, arms pinned to the bed by Leigh's arms, held captive by Leigh's prick, staring up at Leigh.

The handsome face swayed before him, tanned, flawless...

Then faded. Replaced by grey, amorphous tissue. No blood. The reek of formaldehyde. A single shard of bone poking through the mess. One pink lip dangling helpless from a disembodied head, ending in a white sheet, just above collarbones. Cold, fluorescent light bleaching the tanned skin. Vomit rose in Jas's throat. He swallowed and turned away...

Light on his face. Jas blinked. Sunshine leaking in through the heavy iron gate. He grinned, enjoying the warmth. A hand on his forehead, soothing, caressing. A cool soft hand. Then a voice: 'Jas?'

He peered through the light, unable to move, unable to see.

'Jas? Jas?'

Leigh's voice filled his head. He tried to sit up. Muscle rebelled, holding him down. His prick was hard in response in the dreams, the voice. In the distance, the rustlings returned, accompanied by whimperings.

Jas opened his eyes.

Inches away, two yellow pinpricks flashed in the dark.

He turned over onto his right shoulder, inhaled sharply as pain needled his body.

A whine, then whimpering again. Closer now.

Jas resumed his original position. A warm body nestled in at his side. He smiled and sailed back into black...

Cold woke him up. Jas shivered and opened one eyelid. The other remained glued shut.

Daylight...or at least, daygloom.

He tried to move, then stopped and looked down. Not his body, his legs or arms. The jacket had fallen off. A small white dog with one black eye lay curled at his waist. Jas straightened his knees, gasping as cramp spasmed in his thighs.

He knew the cure. Like stripping off sticking-plaster. Closing one eyes, he clenched his fists and wrenched himself upright. Red haze pulsed on his eyelids. He staggered towards a wall, leant against it for support. Under leather and jeans, his body was an open wound. Fire blazed through limbs, making his eyes water.

The sticky lid unstuck itself. Jas blinked, grinned then scowled. Even his mouth hurt. But at least now he had another functioning eye, and a semi-functioning body.

A low growl.

He looked around. The Jack Russell had retreated to a corner, from where it one-eyed him suspiciously.

Propped against the wall, he began to stretch. Starting with legs...

Not too bad. A muscle palpitated in his left thigh, but after several knee-bends even it subsided. Soon, only stiffness remained as a warm glow spread upwards.

The arms were a problem. The left eventually loosened up, but the right refused to move at all. It hung, prosthesis-like, from his right shoulder, alien, outside his control.

He clenched his teeth, tried to make a fist.

Fingers quivered rigid, knuckles refusing to appear. Jas rubbed the bare goose-flesh with his left hand.

It reddened slightly, but remained inert.

"Fuck!"

The oath echoed, then dropped like a stone. He turned swiftly and, using the momentum and the anger, struck the errant limb against a granite wall. Agony exploded in his head as reflex took over. He hugged both arms to his chest. A low, feral growl resounded in his ears. Blood coursed through the damaged arm, banishing stiffness.

Tiny paws on his right leg. Jas looked down. Concern and fear in the canine eyes. The dog stood on two back legs, gazing worriedly up at him.

He smiled, made a soothing noise through dry lips.

The dog resumed four legs and trotted back to the corner.

When his breathing had returned to normal, Jas rotated both arms, raising and lowering his shoulders. He had control...of his body, at least.

Slipping down the wall, he settled in a crouched position and reached for the mobile. As he moved, something tugged at the skin of his lower abdomen. He unzipped jeans and looked down.

Crystals of spunk crested pubic hair, prick and stomach.

Jas scowled. Wet dreams of dead men. At least one member was still fully functioning. He grabbed the mobile and punched in Andy Clark's home number.

After three rings, a sleepy voice: "Yeah?"

Relief overcame the last dregs of pain. "Andy? Ah need another favour..."

Twenty-Four

Jas looked at his watch: 7.53am. Andy had said to phone back about noon. He frowned. Time...everything took time. Too much time, time he didn't have. Even here, in his lair, he was vulnerable. He reached for the biker's jacket and 'G''s letter.

Seven years of CID training etched on his brain. Seven years of logical reasoning. Seven years of the police-mask.

Slowly, the DS in Jas Anderson surfaced.

A plan...A pattern...A profile of 'G'...

He narrowed his eyes and began to read...He stopped twice, as blue script leapt from the page and jigged before him. He closed his eyes, opened them again and held the letter further away. The jig slowed to a sedate two-step, then the dancers stopped completely and became wallflowers. He refocused and read on.

After four readings, he laid the letter of the flagstone floor. He could recite the words from memory, but could not relate them to the picture of 'G' in his head.

Gay or bi: hard to profile.

Partial to pretty boys: so were thousands of others, himself included.

Scottish: so were millions of others, himself included.

The suit: businessman? As opposed to...what – manual worker? Everyone wore a suit at some point – even he wore a suit sometimes. The suit on its own meant nothing.

The hotel: that meant something. There were plenty of hotels cheaper, less flashy that the Kensington Park. 'G' had money, a well-paid job. The letter written in February was dated mid-week, indicating possible business usage. Suited, not uniformed usage.

Two dates. One name should appear, if Andy could gain access to the Kensington Park Hotel's guest records.

The uniform fetish...?

Jas sighed and licked dry lips.

...maybe meant nothing.

The dog, which had been snoozing on his jacket, stirred, stretched and yawned, then padded over to him, leaving faint paw-marks on G's letter.

Gently, Jas lifted the animal one-handed and set it down in his lap. With a damaged right hand, he stroked the smooth coat while brushing dried mud from the letter with his left. Then he stopped.

Peering, Jas examined words from a different angle. He'd seen experts profile personality-type from information concealed in the seemingly random sweep of a pen.

G's writing was formed by small, neat characters, no extravagant swirls. He reached over, fumbled in the pocket of the biker's jacket and produced two other letters.

Edwards's script was tight and controlled. Like the man himself.

Leon's was flowing and florid, like the language in the letter.

Jas looked at G's. By the same logic, what appeared?

An organised man – in the forces, perhaps, like Leslie Edwards? A powerful man, a man used to getting his own way? A man who had found out he was sharing Leigh and, unlike Richard Beatie, took his objections out on the disputed object?

A jealous man? A man who knew how to use a gun?

Anger throbbed in Jas's head. His guts contracted, then rumbled. Hunger, not emotion.

His throat burned. Thirst, not emotion.

Jas looked down. The dog in his lap looked up. He smiled, gripped the warm, relaxed body. "C'moan, boy. Let's git somethin' tae eat." He set the dog down on the floor. The Jack Russell wagged a stump of a tail, then trotted through the open iron gate.

Jas pulled on the baseball cap, eased himself into the jacket and left the mausoleum. It was a little before 9am.

At a fast-food caravan a few yards from the Royal's Accident and Emergency Unit, he waited in line behind two green-gowned figures before buying a hamburger and two bottles of Lucozade. He was suspicious of the unknown meat which lurked between the roll-halves. He studied the pink, grease-smeared substance, then glanced at the munching green-gowns.

Jas shrugged. If sugeons could stomach it...he took a bite, chewed, scowled then spat.

Dog-meat. The Jack Russell darted from between his feet and seized the semi-masticated gobbet. He tossed the rest of the hamburger to the ground, then sat down on a low wall beside a row of ambulances. The dog devoured the meat greedily but left the bun. Jas unscrewed one of the bottles and drank half.

The green-gowns finished their breakfast and went back inside.

Jas drank and watched.

Even on a Monday morning, the results of Sunday night's fun was still evident. Three young men breezed past him, one holding a blood-smeared rag against an eye. His companions talked animatedly, slapping his back.

A solitary, pale-faced youth emerged from swing-doors, arm in sling. A thin girl with a black eye ran after him, sobbing. The youth swore, pushed her away and walked on.

A stocky nurse, one grubby dosser clutched firmly in each fist, appeared: "An' don't come back!" She thrust the coughing, tubercular-sounding bodies from the warmth of the doorway out into damp, morning air.

A diesel engine made him turn.

Two girls in last night's finery scrambled from a taxi, half-carrying another between them. All three were gore-splattered, as blood poured from a recent knife wound in the middle girl's thigh. A taxi-driver shouted after them, wanting to be paid. One turned, cursed him, then walked on.

Leaning back, he watched the weekend warriors come and go. He drank the rest of the Lucozade. The dog sat patiently at his feet, one paw raised.

A passing paramedic approached, crouched and extended a hand towards it. The dog snarled and darted forward, snapping viciously. The man swore, the hand quickly withdrawn, and walked away.

Jas lifted the growling animal, smoothing spiky white hackles. It whimpered and tried to lick his ear. Jas smiled. "Jist you an' me, boy – eh?"

The dog began to wriggle in his grip, struggling. He replaced the Jack Russell on the ground, where it squatted then urinated urgently.

"Sorry...girl." Jas sighed: he was always getting things wrong...He stood up and walked back down John Knox Street to the necropolis. No one glanced twice at the down-and-out with the mangy dog. Jas grinned: he might be down...but he wasn't out.

Within the iron palings, he paced restlessly up and down the streets of the dead. His headache had returned. The dog sniffed a patch of grass then raced ahead, sensing rabbit or fox.

Terriers were hunters, tireless trackers of prey. Once they got a scent, they pursued relentlessly, often until death.

Two hunters. Only one had a fresh trail to follow. But instinct could do only so much. Technology could do more. Jas looked at his watch. Two hours to kill. Ignoring the headache, he began to climb, focusing on his surroundings.

In the 1870s, while thousands starved outside its walls, wealthy dead Victorians and their descendants built marble castles in the air atop this Golgotha. It wasn't enough that they had lived well: they had to die well, too.

Important in life, imposing in death. Jas smiled through pain. As if rusting iron and crumbling sandstone could replace bone and flesh. He paused.

They had problems with their mortality, the Victorians...

His mind drifted back to the Western Infirmary. Jas shivered.

...so what had changed?

A white bullet tore towards him. The dog stopped inches away, dropping a flattened Evo-Stick tube at his feet.

Jas picked it up and tossed it over the wall which separated upper from lower level. The tube lodged in a dense bank of ivy.

These days, his necropolis saw the odd burial, but was used mainly by addicts and those requiring to hide the spoils of bank jobs. Folklore claimed over a million pounds was hidden somewhere within the rotting cemetery, the thieves having been apprehended and imprisoned before being able to retrieve their ill-gotten gains. As a kid, Jas had half-heartedly searched himself, from time to time, as had others, more earnestly. Urban mythology: no one ever found anything.

He continued to wander along tightly-ordered rows of monuments. All show. The bodies below were dry dust, but the casks remained. Nothing lived for ever. The prosperous businesses which had financed a folly were gone.

Jas paused at a hulk-shaped marble structure, the final port-of-call of a wealthy ship-owning family. The only shipyard still functioning in Govan was Scandinavian-owned.

'Why seek ye the living amongst the dead? He is not here. He is risen...'

He scowled, unscrewed the top of the second Lucozade bottle and drank. The sugary liquid felt good in his mouth, fulfilling a need. He stared around.

The necropolis looked...different. Maybe he was different. Jas rubbed his face and zipped up the biker's jacket.

At least the rain, like the sweating, had stopped. Crouching against a thick, granite column, he gazed at the city's outline and shivered. Somewhere out there was 'G'. Somewhere out there was Leigh's killer. He continued to stare, lifting his eyes upwards to grey, leaden clouds. He stared unseeing, then glanced at his watch. The sky had grown blacker.

Noon...darkness at noon.

He removed the mobile from his pocket, punched then waited.

It was answered almost immediately. "Jas?"

He smiled. A friendly voice.

"Jas? Are you there?" Slightly concerned.

It made a change. "Aye, pal. Ah'm here..."

Relief. "Look: if you're still in London, stay where you are. The Met are involved now, they're watching airports and stations."

Suspicion returned. Could he trust this man, this virtual stranger? He had to. "Ah'm back in Glasgow, Andy." Why didn't he know? The cop Marie snouted for knew...

Shock. "I don't know how you managed that!"

Jas clenched a fist. "Ah've no' got time fur aw' this, pal. Can ye git me whit ah need?"

Sigh. "Thought I had it already. The Met have interviewed the manager of the Kensington Park Hotel, and one of his staff, since you were so interested in certain dates in their records." Angry. "I could have done that for you by phone, Jas. Why didn't you ask me? It would have been much safer."

Because I didn't fuckin' think! "Nae time, Andy. Ah wiz there an' ah had tae know..."

"The details were faxed up last night, but I can't get my hands on them." Harsh laugh. "For Sloan's eyes only, it seems. Anyway, I'm at the terminal in Pitt Street's 'Missing Persons'. It's always quiet. Fire away, and I'll see what I can do..."

Jas fired with the first date, then waited.

"Don't know if my computer skills are up to this, but I'll try to access both months, then cross-reference. What's the second date?"

He removed G's letter from his pocket. "Twenty-seventh of April, this year. There's an initial 'G', but ah don't ken whether that's first or second name. Could even be some sorta nickname..."

"The computer won't need that, it's...Christ!" Sigh. "Sorry – bloody thing's gone haywire! You'll need to give me that again." Self-conscious laugh. "I'm more of a laptop man – don't know this system and...the bloody screen's flooding with station expense-requests from the conference. Hold on and I'll see if I can clear it. Now: April the...?"

"Whit conference?" Jas tensed.

"Just let me clear the screen and..."

"Leave it, pal! What conference?"

"The one on the new Police and Criminal Evidence Act. Paul Condon was chairing. A lot of the big brass from here went..."

"When?"

"It's all here on the screen, Jas, but why...?"

"Jist tell me!" Something was starting to make sense.

Sigh. "Okay, okay. I'm surprised you don't remember all the fuss it caused. Anyway, the conference lasted four days: twenty-fifth to twenty-ninth of April. It was held at New Scotland Yard..."

Jas remembered, but not the details. "Who went fae here?"

"The usual pen-pushers, but I don't see what this has to do with..."

"Names, pal."

Confused. "Sure. Well..." Pause. "According to this, five attended from Strathclyde. McDade from 'A' Division, Baxter and Murphy from CID, DI Monroe...oh, sorry: he didn't go, pulled out at the last minute."

"The last two?" Something pulsed in his head.

"The big chief, Commissioner White, and Sloan – who took Monroe's place – reluctantly, if I remember correctly."

The pulse moved from head to heart. "Git back tae the hotel records."

Pause, then irritated. "It'll take a minute or so for the screen to clear. God, the expenses some of them put in, they must have taken taxis to London and back!"

Jas scowled, impatient. At his feet, the dog was back, a still-trembling baby rabbit between smiling jaws.

Andy talked on: "You know what the big brass do, of course: most stay with relatives then claim a whacking great bill from a hotel in London. They can make more out of a so-called business trip than you or I take home in a month. I see Assistant Chief Commissioner Sloan pushed the boat out a bit more than usual..." Silence. Then: "Jas? Why do you want to see the Kensington Park Hotel's records?" Suspicious.

"Jist a hunch. Why? Whit is it?" With his left hand, he managed to remove the rabbit from the dog's mouth. It was dead.

"From the expenses he put in for, Sloan stayed at the Kensington Park for the duration of the conference." Thoughtful. "Let me cross-reference that with the hotel's own records." Pause, then: "Confirmed. He actually did stay there." Another pause. "January two years ago was the other month you wanted to see? I'll do 'Search and Find' with his name."

Jas tossed the furry body away and waited. The base of his skull pulsed with life.

Eventually: "Sloan stayed three nights that January. Want me to flick back to station records, see what the occasion was that time?"

A new betrayal grew in his heart: new, and old. "No, but there is wan other thing, pal. Whit's Sloan's first name?"

"Er...Gregory, I think...yes, Greg." Curious. "What's this all about? What do you need this for?"

"Is Sloan at the station, Andy?"

"No, Monroe's in charge today. Sloan's at home with paperwork, I think..."

"His address."

"Clarkston, somewhere, I think. Want me to access his file?"

"Aye..."

Pause, then: "Here we are. Telephone number 768-9832. Address...18 Marchbank Avenue, Jas..."

"Thanks, pal – ah owe ye wan."

Suspicious. "What's Sloan got to do with all this?" Worried. "I hope you're not going to do anything stupid – remember Beatie? For all his braid and bars, Sloan's still a cop, like us. I know you didn't kill Leigh, but Sloan's just doing his job, with this case. It's nothing personal, I'm sure and..."

"Bye, Andy...an' thanks." He severed the connection, mid-sentence.

'...just doing his job...nothing personal...just doing his job...'

Sloan hadn't been doing his job, when he picked Leigh up, two years ago, and brought him back to Glasgow.

Sloan hadn't been doing his job, when he'd fucked Leigh.

Sloan hadn't been doing his job, when he hadn't admitted to an interest in the case.

'G' was Greg Sloan, Assistant Chief Commissioner Sloan, second-in-command of Strathclyde Police, at present the officer in charge of the investigation into Leigh's murder.

Was it coincidence that two men who had shared another came from the same stable, but were now on opposite sides of the fence? The hunter and the hunted.

Jas reached down and patted the Jack Russell.

Greg Sloan: a cop.

So much in common...including a lover.

A dead lover.

He patted his jeans pocket. Money jangled. With trembling fingers, he punched in a telephone number. After three rings:

"768-9832. Greg Sloan speaking."

Jas stared at the phone. A memory: 'Is he dead...?'

The voice of Assistant Chief Commissioner Sloan.

The voice of the mobile-phone owner.

The voice of Marie's new guy.

The voice of the man who'd tried to have Jas killed.

The voice of 'G'.

The voice of Leigh's killer?

He severed the connection, replacing the phone in his pocket.

This wasn't professional: this was personal.

Clarkston: about five miles away. Taxi was safest. Taxi-drivers didn't like polis. But Jas wasn't polis anymore.

He was a murderer...or if he wasn't, he soon might be.

Twenty-Five

THE JOURNEY to Clarkston was swift and uneventful. As the taxi sped from Glasgow's city centre into suburbs, the middle-aged driver burbled merrily on about the weather, the football and the murder – in that order.

Jas tried to clear his head of cotton-wool and a persistent ache. He had no idea what to expect from Greg Sloan. He had no idea if this was a good idea.

Would Sloan be Richard Beatie revisited?

There would be one big difference: Beatie was out. Jas and Sloan were two of a kind, at the back of a closet stocked with serge. That alone bonded them.

He sighed and rubbed his face. Greg Sloan was the last link in the Leigh-chain. Jas had to talk to him face-to-face.

Up until now Sloan, like Beatie, had had Jas at a disadvantage. Both men knew about him: he had known neither.

His unannounced arrival at Sloan's home should redress the balance.

Surprise. It had worked with the others, in London. It would work with Sloan.

The taxi pulled up at traffic lights. Inches away, two beat-cops ambled past, chatting.

Jas lowered his head and looked away. The lights changed to green and the taxi pulled away. He sighed.

As senior officer in charge of the murder inquiry, Sloan could have had Jas arrested at Marie's flat.

Instead he'd tried to have him killed.

For Beatie's BMW read Felix Hunter and the boys?

Another lover, another murder attempt? Why? Another lover aware Leigh was shared? Another lover determined to free Leigh? Or was Sloan directly involved in the ultimate 'freeing' of Leigh?

"Whit's the address again, son?" The driver turned left and cut across his thoughts.

Jas scowled. "Marchbank Avenue. 18."

Nod. "Aye, ah ken it. The big hooses." Hearty laugh. "Ah dinney git many fares fae your end o' toon tae ower here."

Jas shrugged. Affluent retail Clarkston became affluent residential Clarkston as small, exclusive boutiques became large, Georgian mansions.

Not tenements, not Dennistoun.

Detective sergeant: Assistant Chief Commissioner.

Jas and 'G': poles apart.

The job in common.
Isolation in common.
Leigh in common.
Leigh's death in common.

"Here ye go, son." The diesel engine idled noisily.

Jas stared from the window at iron gates and a shoulder-high box hedge. A clump of tall pampas grass waved above green. Beyond, an imposing three-storey building. Greek-Thomson-style sandstone pillars flanked a half-open door.

"Call it a fiver, son."

Jas thrust a note through the grill. "Keep the change."

The driver stared at the blue, then scowled. "Funny, son...very funny!"

Jas got out, walked towards the gate and 'G'.

In front of a heavy, hardwood door he paused and pressed the bell. No nameplate, just a number.

A tinkling sound from inside. Seconds later, the door pulled fully open. A teenage girl in jeans and a Daniel Poole T-shirt. Dark hair centre-parted, unmade-up, pretty face ruined by a sulky pout. Startling, emerald irises.

Jas avoided the green eyes and modified his accent. "Have I got the correct address? I'm looking for Assistant Chief Commissioner Sloan."

She looked him up and down, frowned, then turned her head. Bored voice over shoulder: "Dad? Another one of your tatty detectives is here." To Jas: "In there..." She stood aside and pointed to an open door and the end of a wide hallway. Careless, Laurel-Bank-Girls'-School vowels. "...he'll be down in a minute." Eyes on his neck as he walked past. Snotty voice: "You've got your T-shirt on inside out – do you know that?" She stared at the rough, exposed seam.

Jas ignored the remark and continued down the impressive lobby. Sloan had at least one child and, presumably, a wife. He lived here with his family, occupying the whole three floors.

Another of Leigh's married men. A uniformed, married man. A cop.

He sighed and walked through the doorway.

The room to which he had been directed was some sort of study. Airy. Lots of natural light. High ceiling. Books lined one wall, a sturdy leather-topped desk sat in the far corner. On it, a compact PC. Business-like.

Jas took off the baseball cap and looked around. The other furnishings had been chosen by a less austere eye. Two comfortable-looking sofas, rugs, vases of dried ferns and pampas grass. Flowery, soft, more feminine than the 'den' aspects of the rest of the room. He ran rough fingers over the frill of a chintzy cushion.

A voice from the hall. Mellow tones. The tones on the phone. Greg Sloan's tones. "Thanks, Ashley. Tell Mum I'll be with her shortly."

Jas turned towards the voice and stared.

The rear view of a tall man. A strong neck topped by steel-grey hair. The tones continued, irked. "I left strict instructions with Sandy Monroe that..." The head spun round, the lips stopped moving, a face stared. A vaguely familiar face.

Greg Sloan walked swiftly into the room. He closed the study door behind himself, locked it, never turning his back.

Jas tensed. Emotions fled his body like lemmings. He was empty, could summon no response to this man. He studied Leigh's lover like a rapidly-assembled photofit.

Late forties, early fifties. Slightly flabby now, but evidently had been fit, once. Pink, undistinguished face, a little wrinkly round the mouth. The word 'freeform' flashed into Jas's head. He pushed it away. Sloan's face was an ordinary face. But the eyes...

He looked at the rest of the man. Pringle golfing sweater, well-cut dark slacks and black brogues. A large hand held a box of tees.

He looked back at the eyes. The same piercing green eyes as his daughter. Powerful eyes. Hard eyes. Cold eyes. Unblinking eyes. The windows of the soul were behind three-inch steel shutters.

Jas sighed: like his own soul had been shuttered, locked away, until Leigh had torn off that protective covering...

Sloan remained motionless, his back to the door.

Jas cleared his throat, fingering the brim of the baseball cap. "Sir." The respect was instinctive.

"DS Anderson. Sit down."

Nothing in the voice. No anger, no surprise, no hate. The professional police-mask.

"I'll stand." Jas walked to the fireplace.

"Suit yourself." Sloan moved to the desk and stood beside it, placing the box of tees on the leather-covered surface. Sigh. "There was no need for you to come here, you know. I intended to contact you at the usual place, to take care of things."

The man had worn masks for so long, this one was glued in place. Jas mirrored the tone. "I'm not at Marie McGhee's flat now. Surely you know that?"

Ghost of a smile. "I was referring to the hotel, Anderson. As for Marie, she's long gone, I'm afraid." Sloan was a block of frosted ice: cold, opaque, impenetrable. The temperature in the room was dropping. Jas considered the unconsiderable: was the uniform the only aspect of this man to attract Leigh? "Have you taken care of Marie, the way you tried to take care of me?" The way you took care of Leigh?

Sloan sat down behind the desk and opened a drawer. "I've no idea where McGhee is. I don't keep tabs on my snouts – they're usually there when I want them..." He produced a cash-box. "...but she was getting rather unreliable. As for...taking care of you, as you put it – do you blame me? What would you have done in my position?" Sloan stared an unflinching Sloan-stare.

"I like to think I'd have had you arrested."

Another phantom smile, half-formed, no substance. "Oh, very good! You've got bottle, Anderson – I'll say that for you. I knew, the night we met at London Road."

Jas stared.

The mouth a thin, red streak. "Oh, come on! Sunday, two weeks ago..."

Two weeks...

Two weeks...

Only two weeks? It seemed a lifetime away...Leigh's – his – lifetime away.

"You'd given the Mygo-character a beating. We took the lift together." Laugh. "You still look a mess." Frown. The mask back. "I didn't know then what I know now, of course." Hand into pocket, then withdrawn. "So..." A key produced from another drawer. "...how does ten thousand sound to you?" The cash-box unlocked and opened.

Jas blinked.

Sloan regarded him, impatient. The first sign of emotion. "Well, Anderson?"

Jas rubbed his face. The headache was back.

Sloan, cold and calm. "Don't try to push it, I haven't got time for all this."

Jas tensed. "I want to know who killed Leigh."

Sloan-shrug. "Who cares? He's dead. I must admit to feeling a little sorry for you, my friend..."

Jas lunged across the desk and grabbed Sloan's throat. "Ah'm no' yer friend, pal! Did ye set me up, ya bastard? Ye ken ah didney kill Leigh!""

A surprisingly strong grip on his weakened right arm, pulling the hand away easily. "Calm down, Anderson. This achieves nothing." The grip relaxed.

Jas stepped back, nursing his wrist.

"No, I didn't set you up." Full parody-smile. "You managed that all by yourself. And yes – I know you didn't kill Jason, or Leigh as you've chosen to call him." A hint of anger. "But you must have your suspicions who did." Sloan-scowl. "I thought he was alone – I'd no idea there were two of you." Low words, whispered. "My own fault, I suppose. I should have known..."

"Known whit?" A myriad lies swam in his head.

Suspicion. "You're not wired, are you? You've not done some

sort of deal with that Clark character from CIB, have you? I knew he was up to something! Take your jacket off, please." Brisk, business-like.

Twelve years of obeying orders took over. Jas tossed the biker's jacket to the floor and stretched out his arms.

Sloan rose, moved out from behind the desk and stood in front of him. Expertly, he ran his fingers over the damp T-shirt, then patted up and down Jas's legs, lingering over the crotch area.

Jas shivered. There was nothing erotic in the sensations coursing through his body.

Apparently satisfied, Sloan straightened up, back in control. "Excuse my caution. You must appreciate my position."

The headache was lifting. Jas looked into icy, green eyes.

Sloan absently rearranged the neck of the 'I ♥ London' T-shirt, then walked back to the desk. He began to count large denomination notes from the cash-box onto the smooth leather. "Fifties all right?"

Jas picked up his jacket, withdrew Sloan's letter to Leigh. He crushed it between sweating fingers. "Ah dinney want yer money."

Sloan stopped counting. He looked up. "I don't know what kind of game you're playing, Anderson. If the money's not enough, I can arrange other..." He glanced down casually at neat, short fingernails. "...favours. You can leave Glasgow, go anywhere. I'll guarantee you safe passage wherever you want. Just say the word..."

"Ah only want wan thing fae you."

Losing control. "Anything. Name it. Just give me the negatives."

A cloud of understanding burst in his head:

Harry from Walthamstow's relief at the news of Jason's death.

Leigh had been playing the most dangerous game of all. Jas frowned. "Whit did he huv on ye – dirty pictures? Threatened tae tell yer wife an' kids aboot yer wee arrangement?"

"What do you mean, Anderson? There was nothing in the letter about involving my family."

"Whit letter?" Jas waved two crumpled sheets of paper. "Yer wee love-note tae Leigh?"

"I'm getting rather tired of all this." Sigh. "The letter I received from you last week. Like the other demands, over the past two months. You and that little bastard..."

"Whit makes ye think ah wiz involved..." His own voice rang in his head. "...that ah'd huv onthin' tae dae wi' blackmail?" Jas ran a hand through his hair. "Christ!" Hatred for Leigh and what he'd done filled his throat. He finally managed to speak. "Ah lived wi' him, but ah kent nothin' aboot you, or this..." He stared at the wad of money, then closed his eyes.

Or Beatie.

Or photographs.

Or exploiting dying men.

Or blackmailing senior police officers.

Or Leigh Nicols.

A low laugh filled the airy room. "You're joking!"

Jas opened his eyes and scowled.

Sloan nodded slowly. "Okay, you're not joking." He began to stuff money swiftly into the cash-box. "What do you want, then?" The box disappeared back into the drawer, the drawer relocked. Sloan drummed elegant fingers.

Jas clenched his fists. Blackmail victims had strong motives for murder. "Tell me aboot Leigh, aboot the photographs." He scrunched the love-letter into a tight ball.

Sloan walked over to a small drinks-cabinet, opened it and poured himself a whisky. "You really didn't know about the blackmail?" A hint of worry. "Whoever Jason was working with is still out there. That letter came..."

Jas growled. "Tell me whit he had on ye!"

Sigh. Sloan sat down on the sofa. Eyes on Jas's hand. Cold, calm words. "That letter, which I foolishly wrote to him months ago, and a quantity of photographic material." Frown. "I've seen a sample. Jason threatened to send the photographs to the Scottish Office. If that happened, my career would be over. You, of all people, know the score, Anderson. My position would become untenable within the Force, should my...sexuality be made known." Icy, humourless smile. "I think you've already had a foretaste of what life would be like as an openly gay cop." He tapped the whisky glass with his fingers. "Consider my predicament, man. In four years' time, I can apply for early retirement. Until then..." Pause. "...with rationalisation in the air, the rank of Assistant Chief Commissioner will be one of the first to go. Cost-cutting again, I'm afraid. Those in charge of budgets are looking for excuses. If I can last the next four years, there's a good pension and a lump sum in it for me. If I..." Scowl. "...blot my copy-book, as it were, before then, I'll be dismissed, out on my ear, the last twenty-five years counting for nothing..."

No 'my wife mustn't know.'

No 'my kids mustn't know.'

Sloan: the career-cop. Nothing else mattered to him. Jas knew the feeling. In the beginning, the job was his life, too.

Then Leigh became his life.

Now? He sighed.

No lover...no job...regardless of the test-results, no life. He refocused on Greg Sloan, and all this man had to lose. Leigh had gone for the big-time. "When did ye last see him?"

Sloan-shrug. Sloan-smooth. "Oh, of course: you don't know any of this, do you...?" Pitying look.

Jas wanted to take the pity and stuff it down the Sloan-throat.

"...no reason not to tell you, I suppose. You can't do anything with it." He gripped the whisky glass. "Tuesday night. I was feeling quite pleased with myself, Anderson. I'd finally tracked Jason down to his lair. Oh, he was clever! We always met in a hotel, in Kersland Street: he insisted on it. In the beginning, to do the business..." Frown. "...then to do another sort of business. I knew he wasn't living here. I rented a flat for him, after he came up from London, but he moved out three months ago." Sloan-stare. "No one blackmails me – no one! At least, not for long." Whisky glass to thin lips. "I followed him back to the Eastercraigs address. Your name meant nothing to me, at that point, so I presumed Jason had set himself up there..." Raised ironic eyebrow. "...impressive detective work, for desk-bound brass, eh, detective?"

"Amazin'..." The letter grew hot in his hand. Sloan had been taken for a ride, as Jas had: only the route and the destination differed. Pain buzzed in his head. "Ye loved him, didn't ye? That's whit hurt, more than the thought o' losin' yer job..."

"Love?" Frozen fury. The police-mask ripped away. "You think I loved him, Anderson? He was nothing. A good fuck, maybe ...but a very expensive one, as things turned out!" Cold eyes. "When I read the autopsy report, read the state of what I'd been fucking..."

"Did ye test?"

Brief armistice. Nod. "A discreet GP, an old family friend..." Common ground became no-man's-land again. Low, seething anger. "If my wife and family had been at any risk from..." Heavy breathing, groping for control. Finding it. "Negative, thank Christ! But no thanks to Jason. I insisted on the condoms." Twisted smile. "Jason preferred to be ridden bareback."

Leigh: 'Yours...only yours...'

Pretty-boy had pretty well met his match in Greg Sloan. There was no rationalisation of emotions here. An Assistant Chief Commissioner had availed himself of a service. Nothing more, nothing less. Jas clenched his fists. "Tell me the rest!"

"I wanted those negatives, and I was going to get them. Jason had no intention of ever handing them over, I knew that. So, last Tuesday night, I waited in Alexandra Park, for my chance. I knew he was in the flat: checked. You arrived about six, left about ten..."

Pain pulled at his heart. Four hours...his last four hours with Leigh...Leigh's strong body...

Smile. "You know, I thought you were one of his other victims, Anderson!" Soft chuckle.

Ah wiz, but no' the way you mean.

A knock at the door. Woman's voice: "Greg? Will you be much longer? We're booked in for three..."

"Something's come up, dear." Sloan was cool. "You go on ahead."

To Jas. "I had to get Jason out of the flat. So I phoned him, asked for a meeting. He agreed. I waited over an hour for him to leave. Nothing." Frown. "It seems I wasn't quite clever enough, Anderson: there's no back gate in your building, but there's a wall. Jason must have left that way, for our fictitious rendezvous. Next thing I knew, he was walking back in through your controlled entry. I'd missed my chance." Sloan refilled the whisky glass. "I waited a bit longer, just in case, then my luck changed. I was about to give up when I noticed someone leaving your building." Sigh. "I suppose desperation made me think it was Jason. The rain was heavy that night, I could hardly see. I wanted it to be him badly enough to risk approaching the flat. I rang your bell, no one answered. Both doors were unlocked, so I went in."

Jas closed his eyes.

Emotionless. "I found him in the bedroom. He was dead, of course. I suppose whoever I'd seen leaving the flat killed him."

"You phoned Baird Street?" Jas opened his eyes and stared.

Cool. "Eventually. This was my chance to find the negatives." Smile. "Nice flat, by the way. Very tasteful, Anderson..."

Jas scowled. "Ah take it ye didney find onythin'?"

Whisky glass replaced on drinks-cabinet. "Nothing." Shrug. "But at least he was dead. I just had to hope the photographs wouldn't come to light." Sigh. "Then the demands for money started again..."

Fury and frustration throbbed in his head. "Ye ken ah had nothin' tae dae wi' the blackmail!" Jas looked into inhuman eyes. "Ye saw me leave – ye ken ah couldn't huv killed Leigh! We could work together, nail the bastard who did."

Head shake. "I don't think so, my friend. Do you honestly believe I'd come forward – even now – to get you off the hook, only to offer my own private life up for public inspection? You're very naive, Anderson."

And you're a cold bastard, Assistant Chief Commissioner Sloan. Jas swallowed hard. His heart was pounding. "No one deserves tae die the way Leigh did." The words came before he could stop them.

Laugh. "I think Jason got exactly what he deserved, Anderson, and I'm rather surprised you don't feel the same."

Jas was surprised too. He wanted to smash the smug Sloan face, without knowing why.

"Anyway, none of this solves my little problem..." Hard smiled. "...or yours, come to think of it." Thoughtful pause, then: "Let me run something by you."

Jas sat down and buried his head in his hands. He was no nearer to fining Leigh's killer. Sweat cooled on his face and trickled down his neck.

In the background, Sloan's slow, deliberate words. "I've searched Jason's old flat, the hotel and given your place a cursory going-over

– as have our...uniformed colleagues. Nothing. Whoever Jason was working with – whoever sent that letter – is still out there, but I've got a feeling he may be bluffing about the negatives. Jason must have hidden them somewhere." Pause. "Your flat is as good a starting place as any." The voice closer now, near his ear. "We can help each other, Anderson. You need me..."

Jas raised his head and stared into emerald eyes. "Ye've withheld vital information in a murder inquiry: you found Leigh's body. Ye huvney disclosed a personal association with the victim: ye wur fuckin' him an' he wiz blackmailin' you." Ye've got motive..." He held out the love letter.

"And you've got no proof, Anderson. The letter's nothing, without the photographs and negatives. You've assaulted two other men, you've no alibi, your fingerprints were on the murder weapon. Any accusations you make in my direction will look like the ravings of a desperate man." Laugh. "And who would you tell – Sandy Monroe? You wouldn't last five minutes in custody! There are a lot of angry men waiting at London Road for the chance to be alone with you." Smile at the ambiguity. Sloan walked to the desk and lifted the phone. "Want to risk it?"

Jas stared at the expressionless face. Any shred of sympathy he had harboured for the man, as a fellow gay cop, tore loose and floated away. But Sloan was right: Jas had everything to lose and nothing to gain by going to the police. He was defeated, and it showed. He shook his head.

With a cop's skill, Sloan exploited the weakness. He replaced the receiver, sat down. "I want something. You can get it for me. You know your own flat better than I do.."

"Why don't ye look fur them yersel'?"

"Your flat's still under surveillance, has been for a week now. I can't risk sparking off a new line of inquiry: Monroe has his case and, frankly, it suits me."

Betrayal...more betrayal. Jas closed his eyes, wanting to blot out this man, for whom 'the job' was more important than anything else...including another's life.

Sloan continued: "I don't care who killed Jason, but I need those negatives, and any other material. Due to the twenty-four hour surveillance, there's a good chance Jason's partner hasn't had the chance to retrieve them either." Bargaining. "Search the flat for me, Anderson. I'll keep Monroe off your back for the next, say, twelve hours. Get me what I want, and you can do what you like with anything else."

He opened his eyes and met a glassy stare.

"If Jason was blackmailing me, there were almost certainly others." Persuasive. "If you really want to clear your name, one of them probably killed him. Anything you find on anyone else is yours. Go after them yourself, or turn the information over to Monroe and take your chances. Just keep my name out of it. The rest's up to you. If you decide to leave the country afterwards, my offer still stands." Sloan drained the glass. "Come on, Anderson. It's the best offer you'll get. The only offer."

A muscle pulsed on his neck. Jas shivered. He'd found Leigh's address-book and letter. Both Sloan and the uniforms had missed the handcuff box. There were a couple of other places he could try, he knew that. But the only way to get the chance to do so, was to agree to Sloan's suggestion. Jas stared into green, snake eyes and frowned: he didn't trust this man, but he had no other option.

Sloan read him like a book. "Good! Now...I think Sandy Monroe will agree to easing-off the surveillance on Eastercraigs. After all..." Cold smile. "...you are supposed to be in London, and the man-hours can be better spent elsewhere." He stood up, looked at his watch. "I'll give you until five tomorrow morning – does that sound fair? Ring me here, as soon as you find anything. Goodbye, Anderson."

Dismissed like a rookie, Jas walked numbly from the room.

Twenty-Six

THROUGH THE back window of the taxi, he gazed up at a pewter sky. Outside, it was raining hard, and the light had a heavy quality to it. Clarkston receded in the distance like a bad dream. He looked at his watch: 4.34pm.

"Is it the flats in Wishart Street, pal?" Young driver, this time, and female.

Jas scowled. "Jist Wishart Street. Ah'll tell ye when tae stop."

"Fair enough, pal." The taxi picked up speed.

Sloan and Leigh filled his head. Hatred for both victim and victimiser washed over him in waves. Leigh had lied to him. Leigh had been blackmailing a vulnerable man, possibly several vulnerable men.

As an equally vulnerable man, when would Jas's own blackmail have begun?

Sloan: the professional cop. Sloan had seen Jas leave the flat, and had said nothing. Sloan knew Jas was innocent, but would do nothing.

He rubbed his face slowly. Sweat slicked under his hand.

Sloan was saving his own skin at Jas's expense, using him, manipulating...the way Leigh had used and manipulated...

A tool...everyone's fuckin' tool.

The taxi took a corner too fast.

Pointless self-recriminations slid to the far side of his mind. Jas clenched his fists.

Leigh had a partner.

Who else had Leigh and this partner been blackmailing?

If Sloan's supposition was correct there could be armies of frightened ex-lovers all eager to see Leigh dead.

At traffic lights, two kids and a dog carefully crossed the road.

Jas sighed. The blackmail explained a lot. Leigh had managed to live well on a lab technician's wage. Little extras took on a new significance. The expensive, clothes, the Patek Phillipe watch Leigh had owned; a gift from his parents, he had claimed. The oyster Rolex – good copy, Leigh had insisted – which Jas had received last Christmas as a present.

He paid the mortgage – or rather, Strathclyde Police did – and Leigh bought the food. Good food. Even the offer to pay half the holiday to LA.

Jas closed his eyes. He had lived for nearly two years with a blackmailer and hadn't known: so much for police training.

So much for insight.

So much for trust.

So much for so little...

The taxi slowed, then pulled up. "Four quid, pal."

He rummaged in his pocket. Only loose change appeared. He counted out four pounds in fifty, twenty and ten pees.

The driver grinned. "Been fiddlin' the meter?"

Jas thrust the money into the woman's hand and got out of the cab. He looked across at the necropolis. A low bank of grey cloud shrouded Monteith's mausoleum. It was unnaturally dark, for a July afternoon – even for Glasgow.

As the taxi pulled away, he knew he had to give Sloan time to cancel surveillance on the Eastercraigs flat. Crossing Wishart Street, he climbed through the hole in the fence, up two steep banks and into his den. The dog was nowhere in sight.

Like an injured animal, he retreated to the back of the mausoleum, curled his aching body into a defensive ball. His aching mind was another matter. But eventually, sleep came.

A line of faceless men, each holding a gun. Leigh handcuffed to the bed. Jas at the back of the line. A crack resounded. The queue moved forward. Another crack. The queue moved forward. Eight shots later, he stood before Leigh. There was nothing left of the handsome face. Jas raised the gun and fired into bloody mush. A scream circled in his head...

He blinked awake, breathing heavily. He shivered, looked at his watch: 8.30pm. Jas frowned, aware he'd wasted at least two hours searching-time. Standing up, he shook stiff limbs, testingly. His right arm felt better, but his skull was throbbing again. He smiled.

Maybe Sloan wasn't as clever as he thought. This arrangement would give Jas first look at the blackmail material. How did Sloan know he wouldn't keep it, use it himself?

Jas scowled. Sloan knew.

He shrugged and left the mausoleum. He didn't care about Sloan. He didn't care about blackmail. He didn't care about Leigh. He did care about whoever killed Leigh.

He cared about his own life...

A shiver racked his body.

...or did he? Jas walked on. An artificial night had fallen. It was still raining, and Wishart Street was empty.

Another wet night. Walking back to Eastercraigs to find Leigh dead.

Jas walked back to Eastercraigs now to discover how Leigh had made a living.

Alexandra Parade was a grave, as he made his way home.

Home. His home. Their home.

The house from which Leigh had run an extortion racket.

At the corner of the Parade and Eastercraigs, he paused, patting his pocket.

The house-keys were still there.

He walked on, until he could see Seven Eastercraigs. How long had it been – a week? Two? It was a lifetime. Literally. When he'd left the flat two weeks ago, he'd had a life, a lover. Leigh had been alive.

When he'd returned, Leigh had been dead. A victim of his own success?

Jas scanned the street. No cars, no solitary figures lurking conspicuously in 'plain' clothes. On the ground floor of Number Seven, he noticed paper blinds were drawn behind Miss Dunlop's familiar net curtains.

Another death.

Jas opened the outside door. The tiled close smelled of disinfectant. Someone was late washing their stairs.

He climbed two stone flights and paused outside 2B. The small name-plate read: J. Anderson. Underneath, printed neatly on faded paper: L. Nicols.

Jas ripped the card from the door and crushed it. He inserted two keys in two locks, turned twice and pushed.

The door swung open.

He stepped inside. The familiar hit him like a blow. Outside these walls, his world had changed beyond recognition. In here, everything was the same. He walked into the lounge. Someone – uniforms? – had tidied up a bit...or was the mess in his memory? In the kitchen, a small red light blinked at him. Someone had done a wash. A vague memory of loading the machine.

Jas crouched and pressed a switch. The red light blinked off. He waited the two minutes for the door to unlock, opened it and began to unload damp, mildewed clothing into the laundry basket.

Then he stood up. The sudden movement drained blood from his brain. Sparks flashed before his eyes. Jas clenched a wet sock in one fist and swayed. Regaining his balance, he kicked the plastic laundry basket and turned away.

This wasn't home, this wasn't routine. He was here for only one reason.

Find the photographs. Find another direction in which to look for Leigh's killer. Jas switched on the overhead light and began to search the kitchen. It was almost nine pm.

Two hours and three rooms later he paused and sighed. The sound of his breath floated around the room. Nothing.

He had looked under carpets and floorboards, in the freezer, in the fridge, under and inside the washing machine, in and on top of six cupboards, in and behind the TV, inside books, magazines, CDs, in the fireplace, behind wall-prints, under and in furniture, under the shower, inside the cistern, in the spare bedroom. Jas rubbed his eyes. He'd looked in places he'd forgotten were there.

He had searched every room but one.

Jas sighed again. The sweats were back. He'd already taken off the biker's jacket. Now he took off the T-shirt. 'I ♥ London' laughed at him. He tossed it to the floor. Gritting his teeth, he walked slowly through to the bedroom.

The smell... He glanced down. A bottle of Lacoste lay on the floor, spilt by some clumsy cop. The lemony-limey odour was everwhere. He coughed and looked around.

The room swayed violently. He sat down on the bed. Memories of the last time he'd sat – lain – on this bed bled into his mind, memories of Leigh, Leigh's body shadowing his own, Leigh's...

Jas blinked the thoughts away. Other, more useful ideas filtered in.

Leigh had been shot here, at close range, by someone he had let into the flat. Leigh had known his killer. But not merely as a lover. As a victim: someone driven to kill through desperation and betrayal. Not Sloan. Who?

Blackness rose up before him, threatening to drown him. Jas shook his head, got up and walked round to where the handcuff box was hidden. He knelt, pulled back the rug, eased up a floorboard and fumbled.

Still there. He lifted it out.

Leigh's task. Jas had never really looked at this box properly. He sat back down on the bed and raised the lid.

A clutter of metal and hide stared up at him. Jas plucked out two spare sets of handcuffs; a G-string, the leather stiffened by sweat and spunk; four straps; three cockrings, a couple of gags and a brown envelope. He tipped it onto his palm.

A blister pack of lozenge-shaped pills. Jas read the printed foil: Prozac. Leigh's voice echoed in his ears: 'Got them from a guy at work. Don't you want to try them, Jas? Come on, let's have some fun...'

A smile played on his lips. Leigh the Experimenter, always trying to surprise him. The smile twisted into a frown: who'd got the bigger surprise, last Tuesday night? He peered into the box.

Lying face down, a photograph. Jas tensed, lifted it out. Heart bursting, he looked at the polaroid.

More memories. Christmas, here in the flat. Leigh's new camera. A present from Jas. Taken by the timer-mechanism, the snap showed himself and Leigh.

Not naked. Not in bed. Not even touching. Laughing. Jas remembered the shared occasion, the shared moment, the shared joke. The smile teased dry lips. He tried to chase it away, but it stuck stubbornly.

In the snap, Leigh was wearing a tight black polo-neck and black Levis. Pony-tailed blond hair hung over one shoulder. A slender, tanned hand held a red-and-foil Christmas cracker, which he'd been trying to get Jas to pull with him. As an incentive, Leigh had offered to let him wear the paper hat, contained inside. The handsome face smiled innocently up at him.

Jas relived the moment. His brain wanted to forget; his heart was a different matter. He sighed, stroking the photographic image...

Betraying, lying Leigh receded in the face of this Leigh.

Blackmail. With a partner. A new possibility emerged...partner as killer...greedy partner, wanting more, wanting it all. Did this partner have something on Leigh himself?

Leigh: easy-going, easily-manipulated Leigh. Frightened, in over his head, hating the lies but forced to go on, by a more determined accomplice. Trying to break free, wanting to tell Jas everything. Prevented from doing so by a single bullet.

Jas fingered the photograph, stared at his own relaxed face, then Leigh's handsome face. The smell of Lacoste was bewitching him, twitching and twisting his soul. Why had he been so eager to believe the worst of Leigh?

Sweat flooded from his forehead. The headache was back, worse than ever. His chest tightened, a huge weight pressed down on him...couldn't breathe, couldn't think.

He tried to stand. Tinder legs crumpled. He fell heavily, head glancing off the brass bed-frame. Flailing with useless arms, Jas hit the floor and plunged into a glittering sea...

Fragments of Leigh swam through his mind. Snatches of conversation floated up to join them in a sparkling, sequined soup. The smell of Leigh, the feel of Leigh's long, taut muscles, hard tight buttocks. Leigh's voice: 'Jas?'

His prick responded like one of Pavlov's dogs. He saw the handsome, flawless face before him. He began to harden.

A cool hand stroked his forehead. 'Oh, Jas...' The caresses continued, soft lips on burning skin.

Jas moaned. Nimble fingers were unbuttoning his jeans, freeing his prick. He tried to stand, couldn't. Denim pushed down onto thighs. Leigh's mouth on his mouth. Hot tongues colliding hungrily. His stomach flipped over. He leaned up into the kiss. Long fingers played with his balls, teasing, taunting. Jas grabbed the hand and moved it to his prick.

Under his own rough fingers, Leigh's fingers began to move expertly up and down the length of him. With each familiar stroke, Jas died a little. No more of this. No more Leigh.

No more job...only pain and endless days of searching for a killer he'd never find.

Leigh's strokes quickened. Jas removed his own hand and seized a fist of soft, blond hair. Mouth pulled away, saliva licked from lips. 'Come to me, Jas...' The hand continued to move up and down his prick.

No more lazy mornings in bed. No more sweet kisses. No more love. No more life.

Leigh's mouth was on his neck, now, licking and nibbling. A voice in his ear: 'Come to me, Jas. Come with me...'

He moaned and closed his eyes. What was there for him here?

Pain. Hurt. Hate. The test results. A slow, lingering death alone.

Lips brushed his ear-lobe. 'Come on, Jas...'

His prick throbbed with unreleased tension. He slipped a hand under Leigh's T-shirt, groping for nipple-rings. He rubbed the warm metal and flesh between thumb and forefinger, as another thumb and forefinger ringed his aching prick.

An eternity of pleasure flashed through his tired brain. At worst, what was death – blackness? A void?

He had that in life.

Death could be a long, wet dream going on for ever. An after-life after-glow with Leigh, stretching to infinity. A breath caught in his throat. Jas opened his eyes.

The blade of a knife floated in front of him. So easy...so easy. Slice away the life, the pain, the loneliness.

Jas blinked. Blue eyes. Leigh smiled lazily and continued to caress.

So close now...so close. He pulled Leigh closer still. Pain flashed down the injured arm. He gasped, eyelids closing against the agony.

Leigh's mouth soothed the pain. Then words: 'Come on, Jas...'
At the moment or orgasm, he screamed one word. "No..."
Leigh was dead. That was wrong.
Someone had killed him. That was wrong.
His killer would escape justice. That was wrong.
Too many wrongs...too much still to do. Shivers of pleasure coursed through him, as his balls contracted, spurting semen from prick onto stomach and Leigh's tanned hand.
Jas opened his eyes.

The dream refused to dissolve. He looked down, his still-hard prick still clasped by strong fingers. White, sticky fluid dotted the skin. He looked up.

Blue eyes smiled at him from the handsome face. Above the right cheekbones, three small healing scratches. "You want to come with me, don't you Jas?"

Leigh's voice. Leigh's face. Leigh's body.

Jas shook his head. "Ah can't, Leigh...ye ken that..."

The dark came back, thick and suffocating. In the pitch, a glint, then pain. New pain, sharp and stinging in his damaged arm.

His brain cleared. He lurched upwards, pushing Leigh away, pushing the dream away. He dragged jeans up with one hand, steadying himself with the other.

Leigh sat a few feet away, watching.

Jas got to his feet.

The dream dissolved into nightmare.

Twenty-Seven

JAS STARED.

Leigh produced a packet of cigarettes and lit one. He inhaled, then exhaled noisily, blowing blue smoke over his shoulder.

Jas blinked. "You're dead..."

"Sorry to disappoint you." Hint of a smile. Leigh got up from the floor and stood inches away. A hand extended, fingers brushing matted hair from Jas's face, gently touching bruises.

Jas stared. "Whit is aw' this?" Thunder in his ears.

Sigh. Leigh sat down on the bed. "Christ, I'm glad to see you! I didn't know what to do."

He stretched out a damaged hand and touched the tanned face, feeling warm, smooth skin. Above a golden cheekbone, three small scratches bore further testament to mortality.

Leigh grasped the hand and pressed it to his lips. "I've missed you...you don't know how much." The cigarette dropped on the polished floor.

Jas ground it out with the heel of his biker's boot, then took Leigh's other hand and pulled him upright. Strong, slender arms wrapped themselves around his waist. Jas rested his chin on a soft shoulder and breathed in the scent of cigarettes and Lacoste. His brain wouldn't work, but he didn't care.

Leigh was alive.

He pressed the impossibly warm body tighter against his own. The past fourteen days drifted away on a sea of longing. After several minutes, he loosened his grip. "Whit happened? Ah don't understand..."

"It was awful." Leigh lowered his head to Jas's chest. "Those guys..." Fear in the voice.

Jas rubbed the broad back, soothingly. "Ah'm here noo, Leigh. No one's gonny hurt ye. Whit guys?" He stroked the blond hair.

Hesitant. Fearful. "The guys who were after you. They came here, looking for trouble...Johnstone, I think..."

Jas sighed and ran a hand over the ponytail. His instinct had been right. Liam and Michael's lackeys were somewhere behind this mess.

"...three of them, said you'd hurt their brother. They wanted to know where you were..."

Jas frowned. He knew from Marie that the Johnstones themselves had alibis for that night. Through the joy in his heart, brain began to function. Sloan...

"...I wouldn't tell them, Jas. They had a knife..."

Sloan said...

"...they were big guys, Jas, bigger than me. They said they'd make me..."

Sloan said only...

"...tell them. I couldn't handle it, Jas..."

Sloan said only one...

"...they were going to wait for you to come back. Then they started on me..."

Sloan said only one man...

"...I had to defend myself, Jas..."

Sloan said only one man entered...

"...I didn't know what to do. Then I remembered the gun..."

Sloan said only one man entered and...

"...it was still under the bed. I managed to get to it..."

Sloan said only one man entered and left...

"...I didn't want to hurt anyone, Jas, but I had to..."

Sloan said only one man entered and left the...

"...just pointed the gun, closed my eyes and pulled the trigger.."

Sloan said only one man entered and left the flat...

"...must have been too close, Jas. I only wanted to scare them, didn't mean to kill anyone. There was a lot of shouting..."

Sloan said only one man entered and left the flat that...

"...the other two must have run off. I heard the outside door slam. When I opened my eyes, he was just lying there..."

Sloan said only one man entered and left the flat that night...

"...there was blood everywhere, Jas. I didn't know what to do. I suppose I panicked..."

Sloan said only one man entered and left the flat that night. Sloan, like all Glasgow cops, knew Liam and Michael Johnstone well. If the brothers had been here, Sloan would have seen them. Jas's arms dropped like stones. "Ye say these guys were the Johnstone brothers, Leigh?" Had Sloan lied?

Nod. "The one I shot...think the others called him Neil..."

Neil Johnstone was in Barlinnie Prison, had been there for the past eighteen months. Jas backed away. "Neil, ye say?"

Vigorous nod. "Yes, Jas, it was definitely Neil. I didn't mean to hurt anyone – you must believe me, Jas. I did it for you. They were going to kill you..."

At arm's length, he cupped a hand under the penitent chin and raised the blond head. Eyes locked, staring.

The Game...The Game...

Leigh broke the gaze. "I was stupid to run, but I panicked. Look: I know I've probably got you into trouble, but we can both leave now, get away from here. Come with me, Jas. We can go to LA like we planned..."

With his left hand, Jas pulled back and slapped the handsome, lying face.

Shock. "Jas! What's wrong...?"

Another slap. "Don't lie to me, Leigh."

Shrinking away. "I'm not lying – Christ, I saved your life! If I hadn't shot that guy..."

"The Johnstones were never here lookin' fur me, Leigh, an' none o' them are deid! None o' them huv blond hair. None o' them look like you. Who did ye kill, Leigh? Who's the guy in the morgue?"

"Who cares?" Head up, defiant. "Some low-life you rubbed up the wrong way." Leigh's lips were moist. "I've missed you so much, Jas, missed you fucking me..." Soft smile. "...missed fucking you. Remember what it felt like, remember..."

"Who's the guy in the morgue?" He pushed away memories of Leigh's prick and what it had made him feel.

He couldn't feel now...couldn't risk it.

Beguiling eyes. "Forget him! Let's get out of here..."

Jas moved towards the tall figure. Trust vanished like a ghost. "Ah'm no' goin' onywhere, Leigh..an' neither are you..."

Confusion. "But the police, Jas – we've got to..."

"Tell me the truth, Leigh..."

"That is the truth! Why would I lie?"

Jas tensed. One last chance. "Tell me about Sloan, aboot Beatie, aboot aw' the rest. Ah don't care..."

"Who?" Unflinching blue eyes. "I don't know any Sloan or...what was the other guy's name?"

Blackness filled his mind. He stared into clear eyes. "Tell me somewan made ye dae it, put pressure oan ye..."

"I'm yours, Jas, only yours." Leigh stepped forward, pressed a hand to Jas's crotch and traced the outline of his still-hard prick. "And you're mine – there's no one else for either of us, you know that..." He kissed him softly on the mouth.

A Judas kiss. Jas pushed him away and spat. "Ya lyin' wee..."

Shrug. "Suit yourself." A hand into back pocket, then a blade flashing through the gloom. A healthy, fit Leigh darted towards him, knife in hand. Cold blue eyes glinted.

Jas watched, motionless. It had been a long time coming, but here it was.

The real Leigh.

He laughed, instinctively reaching for the weapon with his right hand. It trembled and refused to obey.

The blade twisted upwards, entering the biceps. Pain shuddered. Jas ignored it and slammed his left fist into the side of Leigh's head.

Leigh gasped, let go of the knife and clutched his face. No further sound. The lean body crumpled to the floor.

Jas seized the handle and tugged the blade from his arm. Blood pumped from a deep wound. He pressed the palm of his hand to the cut and scanned the room.

On the bed, the leather straps caught his eyes. He lifted one, bound it tightly just above the muscle. Then he saw the handcuffs. Clenching teeth against the pain, he grabbed the metal bracelets, then turned back to the slumped body. Expertly, meeting no resistance, he secured each of the cuffs to a tanned wrist. Jas gripped the inert form and hauled Leigh onto the bed. He fastened each of the reinforced steel cuffs to the brass bed-head.

A sound. Leigh was regaining consciousness.

Jas leaned over and picked up the knife.

Leigh's eyes blinked open, eyelids fluttered then closed.

Jas brought the blade level with the tanned neck and paused. Blood from his arm-wound dripped down onto white lycra. It would be easy, so easy... He scowled and dragged the knife lightly down the length of Leigh's T-shirt. Tight, body-hugging fabric parted, revealing the bronze, hairless chest and glistening nipple rings.

Leigh was mumbling something.

Jas ran a hand over hard sinew.

Leigh's words were audible now. "You want to play, do you?"

He looked down at Leigh's groin. Seven hard inches were clearly visible under the denim. "Ah want the truth, Leigh."

"A truth-game, huh?" He smiled and spread heavily-muscled thighs.

Jas toyed with a nipple ring. The knife hung limp in his right hand. "No games, Leigh. Jist the truth." He looked at the handsome face.

It smiled. "I know what you like, Jas..."

The truth. The truth. He scowled. "Whit ur ye, Leigh?"

Exquisite tension painted the exquisite face. "An animal." The voice was low, throaty, expectant.

Jas tweaked a nipple. "Whit kinda animal, Leigh?"

"A bad animal..."

"And?"

"A dirty animal..."

Games, games, vicious games...

Rage pulsed in his throat, as Leigh continued, trying to control him, manipulate him. Jas tugged on the nipple ring. His voice came harsh with another emotion. He finished the ritual. "A lyin' animal..." Hate throbbed in his veins. "...a blackmailin' animal..." His fingers tightened and twisted. "... a murderin' animal..."

Leigh screamed.

Jas relaxed and raised his hand. Between two fingers, a tiny gold ring and the bloody remnants of a nipple. A scarlet trickle made its way over tanned skin. He grinned. "Now, Leigh. Let's start at the end an' work back tae the beginnin'..."

Panic stained the handsome face. "Christ...!" Blue, terrified eyes looked down at the fleshy mess. "I'm bleeding ..."

A back-handed slap sobered the voice.

Leigh coughed. "Okay."

"Whose body did ah identify?" Tracing the blade over the well-muscled pectorals, he closed his eyes and waited.

Leigh coughed again, then: "Jason's – my younger brother. He's – was – twenty-two. I didn't mean..."

"Tell me aboot the blackmail."

Saliva dribbled from the side of Leigh's mouth. Words came slowly at first. "The whole thing stared about four years ago in London. I was in the second year of a BSc in Chemistry at Sussex Uni. Jason was doing what he always did: fucking anything that moved, selling himself on the streets. Money was tight. I moved in with him when my grant ran out. He was hard-up, too. Business was tailing off. AIDS was scaring people. I suggested to Jason that he pal up with guys, instead: specific guys. HIV-positive guys."

Faint smile. "Suppose you could call it target marketing. They didn't have long, anyway – or they thought they didn't – and Jason was a real charmer. Where was the harm? He made them happy, and they were grateful. We used to sell the presents they gave him..."

"Tell me aboot later."

Sigh. Earnest words. "We were desperate, Jas. Then it occurred to me. Jason was still trolling bars on the side. He'd tell me about his tricks: this one had a wife, that one was a closet-case...you know the sort of thing." Cough. "Jason had no business sense at all. But I could see the potential. I suggested we expand our business plan a little, to include married men, men with something to lose, men with jobs where their orientation would be frowned upon, should it come to light. That's where the money is, you see Jas. The real money..."

"Blackmail money, dirty money..."

"Money's money, when you don't have it, Jas. We invested in a camera, moved to a bigger flat and began the business. That's what it was: a business arrangement. Jason would bring tricks back, I'd photograph the proceedings, then send them a little memento of their hour with Jason."

Jas clenched his fists. "Go on."

"It was a nice little earner, but Jason was no actor. Kept getting involved with his tricks, and that, of course, ruined things. Your original tart with a heart, that was Jason..."

"An' whit aboot Sloan?"

Blue eyes widened. Laugh. "That really was an accidental meeting – one of those things you dream about! Jason was on a break, in the Kensington Park's coffee lounge. Greg Sloan was down for some conference. He picked Jason up. When I found out he was a cop...!" Laugh dissolving into cough. "The money we'd been making from the others was peanuts compared to what someone like Greg could pay..."

"You met him?"

"Me? Christ, no! I was the...silent partner, the brains, Jas. None of the tricks ever knew about me." Distaste shadowing the handsome face. "I'd never sleep with boring, disgusting, disease-ridden old men..."

Sick, dying Leon Marshall flashed before his eyes. Jas scowled, gripped the knife more tightly. "An' the rest!"

"Sloan wanted Jason to come to Glasgow with him. Said he'd set him up in a flat. Jason agreed, and I came too. Assistant Chief Commissioner Sloan was the big-time, Jas. A cop...a married cop with kids. I made Jason keep him sweet for quite a while. He was a long-term investment." More confident now. "Glasgow was pastures new, ripe for exploitation. You're all so repressed, up here. I bought a video camera..."

Not photographs, not negatives. Jas sighed.

"...much better than still-life, so to speak. On video you get sound and movement, Jas. Much more effective. And the stills made equally persuasive mementos for the tricks. After only six months, we had five new clients: a social worker, two prison officers, a primary-school teacher and a Free Church minister." Almost proud. "Now we've – I've – got two judges and an MP on the books!"

Jas stared at the tanned face. "An' whit aboot me? When were ye gonny start oan me...?"

"Don't be stupid!"

Jas back-handed the face again. His knuckles stung.

Leigh gasped. Fear. "You weren't business, Jas: you were pleasure. There was never anyone else for me. Jason was the tart. When I met you..." Pause. "We hit it off straight away, you know that. Okay, it was great sex, but you were so much more – everything I'd ever wanted. We're two of a kind, Jas. We both know what we want, and how to get it." Sigh. "Jason isn't – wasn't – any great shakes, in the brains department. I had no one to talk to." Frown. "But I knew you were a cop, that you'd never accept what I did for a living. So I made up the lab job, gave you what you wanted to hear. I know you won't believe me now, Jas, but I..." Embarrassed. "...fell in love with you. I was never unfaithful to you, never wanted to involve you in all this."

Jas closed his eyes. Where did the lies stop and the truth begin?

"If you need proof, look in the kitchen, behind the cracked tile."

"Why should ah?"

Insistent. "Just look, Jas."

Like an automaton, he got up and walked from the bedroom.

The tile he'd always meant to replace came away easily. Behind, a small plastic-sheathed book. He removed the cover. Bank of the Cayman Islands. The balance read £56,715: business had been brisk. Jas sighed and returned to the bedroom. He threw the book at Leigh. "Whit's this meant tae dae fur me?"

Pleading eyes. "It's for us, Jas. Just you and me, now – always was, really. That business with the Jimmy Mygo guy...I wanted the police to throw you out, Jas, wanted you to decide that being with me – being out was more important than that stupid job. We'd go to LA and never come back. Now...?" Licking dry lips. "Be sensible. No one will believe I didn't mean to kill Jason. They'll put me in prison." Pout. "You know you wouldn't like that – we're a once-in-a-lifetime thing! Let's just go, leave this mess behind. We can start again in..."

"Whit happened tae Jason?" Jas lifted the knife and pressed it to Leigh's throat. "Why did ye hiv tae kill him?" A tiny droplet of blood pooled beneath the blade's point.

Leigh inhaled. "That wasn't meant to happen, I swear..."

"Ye did shoot him, then?"

Nod. Swallow. "I had no choice..."

Jas slapped him hard.

Leigh's head flipped like a rag-doll's.

Jas seized the strong chin and turned the face towards him.

Tears sparkled on dark lashes.

Jas felt the guts wrenched from him. He scowled. "Come on, ya..." Words were inadequate. He pulled his hand away and rubbed his eyes. "Tell me why."

Leigh sighed. The bottom lips trembled. Low words. "Jason wasn't well. He'd probably been positive for years, but had never tested. Richard Beatie turned out to be a bad bet – he was out, there was nothing we could use against him. Worse, he made a big impression on Jason. There's nothing more sickening than a rent-boy in love, Jas. Beatie made him test. After that, Jason became unmanageable. He was getting soft – wanted to stop working and go and live with Beatie." Frown. "After all I'd done for him, Jason was going to leave me. I couldn't have that. I needed him, and he needed me." Laugh. "I'm sure Beatie would have wanted nothing to do with Jason, had he known what he did for a living."

The BMW. Richard Beatie's distraught face. Leigh was the partner who wouldn't let Jason leave. Business partner.

Jas flinched: Beatie's love for Jason was an emotion someone like Leigh would never understand.

"Jason started getting stroppy. Kept pleading with me to let him go. I couldn't do that, could I? There was a lot of time and money invested in Jason. Last Tuesday, after you'd gone to the hospital, he came here. It was pathetic. He was crying like a kid." Scowl. "On top of that, Sloan had somehow got this number, and that was bad news..."

'Come out or get out.' Jas rubbed his face. Advice given for his sake, or because Leigh knew Sloan was closing in on him?

"...and now Jason was at it too, threatening to tell you about our little business venture. I was stupid, Jas – I realise that, now. I should have called his bluff. But you meant so much to me, I couldn't risk losing you. My life was falling apart. Then I remembered the gun..." Handsome face frozen in memory. "...only wanted to scare him, but he tried to take the gun away from me. Jason was desperate enough to really try to use it. One minute we were wrestling, then there was a sort of muffled bang and he was dead. Christ, Jas! It was terrible. I must have been too close...my fingers were burning and there was nothing left of his face." Breath quickening, rushed words. "I wanted to tell you everything, I wanted to wait until you got back, but I didn't have the stomach for it. Please believe me, Jas..." Repentant blue eyes stared deep into his. "You know how much you mean to me..."

Jas back-handed the words away. A dark, red print etched Leigh's cheekbone, above the scratches. He thought of the mushy ruin of a face which had lain on this bed, seven days ago. Lies, lies...too many lies. He tensed. "Where huv ye been fur the past week?" The point of the blade traced a paling cheek.

Shiver. "We had a place, in the West End. Only Jason and I knew about it. I was scared, Jas, and I had no money. Thought Sloan would be good for another couple of payments, but he never turned up for the meet..."

Jas remembered cold, green eyes. Desperate eyes. If Sloan had turned up, Leigh would not be alive.

"I was trying to find you, Jas. Didn't know where you'd gone. I wandered round our cemetery, came back here a couple of times, but there were always badly-dressed detectives watching. So I hid up West, coming back every night, waiting for you. Where were you, Jas? Did the police arrest you?"

The police. Sloan. Jas closed his eyes. "Where's the blackmail stuff?" He opened his eyes.

Smile. "Didn't think you were into voyeurism..."

Jas stood up, dropped the knife. He looked away: Leigh was unbelievable! "Where is it?"

"Put the video on. We can watch together, if you like..."

He walked from the room and into the lounge. Crouching before the VCR, he switched it on. Static, then grainy black-and-white. Then Leigh...Jas peered at the screen...not Leigh. A tall blond boy in a leather G-string lay on his side. Not Leigh's face, the body not as well-muscled as Leigh's. No pierced nipples. Jason ran a pink tongue over pink lips, and turned over onto his back. Another body appeared. White, unhealthy flesh. The rear view of a crew-cut grey head was visible. The head turned, smiled to itself, then turned away. Greg Sloan.

Jas switched off the tape. He didn't want to see anymore. A number of videos in ex-rental boxes lay scattered on the floor. He picked up *Terminator Two*, ejected then inserted.

A body far removed from Schwarzenegger appeared on-screen. Baggy. Old. Face straining with pleasure. Between flabby grey thighs, a blond head was busy. Jason's blond head.

Jas switched off. Disgust spread through his body like a plague. He sighed, returned to the bedroom and looked down at the spreadeagled body. Prick throbbed with a mind of its own.

Leigh was smiling. "Not a pretty sight, Jas, you'll agree..." The metal bracelets rattled.

Jas scowled. No regret, no remorse, no tears...at least, not for his brother. The shooting could well have been an accident, but Leigh was too clever to miss the striking resemblance between Jason and himself. Jas had been set up. Jason was shirtless and shoeless, when the body was found. That was no accident. "How could ye dae that, Leigh?"

The wrong answer. "Blackmail's only possible when there's

something to hide, Jas – you know that. Society's so-called norms make it possible, the same norms which make it impossible for us to be accepted. We're excluded from society, so why not use society, use the rules to our advantage?"

"But ye were hurtin' people like us..."

"We're not like Sloan..." Laugh. "...or any of the rest of them, Jas. We live our lives in the open..." Sly smile. "...or, at least, I do. But I'm not talking discretion, here. I'm talking lies, double lies, cowards who want the best of both worlds. Sloan fucked Jason, then went home and fucked his wife. He was lying to her, to his kids, his colleagues. If he came out, as an example, there would be no scope, no blackmail. He brought the whole thing on himself: honest men can't be blackmailed. Sloan deserves all he gets. People like him make life harder for the rest of us..." Blue eyes locking with his. "...you know I'm right, Jas.

Lying...lies...honesty...

He pictured Sloan's sulky daughter, heard the warm voice of Sloan's wife. He thought of Ali, of Mrs. Rehmandi, of Big Rab and the boys at the gym, of his police colleagues, men he had worked with for twelve years.

Omissions of truth were lies just the same. How far would he himself have gone, to protect his own private life? He frowned, recalling the bargain with the Assistant Chief Commissioner. "That aw' there is?" He nodded to the lounge.

Raised eyebrows. "Christ, no"! The copies are hidden..."

Jas grabbed blond hair, delivered another slap. "Where?"

"What do you want them for?"

He tightened his grip on the hair.

Leigh yelled. "The necropolis!"

Jas loosened his grip. "Where, exactly?"

Leigh smiled. "In our mausoleum, Jas. the big flagstone in the left-hand corner's loose." Grin. "Remember that summer, remember how good it was? Fucking in the open air, Jas. There's nothing quite like it...remember how it felt?" Desire in the blue eyes. "Christ, I need you in me, Jas." The bruised face stared, beseechingly. "Fuck me, Jas. Fuck me now, here, like this..." Swollen lips parted further. Breathing laboured. "I love you, Jas..."

The three words spiralled in his head. The heat in his groin almost melted the ice in his heart. Jas clenched his fists. Too many lies...

Slowly, he checked the handcuffs. Leigh flinched, sighing at his touch. Jas turned and began to walk away.

Panic. "Where are you going?"

Without looking round. "Tae check yer story, Leigh. But don't worry. Ah'll be back."

"I'll be waiting." Fear, anticipation and lust tinged Leigh's words.

Twenty-Eight

ALEXANDRA PARADE was a wet blur as he made his way back to the necropolis.

It had all started in a cemetery. It would end in a cemetery.

Rain began to fall. Jas turned up the collar of the biker's jacket and thrust hands deeper into jeans pocket.

Something cold touched his fingers. He rubbed the cold between thumb and forefinger, then withdrew his hand.

A single nipple ring. He looked at the gold circlet and its fleshy companion, then replaced both in a zip pocket.

He didn't want to think...didn't want to do anything. He walked on until he reached Wishart Street...

Inside the grounds of the necropolis, double darkness embraced him. Pupils expanding in the velvety tar, he saw the mausoleum was as he'd left it. A whimper greeted his arrival.

Two shining eyes glinted in the gloom. The Jack Russell got up from a corner, stretched and padded towards him. Jas smiled and patted its head. The dog licked his hand.

He walked to the back wall and prodded the floor with a foot. The flagstone was loose. He edged it to one side with a biker's boot then knelt, thrusting a hand into the space beneath.

Nothing...then something. Smooth.

He grabbed a corner of the bin-bag and pulled it out.

The dog snarled at the slithering sound.

Five video-tapes clattered noisily on the stone floor.

Plunging his left arm deeper into the bag, he searched. Paper...shiny-feeling paper. He drew out a handful of 8" x 10" photographs and stared at the glossy surface. In this light, he could see nothing. He didn't need to.

Jas sighed, stuffed the videos and the stills back into black plastic and replaced the bag under the flagstone. He crouched down.

The Jack Russell leapt onto his knees. Jas rested his right hand on the wiry hair of the dog's back. Tiny shivers of pain scuttled up and down his arm. The dog inhaled, then sighed noisily.

Jas tried to think. He needed to think, now. His brain refused to work.

Procedure: action without thought. Police procedure. His head spun.

The dog whimpered, retreated to a dark corner.

Jas shook doubts away and left the mausoleum.

On Wishart Street's cracked pavement, footsteps behind him.

He turned. No one. Something touched his legs. He looked down. Two small black-and-white paws were braced against a biker's boot. Ears flattened against skull, the Jack Russell smiled up at him.

Jas bent down, patted the dog then walked on. Crossing Hanson Street he scowled, stopped and sat on the cigarette factory's low wall.

He knew who'd killed Jason.

He knew he was off the hook. Why didn't he feel happier? Jas knew with his own testimony and that of others, Leigh Nicols would go down for a long time. He shivered.

The boys in Barlinnie didn't play games. They played for keeps.

He got up and walked on. He wanted the Parade to stretch into infinity, counted and named the intersections as he crossed them. The headache was back. So was the Jack Russell. Jas shooed it away.

Leigh's bank book.

LA. Sun, sand and...

'Yours...only yours...'

A smile teased bruised lips. At least that much had been true. Or had it? Jas walked on.

So many lies...so much pain.

Leon Marshall, Harry from Walthamstow, Richard Beatie, Greg Sloan, countless other men...even Leigh's own brother.

He thought of Jason. A picture of an ill, vulnerable boy seared his brain.

No one deserved to die that way. Victims. Used and manipulated. Part of Leigh's plan.

Jas couldn't live with that. He broke into a run, before strength abandoned him completely.

The trees of Alexandra Park appeared ahead. He swerved left, tearing into Eastercraigs.

Just because Leigh could give him a hard-on didn't mean he could lead him around by it.

And that's what it came down to: hard-ons.

No...trust.

No...respect.

No...love – how could he love someone he didn't even know? Outside Number Seven, Jas breathlessly fumbled for keys.

A voice behind: distant, indistinct. His name.

Blood pounded in his ears. He frowned, rubbed his face. Not Leigh's voice. A female voice? He looked down, then turned.

Across the road, the dog was sniffing at a tree.

Jas sighed, ignoring all voices except the one in his head. He leant against the door. It opened under his weight.

He walked slowly into the close and up two flights of stairs.

The door to 2B was ajar. The ghost of a smell drifted out to meet him.

Lacoste, dampness and...metal?

Another night. A week earlier.

The flat was silent. Jas walked through to the bedroom. In the gloom, he could see Leigh was asleep. But smiling. The other smell was stronger here. A sour smell. An animal smell. He moved to the bedside table and turned on a single spotlight.

Two brown arms still cuffed to the bed-head.

Handsome face gazing upwards through blind eyes.

A second smile, inches below bluish lips.

Red wetness soaked the white lycra T-shirt. The mattress swam with it. Leigh's knife rested amidst the mess.

Above, on the mirror, five red words. Smears, more than words. Almost illegible...but not quite: 'I always pay my debts.'

He stared from the taunt to the wide gash across Leigh's throat, turned and ran from the flat. His face was wet. Salt was in his mouth. Outside, he tripped and fell.

His last memory was of gloss PVC boots.

August brought more sunshine.

In the necropolis, Jas sat on an overturned headstone and watched five boys play a half-hearted game of football. The white shirt was crisp and stiff against his skin. He could still smell the hospital.

Fuckin' Hepatitis A and concussion! Four days of liquids and anti-biotics had cleared that up. His right arm was another matter. Under white bandage and half-inch plaster, which ran from shoulder to wrist, his skin itched unbearably. The consultant wasn't optimistic: 'The bones may knit, Mr. Anderson, but tendon damage is less easily repaired. The numbness should subside with time, and you could experience a tingling in the fingers, but I'm afraid you'll never really be able to use the arm again...'

Jas tried to make a fist with his right hand. Fingers quivered, but refused to move.

A football rolled towards his feet. He stood up, kicked it back, then sat down again. At least he was alive, and expected to remain so for some time. In the Royal's male surgical ward, where he'd been for the past week, he'd had five visitors.

The first two were Andy Clark and his son. Ricky Clark had grown into a handsome young man. The fifteen-year-old boy Jas had dragged from the Calton cottage three years before was almost unrecognisable in the eyes of this mature, confident adult. After squeezing Jas's good hand, Ricky had remained tactfully in the background, while his father had probed for information Jas knew he couldn't provide.

A bargain – even one with a bastard like Greg Sloan – was still a bargain.

His third visitor was Marie, who brought news of the test results and a bunch of chrysanthemums. Leigh had been negative. So was Jas. Through a haze of anaesthetic and resentment, he had listened to her words and apologies without hearing any of them. The scarred face floated in front of him. He would have turned away, had he been able to move. Eventually, she'd left, after kissing his forehead: "Ah'll see ya aroon', Big Man..." Slipping something under his pillow. Leigh's bank book.

His fourth visitor arrived two days ago, in full dress uniform. Jas's mind had been clearer, by then. He'd regarded Greg Sloan's emotionless eyes: "Well? Did you get what I wanted?"

Jas had stared. "Maybe..."

"Don't hold out on me, Anderson!" Sloan had unbuttoned the dark serge jacket. "I've kept my part of the deal. Meet me... day after tomorrow. Bring the material with you. Your choice of place."

Jas had chosen 3pm in the necropolis. He didn't know why, but it seemed appropriate.

His fifth visitor was an ever-present blond wraith, haunting his dreams and torturing his body through the physical pain of slowly-healing injuries.

Discharged yesterday from the Royal, Jas had booked into a small hotel. He hadn't returned to the Eastercraigs flat, doubted if he ever would. After a shower, he'd tried to sleep, then watched TV. The local news briefly mentioned that a man had been charged in connection with two deaths in the East End of Glasgow. No names, no details...

...the sun hurt his eyes. Jas nudged the duffle-bag with one foot.

Four video tapes and a quantity of photographic material. Jas had a feeling there would be a couple of resignations and at least one emergency by-election, if this lot came to light.

The stab-wound tingled beneath the plaster-cast. Like Leigh, it would scab over, given time. Jas wondered vaguely who had killed him. Only vaguely...because it changed nothing...

...an eclipse. The sun was momentarily blocked out. "Good afternoon, Anderson."

Jas looked up. The tall, backlit figure of Greg Sloan loomed over him. He blinked and looked away.

Sloan sat down beside him, on the headstone. "How are you feeling?"

Jas scowled. "Fine."

"And the arm?"

He gazed at the stiff, useless limb. "It's comin' on..."

Laugh. "I like your style, Anderson. If we had met under different circumstances..." Unfinished, the sentence hung in the air then drifted away.

Jas swallowed, stood up and grabbed the duffle-bag.

Sloan stretched out in the sunshine, then eyed the bag. "My

property, I believe."

Jas moved the bag out of reach.

Frown. "I kept my part of the deal, Anderson – even got you off the hook..."

Jas looked at the cold eyes.

"...got you to hospital too, didn't I? Just as well I sent Marie McGhee to keep an eye on you. We've got Jimmy Mygo in custody..."

"Whit?" He sank to a crouch.

Sloan casually lit a cigarette and exhaled. "You heard. Marie McGhee saw the whole thing, and has made a statement to that effect. Jimmy Mygo's confessed. Seems he was holding some sort of grudge against you, after all."

'I always pay my debts.' The whole thing had come full circle. Jas looked at Sloan, relaxed in jogging-pants and a denim jacket. "And whit aboot Jason? How're ye gonny explain him?"

Sloan ground out the cigarette. "Oh, the Johnstone character's confessed to that too – didn't I tell you?"

Jas clenched his fists. The fingers of his right hand spasmed, but remained straight. "Jimmy wiz naewhere near..."

"He's confessed, and Sandy Monroe's happy with that. No jury trial, no fuss. James Johnstone will appear for sentencing next week, then join his brother in Barlinnie. Another piece of scum off the streets, Anderson – isn't that what policing's all about?" He glanced at the football game then back at Jas.

"Jimmy didney kill Jason. Leigh did..."

"I know, but this is much more convenient for everyone. You must see that."

Leigh had received justice, of sorts. But Jimmy?

Convenient...like Jas had been convenient. "Did he huv a solicitor?"

"Didn't want one, said he needed to get the whole thing off his chest." Hands thrust into pockets.

Jas could picture the scenario. An interview room of cold, threatening eyes. Blows delivered where they wouldn't show... or worse. The tape-machine propitiously out-of-order. Jimmy Mygo wouldn't have stood a chance. He sighed.

Sloan reached for the duffle-bag.

Jas stood up. "An' whit aboot me?" He kicked the bag away.

Sigh. "Let's be sensible about this. Johnstone can be persuaded to drop the assault charges against you, but Richard Beatie's a different matter. I've talked to him – on your behalf. All he really wants is your resignation." A hand touched the plaster-cast. "You're not fit for duty anyway – I have the doctor's report. Resign, and I'll personally see you receive a generous invalidity settlement. You've no other option: officially, you're in the clear, but I don't envy your future in the force. Suppose I could find you a desk-job, or something in Community Relations, but do you really want that?"

What was always there in the background? What had seen him through life, before Leigh? What would be a lifebelt now, when he most needed it? "Ye ken whit ah want! Ma old job back."

Light laugh. "Not possible, Anderson. No one would work with you. If you hadn't blown your cover so dramatically, in the first place, there might have been a chance. But you know as well as I do: officers like Sandy Monroe are far from unusual in their...attitude."

Jas stared into middle distance. "An' you? Whit's your attitude?"

"We've never met. I knew nothing of you, Jason or Leigh Nicols. Now, give me the bag."

He passed four videotapes and a ream of photographs to Assistant Chief Commissioner Sloan, who featured in none of them. "Ye've got the two from the flat?"

Sloan opened the bag and peered into it, before replying. "Yes, I found them."

Before or after you phoned an ambulance for me? Before or after you checked Leigh's body for a pulse. "So whit dae ye dae noo?"

Smiled. "Me?" Duffle-bag hoisted onto shoulder. "Dump this lot in an incinerator, then a little holiday. My wife and I are off to Greece..." Laugh. "A sort of second honeymoon."

Jas stared. "That's it? Two murders; Jimmy Mygo fitted up fur wan o' them; ma fuckin' arm useless, thanks to Felix Hunter and his pals...an' you're aff oan holiday?"

Frown. "What did you expect? A touching gay-pride scene, in which you and I face the massed ranks of Strathclyde Police together?" Laugh. "I think not, sergeant...or, rather, ex-sergeant."

Jas stood up. He was a fool to even consider any other course of action. "Ma resignation'll be on the Commissioner's desk the morra."

A hand on his shoulder. "Good. You know it's for the best." Fingers massaged the muscle. "You're a young man. Ex-police have no trouble in the employment market.

And gay ex-police? Disabled gay ex-police? Jas shrugged off the hand. "Ye've got it aw' worked oot, eh? Nothin' touches you, pal..."

"And nothing ever will." Glacial green eyes. "Remember that." Sigh. "Your flat's been cleaned up, so you can return whenever you want." A hand extended. "Goodbye, Jas – that's what you like to be called, isn't it? As in freeform?"

He looked at the hand, then at the ground.

"Come on, it's over. I only did what I had to...we both did..."

"Hi, mister? Kick the ba' back, eh?" A thin, tanned teenager.

Jas kicked the ball towards him and walked away.

From the lies.

From the corruption.

From Assistant Chief Commissioner Sloan's mocking eyes. Jas knew he had abused his own position by attacking Jimmy Mygo. He had acted in hot blood, but had been prepared to take the consequences.

What coursed through Greg Sloan's veins wasn't hot...not even lukewarm. The Johnstone brothers were candidates for sainthood, compared to Sloan.

A liar. A suppresser of evidence.

Not fit to wear the uniform. The uniform which made him vulnerable. The uniform which had almost been his downfall. Jas crossed the Bridge of Sighs which linked the necropolis to Glasgow Cathedral.

Leigh had got his way, in the end. Jas was out...out of a job.

Leigh was dead: there was nothing left worth fighting for...or was there?

Outside the Visitor's Centre, brightly-coloured tourists were thrusting handfuls of postcards into a postbox.

With his left hand, he pulled a padded envelope from his pocket. Leaning against a wall, Jas located a pencil stub in another pocket and began to write. The address was a scrawl, but a legible one:

The Chief Commissioner of Police,
Strathclyde Police Headquarters,
Pitt Street,
Glasgow.

Inside was a video of Jason and Sloan. Jas thrust it into the postbox's mouth, sighed and walked towards Alexandra Parade.